Dead Man's Treasure

by

Rebecca Grace

Dead Man, Book 2

Dead Man's Treasure

Cover Art by *Jennifer Greeff*

The Wild Rose Press, Inc.
PO Box 708
Adams Basin, NY 14410-0708
Visit us at www.thewildrosepress.com

Publishing History
First Edition, 2022
Trade Paperback ISBN 978-1-5092-4577-2
Digital ISBN 978-1-5092-4578-9

Dead Man, Book 2
Published in the United States of America

When free spirit Freeda Ferguson goes in search of her father, enlisting help from uptight lawyer Patrick Sanchez, sparks fly, but can love overcome a dead man's ghost and a town's lust for treasure?

Dedication

To my sister, Lillie, my brothers, John and Richard and my sister-in-law, Janet. Without their constant support and valuable research help, my stories would not get written.

Prologue

He huddled in the darkness, inhaling the odor of his own blood mixed with the clean scent of juniper. The only sounds were the comforting chatter of crickets and the rustling of wind in the nearby juniper trees.

No! That wasn't wind. Someone was coming through the bushes, stepping lightly to muffle the sound of stealthy footsteps. The person walked carefully, trying to avoid detection, perhaps aware he might be listening. A sudden wheeze, followed by shallow breathing slightly relaxed him before she stepped around the side of a tree.

A small familiar face came into his limited view.

"Did you do it?" he asked.

Rosalie stopped, her breath catching before she spoke. "Yes, I even marked where I put it. But what about you? Are you okay?" No longer concerned about concealing her presence, she stepped toward him, leaning over, panting.

"I'm doing fine," he lied, touching his side where the wound burned the worst. Warm liquid seeped over his hand. He knew from its scent that it was blood, but the night was too dark to see the red flow. He didn't want to think about the searing pain that had blinded him when the car windshield smashed across his face or the flames that tore at his shirt as he struggled to free her and pull her from the car.

She reached out to touch him, but he held up his hand to stop her.

"Don't worry about me. I'll be all right," he insisted, wheezing. "Just…ah…needed to rest for a couple of minutes…"

"The commune is not far…maybe a mile or so beyond this ridge," she whispered. "I could see the lights from the top of the hill. Can you make it? I can go there and get help if you want."

"No, we can't wait." He drew a quick breath and struggled to his feet, looking back in the direction from which they had travelled. "They'll be coming. We have to move." He almost expected to hear the baying of hounds in the distance, following their trail. "Let's go. But…if I don't make it…I want you to know…how much this means…how much it's meant to have you as my friend…"

Her crooked smile was visible in the low light of the moon. "I *am* your friend. That's what friends are for. And when you *do* make it, which I'm sure you will, I want *you* to know that. I will always do anything for you."

For a few seconds, the ache in his soul matched the pain that burned his lungs and his eyes. If only she could have meant more to him. If only he had been willing to do anything for her. He twisted around to glance back at the burning wreckage of the car one more time. They had to get moving.

He needed to move on too, in both his head and his heart. He needed to forget the past. She was his future. Yes, the time had come to go forward—no matter how many regrets might lurk ahead.

Taking a shuffling step forward, he beckoned her with his hand. "I'm ready. Let's go."

Chapter One

Freeda Ferguson kicked the tire of her Aunt Lottie's blue sedan and winced. She bent forward and muttered a curse at the immediate shot of pain in her foot, but she might as well have been yelling. No one would hear her. That thought alone provided an excuse to holler.

"Damn!" she shouted in frustration, as loudly as she could, twisting her head to look up and down the deserted two-lane highway. Sometimes she absolutely hated rural New Mexico. If only she was back home in Los Angeles. The cars might speed by, but sooner or later, a helpful highway patrolman might stop, or roadside assistance people would come by. Heck, help was only a cell phone call away at any hour of the day or night.

But here? The surrounding prairie was silent as death and might as well be devoid of any living creatures, though she knew prairie dogs and lizards scurried around somewhere in the scrub brush. She glanced down at her cell phone again before lifting it in different directions. No matter which way she turned, it still read *No Service.* Heck, even the darn cows grazing in the nearby thin layer of grass didn't lift their heads at her shouting. She should have known better than to borrow her Aunt Lottie's fifteen-year-old car.

If only Cere wasn't out of town. Her cousin might have understood the circumstances and given permission to borrow her car. Freeda had considered simply taking it, and in the past, she might have done that. However, their relationship was different now. Cere's husband was the sheriff. Walking into their house and taking the keys off the peg by the door might have landed her in jail. Sheriff Rafe Tafoya was a by-the-book type of guy who didn't approve of people who ignored the rules. At times, Freeda didn't think he liked her or her influence over Cere.

Freeda kicked another tire—harder this time. Wincing again, she leaned over to rub her foot. Damn, that was a stupid idea. Kicking tires with her sandals wasn't going to make the car work. It wasn't getting her anywhere, except to make her toes hurt. What was she going to do? She hadn't seen a single car along the road since she left Rio Rojo half an hour ago.

"Must have missed the morning rush hour," she grumbled, scanning the yellowing grassy, rolling plains around her.

"Where are you, cute cowboy?" she shouted through gritted teeth, needing to hear something, *anything!* Even the sound of her own voice was preferable to the overall sensation of stillness. The only sounds were the breeze whispering through nearby juniper trees and the rustling of tumbleweeds as they bounced through tufts of buffalo grass. She hadn't realized how much she needed outside noise until she came to New Mexico. The steady drone of traffic, people yelling into their cell phones, a loud TV, or pounding music from next door neighbors had all been mere background sounds that she hadn't appreciated until their sudden absence. Silence pressed down on her like a pile of bricks.

How far was it to the turn off that led toward

Albuquerque? It should have been coming up soon. Hadn't the last sign said five miles to the junction? Was there a gas station at that location? She couldn't remember, but even if it held nothing, perhaps she could see something in the distance along that stretch of the road—at least some indication of human habitation. At the rate of speed she'd been driving, she was a good 40 miles from Rio Rojo. She sure as hell couldn't walk back there. Maybe she shouldn't have been speeding. Or maybe she should have turned around when the car first started smoking.

Freeda peered forward, as though just by looking, something might suddenly appear. Was there anything down this road? She should have studied the map ap on her phone or tablet before heading out. She again lifted her cell phone from her pocket. Still no sign of a signal. Maybe if she walked to the top of the next hill, she might find something.

The road dipped and rose to a plateau. Squat juniper and pinon trees on either side of the road couldn't hide anything like a ranch house or even a barn. A lone windmill spun in the distance, but as she had come to learn since she arrived in New Mexico, the towns in the northern part of the state were few and far between. She was more likely to find a herd of cows gathered around that windmill with no sign of a living person.

As she surveyed the horizon, a sudden burst of dust rose in the distance. A dust devil? No. The faint sound of an engine came to her as the dust moved in a straight line toward the highway. Hadn't she passed a turn off from the highway a mile back? Maybe the vehicle was headed there.

No matter who it was, the moving dust meant

humanity. Perhaps Rafe was out on his rounds. He regularly patrolled this area. What was down that road anyway? But no matter. She needed a ride. She sprinted in that direction. Perhaps the driver had a phone that worked out here. She arrived at the fence gate where the road met the highway just as the pick-up approached.

Her hopes sank as a lanky man of medium height hopped from the truck to unlock the gate. She didn't need to see the *No Trespassing* sign beside the gate to know where the road led—Tres Padres, the largest ranch in the area. And she knew the man.

Diego Diaz.

She grimaced and wrinkled her nose in distaste. *Damn!* Just what she *didn't* need. The one person she did not trust, had never liked, and she knew he probably felt the same way about her.

Diaz grinned at her, but his smiles never appeared welcoming or sincere. The curl of his full upper lip always struck her as sinister. As usual, he wore very dark aviator sunglasses under his worn cowboy hat. Despite the warm Indian Summer weather, he was dressed all in black—his normal attire. Black plaid western shirt with metal snaps, faded black jeans, black hat, dusty black boots. Like a villain in an old-time cowboy movie, she'd always thought. The only thing he lacked was a curling mustache. The thought made her smile.

He probably was a villain—though at times he probably considered her one too. Slightly above medium height, thin and rangy, he reminded her of a man who could have starred in movies as the bad guy with a bad motive who dogged the hero until the end. One side of his dark face was scarred, while the other side was weathered from too many days under the hot New

Mexico sun. She had seldom seen him without the dark glasses—even inside. She had decided he wore them to conceal a patch over the eye on the scarred side of his face.

He spoke first—in a soft raspy voice that sounded as spooky as any film bad guy. "Well, well, what have we here? Miss Freedom Ferguson."

She rolled her eyes. "Well, well, Mr. Diego Velasquez Diaz," she shot back in the same tone of voice.

Her aunt had made a critical mistake when she explained to him that Freeda had been the offspring of two people still wishing they'd been part of the flower power generation, and her birth certificate read *Freedom*. Freeda might have been born in the 90s, but her parents had remained afficionados of the 60s and 70s. In the few pictures she had seen of her deceased mother, Jane Ferguson had worn her dark hair long and straight, while Freeda's dad still favored fraying jeans and a leather vest or jacket. She had never learned why they named her Freedom, though her father eventually shortened the name. Now only the incorrect spelling remained, but this man had no business teasing her about her name. People never called him by his real name. He had always made it clear he preferred Diaz or the simple initials D. V.

"What are you doing all the way out here alone?" Diaz asked as he pulled open the gate.

She gestured toward the car. "My car broke down."

"Your *aunt's* car," he corrected in a tone filled with sarcasm. "Does she know you would be driving it all the way out here? That thing is a pile of junk."

"Tell me about it. I think it overheated."

"I doubt Lottie realized you'd be coming out this far.

Doesn't she only use it around town for quick trips?"

Freeda grimaced, refusing to admit that while Aunt Lottie had given her use of the car, she had also cautioned about driving it outside of town. But this was an emergency!

"I don't need a lecture, dammit, I need a ride."

"Not heading to Rio Rojo. I'm heading over to the east gate…" He tilted his head to the east.

Freeda had no idea where the gate was, though she knew the Tres Padres ranch where Diaz worked stretched from Rio Rojo to near her destination. "Great! Do you mind dropping me in Casitas?"

"Much as I'd love the pleasure of your company," he said coolly, "I'm not going all the way into town. The east gate is just a few miles up the road. By the way, have you seen your daddy lately?"

Freeda drew a quick breath as her pulse rate increased. "No, but do you know where he is? Someone said they saw him in Casitas. Have you seen him?"

He grunted as he shook his head. "Nope, not lately, and you better hope I don't."

That comment appeared ominous, and she shivered slightly. "Why?"

"That's between me and him. He doesn't tell you everything, does he?" His thin lips lifted in a crooked grin.

A flush of anger rushed through her. Diaz probably knew she had not seen her dad lately. He also knew her search for her father was a vulnerable point he could exploit. As she turned away, she caught sight of a sparkle in the distance. Sunlight glinted off something moving– a car. It had just come over the top of the rise to the east and was headed toward her and Diaz.

The hell with him.

"Never mind." Freeda walked toward the edge of the road to await the car's arrival. The oncoming vehicle was only a faint glimmer, but she would wave it down if she had to stand in the middle of the highway to do it.

Diaz drove through the gate and stopped beside her. "Why don't I look at your aunt's car? See if we can get it going?"

The unexpected offer surprised her, but she was not going to argue. Perhaps he could get her back on the road. "Would you do that?"

He waved a gloved hand at the car. "I don't mind. I have time and I keep a tool kit in the truck. Lottie doesn't need another headache."

She wanted to stick out her tongue at him for his comment, knowing he classified her as the "other" headache. She refrained from the childish gesture only because he might change his mind about looking at the car. The guy was totally unpredictable, but he might be able to get it running—if only as a convenience for her aunt.

He parked his truck beside the gate and relocked it before grabbing a toolbox from the back of the pick-up. Following him to the car, she explained how the engine had simply died.

"Does it have gas?" he asked, his tone mocking.

Naturally that would be his immediate thought, and she bit back an impulsive reply that might include a couple of swear words. "I'm not that stupid, *Mr. Diaz,* and I always fill it up before and after I borrow it, for *your information.*" She applied her own best derisive tone to her final words. Two could play at his game of sarcasm!

He chuckled as he removed his sunglasses, revealing the black patch over one eye. The other was a light shade of green. "Well, well, who knew?" he said, demonstrating his own tone of sarcasm. "Anyway, if I can't get it going, I'll push it behind the gate, so it's locked up. You don't want to leave it by the road out here."

"I'm certain my aunt will appreciate your concern," she shot back. To her surprise, his tanned face flushed darker, and the green eye shifted to the ground.

Well, well, himself! She'd always suspected he had a soft spot for Aunt Lottie, but she was not going to tease him—not if he helped her. She'd save that comment for another time. He was probably heartless enough to leave her stranded if she angered him.

Nervously, she watched him work under the hood. After chewing off several fingernails, despite a fresh polish job, and a few anxious glances at her watch, she began to worry. The first chance she'd had to see her father in several years, and she might miss it! Why couldn't Diaz just agree to take her into Casitas as she had requested?

Freeda was about to ask him to reconsider a trip to Casitas, but the car she'd spotted in the distance was coming nearer. If Diaz wouldn't take her, maybe this driver would. She marched to the middle of the road. She wasn't worried the driver wouldn't see her and might hit her. Hell, the person had a mile to spot her frantic waving. Just to be on the safe side, she began to jump up and down and shout, waving her arms wildly as the car approached. No use making light of her situation and letting the person try to ignore her and drive by.

Diaz jerked his head from under the hood. "What the

hell are you doing?"

"There's a car coming, and I need to get to Casitas!" she insisted.

He sighed and shook his head. "That car is going in the opposite direction. In case you didn't notice, it's going *to* Rio Rojo. If you want a ride in *that* direction, *I* can take you."

"Didn't you say you were going the other way?"

"I am, but Rio Rojo is close enough that it wouldn't take me long to drop you off."

He was being contrary, she decided, and shook her head. "Maybe this driver is a nice person who doesn't mind going a few extra miles in the *other* direction," she shot back.

"Or maybe the driver is a mass murderer," he retorted in his familiar raspy voice. The green eye blazed at her. They stood in a silent standoff, glaring at each other until he waved his good hand in dismissal.

"Ah, hell, do what you want." He ducked back under the hood.

He didn't see it, but this time she *did* stick out her tongue at his lowered head before turning back toward the road. The car grew closer and slowed as it approached. Her pulse rate quickened as the vehicle pulled to the side of the road a few yards from her.

Success! Freeda hurried toward the car, though wariness slowed her for a few seconds. She shook off the fear. *No,* she needed to get to Casitas. Besides, Diaz, obnoxious as he was, stood within shouting distance. He might not like her, but she doubted he'd let someone hurt her. Aunt Lottie would never forgive him.

A lone, dark-haired man sat inside the sleek silver sedan. The window slid down as she approached.

Freeda pulled on her most pleasant smile. "Hi there, I'm so glad you came along. I need help," she said, breathless from jumping.

His tan face turned toward her, but a pair of black sunglasses shaded his eyes. "I see. Your car broke down?"

"Yes, he's looking at it, but I need to get to Casitas and he's not going there. Can you please take me? It's back that way." She pointed in the direction from which he had come.

"I'm headed to Rio Rojo. Maybe I can give you a lift in that direction?" He removed his sunglasses, revealing very dark eyes and craned his neck toward her car as if to see what Diaz was doing.

"No, no! I'm *coming* from Rio Rojo," she protested. "I need to get to Casitas. It's a matter of life or death."

Okay, perhaps that was exaggerating slightly, but she did need to get there within the next hour. After the delay of the car problem, she didn't have time to go back and forth with him. She doubted her dad would be in the diner beyond 10 A.M. and it was already past nine.

"Life or death?" The man drew back, his tone skeptical, his eyes cool and watchful.

She adopted her most pleading voice. "Yes. It's an emergency with my dad." At least that part was sort of honest. "*Please, mister,* I need to get to him as soon as possible."

"Can't you call him? Where is he?" The man's voice had grown gravelly and impatient. He leaned forward to look toward her car. "Were you in an accident?"

She ignored the questions. Time was passing. "Please, I'll pay you. Um…a hundred dollars?"

Of course, she didn't have that much money on her.

She'd have to borrow it, and hopefully he didn't demand it up front. But then, he didn't look like he needed money anyway.

Freeda studied the driver, trying to decide how to best appeal her case to the guy. He had a narrow handsome face beneath thick dark hair that was cut short. He wore a blue cotton shirt that she would bet was purchased in a store where men ordered custom shirts, as opposed to pulled off the rack in a department store. The sleeves were rolled up on tanned arms covered by a thin layer of black hair. His eyes were sharp, like sparkling pools of dark cola, as they darted around, appraising the situation.

Long, slender fingers tapped the steering wheel in irritation. and she noted his fingernails were so perfect they might be regularly manicured. The ring finger was bare. Not that it mattered, but who was this guy? He didn't look like any of the other men she had met during her four-month visit in New Mexico. At least he appeared more trustworthy than that damn Diaz whose attention remained on the disabled car.

Freeda leaned forward, gripping the edge of the window and speaking softly. "I need to get to my dad. It really *is* critical."

"And I need to get to Rio Rojo," the man replied in a crisp, clipped tone, waving his hand forward. "That is critical for me."

She sighed and fought back frustration. "What's so damn important in Rio Rojo? It's a little hole in the wall place. Nothing ever happens there. I've been coming and going for months, but I never stay long because it is so damn boring. I only keep going back because my cousin and aunt live there, and I sometimes miss their company."

His jaw tightened and a nerve jumped in one lean cheek. "Unfortunately, things *do* happen in that little town. It is not immune to violence. My grandfather was murdered there not long ago."

Freeda blinked in surprise and started to protest. "Murdered…no, not lately…Oh, wait! You don't mean Naldo Sanchez, do you? He's the only murder victim I know of, but that happened several years ago."

His head jerked up, and the look of distraction vanished. His dark eyes zeroed in on her like black pinpricks. "You knew him?"

She shrugged, uncertain how to answer. Freeda had only seen the old man a few times, but she had never been introduced to him formally. Still, she knew the circumstances of his death.

"Well, no, I didn't know him personally," she admitted. "I arrived in town days before he was killed, but I do know what happened. Heck, my cousin caught his killer."

The dark eyes blinked again. He tilted his head toward the passenger side of his car. "Get in. You can tell me the details while we drive."

She pointed in the direction from which he had come. "I'll give you the details while you drive me to Casitas. It's only maybe ten miles out of your way."

He twisted around to look back down the road. "A little farther than that. As I recall, at the turn off from Albuquerque a couple of miles back, I saw a sign that said Casitas, fifteen miles west and Rio Rojo, thirty-five miles east."

"See? Casitas is closer. It will only take you an hour or so to get there and back. I'll tell you everything I know about what happened to your grandfather." She clasped her hands together in a praying motion. "You'll want all the details before you go into that town if you aren't from there. It's a strange little place. No one will tell you a damn thing. They don't like strangers …."

She paused, realizing she might be making a mistake by disparaging the town. Despite the fancy duds, he might be a native who had left years earlier. She hadn't heard anyone mention that Naldo had a grandson, but she wasn't exactly plugged into the town's gossip line. "Are you from there?"

He shook his head. "Haven't been there since I was a boy. I was born and raised in Albuquerque."

So! City guy. Maybe the promise to feed him information about his grandfather was not enough. "It's not just a ride I need. Please, mister, don't leave me alone out here with that guy…"

Chapter Two

Freeda stifled a smile as the man jerked his head and twisted in his seat to look toward her car where Diaz bent over the open hood. Her words were having an impact, so she rushed forward with her most entreating tone.

"I don't trust him," she added, keeping her voice low. "And there's no telling when someone else might come along…"

"Oh, all right," he agreed, sighing. With a quick motion, he cleared off a newspaper from the front seat and leaned forward to pick up a leather briefcase from the floor. He deposited both items into the back seat and gestured toward the passenger door. "Get in. I'll take you where you want to go."

Relief swept through her, but only for a few seconds. Freeda peered around the deserted area. "Turn your car around first."

"What? Don't you trust me either?" Surprise filled his voice.

"I don't trust any man," she replied honestly. "Turn the car around, and then I'll get in."

While he made a U-turn in the middle of the deserted road, she walked back to her aunt's car as fast as she could, wishing she had not chosen to wear such damn impractical shoes. Three-inch high-heeled sandals and long stretches of pavement didn't mix.

Diaz leaned over the engine, testing connections and

wiping his hands on a dark blue handkerchief. He did not look up from his work as she approached.

"That guy says he can take me to Casitas," she said, momentarily reconsidering her actions. She didn't like leaving the car in his hands, even if it was old and didn't belong to her. "Do you think you can get this thing running?"

"Don't worry about the car," he replied gruffly without looking up. "If I don't get it started, I'll let your aunt know what happened and see that it gets towed into town *for her.*"

His emphasis on the last two words made it clear he was doing the favor for her aunt. Freeda was again tempted to tease him, but she kept her reply simple, forcing a false smile to her face. "I'm certain Aunt Lottie will appreciate that, Mr. Diaz. Who knows, I might even ask her to cook you some of her famous chili in return."

He leaned around the side of the car and jerked his chin in the direction of the stopped car. "You're not worried about taking a ride from a stranger?"

For an instant, his gruff tone switched to one of concern. He had removed his dark glasses to work on the car, but without them, he appeared even more sinister with his watchful light green eye boring into her. The other was hidden behind a black patch.

She flashed a confident smile before opening the front door to get her backpack and jacket. "He's not exactly a stranger. He says he's old Naldo's grandson. Looks like he has money. No wonder he has never been around."

Diaz jerked up so rapidly he almost hit his head on the upraised hood of the car. The green eye trained on her and then shifted around to the stopped vehicle across the road. He wiped his hands on the rag he'd been using, dropped it on the radiator and walked toward the other car. She grabbed her backpack and followed.

Patrick Sanchez was ready to simply step on the gas and be on his way if the woman continued to be so demanding. He had an uneasy feeling about stopping along this deserted stretch of state highway.

As he often did with witnesses in his court cases, Patrick had studied her when she first approached. After turning his car around, he viewed her in his rearview mirror as the woman walked back to get her possessions. She was of medium height with thick black, curly hair that bounced around her shoulders. Her quick, animated way of speaking hadn't sounded like a New Mexico native. Her clothes didn't look that way either. She wore a tight black leather skirt, high-heeled sandals and a silk shirt that appeared to be a size too small.

Was stopping a mistake? He sighed—it was too late to consider that now. No, Patrick determined he had done the right thing. He would have felt more guilty leaving a stranded woman alone in this wilderness with someone who frightened her.

Besides, he had promised his mother he would get the situation regarding his grandfather's property resolved, and he didn't have much time to accomplish that task. If this woman could give him information which might make the resolution go more smoothly, the side trip might be beneficial to his interests too. She was correct about one thing. This side trip would only take him an extra hour and he might learn more from her in an hour than he would from a day in Rio Rojo.

He tensed as the man who had been working on the car abruptly jerked up from his efforts and strolled toward him. Perhaps his initial impression was wrong, and the pair was up to something together. Patrick would be a prime target—alone and driving an expensive car. He should have rented a vehicle for this trip.

His fears lessened somewhat as he watched the man's approach across the highway. He was of medium height and wiry, but he stepped forward with a slight limp. Why was the woman afraid? The man wore dark glasses, a worn cowboy hat, faded black jeans, scuffed boots and his appearance was like any cowboy who might work at one of the ranches in the area. His nearby pick-up was weather-beaten, and the faded green paint job showed that it had spent years under the hot New Mexico sun.

As he neared the car, the man touched his left hand to his hat. A slight smile lifted his lip on the left side, and Patrick realized he wasn't wearing glasses. His right eye was covered with a big black patch. Graying hair sprouted around the side of his faded black cowboy hat.

"Hi there. You're Naldo's grandson?" The man spoke amiably with a drawl in a soft, raspy voice.

"Yes." Patrick nodded slowly, feeling less wary.

"Diego Velasquez Diaz. Folks call me DV." The man wiped his hand on a blue handkerchief, but he didn't hold it out. "I'd like to shake your hand, Patrick, but I'm greasy from working on that car. I just want to let you know how sorry I was 'bout your granddaddy. Naldo was one of the good guys. One of the best men I've ever known. *Gente muy bueno.*"

Patrick noted his sudden use of Spanish. Many people in New Mexico did that, lapsed into dialect somewhere between English and Spanish—or *Spanglish*. Patrick was more surprised that the man knew his first name. He had not given it to the young woman.

"*Gracias*, Mr. Diaz. I'm sorry I didn't get to see him as often as I would have liked, and I was living back east when he died."

Diaz waved a hand and shook his head in dismissal. "Didn't matter none. That old man was proud of you, son. Damn proud! Kept your college graduation picture on a shelf next to his wedding picture. Loved telling the story of how if he ever got into trouble, he would call his lawyer grandson to set things right." He emitted a grunt and chuckled. "Not that he was ever gonna get in much trouble. Shame what happened to him…damn shame. He was a harmless old man who was always ready to help. Sometimes too much…"

Another twinge of guilt ran through Patrick at his lack of knowledge about the past, and that what he did know about his grandfather came from newspaper clippings. Even his mother had not known the old man that well.

This close, he noted that the man's smile didn't extend to the right side of his face, and that the skin around the eye patch was smooth, while the left side of his face was rugged and wrinkled with age. Diaz appeared to be in his 60s. Why was the woman afraid of him?

She approached the car carrying a large black backpack. "Thank you for taking care of Aunt Lottie's car, *Mr. Diaz,*" she said, giving him a stiff smile and holding out a set of keys.

A smile as fake as hers creased the man's face as he took the keys. "Like I said, *Miss Freeda*, no problem. You might warn her about allowing you to take it out of town. I'm no mechanic but that thing…" He shook his head.

She stiffened. "I'm certain she'll appreciate your concern *for the car*," she replied coldly, walking around to the passenger side of the car and climbing inside.

Diaz ignored her and turned toward Patrick. "You gonna be in town for a few days, Patrick, or are you heading back east right away?"

"Actually, I live in Albuquerque now, but I'll only be around long enough to check on the house and get the property on the market," he said and immediately regretted that he sounded so formal. The man had been extremely cordial.

Diaz tapped the side of the door with a finger. "Tell ya what, Patrick. I work up the road at the Tres Padres ranch, but I get into town frequently. I'll look you up in a coupla days when I come into town in case you're still around. Be happy to buy you a meal and answer any questions you might have about your grandaddy."

Patrick leaned forward, took a card from his pants pocket and handed it to Diaz. "Thank you. I look forward to hearing from you."

Diaz read the card before leaning forward to flick a pointed index finger toward the woman who was pulling a small purse from her worn backpack.

"Maybe I'll see you too, Miss Freedom. You take care of yourself. Don't go taking crazy risks for no good reason. And you can tell your daddy when you see him that if I catch him anywhere he shouldn't be, I'm going to have his sorry behind thrown in jail."

He stepped back and touched his finger to his weathered hat before turning and limping back toward the disabled car.

Freeda stifled the urge to stick out her tongue at him

as she watched him walk away. Somehow, he always seemed to engender her childish urges. Instead, she wrinkled her nose and made a face at the departing figure. "I hope I don't see you again for a very long time, Mr. Busybody," she grumbled through gritted teeth as she dropped her purse on the floor and sank onto the soft leather seat of Patrick's car.

Twisting around, she leaned over to place her backpack on the backseat, but her mind remained stuck on Diaz. Why was it that guy always gave her such a hard time every time they ran into each other? Beside her, the man Diaz had called Patrick concentrated on starting the car. She'd had no idea Diaz was that well acquainted with old Naldo Sanchez.

"He probably made up that comment about knowing your grandfather," she said, buckling her seatbelt as Patrick guided the car onto the highway. "I don't think he has been around here that long."

Patrick glanced toward her, his brow furrowing. "Why do you say that? I thought he appeared to be a nice guy."

"Hmph! You don't know him." Freeda blew out a quick breath, rolling her eyes. "If you're smart, you won't trust him or believe a single thing he says."

He drew up straighter in the seat, stiffening slightly. "I'm an attorney. I make it my business to study people, even upon first acquaintance."

Stifling her immediate inclination to protest, Freeda instead made a quick study of the driver. His comment and tone struck her as condescending, and the more she studied him, the more his entire appearance confirmed her initial impression.

She also surmised that the attorney was inwardly

laughing at her, though she wasn't about to tease him or contradict him on anything. She needed the ride, and Patrick Sanchez, driving his fancy, air-conditioned car with the soft, comfortable leather seats was just the right ticket to get her to her destination.

Still, she disliked men who thought they knew everything, and the more he talked, the more that opinion of him grew. He might be from Albuquerque, but he spoke with an eastern accent. If his grandfather really was old Naldo Sanchez, where had Patrick picked *that* up? Hadn't he just told Diaz he'd been back East? Was that where he had gone to school? How had he afforded that sort of an education? The man appeared to have money. Heck, even his cologne smelled expensive. That smell wasn't purchased on a drug store shelf.

"So, what's your story? Did your father give you a share of Marco's stolen money?" she blurted, curiosity getting the better of her. "Is that why no one has ever found it? Is that why no one has seen him since Marco died?"

"What?" He jerked upright in his seat. "Who the hell is Marco, and what does my father have to do with him? I have no idea where my father is. He disappeared years ago…" He paused, drawing a quick breath. "My family's history is nobody's damn business! Pardon my French."

Freeda stifled a smile. She could see that she had surprised, or perhaps even startled the man. His cool exterior had been penetrated by her personal inquiries, and he appeared flustered. She hesitated only a couple of seconds before continuing.

"Okay, let's talk about the present. Why have you never been around? I've heard Naldo's grandson had never been to Rio Rojo. That's a direct quote. Never visited once. But now you're suddenly going there? Years after your grandfather died? Why is that? Did he ever tell you the truth about Marco or…?"

She stopped, unable to follow through with the accusation she had been about to make—the rumor that his father, Berto, had been the person who killed the town bad boy, Marco Gonzales. Former Sheriff Bradley Foster had engineered the events, but Patrick's father was rumored to have either carried out the dirty work or helped Marco commit suicide. The exact end of Marco remained a mystery.

Patrick shook his head, the glistening dark hair shifting slightly before falling perfectly back into place. "Where are all these questions coming from? I have no idea what you're talking about, and I don't know about any guy named Marco. All I've ever known was that my grandfather was killed over some lost or stolen money. I do not believe rumors that he buried money in the yard or stashed money in the walls of the house as everyone seems to think. Yes, he operated a pawn shop, but that was many years ago, and he didn't hoard gold coins or stash stolen money. If he did, where did it all go? I've never seen it. My mom never saw it. She's worked in a dress shop as a seamstress for 40 years."

"But you got an Ivy League education?" she asked, acting on a hunch about his accent.

The man's full lips pressed together into a straight line before he replied. "Who said that?"

Freeda shrugged, uncertain now about her guess. She had never heard anything about the old man's grandson. She hadn't even known he had family still living. "You talk like you're from the East. You told Diaz that's where you were when your grandfather died."

"That is where I went to school. I got a scholarship and worked every day to get through college. I sat out a year to earn enough to get through law school." He took a quick breath and continued in a defensive tone. "I don't think my mom and I would have had to struggle so darn hard if we'd had a secret stash hidden somewhere, all right?"

"Okay, okay," she said, holding up her hands in a gesture of surrender. "I'm simply telling you what I've heard. It's people in that crazy town who keep spreading weird rumors."

"I haven't been *in* that town in years, so I don't know them, and they do not know me. What have *you* heard? You said you'd tell me if I drive you where you want to go. So, enough equivocation. We're driving in the direction you requested. It is time for you to hold up your end of the bargain."

Drawing a quick breath, Freeda decided to try a different approach. "Yes, sir, Mr. Attorney. Don't hold me in contempt or fine me. I'm not looking for jail time." She leaned forward, smiling at him, waiting for his body to relax.

Slowly, the edges of his full lips turned up, and his hands loosened on the steering wheel. He twisted in his seat to glance at her and grinned, a look that softened the hard lines of his lean face. "Then give me the truth and nothing but the truth."

Freeda laughed, stopping herself from telling him he became much more handsome when he loosened up. He might take it the wrong way. Better to simply start talking.

"Well, okay, like I told you, no one seems to know

where all this alleged missing money came from or went, but the mystery appears to involve your father and grandfather."

"But there is missing or hidden money?" he asked.

"That's what *they* say, but who knows who started the rumors? Your grandfather was rumored to have all these gold coins that he accumulated when he ran a pawn shop. No one's ever found any since he died, but various people around town claim they had seen them—that he liked to show them off from time to time when he was alive. There was also talk of a stash of bills and coins, rumored to have been kept in a bag or box that he buried somewhere. Some people say he may have forgotten where he put the bag. His memory apparently wasn't very good right before he was killed. He supposedly dealt mainly in cash and didn't believe in keeping it in the bank."

"That's what my mother says too," Patrick replied. "She told me that he had been that way for years because of runs on the banks that happened even before he was born. He was raised not to trust banks…" Patrick paused and turned away from her.

"No secret safe deposit box or anything?" She asked, but then would a careful attorney admit that, even if the old man did have one? And would he admit it to a stranger?

"All that is part of what I need to look into," he said quietly. "What else have you heard?"

She hesitated but decided to plunge forward with another account. "There's also a crazy story that your father took all the money and coins when he ran away. There's even a version that says he came back later and dug them up after your grandfather was murdered. Heck, there are even some people who think he came back and killed your grandfather for it."

When he scowled at her, she plunged forward. "I know that sounds callous, but the folks around here love stories and legends, especially about missing gold and treasure. There are tons of books in the local bookstores about New Mexico's hidden secrets. All you need to do is visit a store or gift shop to find the latest treasure map. I did a magazine article on that subject not long ago, and every store I visited swore that the books they carried were what I needed to make a fortune." She laughed, waiting for him to join her, but his scowl remained. "This place is a treasure hunter's paradise. Didn't you know that?"

Chapter Three

Patrick blew out a quick breath at her comment, but he chose not to respond. Yes, he knew about the many legends of missing or lost treasure in the New Mexico wilderness, but her statements about his father being part of a local treasure legend were new to him. His father supposedly had run away but might have come back? Why had his mother never told him that? Why had she also never mentioned that his dad's disappearance might have played a role in his grandfather's death? According to his mother, the murder of his grandfather had involved an old tragic mystery, but did that mystery itself also involve his father?

He released his breath as a long sigh. Patrick had never blamed his mother for not knowing all the details about his father's disappearance or not telling him much about the past. This was all on him. Yes, he'd been in Boston working on a case when his grandfather was killed, and he'd been unable to take a break for the funeral. But upon returning to New Mexico, he had still not taken the time to find out more about what had happened to the old man. All he'd read were a few newspaper accounts, and the Albuquerque newspapers had not been that interested in the murder of one old man in a town more than a hundred miles away.

His mother had been uninterested in anything beyond what happened to the property and whether the old man had left anything of value. She visited Rio Rojo after the funeral only long enough to check on the legal situation and find a local attorney to manage the old man's property. When no hidden bank accounts or stashed money was found, she let the matter go. Or had she? There were times he thought she hung onto ownership of the house in case something of value was discovered. Now, after spending more money repairing and keeping the property livable, she had finally decided they should dispose of it. She had never mentioned his father in discussing the property. As far as he knew, his missing father had never reappeared.

"From all I've been told, no one has seen my dad in years," Patrick admitted quietly. "But, please, go ahead with your story and what *you've* heard about him. Tell me everything you've been told since you came here. Don't leave anything out."

"Some of it goes back years," she warned.

"We have time," he prompted, waving toward the open road stretching in front of them.

Freeda drew a quick, sharp breath. "Okay, here goes. The old mayor of Rio Rojo, Bradley Foster, claimed your father helped frame this guy, Marco Gonzales, for burglaries that were committed thirty years ago."

"That far back?"

"It goes back farther than that. From what I've heard, Foster hated Marco since he was a boy and Foster was a deputy in Rio Rojo and supposedly caught him breaking into stores. Marco claimed he was innocent, but he was convicted and went to jail. Years later, he came back. Foster was sheriff by then and wanted to get him out of town because the reformed Marco had become a political activist and was stirring up people. This is where your father, Berto, apparently comes into the picture. The story goes that Berto was recruited by then Sheriff Foster to commit a series of burglaries similar to those Marco had been convicted of committing years earlier. Berto supposedly got to keep the money, while Foster blamed Marco so he could send him back to jail. Eventually, the pressure was so great, Marco killed himself or someone killed him. His death has never been fully explained, but your grandfather knew the truth, and that's why he was eventually killed. It was all a big damn, cover-up. In the end, Berto disappeared so no one has ever learned exactly what happened."

Patrick disliked hearing from a stranger about the unhappy truth regarding his father. His mother had informed him about his father's dubious past when he was young. However, she had never provided names; she merely told him that Berto Sanchez had been accused of committing a string of burglaries before Patrick was born and had gone to prison. After his release, Berto never returned to his wife and baby son in Albuquerque. He returned to his hometown and disappeared after a new string of burglaries and the mysterious suicide of one of his friends. After hearing of the reason for his grandfather's murder, Patrick had begun to wonder if his father stayed hidden for so long because he feared going back to jail because he might have committed the more recent burglaries, or if someone might take revenge on him for getting a man killed.

Knowing about his father's criminal past, Patrick spent years trying to demonstrate he was nothing like the lawbreaking criminal in the story. Hearing later that his father might also have been involved in the coverup which led to the death of his grandfather, had been even worse.

Going to Rio Rojo now meant facing those events of the past. His mother didn't like to discuss her former husband, but Patrick now felt like the time had come to learn the bitter truth. Perhaps this was the best way to cope with the problem—discussing the story with someone who didn't have loyalties tied into the town.

"Tell me what you know about my grandfather's death."

She hesitated, and he could feel her studying him. "You don't know the details of your own grandfather's murder?"

"Well, I know what I've read in the old newspaper stories, but…" His throat had grown dry, and he reached for the bottle of water in the cup holder. She appeared to sense his need and took it from him. She opened the bottle before handing it back to him with a sad, understanding smile.

He took a quick sip. "News stories don't always provide all the details. I don't recall reading any accounts that linked his death to my father's disappearance. What have you heard about him other than he might have broken into a number of businesses and then disappeared?"

"The story is that after Marco was released from prison, he returned to Rio Rojo. When someone began breaking into stores again, he immediately became suspect number one. The real story behind those break-ins was that the sheriff decided he didn't want Marco around at all. He wanted him gone permanently, so he asked your father to begin committing the burglaries again. However, this time your father was supposed to kill Marco eventually and make it look like suicide. People still argue about which it was, but Marco was finally killed or killed himself. However, your grandfather knew the truth—that someone, maybe your father—had been paid to kill him. When my cousin. Cere, started asking questions about that old Marco case several years ago, your grandad decided it was time to be honest about what he knew."

"Why would she want to do a story on an old murder case in a small town?"

"The assignment didn't start that way. She was supposed to do a supernatural story on a ghost appearing at some old dancehall—supposedly the ghost of Marco. It turned into a murder mystery when someone killed your grandfather."

He shook his head. "This is confusing."

"Yes, it is. The original story was that Marco committed suicide at the dance hall because he knew the sheriff was going to arrest him for the burglaries, and he didn't want to go back to jail. Years later his ghost supposedly began haunting the place because Marco hadn't committed those crimes or killed himself. That's what everyone said—that his innocent spirit needed to be set free. When Cere started asking questions, your grandfather decided to tell the truth—that if Marco *was* appearing out there, it was because he not only didn't commit the burglaries, he also didn't kill himself. He'd been framed by your father and the sheriff and murdered by either the sheriff or Berto. Your grandfather supposedly wanted to give peace to Marco's ghost by finally telling the truth. Instead, his actions got him killed. But who knows what the truth is? No one has seen your father since then, so it makes sense he went on the run to stay out of jail on a possible murder charge, and I don't think anyone has seen any ghosts since then either, so maybe that was the end to the story. Marco's ghost is finally at peace."

"You don't believe that whole ghost story?" he asked, glancing at her.

"Who knows? The bottom line is that the building burned down, and the ghosts are gone. Anyway, there's still the lost money angle. No one has ever found the money that was stolen. If Marco did take the money, what did he do with it? Where did he hide it? People keep digging around town, looking for it. Did Berto take it and run away? Both Berto and Marco were living at your grandfather's house. One died, the other ran off. What happened to the money?"

"That's why people think it's hidden around my grandfather's house," he muttered with a grimace. Patrick had been told some of the story previously, but he welcomed the opportunity to hear it from someone who had been a witness to the most recent events. The more he knew, the better off he would be when he finally arrived in Rio Rojo. He had delayed coming to town to settle his grandfather's affairs, but perhaps it was time to acknowledge that his father, Berto, had not only abandoned his family, but that people suspected him of being a thief and a possible killer. Had the mysterious Marco killed himself or had his father killed him and taken off with the stolen cash as this woman seemed to be suggesting?

"Go on," he prompted softly. "Please tell me what you know about the specifics of how my grandfather was murdered."

She leaned back in the seat, crossing her legs as she

began to tell the story. "Cere received a note from him that he wanted to talk to her. I guess he felt guilty after all these years and wanted to tell the truth. He knew how everything had happened, but he never told anyone the truth because he wanted to protect his son. When Cere came to town to do the story and started asking questions about the past, apparently your grandfather decided it was time to be honest. I don't know if he was still in touch with your father. We never found out. Your grandfather left a note for Cere, saying he wanted to talk about Marco's death. Unfortunately, he trusted the wrong person about his decision to tell the truth, and that was what got him killed."

Pausing, she tapped an unopened bottle of water in the cupholder between them. "Mind if I take a sip? I left my water bottle in the car."

"Go ahead. I keep a supply in the trunk when I travel."

She rolled her eyes as she opened the cap. "Now how could I have guessed that, Mr. Organized, Perfectly Pressed Shirt Guy?"

Patrick shot her a quick warning look, and Freeda decided she needed to be less sarcastic. Blowing out a quick breath, she took another sip of water before speaking, though she couldn't resist a final dig laced with a touch of flirtation. "Yeah, not like you came back to deal with things when he died or anything. I was here then. I didn't know many people, but I would have remembered your great smelling cologne."

His body tightened, and he steeled himself to ignore her gibes, wishing he didn't feel the need to justify himself. "I don't know anyone in town, and I was in the middle of a major case in Boston. As I've already mentioned several times, I never spent much time with my grandfather."

"Okay, okay, no need to be defensive. I don't get to spend time with my dad either, which is why I need to find him." She took another sip of water before resuming. "Anyway, that's your grandfather's story. Mayor Bradley Foster was trying to keep the poor old guy from revealing the truth—that Foster had paid your dad to kill Marco and keep the stolen money to get away. What did your dad do with it? Take the loot to Vegas and turn it into a fortune? What is he doing these days? Did he hear about the mayor's confession and that's why he never came to your grandfather's funeral? He knew he'd be arrested?"

Freeda stifled a smile as the man grimaced, his lean body stiffening. She appeared to have made the cool, collected man uncomfortable.

"I have no idea where my father is or what he's doing," he replied in a clipped tone, through tightened lips. "Nor did I ever get anything from him. He deserted me and my mother when I was a baby."

She could feel the tension in his body even across the console between them. Obviously, the issue of his father was a sore point for him. Still, she had to ask, "Because he had that stolen money so he could do anything he wanted or go anywhere he chose?"

Again, the answer came through stiff lips that had lost all color. "I have no idea. Could be."

"Uh, huh." She forced as much skepticism into her voice as she could summon. "Sure, Mr. Men's Wear Daily."

His earlier smile dissipated completely, and he turned to her, sparks flitting in his dark eyes. "Are you asking to be dropped off?"

Freeda blinked. *Oops!* She had gone too far. "You wouldn't!"

"Call me all the names you want. My mother calls me, Mr. Hard Ass without a Heart. So do some of my best friends."

"Your mother really says that? To *your face?*"

The hard lines of his lean, tan face didn't lessen. "Mom's a realist. But every penny I've ever had, I've earned myself and everything I've ever purchased was done on my own dime."

She wriggled back on the soft leather seat. The harsh tone of his voice told her she had ventured into dangerous territory beyond simple teasing. His profile appeared to be as hard as a granite statue, his lips set, his jaw rigid. She'd like to call him on it, but that grim look said she needed to shut up and enjoy the ride before he dumped her miles from her destination.

"I see," she replied in her best meek voice, wishing it didn't sound so squeaky.

The grim look softened slightly as he barked out a laugh. "That stopped you?"

"No, the thought of having to walk ten miles did," she said. "Haven't you noticed my shoes?" Freeda held out her leg, pointing her high-heeled sandals at the center console.

He glanced at her leg, and heat exploded in his dark eyes. He was looking at more than her sandals. She took her time lowering her leg, but she could sense the tension in the car shift from anger to something else—sexual awareness perhaps?

"Does that mean you plan to behave?" he asked.

"Hey, I'm very well behaved. Well, most of the

time." She grinned and winked at him, and the playful gesture appeared to relax him.

He turned back to the road. "Let's go back to what happened to my grandfather. I know you said Diaz wasn't close to him, but I have to disagree with that assumption. He knew where my grandfather kept my graduation picture. How would he know about that picture if he hadn't seen it inside the house?"

She blinked in surprise. "Diaz said he saw it?"

"He told me Gramps kept it on his mantle. That would be easy enough to check, so why would he make that claim if it wasn't true?"

Her face grew thoughtful as though considering the information. "Well, I guess that's possible. To be honest, I don't know much about Diaz except he likes to tease me, and he's always after my dad."

"But he frightens you?" he chided.

She blew out a quick breath. "He doesn't scare me as much as he irritates me. I think he does it on purpose. He used to do it to my cousin, Cere, when we first came to town. After he helped her when Mayor Foster died, she changed her opinion. Now she even seems to like him. So does her mother, my Aunt Lottie. To me, he's always been a spooky guy, but I think a lot of his tough guy approach is an act. He's been genuinely nice to Aunt Lottie. You saw him back there, so damn protective of that old car simply because it's hers. Ask Rafe about him. Rafe's the sheriff. He's married to my cousin, Cere." She reached over to tap his shoulder as though she had a sudden thought. "Actually, if you want more information about your grandfather, you should also talk to Rafe. He was very protective of that old man. Ask him about your graduation picture and see if he says the same thing as what Diaz told you. He has said that he used to visit him all the time."

"I do plan to get in touch with Sheriff Tafoya. He called me after Grampa died. Most of my arrangements have been directed through him. He's been very helpful."

"Oh, yes," Freeda agreed enthusiastically. She'd grown to care about the man she'd once feared, though she knew at times her actions irritated him. "Rafe is definitely helpful and nice. He puts up with me. He and Cere became involved when we came here to visit her mother. She decided to stay with him instead of going back to California. Can you believe it? She gave up a budding career as a television reporter to marry him. But as it turns out, it was a good choice. She loves living here. You should ask him about Diaz too. Rafe has several theories about that guy. He won't tell me what they are, and if he's told Cere, she refuses to pass it on. But like I said, Rafe knew your grandfather pretty well, and now that I think about it, he mentioned once that he suspects Diaz knew your father too."

Patrick jerked toward her, surprise showing on his face. "Diaz *knew* my father?"

"I think Cere once told me Rafe said something like that. The more I think about it, the more I'm convinced you should track Diaz down later and see what he says. Just be careful. He has a way of changing his mind from minute to minute. One day he'll be very pleasant, the next day, he'll look right through you. If he talks to you about anything, see if you can find out how he ended up with that eye patch."

She was rambling, but he appeared to be curious, and she wanted him to know his trip to Casitas wasn't without its benefits.

"What about *your* dad?" he asked.

She jerked up. "What about him?"

"Is he sick? Why is it a matter of life or death?"

Freeda hesitated, taking a moment to formulate an answer. How could she tell him the truth? He might dump her back on the road. "Well, no, he's not sick," she admitted.

"But you're in a big rush to get to him?"

"He's going to be at a certain place until ten this morning, and I don't want to miss him."

"Can't you call him and let him know you're running late? Check your phone now and see if it works." He pointed at her purse.

She grimaced, touching her bag—not that it would do any good. "I…don't have any way to reach him."

"You don't have his number?"

Time to come clean, she decided. At least partially clean. "Um…no. I don't even know if he has a cell phone."

"I see."

His tone sounded skeptical, and she waited for him to protest, but then she remembered his earlier comment about not having seen his father since he was a baby. "It's actually kind of like your deal. Well, maybe not as bad, but a lot like it."

"Meaning?"

"I haven't seen my dad in years. I don't even know for certain where he is. He used to live here in New Mexico. He left me at Aunt Lottie's when I was only seven. Nena, my grandmother came from California and took me to live with her." A shiver ran through her. She hated telling the story. "I'd rather not talk about it."

"But you're looking for him?"

"Wouldn't you find your dad if you could?" she shot back. "Wouldn't you like to spend time with him and find out why he disappeared? Wouldn't you like to know why he just left you and your mother?"

Chapter Four

Freeda's question appeared to unnerve Patrick. His head jerked, and his jaw tightened. She almost regretted asking such a personal question.

For a few seconds he remained silent as though thinking through the question before answering in a soft voice. "I haven't really thought about it beyond the fact that he's never been around. I would like to know what happened to him. I regret that I never spent time with my grandfather. My mother has a big family and they made up for not having a dad around. I liked that my mom and I have always been a team."

"See?" she said, frustration swirling inside her. "You had folks around you, plus your mother. I never had a mother around, and my father has always been on the move. Yes, I had family members all around me, but they all had their own families. I had my grandmother, but I shared her with all of them. Well, now I want to find my *own* dad and maybe spend some time with him. I mean, it's not like I haven't seen him since I was young. He turns up every few years and sends me postcards and birthday cards from various places he visits, so I know he does think about me from time to time. I know that he cares about me. He always says in his letters and cards that he wants to see me, and he says *maybe someday* we can spend some time together. Well, enough with the delays. I am tired of waiting for someday. I don't want to delay any longer! I want to see him *now* and I'm going to do it *now*. This time I might even ask him why he is always on the move. Is he trying to find something or is he running from something?"

"I see." His face grew thoughtful as though he understood.

Perhaps she had said too much, but she wasn't sorry for getting so upset or emotional. The thoughts had been swirling inside her for too long. Perhaps it was best to vent them on a stranger who would probably forget about her the minute they parted. She glanced over at him. His face had grown thoughtful.

"At least you had your mother. I love my Nena, but she had nearly a dozen grandchildren besides me. You were lucky to have someone all to yourself."

His smile was slow and sad. "Yes, I guess so. We are alike that way, not having our fathers around. People are always complaining about their parents, but to me, well, I think it might have been nice to have had that chance for a real family. I'd like to give that to my own kids one day."

His comment surprised her. "You have kids?" she asked. "You take them riding in this fancy car? I don't see any ice cream stains."

His smile widened. "No, no kids. I'm not married yet, but that's what I want when it finally happens. I know what I didn't have growing up, and I'd like the opportunity to share that sort of life with someone who feels the same way."

Freeda considered his answer. "Me too, I guess. Someday. And see, this is why I am trying so hard to get to Casitas. I want to see my dad. I want to get to know him better while I can. I was told he eats breakfast every day at this same restaurant, and he's usually only there until 10. I need to get to that restaurant before he leaves."

He glanced at the clock on the dashboard. "Even without speeding, we should make it with at least ten minutes to spare."

Freeda pulled up her purse from the floor, opened it and began to go through it. "Don't watch. I need to fix my face."

He chuckled gently and flashed a wide smile. "Fix your face?"

She dug out her brush and waved it before fluffing her unruly curls. "You know, freshen up. Make myself presentable. I'm not meeting my dad for the first time in years looking like I was jumping up and down on the road begging some strange guy for a ride. I bet my lipstick is all messed up." She turned down the visor and checked her face in the mirror behind it. Her cheeks were flushed, but she didn't look too bad. She wiped away a smudge of mascara and applied a fresh coat, as well as another coating of Perfectly Cherry lipstick.

"What if he's not there?" he asked, glancing in her direction.

"What?" her voice came out like a squeal, but she couldn't help herself. "Why the hell would you say that? Do you want to jinx me? Of course he'll be there. He has to be!"

"I told you my mom calls me a realist.".

"A hard ass, you mean," she shot back.

Patrick nearly laughed at her harsh assessment but held his face expressionless. He didn't care to explain why his mother said that, but Freeda was probably right. Not that his mother wasn't equally as forceful. If she hadn't been, she couldn't have talked him into making this trip to check on his grandfather's affairs. To discover his grandfather might have things hidden or buried was not something he wanted to contemplate, though he knew it was possible.

As Sheriff Tafoya had suggested years ago, Patrick had hired movers from Santa Fe to pack up the contents of his grandfather's house and put the boxes and furniture into storage. The work had been done under the sheriff's supervision so Patrick didn't worry that someone might have stolen anything.

While he hated the constant vigilance regarding the house, Patrick knew there was some truth to the strange rumors. He'd been told by Sheriff Tafoya that the people who had packed up the house had found small bundles of cash in various locations around the house when they went through it. The number of bundles surprised Patrick but the discovery angered his mother.

His mother decided not to immediately sell the house once the money was discovered. However, the property itself had become a problem after rumors of cash stashed in the walls had gotten out.

For a while, they simply kept it locked. After it had been broken into several times, he and his mother decided it might be better to rent it. Finding renters was no issue, but no one wanted to live there for long. The interior was gutted while the lawn was constantly being dug up. Even the garage and old storm cellar weren't spared. Only the fact that the sheriff lived around the corner had kept it from being completely torn down by frantic treasure hunters. No one seemed to have a ready solution to the dilemma, and that became part of the problem. All anyone knew was money had been found inside the house, and more cash could possibly be anywhere.

Could Freeda's story be the truth about what might have happened to his father? Had he been paid to kill someone and disappeared to keep from being charged? Patrick had never investigated the reasons for his father's leaving but if he had been party to a murder or thefts, it was no surprise he would want to stay hidden.

But his father's disappearance was only part of the unsettling story. There were also those alleged coins Freeda had mentioned. That rumor had also existed for years and was what had his mother in an uproar now.

"They have to still be around," she'd insisted to him. *"Why else would people keep looking for them if they don't exist? Someone knows the truth! We need to find out what really happened to them."*

Inquiries to the sheriff had not revealed any answers. Sheriff Rafe Tafoya had told Patrick he had never seen them, but his mother was growing increasingly adamant that they must exist, or people wouldn't keep vandalizing the house. So here he was—taking time away from work to check out the claims he still believed to be unfounded.

He glanced to the passenger seat. Freeda stared glumly out the side window as she chewed on a fingernail. Her anxious face touched him as did her search for her father. He'd never once considered looking for Berto Sanchez—not that he wasn't aware that his father had spent time in prison on a variety of charges.

At times, when Patrick visited prisons, he wondered if his father might be near, residing somewhere behind the walls. He knew all he had to do was put the name into a state database, and he could probably learn his father's whereabouts, but he'd refrained from doing so. He'd never wanted to think about where the man might have ended up after leaving his wife and little boy.

Recently Patrick had begun to question whether he didn't look for him because he didn't want to discover the truth. He knew his mother had no desire to see her husband again.

Now Freeda had re-opened questions about his father. Could Diaz tell Patrick where his father might be or what had become of him and why he had never gotten in touch with his family? Diaz seemed friendly enough. While Patrick intended to approach him about his grandfather's life, should he also ask about his father?

What Patrick did know about his father was that Berto was an only child, and Naldo's wife died long before her son disappeared. But what had become of the man? Why had he never come forward to claim whatever the old man might have left? Perhaps he had a whole new family, Patrick reasoned. There was also a part of him that feared a confrontation with his long-lost father whom he'd never seen.

Did he truly want to see his father? Patrick had known his father was involved with a killing, but the question had always been whether the man had committed suicide or been shot by Berto. Could he have killed this Marco Gonzales that Freeda spoke of, and was that why he had stayed on the run all these years?

The air conditioning suddenly grew too cold, and Patrick shivered. He had never liked thinking about his father for long. He doubted that would ever change.

****

The outskirts of Casitas arrived in the form of an old drive-in that was recognizable only from the faded sign on the back of a tall torn screen. It probably hadn't shown a movie since the 1960s and it was followed by a junkyard filled with old cars. That was followed by a string of motels on either side of the highway along with a modern strip mall complete with a couple of fast-food outlets and several nondescript stores. Those buildings were followed by a huge warehouse store with a large, partially filled parking lot.

"Where is this place we're headed?" Patrick asked as they reached an area of old retail stores that had the appearance of businesses that had been in business since the 1950s.

"We're looking for a place called *Bernie's Cafe*. I was told it's right along the main highway. Oh! There it is." She pointed to an oval neon sign over the doors of a small white structure that began a strip of aging buildings that appeared to begin the core of the town's central business district.

He pulled into the nearest parking spot while Freeda grabbed her purse and turned around to grab her backpack from the back seat.

"Do you need me to wait for you?" he asked.

"I'll be fine," she said, but he could read the nervous timbre to her voice. After all her brash bravado, she was suddenly flushed and appeared anxious as she craned her neck looking toward the front of the café.

"All right." He pulled his card case from his pocket and took out a card. "Give me a call if you need anything. That has my cell phone number."

She took the card and tossed it into her bag, along with the water bottle she had been using. "Don't worry about me. I'll be fine."

"I'm certain you will be. I'm going to drive over to the gas station on the corner, fill up and then head out.

Maybe I'll run into you in Rio Rojo."

"Yeah, sure." She climbed out of the car, and then abruptly glanced up with a smile as she hefted her backpack onto her shoulder. "I'll buy you lunch or dinner at *El Matador*. That's where you need to stop and ask around about your grandfather, by the way. Dynamite food and it's where all the locals hang out. They give the best gossip. Mention Naldo's name and someone will buy you dinner."

"Thanks, but my first stop will be the courthouse to talk to the sheriff."

"Naturally. But it's only a few blocks from *El Matador*." She gestured with a little finger wave as she slammed the door shut.

"Bye, Freeda. Thanks for the company," Patrick said, realizing he was happy that he had given her the ride. She had made the trip pleasant, and she had been right—he garnered a lot of information that might be useful when he finally arrived in Rio Rojo.

"Bye, bye," she mouthed through the glass.

Patrick chuckled as she turned and walked into the restaurant. He liked the way her nicely formed hips moved, and her curls danced around her head. Nice legs too, but then he stopped. *No! No way*. Even if he saw her again, he recognized that Freeda Ferguson was not his type. She had not even thanked him for the ride. He was lucky to be rid of her so quickly.

He threw the car into gear and pulled onto the deserted street. The side trip had not been a total waste of time. But it had raised a number of questions. The matter of the hidden coins was going to be an issue as he cleared out and closed down his grandfather's house.

Patrick wanted to say the story was all a myth—

except he had once seen one of the coins. As a child, he had visited his grandfather in the summer several times and one evening the old man had dug out a coin from a worn leather pouch he kept stashed in an old cabinet. The gold coin was polished to a bright sheen, and while its origin was unknown. Patrick could see it was not something one might get in an American bank. He also knew it was not the only one his grandfather had in his possession. The old man had jiggled the leather pouch, telling Patrick there were more inside before pulling out a handful and dumping them back into the bag.

"The Spanish Conquistadors brought them when they explored this part of the country," Naldo had said with a broken toothed grin. "They was lookin' for gold, but never found nothin.' Funny thing is, it was all around them, if they'd only taken the time to dig into the hills a little. The gold strikes didn't come until hundreds of years later. Instead, the explorers were killed by Indians or left their belongings. If you look carefully around the canyons, you can still find things like armor, shields, swords…or coins." He'd jiggled the bag again, laughing.

Patrick was still recalling that day as he pulled into a gas station, swiped his credit card, and put the pump nozzle into the tank opening of the car. He probably had at least half a tank, but he didn't like traveling in this rural part of the state without keeping it that way. He could end up like Freeda, waving his arms in the middle of the road.

Damn, he should have asked her if she needed to call a tow truck for her car. No, let her take care of it. She had not been worried about the car, and he doubted anyone would want to steal the thing. Besides, that strange man, Diaz, had said he would see that it was towed into the nearest town, and while Freeda didn't like the man, she had been certain he would take care of the car.

He concentrated on getting the last few drops out of the hose as a familiar exotic, cinnamon scent overpowered the odor of gas. He jerked up as Freeda dumped her bag on the trunk his car.

"Well, my luck just keeps getting better." she said, her voice cracking. "I missed my dad, and now I've lost my wallet."

Chapter Five

Patrick put the nozzle away and held out a hand toward Freeda. "Are you all right?"

She bit back her tears. "I'm fine, but did I drop my wallet in your car?" she asked hopefully, looking toward the front seat.

"I don't think so, but you're welcome to check. Did you go through your bag?"

"Of course, I did. Twice through every pocket! It's not there." She opened the front door and leaned over to dig around. The dark carpet was empty, and she found no wallet under the front passenger seat or in the back seat either. It had probably fallen out before she met Patrick and was sitting on the front seat of her aunt's car, begging any passerby to steal it. She couldn't even remember if she'd locked the doors before she abandoned the piece of crap car. Perhaps Diaz would see it if he glanced inside. At least if he found it, he might take it to Aunt Lottie as a special favor to *her*.

Patrick's gaze swept up and down the block as though he might spot it on the road. "Are you certain you had the wallet with you? Or maybe you left it in the car where I picked you up."

"Thanks, I've thought of all that, but that won't help me right now," she said, immediately regretting her gruff tone of voice. He had been trying to help. "I'm sorry," she added with a sigh. "Everything seems to be going

52

wrong this morning."

He grunted grimly. "Some days are like that. Maybe you should look for a garage to get your car fixed." He replaced the gas nozzle on the pump.

"No mechanic is going to take me all the way back to my car if I can't give him a credit card. Besides, I'm not leaving here without taking some time to look for my dad!" Tears almost overwhelmed her. She had come so close to finding him! Several people in the café said they had seen her father that morning, but no one knew where he was or where he might have gone. He might still be around somewhere. Unfortunately, she didn't know where to start looking around Casitas. Except for the café, none of the stores on the block were open. What could she do?

Against her will, tears edged out of her eyes. She didn't want to cry, but everything kept going so wrong. If only the car hadn't broken down, if only she had left earlier. If only…. She shook her head, still fighting the tears. "I need to find my dad," she pleaded, her voice nearly breaking.

"You said he was gone."

"But he'd been there," she protested. Shivers ran through her as goosebumps rose on her arms. "I was so damn close. They said he left half an hour ago. He might even still be around."

She studied the street as she pulled a tissue from her bag to wipe her damp face. To her horror, her tears had melted mascara into her eyes, making them sting. The result was another flood of tears.

She squeezed her eyes shut, and when she opened them, Patrick kneeled next to her. He held out a snowy white handkerchief and she took it with a mumbled thanks. She didn't know any men who even carried handkerchiefs. Stifling a giggle, her throat constricted, and she coughed instead.

To her horror, Patrick reached for her. She pulled back to escape his touch. She didn't want his sympathy or to show him her sudden weakness. Given her current emotional state she was likely to throw herself against what was probably a muscular chest and then cry all over his fancy shirt. And the whole time, he would probably be inwardly laughing at her weakness. Or even worse, he might try to soothe her. She didn't want either.

As though he sensed her thoughts, he pulled back and took extra time to place her bag in the back of the car and close the door. He washed the windows while she dried her eyes and blew her nose. By the time he finally opened the driver-side door, she had regained her composure somewhat, though her throat still felt tight.

"Do you mind…could you please get me another bottle of water? I left the bottle you gave me earlier at the café. I was so upset about missing my dad."

His handsome face softened. "Certainly."

He walked to the back of the car while she put the handkerchief to her damp face and wiped it. She did enjoy the scent of his cologne, but as she finished wiping her face, she studied the cloth and noted the monogram. Had she ever known any man with such a fancy handkerchief?

But that thought was fleeting. She didn't have time for crazy flirtatious thoughts. She needed to focus on what was important such as what was she going to do about finding her father? Could she convince Patrick to drive her around town looking for him? She studied Patrick through the window, trying to decide if she should ask him. No, he had been in a rush, and she had already delayed him.

He shook his head when she offered him the handkerchief as he climbed back into the car. "Keep it for now," he said, holding out a bottle of water.

Clearing her tight throat, Freeda accepted the plastic bottle. She opened it and took a long drink before replying. "I'm sorry I am such a basket case today. I didn't mean to get so emotional. I don't lose it like that often. But it's been a while since I was this close to finding my dad."

He opened his own water bottle and took a deep drag. "So now what?" The car remained parked under the canopy beside the gas pumps, but they would need to move if another vehicle arrived. She was pleased he hadn't made any move to start the car yet. Luckily, all the other gas pumps were open so perhaps they could stay a few minutes to determine their next move.

"Well, I need to find my dad," she stated softly.

"Yes, and I still need to get to Rio Rojo," he reminded her. "But I hate to leave you here without any transportation and without your wallet."

She blew out a quick breath as she surveyed the street of the small town. Her strength and determination were slowly returning. Freeda summoned her most pathetic voice. She didn't like to ask for assistance, but she had no money to bribe people into helping her find her dad, and she had no idea where to start looking. She might normally be considered resourceful, but at the moment she had no resources and no idea what to do next.

Freeda sighed loudly, hoping for his sympathy. "Um…well…then don't go right now," she said, nearly choking on the words as she attempted a smile.

Patrick watched Freeda, not certain if he was shocked by her comment or if he was pleased by it. He hated leaving her on her own in her current circumstances. His lips twitched, and he fought to keep from smiling. "You want me to stay and help you look for your dad?" he asked. "Is that what you want?"

She had the grace to lift her shoulders in an apologetic shrug. "It shouldn't take long. And believe me, Rio Rojo is going nowhere. Whether you get there in half an hour or later this afternoon won't matter. I just need…" she paused, biting her lip, "I need help right now."

Patrick studied her. "Something tells me you can get all the help you need if you really try."

She inclined her head toward him. "But I'm asking *you*. I don't know anyone here. I don't even know how I'm going to get back to Rio Rojo today if you leave and I don't find him."

"I see." He opened his water bottle and took a drink, his eyes remaining on her. *What was he thinking?* Did he really have time for this detour? His tongue teased his lips, and he was tempted to request she ask him nicely. No, that would sound too condescending or predatory. He touched his tongue to his upper lip, fighting back a quick smile.

She shivered and lowered her eyes. "Please," she said in a soft tone.

"Please what?" he asked, fighting hard now to hold back a smile. For once he felt like he had the upper hand.

"Please, Patrick, will you stay for a little bit and help me?"

He sighed and Freeda watched his nicely formed

lips change into a grimace. "Look, why don't I help you find a mechanic to get that car brought in for repairs. I can lend you enough money to get it fixed. You can pay me back later in Rio Rojo."

She sensed he might be wavering. "Well, my aunt will pay for the car, of course. But I need to find my dad."

"Before finding your wallet?"

Freeda wrinkled her nose in distaste. She needed the credit cards, of course, but they were so damn close to their maximum that even if some thief took the wallet, they'd be damned embarrassed the first time they tried to use them. If some thief wanted to steal her identity, well, so be it. She'd love to be rid of that rotten credit history and blame it all on someone else.

She reached out and touched his bare arm with her fingertips. "Please, Patrick. If you help me, I'll go back to Rio Rojo with you and help you find out what happened to your dad."

He blinked and drew back. She saw some of the color drain from his lean face. For a minute, his pouty lips worked soundlessly.

An attorney without anything to say? She almost chided him, but instinct told her this was a good time to keep her mouth shut. She pressed her lips together and widened her eyes, making a silent plea. Surely he could see how important this was to her.

The air of the car grew hot and stifling, but then he put the bottle of water into the cup holder between them as though putting a brick in place to begin building a wall. He sighed and shook his head, but it wasn't a gesture that said no. It was more a sign of resignation.

"Do you have any idea where he might be?" His head swiveled as he studied the street.

"Well…I was in such a rush, I just took off from that diner, checking the streets for him and then I saw you. Maybe if we go back there, to the diner…I mean the people seemed to know him."

He turned away from her, settling into the seat. "All right. Maybe we can buy a cup of coffee and ask around."

Freeda turned away to look out the window to hide her inner feeling of smug satisfaction.

Bingo!

Patrick drew a quick breath, pressing his lips together. He wasn't certain he was making the right decision in agreeing to help. He could almost hear his mother accusing him of being a sucker for a sob story, but for a few minutes Freeda had been real. He had seen her look of anguish when she said she'd missed her father and lost her wallet. Without all that eye make up her dark eyes had been luminescent and pleading for help.

Now she was busy looking in the mirror of the compact she'd pulled from her purse and repairing her make up. And she was correct—he was in no hurry to reach Rio Rojo. Yes, he needed to find out about his grandfather's belongings and get the house situation straightened out, but she'd also raised some issues he didn't like to consider. Were there answers to his own father's whereabouts in those belongings? Did it matter?

As a boy, he had never asked his mother about his father, and she never volunteered the information. Could answers be hidden in his grandfather's belongings? Sheriff Rafe Tafoya had said he was keeping all personal items locked up in storage until Patrick could go through them. Both he and the Sheriff knew those damn coins might be squirreled away inside some box or mixed in with other items. From Patrick's understanding, his grandfather had never thrown out anything. He had also once run a pawn shop and some of his belongings that he had accumulated might be valuable. At least that was what his mother claimed.

Patrick sighed. Those thoughts could wait.

He parked the car on the opposite side of the street, and they walked across it to the diner. The interior was cool but pleasant. The smell of frying bacon filled the air. Only a few tables held diners while a couple of men sat at the counter. An overweight blonde woman wearing too tight black jeans and a cotton shirt that barely fastened through the bust waved as they entered the room.

"No luck on the search? Well, sit anywhere you want," she said as she filled the cup of a gruff-looking wiry man at the counter. A big straw cowboy hat rested beside him.

Freeda ignored the tables and took a spot one stool down from the men. Patrick sat on the empty seat past her.

"You didn't find him?" a man asked from the door to the back of the diner. His gray hair was long, almost to his shoulders and held back by a net. He had a graying beard that was scruffy, narrowing to a V just above his chest. He wore a greasy apron tied around narrow hips.

Freeda shook her head sadly, pressing her lips together.

"That's a shame." The waitress approached with two glasses of water. "Can I get you something?"

"Maybe a diet cola?" Freeda said.

Patrick opted for coffee, and the woman turned away to prepare their drinks. She wore a plastic name tag that said "Debra," and Patrick thanked her as she placed the drinks on the counter in front of them.

Freeda turned to the man nearest to her at the counter. "Do you know Fergie Ferguson?"

He lifted a hefty shoulder in a shrug. His overly large black T-shirt was ripped in several spots, and his jeans were worn and patched in places. "Don't rightly recall. Maybe."

The other man stepped out from the door to the back and leaned against the counter. "I don't know why he left early this morning. Like I said, he comes in every day." He tapped the counter in front of the other man. "You know him, Ezra. He's in here lots of mornings. Calls himself Fergie. Tall, thin, long gray hair, always ready to chat."

"The hippie lookin' guy?" Ezra asked, lifting his lips from his coffee cup.

The other man put a hand to his chest before speaking in Spanish. "*Si, mi amigo*. A man of the people. That's what he always says. Everyone is his good friend, and he can say it in two languages."

The waitress pursed her lips as she shook her head. "You and Fergie never grew out of the sixties and seventies, Sam."

"Groovy, just searching for peace, stayin' cool." Sam grinned at her as he raised his fingers, to form the familiar Y of a peace sign.

Freeda ignored their antics. "Is my dad working around here?"

The man sitting at the counter grunted. "Don't know if he's working there but he spends a good deal of time hanging out at Tres Padres."

Chapter Six

Freeda whirled toward the man who had just spoken. "Tres Padres? Do you mean the old ranch that's being turned into a resort?"

Ezra set down his coffee cup on the counter with a thump. "So, I hear. Resort spa. Those are just the newest names for what used to be called a dude ranch. Like someone's going to drive those crappy ranch roads just to lay in a damn mud bath or play golf."

Sam tapped the counter. "Don't laugh too hard. I hear they're fixing those roads. But soon, the roads won't matter. Word is they're building an airstrip up there so the big money guys don't even have to drive."

"Yeah, they can fly in on their own private jets," another man at the counter added. "A damned airstrip. Can you believe it? We'll get little planes, jets flyin' over all the time and then some damn plane will crash into a mountain, and we'll have to go search for it, or, hell, they could set off a damn forest fire."

"Air strip ain't gonna work in the wintertime when they get snowed in," Ezra replied.

"Next thing you know, they'll chop down a bunch of trees to build some ski runs. Go after that crowd. Tourists comin' in year around. Mean big tips for you, hon," the other man said, winking at the waitress.

"Pfff…I won't count on that," the waitress replied in a droll tone. "Those types don't come in here that often, and when they do, they don't tip that well. But they expect everyone to jump at their smallest commands."

"Still, turning it into a resort is better than it was in the old days when they had that commune up there," another man said. "Back when I was growing up, we had young folks passing through town all the time, looking for handouts, pitching tents in the park." He shook his head in disgust. "A resort is much better."

Patrick leaned closer to his coffee cup, curious about their discussion of development in the area. His firm had been approached in the past about various development ideas, but that could wait. For now, he had to figure out what to do about this crazy Freeda Ferguson situation.

He finished his coffee and picked up the check.

"Ready to go?" he asked, glancing at Freeda.

She grimaced but drained her own cup of coffee. She gestured toward the waitress. "Can you do me a favor? If he comes back today, will you please tell him I'm looking for him?" she asked, a hopeful note in her voice.

The older woman winked at Freeda. "Sure, hon. Good luck with your search."

****

"What now?" Patrick asked as they settled back into the car. Freeda huddled in the passenger seat, her face downcast, remaining silent. She had not spoken since they left the café. Patrick watched her, uncertain what to say or do. Unlike her upbeat manner when they walked to the restaurant, her shoulders slumped as they returned to the car. Now she sat huddled against the door. He almost reached out to put his arm around her to offer an encouraging word, but the stiffness of her pale face stopped him. Her lips quivered slightly, as she remained silent, giving no indication she had heard his question.

While Patrick had met her little more than an hour ago, he felt a strange, protective connection to her. For all her breezy declarations, Freeda Ferguson struck him as vulnerable at her core, though he doubted she would admit it. At times, he felt like he could read her—or at least he was getting better at it, even after their short acquaintance. She exuded confidence outwardly, and she certainly was quick-witted when she chose to be, but he guessed she also carried doubts inside that she kept hidden.

"Freeda? What do you want to do?" he asked again, but she still did not answer. "I suppose we need to get your car towed into town or I can take you back to Rio Rojo."

She jerked up; her pale face filled with panic. "What? No! I can't leave. I have to find my dad."

An instant spark of irritation ran through him, but he fought to keep his voice calm and reasonable. "But you don't know where he is."

She gaped at him as though he was a slow learner. "How can you say that? Tres Padres. You heard what they told us."

"And they also told us it's 20 miles away," he reminded her.

She lifted her shoulder in a slight shrug. "So?"

"How are you going to get out there without a car or any money?"

Another half shrug. "Hitch. Or I'll find some nice person willing to take me up there."

His eyes shifted to her bare legs. "That's not a good idea, Freeda."

She twisted around, noticing where his eyes were

trained before his head jerked up. Her disgusted gaze met his. "This is small town America. They're mostly farmers or ranchers, not big city users and perverts."

"Ranchers still have hormones."

"I can handle myself," she proclaimed with false bravado.

Patrick drew a quick breath to hide his irritation. "Look, how about if I take you to Rio Rojo to your aunt's house, and you can figure out how to get out to the ranch later. Maybe she'll take you. Heck, if you don't find a ride, I'll take you myself after I talk to the sheriff and find out about the situation with my grandfather's property."

"We don't know that my dad left town," she protested, twisting on the seat to survey the town's nearly empty streets. "He left the café, but he might still be around. Maybe I should visit a couple more places he frequents." Her gaze swept up and down the street, as though gauging which places he might visit.

"Such as?" he demanded, skeptical of that plan. "The jewelry store? The bank?"

She pressed her lips together in frustration before answering. "Yes, maybe the bank, or the grocery store. Maybe he's shopping there right now for food or maybe he stops there regularly. I can check. Maybe the clerks know when he normally comes in or other places he might visit. People in these small towns know everyone and their habits. You heard those guys at the café."

"And if that doesn't pan out? How will you find out where he might be besides the grocery store?"

"Leg work." She pulled down her skirt. "And I don't mean what you probably think."

Warmth flooded his face. Patrick hated when he

couldn't hide his thoughts, and she probably saw the flush that darkened his cheeks. "All right."

"I'll walk around to the other stores and ask people about him. I might find out what places he normally visits when he comes into town. For all we know, he could be staying some place down the block." Freeda straightened in the seat, some of the enthusiasm returning to her voice. "Maybe he's at the drug store, picking up prescriptions, or the library, checking out a book. There are plenty of places to look and probably plenty of people I can ask about him. I can be pretty darn resourceful when I need to be. Talking to people has never bothered me."

While she appeared determined to do exactly what she had said, her plan didn't sound as though it might garnish results. Patrick twisted around to look toward her. "I hate leaving you here on your own."

She grinned at him, her eyes sparkling like bright round gems. "Then don't leave me. Your grandfather is dead, Patrick. Getting to Rio Rojo this afternoon won't bring him back, and you probably won't accomplish a damn thing until I get there and help you anyway."

"I'm planning on talking to the sheriff, then going to the bank to close his safe-deposit box, and finally, to a real estate agent to see about selling the house. I don't need help for that."

Her brow furrowed as she reached over to tap his arm. "You're not curious about the comments people have made about your dad? That he might have been responsible for the death of Marco Gonzales? That he might have been killed himself? Or that he took off with the money?"

"As I've already said, my dad's been gone for a long

time. I never knew him."

"Exactly," she replied in a breathless tone, tapping his arm harder. "Don't you want to know about what happened to him?"

He held up his hand to stop further speculation. "Do not confuse what I want with what you're doing."

Freeda appeared puzzled, shaking her head, but at least she paused her questions. Patrick did not want to get sucked into whatever drama she was outlining, but after a few minutes, he realized her earlier questions about the past had piqued his interest more than he wanted to admit. Until this morning, he had never wanted to know any of the details about his dad or the life he had before he disappeared. Patrick had chosen to walk away from thoughts of the past much as his father had walked away so easily from him and his mother.

Geneva Sanchez had to save every penny when Patrick was in school and only scholarships, loans and grants had gotten him through the university. Grants had again come to his rescue for law school, but he was still paying back the larger chunk of his law school debts. Even though he had been able to help his mother since he got out of law school, he doubted he could ever fully repay her for all the sacrifices she made for him. With that in mind, he didn't want to think about the man who brought him into being but then disappeared.

"Why are you so curious about your dad?" he asked.

"He's here somewhere," she said balling up her fist and pounding it on her thigh. "I just know it. He probably doesn't know how close by I am. I don't want to go back to LA without seeing him. That would be downright rude." Again, she pounded her leg with her fist. Her voice had taken on once more that vulnerable sound, a touch of desperation overwhelming him like a hard punch.

Maybe his mother was right, and Patrick was a sucker for a sob story. And this girl was telling one heck of a sad story.

But something was different this time. He could easily walk away if he chose. And to be honest and fair, Freeda's knowledge might be helpful with his dealings in Rio Rojo.

Still, he hesitated.

"He'll never know you were out here if you never find him," he said.

She drew a deep breath. Her glum attitude dissipated like dissolving fog, and she gave him a sweet half-smile.

"Okay, okay, Mr. Patrick Sanchez. You're a busy lawyer. And you have urgent business. I understand. Thanks for all your help. I'll buy you dinner when I get back to Rio Rojo in a few days."

She took a card from her purse and handed it to him. Before he could reply, she grabbed her backpack and purse and marched away.

"Freeda…" He started to go after her and then stopped. Was it better to let her go? She was right. He did have tasks to accomplish, but there was no time limit to his agenda. Patrick blew out a quick breath as she disappeared around the corner. He'd had this same argument with himself earlier, and she had come back. Damn!

His mother's words echoed in his mind. *"Fate, Patrick. You can't escape what fate has in store for you."* He shook his head in resignation as he started the car and drove in the direction where she had gone.

Freeda was looking up and down the street as though

gauging where she wanted to go next.

He pulled up beside her and rolled down the window. "Need a ride, young lady? I may drive up to some fancy ranch named Tres Padres."

Her face lit up. "Thank you, Mr. Lawyer Man!" she said, reaching out to open the door. "You won't regret it. My aunt's chili will make you swoon."

Patrick's response was a quick smile that made her insides shudder, and she shook her head involuntarily. *Nope! Not a good idea!*

*****

Freeda fell silent as they drove out of Casitas and headed into the hills beyond the town. After a full morning of chatter, she didn't feel like talking. She was so close to finding her father. This time it had to work out. It just had to!

They had made a few inquiries around town, but no one seemed to know where Fergie might be except out at the ranch. No one had seen him that morning. They tried back at the diner, but again, no one had seen him since breakfast and the consensus was that he would have returned to the ranch. After another round of fruitless searching, Patrick bought lunch and issued an ultimatum. If they didn't find Fergie in the next half hour, he intended to leave for Rio Rojo.

"Maybe we should go to the ranch headquarters and ask about him," she suggested. "It's only half an hour away according to that last guy we talked to. If no one there knows where he is, I'll go back to Rio Rojo with you, and come back on my own later once Aunt Lottie's car is fixed."

To her delighted surprise, Patrick agreed. They made a quick stop at a gas station, and she purchased a map of the area. As they drove out of town, she realized it did not provide the information she would need to find where her father might be living. It showed only directions to the front gate of the ranch itself. Once they reached that destination, she would need to ask for more specific directions to his possible location.

As they drove, the grassy plains gave way to rocky hills dotted with pinon and cedar trees. Coming around a rocky outcropping, the landscape transformed again as cactus gave way to grasslands and the stubby trees became slender, triangular fir and spruce trees. The road steadily narrowed as it wound around the base of the mountains, and they reached a gate that spanned the road welcoming them to Tres Padres.

"Wow," Freeda said in a low voice as they made the first turn after entering the ranch. She'd never seen anything quite like the view that stretched before her. California mountains rose immediately from the LA basin, and they could be crossed quickly into the desert. These rows of mountains seemed to go on for miles, each ridge a little higher until snowcapped peaks lined the far horizon.

"Yes, wow," Patrick replied with a chuckle. "Meet the real Rocky Mountains. And this is on the southern side."

"I've never been out this way," she said in a hushed voice. "It's absolutely breathtaking. This area is much prettier than Rio Rojo." While the sweeping panorama touched her senses, her enthusiasm had increased for a different reason. They had reached the ranch! Her father might be nearby! She reached out to touch Patrick's arm. "I can't believe we're finally here!"

A large sign appeared ahead, containing a map of

the Tres Padres Ranch. It illustrated a winding road that would take them to the headquarters in seven miles

Patrick glanced at Freeda, pleased they had reached their overall destination but uncertain about which direction to go. "Which way?" he asked gesturing at the road which branched off in two directions. The paved surface headed straight forward while a dirt road branched off to the right toward a low hill.

"Turn right. If he was in the valley, anyone might see him easily from a car. He probably sticks to the back roads where he can hide."

Patrick made the turn, but his smile disintegrated into a grimace as they rounded the hill. The road became nothing but a wide gravel surface. Tiny rocks pinged on both sides of his car. Damn, this was going to make a mess of his car's paint job. He considered turning back, but Freeda's face had become so animated, he knew he couldn't get her this close to her goal and then deny her the pleasure of reaching it.

As they drove around another sweeping bend, they turned into a valley with a line of steep mountain on the opposite end. The rows of mountains were stunning green waves that seemed to grow to a final row of snow-capped peaks. They were the mountains he remembered seeing with his grandfather. Patrick regretted not coming back to the area sooner.

His mind was still on the past as they rounded the next bend in the road, and Freeda shot up in the seat.

"Oh, my gosh! There he is!"

"What?" Patrick turned to her.

"Over there!"

Not too far ahead of them a tall, thin man in faded jeans and a worn leather jacket ambled along the side of the road. As soon as they had spotted him, he stepped off the road and disappeared behind the next turn, hidden from them by a rocky outcropping.

"Go!" she cried. "That's him. It's my dad!"

They rounded the bend and Patrick slammed on the brakes as a locked gate loomed ahead with a chain link fence on either side. The man was nowhere to be seen, but as soon as Patrick stopped the car, Freeda leaped out and ran to the fence.

"Dad," she shouted, shaking the locked gate. "Dad!"

There was no reply or any sign of the man. He had vanished into the nearby trees. She turned to Patrick with wide sad eyes, her lips quivering.

"That was him. I recognize the jacket!" Freeda cried, turning to shake the fence again as Patrick approached her. A heavy padlock held a chain in place across the gate. She tugged at it. "Damn!" she cried before hollering again, "Dad!"

Freeda turned away from Patrick as tears filled her eyes. "Why does it always have to be so damn hard?" she cried. "Every time I get so close. Did you see him? That was him! I know that coat."

She appeared so defeated Patrick felt his own twinge of disappointment. "I'm sorry."

In frustration, Freeda reached out and gave another fierce tug on the chain. To Patrick's surprise, the padlock flew off. She hesitated for a minute before beginning to unwind the chain.

"What are you doing?" he asked in alarm, but he made no move to stop her.

"We won't be in there long. Just until we find him and then we'll come back out, and he can lock it behind us."

"That's trespassing. They keep this gate locked for a reason." Patrick pointed out, shaking his head.

Freeda didn't appear to care as she continued to unwind the chain. "It's not my fault the gate was left unlocked. I haven't done anything wrong. If someone else left it that way, they can sue them."

He refrained from stating the obvious–that her father had gone through the gate only moments earlier, so if someone left it unlocked, he was most likely the culprit.

"We're not going to do anything that would damage the ranch," she continued, still unraveling the chain. "We'll go in and look around until we find Dad. Then we'll make certain it's properly locked when we come out. He can't have gotten that far."

Patrick eyed her warily. He wanted to repeat that the scenario she painted was still trespassing, but she was determined to get inside the ranch. He doubted they would find her father. The man might not even have come this way. He might have walked along the fence line through the trees. How would he have gotten through the fence?

"Please, Patrick, this is so important to me," she pleaded. "I'm so close I can feel it. I haven't seen him in years, and who knows when I might have a chance to see him again. Just the thought of coming so close and then going back…of not taking those extra steps…can't you understand?"

Not certain how to reply, Patrick simply nodded. Her large hazel eyes were luminous, tear filled, so different from the confident woman who earlier claimed she could take care of herself.

"Do you even know where you're going?" he asked. "This is a big place. Didn't you read that acreage sign back there?" He couldn't recall the exact number, simply that the number had struck him as large for the state.

"Those people in town said he was living in a cabin that was right next to the gate. That had to be the gate. How far could it be?"

He pressed his lips together, frustrated at her insistence, but as she brushed a hand across her cheek, he knew he could not deny her request. She turned her face away from him and wiped her cheek again.

"All right," he agreed, "but if we don't find his place within half an hour, we come out, okay? I don't want to get caught in here."

"Of course!" She grabbed his arm and squeezed it, her face brightening. "I don't want you to get in trouble. And I'm sorry this gravel road might be dinging your car."

He shrugged. "Don't worry about it. This is a leased car and I'll turn it in at the end of the year. I've driven worse roads for my cases at times, so this is no problem."

"Pretty darn fancy for a leased car. Must be nice," she murmured, walking back toward the car. "Let's go."

****

After a ten-minute drive past the gate, they spotted a cabin just off the road, partially shielded by a thicket of trees.

"Do you think he might be living there?" he asked.

Freeda's heart thumped with anticipation. "I hope so! Oh, it has to be It just has to be!"

He pulled into the gravel driveway. The structure was a log cabin that resembled so many of the newer summer cabins that she had seen in the mountains. It had two narrow windows in the front on either side of a tiny porch that framed a wooden door. She thought she saw movement through one of the windows, and she jumped from the car the minute Patrick braked to a complete stop. She choked back the desire to call out for her father.

What if this wasn't where he was living?

No! It had to be the right place.

She ran to the door and knocked, but no one answered. She pounded on it a second time. Still no answer. The air around them was still, as though no one had been around for days.

She glanced toward the side. "Maybe he's around back. I saw a big shed back there."

"Maybe. Or perhaps this isn't where he's living," Patrick said as he emerged from the car.

Freeda refused to contemplate that possibility and instead hurried around the house. The shed door held a padlock and there were no windows to look inside. She turned back toward the front of the cabin and spotted a moving shadow through one of the side windows. Someone was inside the cabin! She ran back to the front door and pounded on it.

"Hello! Dad! Fergie?"

There was no answer, and a stillness fell over the place. All she could hear was wind rustling the nearby trees.

"Fergie," she cried again. "It's Freeda." Her voice sounded desperate even to her, but then she again saw the moving shadow inside, and a tremor ran through her. Someone was definitely inside. "Dad! Are you in there? I've been looking for you! It's Freeda."

A moment later, the sound of a lock sliding came through the heavy wooden door, and it slowly swung open.

Freeda gasped at the sight of the tall, lanky, balding

man for only a minute before she flung herself into his arms and buried her face in his chest. "Daddy! I'm so happy to find you!"

Chapter Seven

Patrick grimaced as Freeda and her father hugged. He wanted to be happy that she had finally found her father, but something about this reunion didn't ring true. The man had appeared dazed when he first saw Freeda, stiff and uncertain instead of appearing pleased. As though realizing the importance of the moment, the man had suddenly grinned and wrapped his long, thin arms around her. To Patrick, his reaction and posture appeared to be more of an act than a sincere gesture of joy. There was no questioning the resemblance between the pair. The shape of the man's face and his bright hazel eyes were duplicates of Freeda's, though he had thinning brown hair laced with gray. Freeda's hair was thick and black.

"What are you doing, gal?" he asked in a raspy voice, pulling slightly back from her. "Let me look at you. Damn, you're lookin' great! So grown up. What brought you up here?"

"You!" She wiped a tear from her cheek, as she stepped back, keeping hold of his large hand. "I've been looking for you for months."

His smile faded somewhat, as he pressed his lips together before answering. "Yeah, someone told me you were in Rio Rojo a couple of months ago, but before I could get down there to see you, I heard you'd gone back to California. I didn't know how to get in touch with you."

"Why didn't you get in touch with Aunt Lottie? She's still in Rio Rojo. Didn't you know that?"

He drew slightly back, releasing her hand. "Well…" His eyes avoided hers, but Patrick knew the answer. The man had been aware of it and had probably known how to get in touch with Freeda all along too. He had simply chosen not to do it. Did Freeda see that reluctance or was she pretending not to acknowledge it?

The man turned away from her and stepped forward suddenly, extending his hand toward Patrick. "I'm being rude. Hello there, I'm Fred Ferguson, but everyone calls me Fergie."

"Patrick Sanchez." He took the large, callused hand and shook it firmly.

"Nice to meet you, Patrick. Are the two of you…" Fergie faltered, looking from one to the other, as though he wasn't quite certain what to say. "Together?" he finally finished.

"I just met him today. He's been helping me find you," Freeda blushed, shaking her head. "He's a lawyer from Albuquerque."

"Lawyer?" Fergie's hazel eyes grew large, and he drew back, his lean body stiffening. Patrick almost expected him to wipe his hand across his shirt as he frowned down at his daughter. "What the hell made you think you needed a lawyer to find me?"

"No, no, you misunderstood. He's helping by giving me a ride. I borrowed Aunt Lottie's car and it broke down."

A slight smile returned to Fergie's thin lips. "I see. Well, I'm being rude. Come inside. Feel like coffee or a soft drink, maybe? I want to hear what you've been up to, Baby. God, I've missed you so damn much."

Placing his arm around Freeda, he led her into the cabin. Patrick's instincts about Fergie told him to be wary. For not having seen his daughter for a long time, Fergie didn't appear pleased to see his daughter. He kept smiling at her, but the smile didn't reach his cool eyes. He was a tall, rangy man with thinning brown hair that was laced with gray and fell just below his narrow shoulders. He wore scuffed cowboy boots, faded jeans and a blue T-shirt below a brown and gray checkered flannel shirt. Hippy from the word go, Patrick surmised. He even wore a thin leather necklace with a metal peace symbol dangling from it.

The large room was furnished sparsely with a worn leather sofa in the center and a roughly hewn wooden table and two chairs beyond it. A small kitchen area took up the back wall. The room held only the basics. Besides the sofa, a chair and desk occupied another corner. A door at one end of the room was open and Patrick could see the edge of a bed in it with a closed door at the end of the room.

"May I use your facilities?" Patrick asked, wanting to leave them alone for a couple of minutes.

"Sure, sure, it's through there," Fergie said, pointing toward the bedroom door.

Patrick stayed inside for a few minutes, flushing the toilet and washing his hands. Damn, now what? Should he just leave her here? He hadn't seen evidence of a garage or any sort of transportation. Hadn't the people in town said he came in every day for breakfast? How did he get around? There had to be a car or truck somewhere nearby.

He came out of the bedroom to silence. Freeda sat at

the table, tears staining her cheeks. Fergie stood at the sink looking out the window.

Patrick wasn't certain what to say, but Freeda pushed herself away from the table and stood.

"Fine. I'll be going then."

Fergie sighed heavily. "Hon, you gotta understand,"

"I don't *gotta* understand anything. You're being a real jerk. After I came all this way looking for you! I haven't gone back to work because I was trying so hard to find you. What a damn waste of time!"

Fergie's face hardened. "Now don't you be talking that way."

"You have no right to tell me how to talk either. You have no right to tell me anything!" she shot back.

Fergie's bony shoulders sagged as he sighed. "No, I guess I don't." He seemed to notice Patrick had come back into the room. "Thanks for bringing her up here, but I have no room for her to stay. Hell, Diaz could show up any time and toss my ass out of here." He turned back to Freeda. "Look, hon, leave me your number, and I'll call you when I have time, when we can spend some real time together."

She rolled her eyes. "You're always saying that, and then I never hear from you. If I leave now, you'll probably disappear again without telling me."

He sighed heavily, running his hand through his thinning hair. "Look, you don't understand. I just can't leave right now."

"But I told you, I can stay," she repeated. "And then I can go into town with you in the morning when you go in for breakfast. The people in town say you come in all the time."

"I *walk* in," he said. "Or I hitch rides. Hon, I have

no transportation to take you around."

"But, Dad, I can—"

"Stop!" His voice grew sharp as he held up his hand. "You can't stay here."

"Your boss won't allow it?" she asked.

"Well, no it's not that…"

"Then why not let me stay? Just for a couple of days and then Patrick could come and get me." She glanced over at Patrick expectantly. "You will, won't you?"

"Freeda, what about your aunt's car?" Patrick asked.

"You heard Diaz," she replied. "He'll take care of it. And when that guy promises to do something for Aunt Lottie, I can guarantee he will do it."

Fergie jerked up suddenly, eyes growing large. "Wait, does Diaz know you're up here?"

"He knows I've been looking for you." She turned away, not wanting to deliver the nasty message Diaz had told her to give to her father, though perhaps she should warn him about the man. She was still debating how to tell him when Patrick spoke up.

"He told us he might have you arrested if he finds you on the property," Patrick said. "You might want to come with us into town in case he comes looking for you. He appeared rather angry."

"Patch man don't scare me," Fergie replied with a grunt. "But I'll tell you what. I'm expecting a friend any time. If he doesn't show up, I may need a lift into town. Why don't the two of you run over to the main house and check it out? They have a visitor area that has a snack bar. Have a cup of coffee and look around. Then before you leave the ranch, you can come back and say goodbye, or if my friend doesn't show, you can give me a lift into town." He glanced at his watch. "He should be here any time. You'd better get going. I don't want to spook him."

Freeda sighed. "Dad, I…"

A buzz came from the bedroom and Fergie's head jerked up. "Just a second," he said and disappeared into the room.

Patrick turned to Freeda. "Perhaps he's right. Let's go over to the main house. Let him meet his friend, and we can come back later. Or we can meet him at the café in the morning. I'll bring you back myself if you promise to buy me breakfast tomorrow." He attempted a smile, but her stoic face told him she didn't like the idea.

Fergie emerged from the bedroom. "Well, that takes care of everything. He's not getting into town until tonight. Let's go driving around. I'll show you the ranch and then you can drop me off in town before you go home. We oughta spend some time together."

"Really?" Freeda's tense face brightened as she jumped to her feet, all traces of distress vanishing.

Fergie's earlier attitude of watchful wariness also dissipated, and his smile grew wide and welcoming. He reached out and patted Freeda on the head as though she might still be a little girl. "Come on, girly, let's become tourists for the day."

"You're not worried about Diaz?" she asked.

"Hell no, I'll be just another tourist wandering around the ranch. He can't toss me out if I'm there as a visitor, can he? He has no idea where I'm staying. And don't you tell him, either. This cabin is so far at the edge, they don't bother to check it until Fall when the hunters arrive. I know every worker's cabin on this ranch and when it gets used. Now let me grab my jacket, and I'll be ready to go."

Freeda kept her head down but at a sigh from Patrick, she jerked upright.

"Do you mind?" she asked, attempting a small smile. "I know you were in a rush, but if you want, you can drop me and Dad at the main house and go on to Rio Rojo. I can find us a ride into town from there and call my aunt to come and get me. She doesn't like driving at night, but…"

Patrick did not answer. He had not decided what he would do. If he left her, she would be on her own, but at least she would be in town where she could reach someone to pick her up. It wasn't like abandoning her on a lonely road. But then again, he didn't trust Fergie.

The tall man appeared from the back bedroom, sauntering into the room. He had changed into a plaid flannel shirt and put on a blue windbreaker over it.

"This is probably for the best," he said. "If Diaz knows you're up here, he might come by and check the cabin just to cause trouble."

"Yes," Freeda said happily. "You might even want to stay in town for the night. I could stay over too so we can go to breakfast together in the morning."

His head bobbed up and down in an affirmative motion. "Yeah, sure, that might be the best solution of all. We can catch up."

Patrick's eyes shifted from one to the other. He could sense that Freeda was eager to spend time with her father. As for Fergie wanting to spend time with her, that was another matter altogether. Patrick had a feeling that once her father met the friend in town, he would not want Freeda around. Patrick drew a quick shallow breath. This was far from the trip he had planned so carefully only a few days ago. He'd intended to talk to the sheriff in Rio

Rojo, look over the house, go through his grandfather's safe deposit box and make the arrangements for a realtor so he could return to Albuquerque. Instead, he had stumbled into an unforeseen drama he could not easily abandon.

As he watched Freeda study her father with a worshipping look in her expectant eyes, he knew he could not disappoint her. He would do whatever she wanted. Patrick had only known her for a few hours, and he wasn't certain what he thought of her or this whole predicament, but something about her touched him. Perhaps it was that blind loyalty she appeared to have for a man who had abandoned her. She talked about staying in town, but had she forgotten that she had lost her wallet and had no financial means to do that? He had a feeling Fergie would not be able to take care of that sort of arrangement either.

Patrick studied Freeda and then her father but said nothing. Maybe spending the day with the man would be enough for Freeda, and she would be ready to go with him when he left for Rio Rojo. His final destination was less than an hour away, and perhaps once Fergie's friend showed up, Freeda would be ready to leave.

A noise reached them from outside, the sound of an engine in the distance. Fergie's head jerked up, and he turned to Patrick with wide startled eyes. "Oh, hell, did you lock the gate after you drove onto the ranch, or did you leave it open?"

"It was unlocked," Patrick said with a shrug. "We left it open."

Fergie walked to the window and peered out. "It's supposed to be kept locked. There are parts of the ranch they don't like left open to tourists."

"You left it unlocked," Patrick shot back. He could tell by the way the man was no longer meeting their eyes that something was amiss. Fergie had aroused Patrick's attorney instincts earlier, but now those instincts were buzzing with alarm. Something was going on that the man didn't want to tell Freeda.

Fergie turned to Patrick with a look of alarm in his eyes. "Look, why don't you drive your car behind the cabin? It would be just like that jerk to tell me to come into town and show up to surprise me because now he knows I am here. I should have known he was lying. First, he says he'll call me in advance so I can meet him at the gate, but then he calls to say we'll meet in town later? He probably just wanted to make certain where I am. Anyway, if that's him driving up here, that fancy car might spook him." He glanced again at the window as the noise of the engine grew louder.

"Dad, we—" Freeda began, but her father waved her off.

"Hell, let's get out of here," he insisted, grabbing a baseball cap from a hook on the kitchen wall and pulling it on. "I'll walk up the road and meet him and we can drive into town. You can move your car behind the cabin and wait until you hear his car drive away. Then you can follow us out. Just lock the gate behind you."

"But when will I see you again?" Freeda asked, her voice quaking.

He waved her off. "Soon, okay? Listen, let's just get going. He's going to come around the bend in a few minutes and see that car." He moved toward the door. "Maybe you should drive your car behind the cabin until I'm out of sight and wait at least ten or fifteen minutes before you go."

"Dad, I can stay and wait in the back room while you talk to him," she offered in a pleading voice. "Then we can…"

"Listen, hon, I'm at the café in town almost every morning. Come in around eight any day and you'll find me, okay. Now, go!"

"No!" she protested, feeling like stomping her foot. The room vibrated with tension until suddenly the sound of the engine lessened. The car was no longer growing closer; in fact, the noise of the motor became more distant as though the car had turned in another direction.

Freeda breathed a sigh of relief, but she couldn't look over at Patrick. She feared a knowing *I told you so* look. She fought back tears again, not wanting to cry in front of her father. *Damn him*, she had spent so much time trying to discover his whereabouts, and now that her search had finally ended, his reaction made her feel worse. Instead of his being happy to see her after their long separation, he appeared ready to let her go because he wanted to visit with someone else—a friend he could probably see any time.

He lifted his large bony hand and touched her shoulder gently, smiling sadly. "You are so damn stubborn, sweetie, just like your mother."

The comparison startled her, though it was the same thing her grandmother often claimed. "Really? Then you know I don't give up easily." Freeda pressed her lips together in a determined line, not certain if she was ready to forgive him for his behavior.

"I'm sorry for being such a damn jerk." He spoke in a low voice as his head twisted toward the wall behind her. Freeda turned and followed the direction of his eyes. A black and white photo was tacked to one of the logs above his makeshift desk.

Her curiosity increasing, Freeda walked to the desk. While she was familiar with graduation and family pictures of her mother, she had never seen this particular photo. In it, Fergie was a tall, lean youth with long curly hair that fell just below his shoulders. Helen Ferguson's long black hair was twisted into dark twin braids that reached her waist. Her facial features were delicate, with high cheekbones and small lips drawn up in a smile, but her dark eyes challenged the camera.

People often said Freeda had her mother's hair and shape of eyes. While her grandmother had shown Freeda plenty of pictures of the young Helen growing up, Freeda had never thought of herself as carefree and confident as her mother appeared in all the photos.

Her father's low voice behind her interrupted her chain of thought. It cracked with emotion; his earlier sense of haste was gone. "Freeda, you know we decided to name you Freedom so that you were always as free-spirited as we wanted to be. Your grandmother never liked that idea, but that's why you're Freeda. Do you remember when you stayed with me a few months when you were very young?"

"I don't recall much about that time," she admitted. "I just know what Nena has told me over the years. That's why I want to spend time with you *now*."

Fergie gently touched her shoulder, his eyes lowering to the ground. "We'll do it then," he replied in a voice that cracked with emotion. "We need to spend some quality time talking, catching up. I've had plenty of hard times, but also a number of real adventures, and I want to hear what you've been doing."

Keeping herself from crying, Freeda was pleased

that he might finally understand that she wanted to get to know him now that she was an adult. While her grandmother had given her a few details about her early life, the old woman had not known about the years when Fergie, Helen and Freeda were a family. All she had known was that Fergie and her mother lived in a commune, and that was where Freeda was born. After her birth, the couple travelled the country until Helen became ill.

Freeda's dim memory of those years was that her mother spent most of her time in bed. Then one day, her mother was gone, and Freeda was taken to live with her grandmother. Fergie departed not long afterward, disappearing from her life for the first of many different times. He returned for another year when she turned eight, but immediately left again. She spent the rest of her formative years with Nena, waiting for Fergie to come back so they could become the real family he kept promising her in his infrequent letters.

Seeing his disregard now, Freeda doubted that he had ever intended on coming back or spending time with her. He appeared totally focused on his own dilemma, not caring that she had searched for him for so long. He paced around the room, checking doors and windows as though he was on the run or in hiding.

Freeda's eyes drifted around the tiny cabin. Did her father enjoy living such an isolated life? Why did he choose this location, so far removed from people he might know? Surely, he had other places he could live.

"So now what?" Patrick asked, breaking into her thoughts.

"I am going to stay with Dad," she insisted firmly, challenging Fergie as she crossed her arms, her lips pressed into a firm line of defiance.

Chapter Eight

The room remained silent for a few minutes as Freeda and her father engaged in a battle of wills without speaking. Tension vibrated in the air in the small cabin. She was determined to remain. Perhaps by staying and spending time with Fergie and having the opportunity to talk with him about the past, she could learn who her father was in the present. Maybe he finally might tell her why he remained on the move for so many years and had chosen not to look for her or get in contact with her. But even as she gazed at him with a silent plea in her eyes, he dashed her hopes.

"Freeda, the bottom line is you can't stay here." He dropped onto a chair at the table across from her. "Listen, hon. I really will call you. Or better yet, how about we get together tomorrow? I can stay over in town tonight and meet you at a café in town, and we'll have time to talk then. Maybe some other time you can come back, or I'll go to Rio Rojo and visit your Aunt Lottie. I haven't seen her in years. It might be fun. I miss the old gal."

She put her hand on his arm. "What is so important that you're throwing me out like this?"

"*I told you.* I have to meet someone, and he should be here any minute. I really need to see this guy. He's driving all the way from Santa Fe. I can't stand him up and I don't have any way to call him and postpone the meeting."

"Wait, that isn't what you told us earlier," Patrick interrupted. "You said you were going into town to meet someone. Then you said he might be trying to trick you by coming out here. You keep changing your story every time you tell it. Which is it? He's coming here or you're going to meet him?" Patrick asked.

His voice had taken on such a demanding tone even Freeda flinched as he walked toward Fergie like a defense lawyer interrogating a stubborn witness.

Her father lowered his head, and his face tightened, but his look toward her was one of apology. "Okay, I just wanted you both to hit the road before he shows up. The truth is, he is coming out here to meet me, and I don't want anyone around who might spook him."

"Why would we spook him?" she asked. This situation was growing stranger by the minute.

Fergie sighed as he ran his hands through his stringy hair. "Can't explain. It just would."

"But why can't *I* stay?" Freeda insisted. "If you're worried he might get spooked if he sees me, I can hide in the back room, or even take a walk until he is gone. He won't even know I'm around."

Fergie shook his head so violently his long hair flew around his face. "No, no, that would never work. Not at all. He…well he's kind of…well…just funny. He made me promise not to tell anyone he was meeting me…it's sort of a business deal."

"What *sort* of a deal, and what *sort* of business?" Patrick asked, his voice cold and filled with skepticism. "Pardon me, but if he made you promise not to tell anyone, that sounds extremely shady to me."

Fergie waved his thin hands, growing more agitated. "No, no, not shady at all. He's the secretive, paranoid type, that's all. He doesn't like people to know his business."

"Perhaps we should both stay. We can sit outside," Patrick announced in a firm voice.

A look of terror crossed Fergie's face. "No! No! That will never work. You gotta get out of here. What if he's watching and he sees you two? Big fancy car? It could spook him."

"What makes you think you can trust him?" Patrick asked, standing firm, his arms crossed.

"No problem there. I *know* I can trust him." Fergie offered a half smile as he reached out to touch Freeda's shoulder. "Look, hon, I promise I'll meet you tomorrow. Hell, if you want, I'll go with you to Rio Rojo, and we can spend some quality time together. That's a promise."

Freeda's face remained set as she glared at him. "Quality time? No. You won't show up and I'll have to come back out here and track you down again. I'm going to wait with you *now* until that man comes and leaves, and we'll spend our quality time together starting then!" She glanced at Patrick "You can go back to Rio Rojo, but I'm staying here."

"Freeda…" Fergie shook his head. "Why do you have to be so stubborn?"

She ignored the question as she whirled back toward her father. "You owe me that much. I don't care if you talk to me or not, and if Patrick tries to take me back to town, I'll jump out somewhere along the way and hike back here. You don't want me interrupting while you're in the middle of your big meeting, do you? Think of how that will be. That will really spook him."

Fergie pressed his lips together, glaring at her; but after several tense silent minutes, with a heavy sigh, he relented. "You're so damn stubborn, but okay. You can stay. You just have to keep quiet and stay out of the way. Don't make a sound until he's gone. And if I go into town with him, just make certain you leave the door unlocked when you go."

Freeda heaved a sigh of relief as she leaped up and hugged him. "You won't be sorry Fergie!"

****

Patrick perched on the edge of Fergie's bed as Freeda paced around the small bedroom like a caged animal. Frustrated, he debated what he should do. He wanted to catch her hand and hold it and try to cheer her up. The rigid lines of her tense face held him back. Why did she have to be so stubborn? Her father had been right about that. He had given in to her, but Patrick had decided to stay as well because he feared she was making a wrong choice. He had only known her a few hours, but he felt responsible for her. He had brought her out to this place. If something happened as a result, something that he could have prevented, well, he knew he didn't want that burden.

Freeda paced from one end of the room to the next. She had been silent since Fergie agreed to let them stay. After hiding Patrick's car inside a nearby barn and promising Fergie they would not come out or make a sound until they heard the man drive away, they had come into the little bedroom and not spoken.

The visitor arrived a few minutes later, and now muted voices came from the living area. Patrick could not make out what the two men were saying. Freeda leaned her head against the door, attempting to eavesdrop when they started talking but finally gave up. The log walls of the cabin were too thick to allow more than the sound of voices to reach them. They could not make out the exact words being spoken.

"This is crazy," he whispered, though he doubted if the pair outside would hear if he spoke out loud. Patrick checked his watch. By the time they left the cabin and drove to Rio Rojo, he doubted be able to accomplish any of the tasks he had planned to complete for today. He would have to stay in town for at least another day.

A door slammed. Was it the outside door? Patrick jerked back as the heads of two men came into view outside the bedroom window. Fergie appeared to tell the man something and walked back toward the front of the cabin. Moments later, Fergie opened the bedroom door.

"Listen, he's going to take me into town. Wait a bit, and then you can go out." He took hold of Freeda's arm and shook it playfully. "Hon, it's been great to see you. We have to get together again. I'll call you in a few days. Write your phone number on the pad on the desk. I'm sorry to have to take off in such a rush, but this business with him may take a while."

"Business?" she questioned.

His hazel eyes hardened. "Yes, business. He might have some work I can do with him. Anyway, I'll get in touch with you in a couple of days when I have more time to spend with you."

"Can't I call you?" she asked.

"I don't have a phone, remember? Trust me, I will call you." He leaned over and hugged her, but his face remained taut, his body rigid, even as she clung to him. Finally, he patted her head. "Don't worry, hon, and if you don't hear from me, well, you know where to find me— either here or at the diner in town any morning."

He pulled back and Freeda let him go reluctantly,

her arms remaining outstretched. "You better call," she said, her lower lip trembling.

He touched the top of her head gently. "Don't worry, little gal, I'm not going to let you get away. You won't lose me again."

Patrick didn't believe the man, but Freeda's face was so hopeful, her eyes wide and questioning, he didn't want to hurt her by asking for a definite commitment of time and place. Fergie turned to him and held out his large, bony hand.

"Good to meet you, Pat. Hope we meet again."

Patrick grimaced. He had always hated the shortening of his name, but he didn't see any reason to mention it. "Good to meet you, Fergie, and I'll make certain Freeda gets home safely."

Fergie turned and walked away without saying anything more, not even giving Freeda one last look. Patrick was tempted to grab the man and shake him, but he didn't make a move. Freeda watched her father wistfully as he crossed the room and closed the door. Freeda and Patrick remained motionless and silent until the car pulled away.

"Well, now what?" Patrick asked. "Are you ready to go home? It's almost two o'clock. Perhaps you should call your aunt and let her know about the car."

She shook her head. "She knows I was going to look for Dad. As for the car, Diaz has probably already gotten in touch with her to let her know about it, and that I'm with you. Maybe we should go back to town and wait around Casitas. What if Dad needs a ride back here later?"

Patrick blew out a quick exasperated breath. "Freeda, do you expect me to play taxi service and wait

94

around all day for him to make up his mind on what he's doing next?"

"No, you can go on to Rio Rojo. I'm just saying if you want to take me into town and leave me there, that's fine. I'll stay and wait until he's finished talking with the guy. Maybe I can help him get a ride back or have dinner with him. I may just stay overnight and have breakfast with him in the morning."

"Where will you stay? You don't have a wallet, remember."

Freeda recalled that dilemma, and she had no idea what she would do if Patrick did leave her, but she could figure that out when the time came. Perhaps her aunt would feel bad about the car breaking down and pay for a hotel room for the night.

****

"Tell me about you and your father," Patrick said as they began driving back toward Casitas a few minutes later. "How much time have you spent with him?"

Freeda was not certain she wanted to discuss her relationship with Fergie again, especially now that Patrick had met him and witnessed her father's indifference. She had been so certain he would be overjoyed to see her and not want to let her go.

Tears clouded her eyes, but she ignored them.

Why couldn't he have been excited or at least pleased to see her? Why did he have to seem so inconvenienced by her presence? Her chest tightened as she rolled up her hands into fists. She wanted to pound the leather seat below her, or the car door—anything! Why had her father acted more interested in the man who was coming to see him than a reunion with the daughter he hadn't seen in years? Freeda's appearance seemed to be an unwelcome interruption. She pressed her lips together, unable to speak, fearing she might cry.

But then again, she should have known better. Even the few times they spoke on the phone, he never seemed to want to talk for long. He always claimed to be busy or had a reason he had to get off the phone. As for visiting, her father had often held her off with various excuses or that he was on the move to a new "opportunity," so he didn't have time to see her.

The last time they had seen each other, he had been coming through Los Angeles on his way to a job in Alaska aboard a ship. At least that was what he told her. They had met for coffee in Long Beach where he asked for five hundred dollars to buy his gear for the trip. She had nearly that much in her savings account, immediately withdrew it for him, and he had gone on his way. She had not heard from him again or where he was, until the rumor came up that he had been spotted in Casitas. Now, he had not mentioned that previous meeting or the loan, though she could understand he might not want to discuss such a personal issue in front of Patrick.

How was he existing now? He had not given them any indication that he might be working. She knew he didn't have a job at Tres Padres since Diaz had threatened to have her father arrested if Diaz found him on the ranch. She wanted to ask Fergie about the bad blood between the two, but since she had such a bad relationship with Diaz anyway, she wasn't certain it mattered that much.

"Freeda?"

She jerked out of her reverie and turned toward Patrick, realizing he had just asked her a question. "I'm sorry. What did you say?"

"You never answered my question about your father. When was the last time you saw him?" he asked.

With a sigh, she told him about the last visit in Los Angeles. Patrick didn't need to know the circumstances, and she had no intention of admitting that she had given him money. "We've never been able to spend much time together because he's always on the move. It's kind of like you didn't see much of your grandfather, but at least you knew where he was."

Patrick didn't reply and they fell into silence until he reached over and turned on the car stereo. The soothing sounds of a jazz ensemble flowed from the dual speakers behind them. Freeda was fine with his action. She didn't feel like talking either. Turning away from him, she gazed out the window, wishing the reunion with her father had gone differently. Disagreements and a tense conclusion were not at all what she'd had in mind for their meeting when she set out that morning to locate him.

****

They spotted Fergie and the man as they drove into Casitas, though Fergie didn't give any indication he saw them. The two men were walking into a bar on the outskirts of the town, a low slung, wooden structure with a big window in front and a neon beer sign in the window. A rusting sign reading *Drift On Inn* hung above the entrance. Several trucks and a couple of cars were parked at various angles pointing toward the building.

"Now what?" Patrick asked.

"Maybe we should go over to the diner again," she said. "I'm a little hungry."

He blew out a quick breath. "I'm not waiting around

to take Fergie back to the ranch," he warned, "in case you're hoping for that. I may not have a timetable to keep, but I really don't intend to spend all my time playing taxi service."

"Then go!" she rasped. "I'll stay here and wait for him. He might need a ride back, and maybe I can help him."

"How will *you* get home once you've taken care of him?"

"I'll call my aunt," she replied in a small voice.

"All right, maybe we can wait a bit," he agreed with a sigh. "It has been a while since breakfast, and I could use something to eat. How about I buy you a late lunch or early dinner?"

Freeda's taut muscles loosened, and she agreed gratefully. She had not eaten much of her breakfast, since she had been so worried about finding her father. "That sounds good to me."

"Do you want to go here or find some other place?" he asked.

"Let's eat here. The other guy won't know who we are. Dad might even be relieved to see us. He'll know we're here for moral support."

Patrick blew out a quick breath, his face tightening. "Okay, but let me repeat, we're not staying here all night. We have no idea if he and that guy have other plans. Besides, I really don't want to drive those mountain roads after dark. I've seen more than one lawsuit dealing with drivers who hit deer on the road."

"I don't expect you to wait and take him back. I can stay by myself and help him get a ride if he needs one. You can go on to Rio Rojo if you want."

"Freeda…"

"Why don't you just go now?" she cried, as frustration overwhelmed her. First Fergie and now Patrick. *Damn men! Who needed them?* "I can do fine on my own."

They sat in silence for long moments before Patrick finally sighed. "I'm not going to desert you. I'll stay for now. It's not like I'm going to be able to do much tonight anyway. We can eat and then if you're ready, I'll take you to Rio Rojo."

Patrick blinked at the dimness of the restaurant as they entered. A neon sign directed them to either the bar on the right or the dining room on the left. The scent of sizzling meat came from the dining room, so he turned in that direction.

He wasn't certain if he was making the right decision in deciding to stay, but he hated the idea of simply leaving Freeda on her own. What if she wasn't ready to leave Casitas after dinner? He could get her a room for the night and continue his journey on his own. But for that matter, there was no reason he couldn't stay over too. He couldn't do anything in Rio Rojo tonight anyway. Whether he stayed here or there didn't make a difference.

After all the talking they had done during the day, both stayed silent through most of dinner. Freeda kept looking toward the bar.

"Tell me a little about your job," Patrick said.

"My job?"

"You said you do freelance work."

"Yes. I come up with story ideas and pitch them to different producers I know. If they want a certain video story, they give me an outline of what they want. Sometimes if I come up with an idea, I pitch it to them.

That was what my cousin Cere did with the Marco story. But then she got all involved with the mystery itself. I keep thinking there's more to that story than what she told. Unfortunately, the old Palladium dance hall burned down and there's not much left out there now. And I can't convince anyone that it's worth doing."

"Maybe you should just do the story and then try to sell it."

She shook her head. "I'd love to, but I need to know I *can* sell it. I don't like doing stories that I can't sell. I mean, what's the point? It only takes up time I could spend on a story that I *can* sell."

"A good story is a good story."

"But a story that can be sold pays the rent and puts food on the table," she retorted. "I mean, don't you ask for retainers when you take on a new client? Would you take someone's case just because it interested you?"

"You make a good point. I guess I wouldn't."

"Damn right you wouldn't. Even if you lose, you're going to get paid, right?"

"Now you're sounding more mercenary than me," he added with a laugh. "I've taken cases where I don't get paid top dollar but I believe in them."

She blinked and leaned across the table toward him. "What? You have a heart? Who knew?"

Patrick chuckled. He had to admit he enjoyed her sense of humor and her quick wit. The day had not been wasted. Her company was enjoyable, and he could see himself staying in touch with her after they parted, if only to verbally spar with her. "Do you ever get into Albuquerque?"

"I flew out of there a few times when I went to Rio Rojo. Not a bad place. Why? Is that an invitation?"

"No, but if you ever get into town, I'll buy you lunch, how about that?"

"Heck, I've gone farther for a free lunch. Why not? I might even buy you lunch if I ever find my wallet."

As they finished eating, Freeda was about to tell Patrick they could leave when Fergie stormed out of the door to the bar, followed by a scruffy looking man. Freeda followed them as Patrick grabbed their check and headed for the front counter to pay.

She followed the men around the side of the building, her pulse racing. *What the hell was going on?*

The man was about her father's age and nearly as tall. He was on the lean side and wore a torn baseball warm-up jacket that had seen better days. It might have once been blue, but now it was a dirty gray. He wore jeans that were faded and hung around his rail thin hips while his boots were scuffed and worn. His long face was lined and haggard as he whirled around to confront Fergie who came up behind him on the sidewalk. The man's grey eyes appeared bloodshot and the hair that peeked out of a grimy baseball cap was thin and stringy. Freeda would have pegged him for a vagrant if she'd met him on the street. What business could her father possibly have with this stranger?

Suddenly the man pushed Fergie backward, making him stumble back against the side of the building, and the man turned to walk away. Fergie regained his footing and followed, grabbing the man's shoulder, but the stranger turned and shoved him again. This time her father reeled before falling to his knees. With surprising quickness, the man kicked Fergie, who curled up in a ball on the pavement.

"Stop!" Freeda screamed.

The man jerked up in surprise and saw her. His mouth dropped open. "This is none of your damn business, sister."

"You leave my father alone."

"Get outta here before I give you a taste of the same damn thing," he shouted.

Fergie was on his hands and knees, gasping for breath. "Leave her...out of this...dammit..." He waved to Freeda. "Go away...this is between...me and him..."

The man whirled back to her father, kicking at him. "You're a damn leech, Ferguson," he yelled. "Always was, always will be. You keep away from me from now on, or you'll be damn sorry."

"You'll be the one who is sorry..." Fergie rasped. "You won't get away...with this."

"Hey!" Patrick's deep voice rang out behind her, carrying a loud note of authority as he appeared beside Freeda. "What the hell is going on here?"

Chapter Nine

Both men jerked straight up, as though realizing they had a growing audience as several other men turned in their direction. The man whirled away from his confrontation with Fergie and stalked away. He climbed into an old black SUV parked at the edge of the lot and drove off, but not before Freeda got a good look at the license plate. The green and white plate indicated it came from Colorado. She began repeating the combination of letters and numbers until she could tap them into a memo file on her phone.

Patrick took Fergie's arm and helped him to his feet. "Are you all right?"

Fergie pulled his arm away from Patrick, his face grim. "Yeah, I'm fine."

"Dad, who was that man?" Freeda asked, approaching him. "Why were you arguing with him?"

His eyes appeared unfocused, and he shook his head. "Don't even ask," he said, taking a deep, harsh breath.

"But Dad…" Her pulse quickened. Violence had always bothered her. It was one reason she shied away from working in news operations like her cousin Cere. Assignments like personal interviews, features, or investigative stories, had always been her preference. To see her father engaged in a physical struggle so soon after finding him sent shivers through her body. Why had the two men argued? How well did her father know the man?

Fergie shook his head so violently his hair flew about his head, and he waved his hands in the air. "Look, I ain't answerin' questions from either one of you." He gasped for air as his breath came in quick breaths. "This whole damn thing is screwed up, and it's all your fault. Both of you." He glared at Freeda. "I told you I had business to do this afternoon, but you had to stick around and screw up everything. Damn!"

A wave of hurt coursed through Freeda. She might as well have been slugged in the stomach. Drawing a quick harsh breath, she struggled not to cry. Instead, she reacted with angry frustration.

"Damn you, Dad," she shouted. "How can you be such a jerk after I spent all this time trying to find you? Trying to help you. Well, go on then. Walk back to your damn cabin, where you're not supposed to be, if you don't want to be around us. Don't worry, I'm not going to beg to go back with you. To be honest, I am not certain that I want to see you again. Screw you!" She bit her lip as she fought back the tears that welled in her eyes.

"Fine! I never asked you to find me or visit me," he replied coldly, hazel eyes blazing before he turned and walked away in long rapid steps. He disappeared behind a nearby building without looking back.

Freeda folded her arms around her midsection, fighting to compose herself. She could sense Patrick's presence behind her, but she couldn't turn to face him. He probably had an "I told you so" look on his handsome face, and she did not want to see it. Luckily, no one nearby had witnessed their verbal battle, though she felt like people in nearby houses and stores were probably looking out, curious about the noise.

A car zoomed by on the road, and from behind her came the sound of Patrick opening his door, setting off the chimes in the car.

"Are you ready to go home?" he asked in a gentle tone. "Your aunt is probably wondering where you are."

Without speaking, Freeda agreed and walked to the passenger side of the car to climb inside. Patrick slid in across from her and handed her a tissue from a dispenser on the console. She took it gratefully and murmured a quick, "Thank you."

"Are you all right?" he asked after a couple of minutes of silence.

"No," she admitted, turning away from him, and looking out the window as she blew her runny nose in the tissue while fighting tears. She hated that Patrick was seeing her in such a vulnerable position. This wasn't who she normally was. The Freeda Ferguson she admired might get herself into jams but normally could get herself out of them one way or another. That Freeda wasn't this vulnerable, needy person who longed for her father's attention. As soon as she had spat out those angry words to Fergie, she regretted them.

Damn! She didn't want to care, but she did. "I can't believe I was so stupid to think things would be different this time around," she muttered, sniffling. "Oh, hell, you don't need to wait. I'll find a place to stay for the night and my aunt can come and get me in the morning."

He blew out a quick breath. 'You're still worried about him," he stated in an accusing voice.

"No, but I—"

"Yes, you are. If you weren't worried about him, you'd go home and make certain Diaz called the tow truck for your aunt's car."

Freeda started to protest, but she knew he was right. Despite her anger at her father, she didn't want to give up on being with him after searching for him for so long. She wanted a little more time with him, even if they had argued. Perhaps that would make it easier to leave him once and for all and get on with her own life. "I'm certain he has already arranged to take care of the car. I can find a hotel here and get a loan from my aunt to pay for the room." She pointed to a sign down the block. "There's one right over there. I can walk that far."

Patrick made a noise of protest. "Why stay? You heard your father. He doesn't care if you come or go. You said you didn't care either."

"I don't! I …" she stopped. Unfortunately, she did care. While her father's final words had hurt her, she could not deny that she had been partially to blame as well. He had asked them to leave, told them his meeting was important, but she stubbornly chose to stay. How would she have reacted if someone had done the same thing to her?

"Besides," Patrick said, interrupting her thoughts. "That place is so run down…"

"Look Mr. Hotshot," she interrupted. "I don't have much money. I can't afford to stay at some upscale, ritzy place. If I'm lucky, I'll be able to convince them to let me stay there without paying upfront. Just drop me off and get going, okay? I know how much you want to get to Rio Rojo. I mean, you've only waited months, heck, years, to get there but now hours might make all the difference in the world."

The words of condemnation hung in the air between them like a thick cloud. Freeda knew she was being harsh, but he was the only person who could help her at the moment, and he was about to turn his back on her.

Patrick drew a quick, harsh breath, and after a few seconds he pounded his palm on the steering wheel. "Oh, what the hell, you're right. I don't need to get to Rio Rojo tonight. I'll stay over too, though I am not certain why."

Freeda clapped a hand over her mouth to hide a sudden smile and drew a quick breath of relief. The truth was she did not look forward to being in this unfamiliar town on her own.

"Thank you," she said in a soft whisper as a feeling of relief swept through her. "I really will pay you back for everything."

Maybe Patrick Sanchez was a good guy after all.

****

Freeda strolled around the hotel room like a caged tiger. She was pleased Patrick had agreed to stay over and was paying for the room—another debt she was going to have to pay back. Unfortunately, he had only been able to rent one room, but she wasn't worried about his motives. Patrick had made it clear they were just sharing a room, not one of the two saggy full-sized beds. With him paying, he had elected to take them part way out of town to a newer chain instead of the rundown motel she had threatened to use back in the center of town. But she was still stuck with his nearby presence. At least if she'd been in her own room, she could have gone out to see if she could locate Fergie. Their angry parting had begun to weigh on her.

Looking back, she had begun to understand why her father might be displeased. She had barged into the middle of his day and totally disrupted his life. Freeda wanted to apologize and see if they could make an arrangement to see each other more often—even if it had to be on his terms. He had been right—she had rudely showed up, expecting him to reorganize his life for her.

As for his heated dismissal of her, she wanted to ask Fergie about that too. Was he angry enough not to want to see her again? She wanted to show him she had not been trying to tie him down. They had been parted for so long, she simply wanted to spend time with him, get to know him again and to show him who she was as an adult.

And then there was Patrick. Her stated desire to see her father again after their blow-up outside the bar had irritated him. She had a nagging suspicion that was really the reason he had bargained for only one room. That way he could keep an eye on her movements. She was tempted to sneak out now while Patrick was in the bathroom getting ready for bed, but she didn't want to risk his locking her out. Then she would have no place to stay. Besides, she had a feeling he was listening for the door. He'd locked it and chained it and she didn't think she could get out without making a noise that would alert him. He probably expected her to go.

Why couldn't he understand why she might want to see Fergie again? Despite their earlier disagreement, she was more worried than ever about her father. The crazy situation between him and that strange man had frightened her as much as it puzzled her. Why was Fergie being so damn secretive? True, she had not seen her father in years, but her search should have convinced him of her dedication toward helping him.

Patrick came through the bathroom door, and Freeda couldn't keep from smiling. The man actually wore silk pajamas. She checked for a monogrammed breast pocket on the pale blue shirt and was almost disappointed not to see one.

He waved toward the bathroom. "It's all yours. I don't suppose you have anything to sleep in? Or a toothbrush? Maybe we should have gone over to the discount store first."

"I never travel without my hairbrush, toothbrush or make up." She dug in her purse for the plastic travel container that held her toothbrush. She pulled it out and waggled it at him. "And I can sleep in your shirt," she said, lifting the garment he'd been wearing all day off his arm.

For an instant, a look of horror crossed his face, and she laughed.

"What's the matter, Mr. Sanchez? Not used to women sleeping in your clothes?"

His caramel face flushed, and he lowered his eyes. Damn, the man actually appeared to be embarrassed. "Well…no, not really."

"Oh, I bet you only date proper debutantes who always have their own silk dressing gowns or they like to sleep naked…" she had no idea what a dressing gown was, but it sounded good.

"It's not that. It's …"

"It's what? Why did you get only one room, Mr. Cool?"

He blinked, looking away. "Not for the reason you might think."

"Which is?" she asked playfully.

"Don't play games, Freeda. I'm too tired to deal with this tonight. You and I both know that the reason we're in this room together is because I don't want to be wakened in the middle of the night by the cops because you've gotten hit on the highway hitchhiking out to

Fergie's place or you're locked up along with Fergie for something stupid."

She had figured as much, but she gave him a wide-eyed grin anyway and bared a shoulder. "And here I thought you were falling victim to my feminine charms."

The look of discomfort on his face and his sudden rigid stance reminded her of holding a treat out for a pet. She couldn't resist the urge to tease.

"You know, I was just thinking, I could sleep in just my panties…like I sometimes do. Or in the nude…like normal…" She grinned at him, lifting, and lowering her eyebrows.

His face tightened, and he turned away. "If you want to sleep in the nude, I don't give a damn. Personally, I can't imagine sleeping naked in any small-town motel room."

The words might have sounded tough, but there was a soft quiver to his voice.

As he turned back toward her, she peeled off her T-shirt, revealing her bra, just wanting to check his reaction.

For an instant his eyes were glued to the curves of her breasts and the deep valley between them. Then something seemed to flicker behind his eyes, and he grinned. He reached over and plucked at the strap of her bra. "Next time you try to seduce a man, you might try French silk underwear. That safety pin doesn't do a thing for me."

Looking down in horror, Freeda cringed. *Oh, damn!* He was right. She was wearing one of her oldest bras held together with a safety pin, because the straps were frayed from use. Not only that, but the color had gone from snowy white to a dull grayish pink color. *Damn,*

damn, damn!

Patrick unfastened his pajama top and held it out to her, a teasing grin on his face. "Why don't you wear this? I've let women borrow it in the past, and I've never received bad reviews." He copied her waggly-brow gesture.

Freeda drew back, and her breath caught. The silk shirt he'd been wearing had been hiding a very nice, muscular chest. Was that what they called a *six pack*? The man obviously didn't spend all his time in the courtroom. He must take time off to spend in a gym. She was tempted to reach out and touch the hard muscles, just to see if they were real.

But as her chest heaved, his eyes lowered again, and this time she saw a strange fire come alive in his dark eyes. She reached for the safety pin, ready to pop it, and he reached over and put warm fingers on hers.

"Don't, Freeda." For an instant he studied her lips, and she realized she was licking her tongue around them. The room grew still. She could have heard the damn pin drop if she undid it. He continued to shake his head. "You're a lovely young woman, but, believe me, I've never been a one-night stand type of guy."

Her breath was quick, and her voice had an unnatural hoarseness to it. "Are you saying I am that sort of woman?"

"No. But I think you like to attract that type of guy," he replied, removing his fingers from hers.

She stared at him, her breath quickening. Of course, he was right. She had never been into casual, sexual relationships. Freeda turned and hurried into the bathroom, clutching his shirt. She washed her face with cold water and brushed her teeth, taking her time. When she came out after changing into his shirt, he was very still under the covers on his bed. She didn't want to ask if he was asleep; she wasn't certain she wanted to know. Instead, she curled up with her back to him, inhaling the wonderful scent that seemed to emanate from the shirt.

"Thank you, Patrick, for everything you did for me today. You're really a nice guy." She spoke in a soft voice, almost hoping he was asleep.

"You're welcome," came the soft reply. "Sometimes a little chaos can be good for a stodgy lawyer. Good night, Freeda."

"Good night." She sighed deeply as she punched the pillow. *What a crazy day!*

Chapter Ten

Freeda rose early the next morning, having wakened at dawn, and was surprised to see the bed across from her empty. Lurching upright, she feared Patrick had deserted her in the night. The sight of his designer suitcase still on the luggage rack near the door calmed her. She stretched, climbed out of bed, and walked to the window to push back the drapes. The sun was cresting the row of hills to the east, sending streaks of gold across the high desert floor. A few cars were parked in the lot and across the highway. A lone runner jogged along the side of the road. She was surprised to recognize Patrick from this distance. Inhaling sharply, she took in the lean lines of his body with his damp t-shirt plastered against his chest and the firm thighs below the shorts. She'd always considered herself into men's legs as opposed to other parts of their bodies. Long, muscular legs had always been her downfall, and that was exactly what Patrick showed.

Freeda pushed back the drapes and glanced toward the disheveled bed. When she first climbed into the lumpy bed, she'd expected to toss and turn as she worried about her father. Instead, sleep had come quickly, and she hadn't wakened until a few minutes ago. Now all she wanted was a shower to wake her up. With Patrick out jogging, she should have time.

After a leisurely shower, she dressed and put on her

makeup. Patrick had not yet returned, and she debated what to do next. Should she stay and have breakfast at the cafe, hoping that perhaps her father might return, and they could patch up their differences? Would he even acknowledge her?

Looking down at her phone Freeda realized she'd missed a call from her aunt. She'd made a quick call the previous night about staying over in Casitas but had been forced to leave a message since Tuesday was her aunt's Bingo night. Freeda knew better than to interrupt her in the middle of a round. Her aunt answered the call quickly, sounding pleased. It must have been a fruitful night at the bingo parlor.

"Good morning, Freeda. How are you, dear? I received your message, but I must admit I've still been a little worried. D.V. got my car towed into town to be fixed, but where are you? Do you need me to come get you?"

"I'm sorry if I worried you, Aunt Lottie, but I found Dad." She didn't want to admit that the meeting had ended with an argument. "We had a pleasant afternoon together, and I want to have breakfast with him before I come home." At least she hoped to have breakfast with him. Fergie might not accept her apology, but she meant to give it to him anyway. "Did D.V. tell you I met old Naldo's grandson? He's been driving me around, and he stayed over too. He'll take me home after breakfast."

"Oh yes, D.V. told me all about him. He made quite an impression on D.V. and you know that cantankerous guy isn't impressed by many people."

Freeda rolled her eyes. No wonder her aunt sounded so calm when Freeda answered. "Oh, yeah, very impressive. Drives a big fancy car. He's a lawyer in

Albuquerque."

"That's what D.V. said. But how did you manage to stay in Casitas last night? D.V. found your wallet on the front seat of the car."

Freeda blew out a quick breath of delighted surprise. "Thank goodness! I couldn't imagine where I'd left it."

"But how could you afford to stay over last night?" she repeated.

"Well, Patrick was kind enough to pay for my room, but I'm going to pay him back when I get home." She didn't mention he'd only gotten one room.

The outer door opened, and Patrick stepped inside. To her surprise, he smiled when he saw her, waving as he picked up a shaving kit from his suitcase and walked toward the bathroom.

She waved back. "I'd better get going, Aunt Lottie. I'll see you in a little while. Give the cats a hug." Freeda hung up as the shower turned on in the bathroom. She finished dressing in the clothes she had worn the previous day and was in the process of putting on her make-up when Patrick stepped out of the bathroom, a towel around his waist.

"Good morning," she said, her face growing warm as she studied his bare, hard chest. When was the last time she'd seen a man with abs that chiseled? "You were up early."

He grinned back at her, as though he was unaware of the effect he might be having on her female hormones. "Always."

"I was just talking to my aunt. Just as I predicted, D.V. took care of the car and got it towed into Rio Rojo. I told you he'd do anything for her." She grinned at him, waggling her eyebrows. "According to Aunt Lottie, he was *very* impressed with you, and that guy isn't impressed by anyone! Even she said so."

Patrick waved her off as he pulled clothes out of his suitcase along with a shaving kit and returned to the bathroom as Freeda burst into laughter. She had not missed the blush that deepened on his already flushed face.

While he dressed, she used the thin phone book on the bedside table to find the number for the café she and Patrick had visited the previous day. With shaking fingers, she tapped in the numbers. She immediately recognized the voice of the woman who answered.

"Hi, this is Freeda Ferguson. I came in yesterday looking for my dad and you said he often stops in for breakfast. Has he come in yet?"

"No," the woman answered. "And I'm a little surprised. He's usually here by now. But maybe he got caught up in that ruckus over at the *Drift On Inn* last night and decided not to come into town. I heard there was a hell of a fight. Bunch of guys got arrested."

Freeda's breath caught in her throat, and she nearly choked. "*The Drift On Inn?*" she said in a croaking voice. "That was where we left Dad yesterday." Her mind flashed on the man who had pushed her father as she and Patrick were leaving. Could her father have been involved in the ruckus? "What did you hear about the fight?"

"One of the guys who was in earlier told us the cops arrested a number of guys, but I don't know who or if Fergie was one of them. It sounded like the fight started between a couple of strangers. Pretty rough though. Someone pulled a knife and one guy got cut up. I don't think anyone ended up in the hospital, but the guys responsible and a couple of others who joined in went to jail. I haven't heard anything specifically about Fergie being involved, but it's possible. Knowing Fergie, though, he could have overindulged and is sleeping in this morning. He does that when he has a late night in town."

Patrick stepped out of the bathroom, so she quickly said goodbye and hung up. He wore neatly pressed khaki slacks but no shirt and carried his jogging clothes. A towel hung around his neck, and he walked toward the luggage rack where he had placed his suitcase. His dark hair was an unruly mass of curls falling across his damp forehead.

Though she was tempted to tease him about the toned muscles of his arms, Freeda kept silent. She was in no mood for humor. She was still worried about Fergie, and she also needed a ride back to Rio Rojo.

"I forgot to mention it before you got into the shower, but D.V. found my wallet in the car and gave it to Aunt Lottie. Now I can repay you when we get back to Rio Rojo. What's on the agenda now?" she asked.

"You tell me," He said, shrugging. "I figure we can have breakfast but then I plan to head for Rio Rojo. You can either come with me or remain here, though to be frank, I don't see why you would want to stay."

Freeda had expected as much. Patrick had no reason to hang around Casitas. But what about her? Should she stay? Could her father have been part of the fight at the *Drift On Inn* the previous night?

"Let's just have breakfast," she said, putting off the question of whether she would go back with Patrick. If her father did come into town, he might have forgotten all about their argument and invite her to stay. From their infrequent interactions she had learned that he had a way of changing his mind from one minute to the next. That was perhaps her most indelible memory of him. As easily as he had grown angry the previous evening, he was just as capable of turning in the opposite direction this morning.

If there had been a fight, and he had been at the bar when it happened, would he even show up for breakfast this morning? He might not want to risk arrest or seeing someone else who had been involved in the melee.

Patrick dressed quickly while she carefully applied her make up. Just in case she did see Fergie, she wanted to look her best. Moments later, she climbed into the car while Patrick went to the front desk to check out. She sent a quick text to her aunt to let her know they were definitely staying for breakfast. They drove the few blocks to the café and found a parking spot in front.

The café was busier than it had been when they visited the previous day. Most of the tables were occupied, while the seats at the counter were filled with men, several in cowboy hats, a few in baseball caps. She scanned the line of men at the counter. No sign of Fergie or the waitress she had spoken to earlier. She and Patrick took a seat at one of the few open tables.

"Coffee," Patrick told the chunky young serving girl who came to their table with a fresh coffee pot.

"Me too," Freeda said, turning over the cup that was already on the table. The woman poured their drinks and walked back to the counter.

As Freeda stirred sugar into the steaming cup, she glanced up and spotted the older waitress from the previous day. They traded waves as the woman began filling coffee cups for patrons at the counter. Damn, maybe they should have taken a spot there so Freeda could ask the waitress if she had heard anything more about Fergie.

Freeda lowered her eyes to the menu, but nothing appealed to her. Her stomach remained queasy even as it rumbled. As she studied the breakfast offerings, she became aware of a sudden buzz in the restaurant. Looking up, Freeda realized several people were watching her and then turning quickly away. No one met her eyes directly; instead, the voices at the counter grew lower, though the heads kept turning.

"What do you suppose is the problem?" she asked Patrick. "People are looking at us."

"Small towns." His upper lip twitched as he shrugged. "These people don't know us. We're strangers. They know that."

"But when we were in here yesterday I told them who we were. Or at least who I was and most of them seemed to know who Fergie was."

He turned to look out the window, scanning the sidewalk out front. "I wonder if he's coming in today."

"I don't give a damn," she replied crisply. Freeda knew she was lying, but could he tell?

Patrick's sardonic smile illustrated he recognized the truth. "You may think you're cool, but down deep you're an open book. You haven't stopped looking for him since we walked in the door."

She didn't want to reply with a nasty comment, but she couldn't stop herself any more than he could stop from looking so damn supercilious. "You would know, Mr. Hard-Hearted Lawyer man."

He emitted a short grunt. "My mother calls me a hard ass except in one instance."

"Lovely doe eyed damsels in distress?" she teased, batting her eyes.

Patrick laughed and pointed his forefinger in her direction. "You got it, sweetie. All they have to do is bat those big, sad eyes at me."

"Typical." Freeda rolled her eyes and leaned toward him. "But I don't consider myself to be in distress, Mr. Lawyer Man. I have two very strong legs to stand on and a wit that can match even the smart guys."

"Really, Ms. Fearless?"

While Freeda didn't consider herself fearless, she enjoyed the thought that he might look at her that way. "Look, I can usually get myself out of any mess I get into. It may not be clean, actually, it may be plenty sloppy, but I can get myself out. I've been doing it for years."

"Oh, now that I believe," he replied with the hint of a smile.

The young server approached their table again, this time with a note pad and paused above them. "Are you ready to order? What can I get you?"

"Bacon and eggs," Patrick replied without batting an eye, handing back his menu. "Over easy."

Freeda hadn't realized he'd even glanced at the menu. She had never been much of a fan of breakfast. She handed back her own menu. "Just toast, and maybe some scrambled eggs."

The woman scribbled on her pad and put the menus into a holder on the table. "Coming up! I understand you're Fergie's daughter. Have you been over to see him this morning?"

Freeda's head jerked up. "Fergie? He's been in already?" She fought back a wave of disappointment as she glanced around the restaurant.

The server shook her head, tilting it sideways. "No, and I guess he won't be coming in for a while."

"Why not?" Freeda asked, her body stiffening in alarm as her fingers began to quiver.

"You didn't know? He's in jail. The guys at the counter just told me that."

Freeda gasped. She felt as though she had been punched in the stomach. "Why would he be in jail? For what? When I called here earlier, the woman I talked to didn't say anything about that."

"Well, I don't know why he might have been arrested. We just heard about it a few minutes ago when one of the deputies came in…"

Freeda immediately thought of the man Fergie had argued with when she and Patrick dropped him off. The woman turned to leave, and Freeda rose to follow her back to the counter, asking about the arrest on the way.

The woman didn't answer, simply holding up her finger until they reached the counter. "Just a second," she said. "I don't know anything about it, but maybe…" She called through the open window into the kitchen. "Hey, Darryl, Fergie's daughter is out here. What did you hear about him being arrested?"

A bulky, barrel-chested man with a day's growth of beard lumbered through swinging doors to the kitchen, wiping his hands on a dingy apron. "Hi, gal. I saw you in here yesterday."

Freeda smiled gratefully, remembering him. "I was looking for my dad."

"Yep, I remember."

"I hear that he got arrested last night?" she questioned. "It wasn't because of the fight at the bar…"

His gaze dropped, studying the speckled Formica counter. "Nah, nothin' to do with that ruckus. But I told you yesterday I thought he was workin' up at Tres Padres and living there? You didn't go up there to look for him, did you?"

"Well, yes, we did. We found him walking up the road. He's living in a cabin just inside the gate."

The men seated at the counter apparently had been listening to the exchange because several of them laughed at her comment.

Freeda turned toward them. "What's so funny?"

"He's not working there," a thin man in coveralls replied coolly. "From what I hear, he's been hanging out at an old hunter's cabin near the back gate. Been squatting there, I guess. Broke in and stayed without asking permission so they had him arrested for trespassing."

A cold chill ran through Freeda as she absorbed what the men were saying. No wonder her father had been so secretive and uneasy when she and Patrick arrived unannounced. It also made sense that he wanted them to keep the car out of sight.

Diaz! Somehow, she knew *he* was the "they" who was responsible. And she had almost been willing to give him the benefit of the doubt! Wait until she told her aunt about this! Unhappily, she thanked them, and walked back to the table, dropping onto the hard wooden chair, her breath coming in quick gasps.

Patrick leaned forward, touching her arm lightly. "Freeda, are you all right? What did they say? Fergie wasn't involved in the fight last night, was he?"

"No," she replied, her lips trembling, "but he is in jail. It sounds like that jerk Diaz had him arrested for squatting in the cabin." Her voice cracked as she fought off tears. *Damn!* His arrest might be her fault. Had all her questions from the previous day alerted Diaz to where her father was staying? If that was true, would her father ever forgive her for getting him into trouble?

Chapter Eleven

Patrick took hold of her wrist and squeezed it gently. "Let's have our breakfast, all right? Then we'll go over to the jail and straighten this out. Here, I grabbed a paper while you were gone." He handed her a section of the newspaper.

Freeda shook her head, shoving it away. No way could she concentrate on anything other than her father's whereabouts. How could she read—or for that matter eat—with the thought of her father in jail roiling her stomach?

"I've lost my appetite. We need to find out what happened to him…let's go now…" she insisted, but Patrick took hold of her wrist and held onto her firmly.

"Freeda, hon, listen, you need to calm down and eat. You barely ate anything last night, and you can't go chasing him all over without taking care of yourself. I doubt they'll even let us in to see him this early." He glanced at his watch and leaned toward her. "Take a few deep breaths and calm down. Read the paper and eat your breakfast. After that we'll figure out what we're going to do. All right? Let's clear our heads and determine a plan of action. I'll help you get him out of jail, but we can't go rushing over there blindly without thinking things through."

His voice was low, soothing, and after he released his grip, he rubbed her arm gently. Freeda doubted she could hold down any food, but as she was about to protest again, her stomach rumbled so loudly he probably heard it even over the din of the restaurant. She drew in a quick breath and blew it out slowly and then repeated the action. Despite her anxiety, she knew Patrick was right. She needed to eat. They needed a plan of action. The next few hours would call for calm, not hysterical reactions. She took another deep breath and blew it out before sipping the hot coffee, barely tasting it, but savoring its warmth.

"Trust me, we can work it out," Patrick repeated from across the table. "They won't be able to hold your dad for long if the charge is just trespassing. He'll probably face a fine. I'll take care of it. Then we can drive him back to the cabin to get his things. He didn't appear to have much, and if they won't let him return to the ranch at all, I'll contact Diaz myself to collect his belongings. We can take him back to Rio Rojo with us and he can stay at my grandpa's place for a while if necessary."

She jerked her head up in surprise, meeting his steady gaze. "You would do that?"

"Why not?" he said with a shrug, shoving the paper at her again.

This time she took it, lowering her head to read but the words blurred before her eyes. All the same, she kept her face down, considering his proposal. Taking her father to Rio Rojo would be a good way to get him away from whatever chaos was happening in Casitas. She could see him, perhaps talk with him, and work out a future strategy for him. She and Patrick sat silently until their breakfast arrived in a clatter of plates. The server placed them on the table and retreated.

For the next few minutes, they busied themselves with their food, until he finally spoke.

"I've been thinking more about your dad," he said as he cut into his eggs. "Since he doesn't have a job right now, maybe he can live in the house and help me clean it out. Heck, I'd even pay him to stay. I'll need to hire some help anyway to get it in shape to sell, and it would be good to have someone constantly on the premises, so people don't continue to break into it once we begin to clean it out."

Would her father agree to do that? But why not? Working with Patrick and living legally in a place for free had to be preferable than having no place to live. She agreed eagerly.

"Patrick, just so you know, my dad does know a little about carpentry if you need any repairs done," she said. "He once built a bed for my dolls and a little cupboard for my dishes when I was young. And I know he's worked as a painter in the past. He isn't a bad man. Irresponsible, maybe. He just can't seem to stay in one place for long. He has always liked to wander…"

He didn't answer, simply watching her over the top of his cup as he took a gulp of coffee.

After a couple of bites, her eggs became tasteless. Even the strong coffee had lost its flavor. In the ensuing silence at the table, she strained to hear the jumble of conversation from the counter. The men were still talking about the previous night, and a new man had joined the discussion.

"But that ain't half the story," he was saying in a loud voice. "They may have arrested Fergie for being a squatter and trespassing, but I'd bet that's only so they could get him into jail. I bet they're gonna get him for murder."

She gasped, her shocked gaze flying to Patrick. "Did you hear that? M-m-murder?" Her voice cracked.

He held a finger to his lips and tilted his head toward the counter. He must have been listening as well. "Just eat and listen," he said in a low voice. His gaze went back to the paper, but she doubted he was doing any more reading than she had been. She twisted in her chair so she could more clearly hear the conversation at the counter.

"Do they know who the victim was yet?" someone asked.

"I heard it was some drifter who had been hangin' around town for the last week. Apparently the fight started with him and Fergie having a loud argument at the bar. Jack was the bartender, and you know how tough he is about arguments. He let the guy stay but tossed out Fergie, and no one saw him after that. But then the guy got into another argument with a couple of others, and that ended up in a fist fight outside. Cops broke it up, but later someone beat the crap out of the guy and left him for dead in an alley just down the street. I heard that someone said the last word he spoke was 'Fergie.' An hour later the cops found Fergie and picked him up."

The man sitting next to the speaker suddenly poked him and gestured with his head toward Freeda. Their voices immediately lowered so she couldn't make out the words any longer.

She put down her fork as her fingers shook so violently she almost dropped the utensil. "Patrick…" A chill ran through her, setting her insides to shaking.

"Shh…Keep cool. Eat your breakfast and we'll go straighten it out," he cautioned calmly.

"Dad wouldn't hurt anyone," Freeda protested, her

voice quivering. She shivered violently. The air conditioning seemed to have grown so cold Freeda didn't think she would ever be warm again. "Dad has always been a pacifist..." From across the room, another man seemed to share that opinion in a booming voice.

"Fergie? Nah, couldn't be him," the man said. "I've never seen him exchange a cross word with anyone. He's always been a buddy to everyone. Other guy musta started it."

"Yeah, I don't see how he coulda done it," another voice protested. "He was so damn blasted when he left the place. I was worried he wouldn't make it around the corner."

"Blasted, my ass," someone else added in a hard tone. "I've never seen anyone who could hold a drink like Fergie, but you're right. He's never been the type to fight."

"They found him passed out, over by that new Hamburger Haven," someone else offered.

Freeda had heard enough. Tears edged into her eyes, and she lifted her napkin to wipe her lips. "Patrick, I can't eat anymore. I need to get over to the jail. Dad...might need...my help."

"We're going to finish eating first," Patrick's voice remained calm though he set down his coffee cup with a thump.

Freeda shook her head, unable to sit still. "You go ahead and finish breakfast...I need to go." She began to rise, but his firm grasp caught her shaking hand. He squeezed it gently.

"Sit," he ordered, his voice uncharacteristically stern. "We're going to finish breakfast. If he is suspected of murder, they're not going to release him on his own recognizance. I doubt the court is open yet."

"But you said you could take care of it."

He leaned forward, speaking in a low voice. "It depends on the charges. Drunk and disorderly is different than being a murder suspect. If that's why he's there, they won't let him go immediately, and we'll probably need to put up some sort of bond."

"Bond?" That meant money—cash she didn't have.

He waved a quick hand at her. "Don't worry. I'll see that he gets out, whatever it takes. Now calm down. We're going to finish eating and then go over to the jail. Having you collapse from hunger in the middle of a court hearing won't help him, okay? Now, eat!"

Freeda knew he was right, and she drew a deep breath as she slumped back down onto the chair. He squeezed her hand quickly before letting it go. She took a gulp of the strong coffee. It was no longer hot, but she didn't care. She wished she had a swig of whatever Fergie had been drinking the previous night to add to it.

Who was the man who had been killed? Could it be the guy who had argued with Fergie earlier? Somehow, she knew that he was the dead man. But he had seemed stronger than Fergie. The guy had shoved her father down and kicked him. Had Fergie gone after him later when the man might have been drunk and vulnerable? She shook her head. No, her father could never become violent enough to kill someone.

Freeda took another small bite of her breakfast and glanced across the table. Patrick watched her with dark unreadable eyes. She wanted to get to her feet and walk over to the counter and question the men about the fight, but she doubted Patrick would let her. Normally she would just do it, no matter what he thought, but she needed his help to get her father out of jail. Angering or upsetting him would only make matters worse. Instead of protesting, she sipped the strong coffee and settled for listening to the bits of conversation she could overhear from the counter.

"Who was the guy who got killed?" someone down the counter asked. "Any of you know him?"

"I'd never seen him before," another man replied.

"Just came into town a couple of days ago," someone else said. "But I think I've seen him with Fergie before last night."

"Yeah, they almost got into a fist fight a couple of nights ago," someone else down the counter volunteered. "I didn't see it, but that's what the bartender said. The guy left without paying his tab and so did Fergie. I'm surprised they let the two of them back in last night."

"Did you see that first fight?" another man asked. "I did. Fergie accused him of hiding something or looking for something or stealing something…they were going at each other pretty hard that night too."

Freeda glanced up and found Patrick watching her. He put a finger to his lips in a warning motion. She again focused on her eggs. She doubted she could eat anything more and hold it down. She lowered her fork and took a sip of coffee instead.

With a sigh, Patrick put down his fork as well. "All right," he said. "Let's go check it out. Maybe they'll let us see him before the court opens."

****

Patrick guided Freeda out of the restaurant and to his car. She couldn't think of anything to say except she couldn't imagine that her father would kill someone. She had seen his anger with Patrick, and she had witnessed his argument with a strange man but she didn't want to think about that. If the two had fought in the bar, others would have known the animosity between them. She shuddered.

"My father is not normally a violent man," she said as they drove down the street.

Patrick didn't reply, concentrating on driving.

"He isn't," she insisted. "Dad has always practiced and believed in peace. He lived in a peace commune for years. It's the one thing I know he really believed in. He might get frustrated sometimes, but he wouldn't hurt people physically. He couldn't even spank me as a child. Now my mother…"

"Look, Freeda," he interrupted. "It doesn't matter who he is, or what kind of a man he might be. That doesn't change the sort of person you are."

The comment surprised her, and for a minute she didn't understand his reason for making it.

Suddenly it hit her. She glanced at Patrick—the driven, successful lawyer. Was he talking about her or his own father? After all, the talk in Rio Rojo had been that Patrick's dad, Berto Sanchez, killed Marco Gonzales many years ago. Heck, the old mayor claimed his dad had taken money for killing Marco and then run off. Abandoned his wife and son. Was that how Patrick explained the actions of his father? It didn't make a difference in the man Patrick had become.

But that situation had nothing to do what was happening between her and her father. "I want to talk to him," she said with a deep sigh.

"I understand."

"No, you don't."

He drew a quick breath. "Okay. Okay. But you need

to see—"

"I don't need to see anything," she protested. "I just want to talk to him. I may not have spent much time around my father, but I know he is not a killer. Maybe that man just fell down. Or maybe someone else saw him getting drunk and attacked him to take his money. And don't be telling me that things like that don't happen in these little towns. Remember, the old mayor of Rio Rojo killed your grandfather. The man shot him to protect his reputation. For all we know, one of those fine upstanding citizens in the café is the real killer, and they're trying to pin the blame on my dad."

"I understand your passion and your dedication to your father," Patrick said, his jaw hard and set. "I'm not saying anything about whether he might have committed the murder. I learned long ago to reserve judgment until the facts are known. Our firm has represented plenty of innocent men who were wrongly accused."

"Okay."

"But we have also at times believed in someone's innocence only to discover later they were very good liars," he added.

Freeda said nothing. From her brief encounter with her father just on this trip, she had seen him lie several times. Patrick probably felt the same way. They both witnessed his tendency to avoid the truth. But she had never seen him display any sort of violent behavior. She had seen him argue or get angry, but to physically attack someone? She could not imagine that.

He pulled into a wide parking lot beside a granite building with bars on the upper windows. A sign outside indicated it was the county building. A similar three-story building directly across the street was marked as the courthouse. Whatever business they needed to do would be in one of these structures. She hopped out of the car without waiting for Patrick. As she rushed toward the courthouse, she spotted a sign reading *Police Department and Jail.* An arrow pointed to a side door. She quick-stepped down the sidewalk and through the double doors.

"How do I go about seeing a prisoner?" she asked the overweight man at the front counter.

He drew back at her question. "Prisoner's name?"

"Joseph Ferguson? I understand he was arrested last night."

"Ah," he said. "And you are?"

"His daughter! I'm here to get him out."

"No bail has been set yet."

"Why not? Someone told me that he was arrested for squatting. Shouldn't he have had a hearing or something? Shouldn't bail be set?"

"I'll get the sheriff for you."

****

Patrick took his time following Freeda into the building, not certain if he was right in agreeing to help her. His experience in criminal court was limited, and if further help was needed beyond getting Fergie out of jail, he would probably need to find someone else to deal with the legal issues.

This was turning into an ordeal, and hell, it wasn't even his business. Why should he care what happened to Freeda and her dad? The man was in jail. That was probably where he belonged if he was squatting on property illegally. Patrick had wondered if something like that was happening when he witnessed Fergie's shifty behavior the previous day.

But then again, Patrick reasoned, he had promised Freeda to help her, and he could not back away from that deal. He had enough knowledge to get her through a simple case of trespassing. Now, if it was a murder charge…he hesitated. If that was the case, he could call his office in Albuquerque and get them to find someone to assist.

What was the deal with Fergie anyway? Who the hell was the man, and what was he really like? As for killing someone, Patrick didn't think the man he had met the previous day was capable of inflicting physical harm, but there was no telling what someone might do when driven too far. There had been open antagonism between Fergie and the man who had approached him the previous day. Patrick had seen it in their stiff body language, like two fighters sizing up an opponent. He sighed in resignation as he walked into the building. He spied Freeda down the long hall and when she spotted him, she hurried toward him.

"They won't let him out," she cried as she reached him, her voice high, tears making her eyes shiny. "Can they do that? Shouldn't they have a bail hearing or something?"

Experience told Patrick someone was purposely delaying procedures. If law enforcement officials thought he was the killer, perhaps they didn't have enough evidence but didn't want to let him go. Patrick hadn't known Fergie long, but from what Freeda had told him, her father had stayed constantly on the go. If Fergie was released, he would undoubtedly disappear. If Patrick put up bail, he would probably lose the money. Fergie would not stay put. But if her father was a viable murder suspect, they probably would not let him go anyway.

For now, even if all authorities had on Fergie was the squatting charge, the sheriff might ask for higher bail as a murder suspect, especially if Fergie had publicly argued with the dead man.

"Look, let me take care of this," he said. "You sit here and don't say anything."

"But Patrick…"

He held up his hand to stop her. "A word of warning…emotion and name calling won't help your father. Let me handle this according to the book. You are far too upset right now. I might be able to do something, but if they are considering suspicion of murder, we may not be able to get him released."

He walked into the door marked as the entrance to the jail and approached the front desk.

"May we visit inmate Ferguson?" he asked.

The man's gaze moved beyond Patrick to Freeda and shrugged. "Sure. We can bring him out to the visitors' area. Can't let him go right now, though."

Patrick walked back to Freeda who sat on a wooden bench, chewing her fingernails. "They're going to bring him out to see you." He pointed to a nearby door. "Go through that door and wait until he comes in. I'm going to see if I can talk to someone about what the charges might be and see what we need to do to get him released."

She appeared ready to cry, but she stood stiffly and lifted her chin in a gesture of determination. Her brown eyes were shiny but unreadable.

"Thank you, Patrick," she said in a tremulous voice.

"Would you rather I went with you?"

She shivered and shook her head. "No, no, I'll be fine. I need to talk to him alone. I'll let him know you're going to help him, but I don't want to upset him."

"I understand," he replied, though he didn't.

"I'll never be able to repay you for helping me through this. If there's anything…" she shivered, and again he wanted to touch her, but he held back. She would probably yank her hand away or slide away from any sort of physical contact.

All the same, the sad look on her face tore at his emotions. He wanted to catch her up in his arms and hold her.

"Take all the time you need. I'll be waiting outside in the car once I get some answers," he said instead.

Taking a quick breath, she drew herself up and followed the deputy through the door into the jail visitors' area. What was she thinking? She had defended Fergie so quickly and so vociferously, but Patrick doubted she knew the man any better than Patrick did. He watched her go, wishing he did not feel like reaching out to her and just holding her close to him and telling her things would be all right. Unfortunately, he had no idea of what might be ahead. As she walked through the door to the visiting area, he knew he couldn't simply return to the car. He walked back to the front desk.

"Who do I need to see about getting Mr. Ferguson released from jail immediately? I'm an attorney from Albuquerque and our firm may be handling his case."

Chapter Twelve

Freeda's heart beat a rapid tattoo as she waited for her father to arrive in the open area behind the glass. Would he be surprised to see her? Happy? After their parting the previous afternoon, she was not certain. The stark gray-green room where she sat was as colorless and cheerless as she felt. The black plastic chairs were hard, the tile flooring a dusty sand color. She shivered at the feel of cool air that came from a nearby vent.

A door in the room behind the glass opened and her father shambled through it. He wore a wrinkled gray jumpsuit, and his thinning dull brown hair was uncombed. His face was drawn and haggard as he moved slowly toward her. She lifted the phone to talk to him with a shaking hand. He seemed to have aged in the past fifteen hours, his face showing lines, his brown hair lank and greasy, his eyes bloodshot. The slumping posture said it all, though she knew with absolute certainty in that moment that he was not capable of taking anyone's life. His lifeless hazel eyes never left hers as he dropped onto a chair across the glass and picked up the phone.

"I didn't do anything," Fergie began, leaning toward her, his voice hoarse. "And I'm not just saying that. I *didn't* do anything wrong except drink a little too much."

She clutched the phone like a golden commodity. "I know, Dad. I believe you and…Patrick…does too. But…who was the man who was killed? Was it the guy who—?"

He held up his index finger and shook his head, cutting her off. Slowly he twisted around to look behind him as though worried someone might be standing there listening. Slowly he shook his head again. "This isn't a good place to talk. You know they bug these phones."

"You've been watching too many crime programs on television," she chided, attempting a smile, but she also realized he was warning her not to mention his earlier altercation outside the bar. That conversation was for another time.

"Bob was an old pal," he said in his rasping voice as a grim smile passed over his face. "I knew him a long time ago. I hadn't seen him in years. I have no idea how he came to be here or why. But I would never hurt him. We were pals. Always had been. Never exchanged a cross word. I can't believe he's gone. I don't know why anyone would want to hurt him."

"I'm sorry, Dad. I understand." She sighed, realizing his comments were about the dead man, not the man with whom he had argued. She attempted a smile, but her lips remained stiff as she put her hand on the glass. He did the same, but the gulf between them was thicker than glass. It might as well have been a brick wall. Freeda was not certain she could believe him, and that doubt bothered her. He could probably sense her ambivalence.

His quick grunt and pursed lips told her she was right. "No, you'll never understand, but it don't matter. We went to high school together. Came to the commune the summer after we graduated."

The comment surprised Freeda. She didn't know that much about his youth. "That was before you went to college and met Mom or Aunt Lottie?"

"Exactly. Bob and I spent several summers working here together in the summer, back in the days when Tres Padres was a real ranch, not this current tourist trap. Old man Landis ran a real cattle operation. Then he made a big mistake and sold part of it. New owner didn't want to live there, so he sold it off in chunks. Part of it became the commune. Bob never left, but I went to California to school. That's how I met your mom…I was talking to a group of kids one day and mentioned I had lived at the commune, and that flirty little babe told me she had spent time in New Mexico and knew all about it. Instant connection. We didn't stop talking for two days."

The memory seemed to turn him emotional, and he lowered his head before wiping one eye with a long finger. "Two damn days," he repeated in a suddenly hoarse voice.

Tears edged into Freeda's eyes as a shiver ran through her.

He smiled sadly. "Bob and I kept in touch over the years—saw each other every so often."

"Where was the commune, Dad? Can you take me to see it when we get you out?"

He shook his head, his shaggy hair flying around his face. "It's pretty much gone now. It was on the other side of the valley, not far from that cabin where I've been staying. All that remains of the place is just the rubble of a couple of old log and stone cabins, foundations of a couple of the main buildings. I guess someone bought all that land years ago and then sold it when the owners of Tres Padres were looking to expand their property, wanting to take it back to the original size. Damn money-grubbing jerks. The land's still the same…still pretty, restful…good grazing land for cattle, but the damn guys also want to chop all the trees into lumber. They won't be happy until nothin's left but cactus and grass. Hell, they'd sell the rock if they could get a few bucks."

She stifled a smile. For a minute he sounded like the old Fergie she remembered from her childhood, full of indignation at the establishment, or better known as to him as "the man." She leaned forward her hand still on the glass. "I'm sorry, Dad."

Lowering his head, he drew a quick breath, though his hoarse voice sounded defeated. "Yeah, me too."

"The guy from yesterday…when we dropped you off, that wasn't the man you were waiting for at the cabin, was he?"

He shrugged and for a moment she didn't think he was going to answer. Finally he nodded, keeping his face down. "Yeah, sort of, but I didn't know it. I was waiting for Perry at the cabin. He was one of my buddies I roomed with in the commune. I didn't know he had also contacted Bob and Jack besides me…Jack has always been a jerk."

"Jack was the guy you arg—" She stopped as he shook his head vigorously, jerking his thumb up and toward a corner. Following the direction of his tilting head and raised eyes, she pretended to look around and spotted the small camera above her. It appeared to be only a black knob on the dull green wall. Were they being recorded? There was probably another camera on his side that would have caught his negative gesture. Of course, he wasn't going to answer her direct question about the argument with Jack.

"So, you hadn't seen Bob or Jack in a while," she said instead, winking at him as she gripped the phone with both her hands.

"I hadn't seen any of those guys. Perry got in touch with me out of the blue not long ago and wanted us to get together with Jack who happened to be traveling through. Perry didn't like the idea of driving out to the ranch so we arranged to meet in town. As for Bob, when I saw him, I figured Perry musta gotten in touch with him too."

"Where are Jack and Perry now? Are they in jail too?"

"I have no idea. Damn jerks headed for the door as soon as the first fight started. I figure they're probably long gone, could be anywhere. Neither one is going to hang around because they know the cops will be looking for them too."

"Do you think maybe one of them might…" Freeda stopped. Again, she didn't want to say too much in front of the camera.

He glanced away, to a spot behind her head. "The hell with those guys. Good riddance! But…I do feel bad for being such a damn jerk to you yesterday. I've been thinkin' about it all night." Sadness edged into his grim eyes. They glistened as he slowly lowered his head.

The tautness in Freeda's body lessened, and she reached up once more and pressed her palm to the glass. "I understand, Dad. Things are hard for you right now, and I know you haven't done anything wrong. You could never hurt anyone physically. Anyone who knows you knows that."

Behind the glass, he lifted his own hand, pressing it to the opposite side for a few seconds, meeting her eyes with his. She smiled at him, wishing she could grasp his hand, but suddenly he lowered his hand, balling it into a fist and pounding on the counter in front of him. "I didn't do anything, dammit! I wouldn't hurt anyone!" he declared with his voice filled with indignation. "Can't you see what's happening here? They need a scapegoat and I'm an easy target."

Freeda jumped involuntarily at his sudden physical show of anger, but she forced her voice to remain calm when she spoke. "Where did you go after you left the bar?" She started to add that he should have called her, but quickly decided that wasn't a good idea. Why would he have tried to get in touch after their final exchange of harsh words? She regretted those emotion-filled moments more than ever now. Again, she put her hand to the glass, hoping to calm him, and he reached over and pressed his to it as well.

"I didn't go anywhere, hon. Someone jumped me almost as soon as I left that place. Coulda been the person who killed Bob for all I know. Maybe he thought I was an easy mark because I was so out of it." He removed his hand to run it though his limp greasy hair, shaking his head. Angry red marks across the back of his hand, and several small bruises were developing on his face.

Freeda's pulse rate quickened at the sight of the cuts. "Dad, were you hurt? Did you tell the police about being hit? Shouldn't you have been checked over by a doctor?"

"Of course I told the cops, but they don't believe I was beaten. They think I was drunk so I stumbled and fell on my head." He paused, shaking his head as he lowered his head, and mumbled, "Okay, so I had a few too many…"

Freeda sighed at his predicament, knowing he didn't want to say much, but she couldn't help him if she didn't know the details of the event. "I know you don't want to talk about it, but is there anything you can tell me that could help you? I want to get you out of here, but I need to know exactly what happened even before you left the bar. Did anyone threaten you?"

Long minutes passed as he studied her before finally beginning to speak again. "Okay, we were all drinking, and maybe I got into an argument with a couple of guys, but it was all cool and we all were fine when I left. Then when I go around the corner, I get jumped."

He held up a wrist displaying the marks—scratches—and she saw several bruises along his thin arm. "See that? The guy scratched me. Coulda been Bob, or hell, it coulda been whoever killed him. I fought back, and the guy took off. Maybe the killer was looking for an easy mark and found out I wasn't it so he went after Bob instead. That damn fool had been flashing around a wad of money."

"Earlier you said he just hit you, but now you're saying you did fight back?" She twisted her head from side to side, fighting to comprehend what he was saying. "Wait a minute, you're not making sense…"

He blinked rapidly, turning away. "Hell, I was drunk. My memory's not real clear…"

"Can you describe the man who attacked you?"

His face scrunched into a frown, keeping his head down. "I know he was as tall as I am, but really can't give you a detailed description. I was out of it. What the hell difference does it make? All I know is that I was bleeding when I woke up."

"Shouldn't you be checked out?" she insisted.

"I'm fine. Just a little knock. Dazed for a few minutes. The guy came at me from behind, grabbed at me, scratched me, and then bonked me on the side of the head. See?" He lifted his lank hair and pointed to a bruise on the side of his temple.

Freeda sighed unhappily. Didn't he realize his story kept changing? Perhaps he didn't remember the truth. "Dad, someone needs to look at that."

"Doc did a little while ago. They say I'm all right. He didn't even believe I was hit. Said he thought I got it when I passed out and fell down." He paused and his eyes widened into angry orbs. "But I didn't fall, dammit! Someone knocked me down."

Freeda put her hand on the glass, wishing she could reach her father. More than ever, she wanted to take care of him. She had always thought of Fergie as a physically strong man who was quick on his feet. This sad graying man with the scruffy appearance, thin arms, bony shoulders, and bloodshot eyes was not the vibrant man she remembered from the past.

"Will you ever forgive me for bein' such a jerk?" he asked in a suddenly raspy voice filled with emotion. A grim sadness appeared in his hazel eyes.

"Of course I forgive you. I know you care about me, and I know you haven't done anything wrong."

"I didn't!" He pounded a fist on the counter, his voice filled with indignation. "Can't you see what's happening here? Someone jumped me. I coulda ended up like Bob. Why doesn't anyone see that?" He held up a wrist displaying scratches along his arm. "See that? The guy even scratched me."

"You didn't get it in the fight?"

His face scrunched into a frown. "No, I don't know anything about the fight everyone keeps talkin' about. I wasn't even there by then. All I know is I went outside to meet Jack, and someone jumped me. I was bleeding when I woke up. I don't know if he did it or if it was someone else."

"So you never really saw the person?"

"Not really. The guy came at me from behind, grabbed at me, scratched me, and then bonked me on the side of the head. See?" He pointed to a bruise on the side of his temple.

Freeda still was not certain her father was medically all right. More than ever, she wanted to get him out of the dismal place and get him to a doctor who could properly examine him. His memory and his repeated but slightly different answers had her worried about a concussion.

"We're going to take care of this, Dad," she promised.

A sly smile crossed his face. "What happened to that guy you were with yesterday?"

The change in topic surprised her. "Patrick? He's right outside. He's going to try to get you released from custody. If they let you leave town, he says we can take you with us to Rio Rojo. He's cleaning up his grandfather's house, and if you help him, you can live there for a while."

He drew up, blinking, but then his eyes grew cool. "Really, and how much rent is he gonna charge me for the privilege of staying in his house?"

"Nothing. Like I said. He needs help cleaning out the place, but more importantly, he needs someone to be on the premises. People keep digging up the lawn and destroying the interior." She didn't want to bring up the possibility of hidden money.

His eyes widened. "Wait—is that the place belonging to the old man who was killed a couple of years ago? That house? Where they say—"

He stopped abruptly and Freeda winced. Damn! She had a feeling he knew all about the stories regarding the house, old Naldo, and the alleged hidden coins.

"Patrick needs help. He wouldn't charge rent and he would pay you for any repair work you can do. I told him about you making me that doll house when I was young."

His smile grew, and his defeated demeanor shifted as he sat up straight and nodded in agreement. The wrinkles on his ruddy face appeared to vanish. "A work of pure joy. A thing of beauty if I say so myself." The sudden change in his posture and attitude shocked her.

"I loved that doll house," Freeda continued slowly. "It must have taken a long time to make. And the workmanship…"

His face softened as he put his hand to the glass. "Hell, honey, not so hard to someone that knows what they're doing. I'm a carpenter by trade—look at these hands—and I'll be happy to help out your friend. Hell, the whole set up is perfect. I wouldn't have to sneak inside to my own bed at night or worry about having a roof over my head or that damn Diaz showing up all the time. Sure, I'll help your guy out. Long as he gives me the supplies, I can clean it, even fix things up. Might need a new toolbox, though. I bet Diaz took off with mine if he went to the cabin and found my stuff."

"I'll get it back." She wasn't certain how she would do that. Then the answer hit Freeda. "Aunt Lottie and Diaz are friends. I'll have her ask him to give it back to you. He seems to like Patrick too. He said he was friends with his grandfather."

He drew up even straighter, focusing on her first sentence. "Really? Didn't know that about him and Lottie. Listen, hon, go talk to your boyfriend. See how quickly he can get me out of here."

Freeda rolled her eyes, but she couldn't resist a smile. "He's not my boyfriend, Dad, but he will fix things for you. Don't worry, things will work out."

"Sure will." Suddenly he grinned and winked as he reached up and placed his palm on the glass between them. "And we'll be able to spend some time together finally. Talk and really get to know each other better."

A rush of contentment ran through her. "Yes! I'd really like that."

The door behind him opened, and a guard suddenly appeared, waving at her. "Sorry, ma'am. Time's up. Gotta take him back."

"We're finished, but what about his injuries?" she asked. "I know he said someone checked him earlier, but—?"

"You could take him to the emergency room when he's released if you don't think he's all right. Doc already cleared him here."

She was about to protest further, but from behind the glass, her father tapped the glass and shook his head. "I'm okay," he mouthed through the window, making a circle with his thumb and forefinger. "Get me out."

Freeda turned back to the guard. "If he isn't released or charged soon, I want to take pictures of his injuries, just in case. And if he isn't okay when a doctor checks him later, I want you to know I have a darn good attorney from Albuquerque. He's a civil attorney, and he's so good he drives a very expensive car. If Dad has been mistreated or is not okay because he didn't get medical help, your department may have to buy one for Dad too."

The guard appeared bored at her weak threat, but he didn't argue. "We'll get him processed and out the door within half an hour and you can take him to his own doctor. To tell you the truth, miss, he usually prefers to spend the night in jail when we pick him up."

She stared at him glumly. "He's been jailed here in the past, I understand?"

"Numerous times," he replied with a grin. "Usually, it's because he has too much to drink, and it's easier to let him spend the night in a cell than worry someone might hurt him if we leave him sleeping on the street. I doubt there will be any major charge against him, but you can have your attorney come by the front desk and check on what's going to happen next."

Emotions swirling inside of her, Freeda walked out of the building feeling drained. Patrick's car remained parked on the street, but it appeared empty.

"Freeda, are you all right?" His voice suddenly coming from so near startled her.

Freeda jumped, emitting a soft cry.

"Sorry." He rose from a bench to the right of the front door and approached her. "You look exhausted. How's Fergie?"

She pressed her lips together, fearing she was going to cry again, aware she was shaking slightly. Despite the early hour, Freeda felt as though she had put in a full day of physical labor. "They're going to let him go." She didn't mention that she had invoked Patrick's presence as a threat.

"Good. I think they mainly tossed him in jail to sleep off the alcohol. From what I've heard from a couple of folks who have come by, they did that to a number of the guys last night. Listen, why don't you go sit in the shade and I'll bring the car around. We can wait until he comes out."

Freeda readily agreed. The less she had to think and worry, the better. She walked to the bench he had pointed out and dropped onto the plastic seat. While she was pleased Fergie had agreed to go with them to Rio Rojo, she couldn't get over a feeling of dread about her father. Had someone really attacked Fergie the previous night, or was he claiming that as a way of explaining his haggard appearance this morning? Could he have been the culprit who killed Bob?

No! She shook her head violently. No! Not Fergie!

Footsteps approached, and she lowered her head and sighed, wishing she had walked to the car with Patrick. She knew the sound of the unsteady gait that approached. However, the softness of the hoarse voice surprised her.

"Hey, gal, are you all right?"

She jerked up her head to face the sunglasses of Diego Diaz. The shiny dark lenses reminded her of a bug about to pounce on a smaller insect

"No. My dad spent the night in jail because of you," she spat out in a cold tone.

He blew out a quick breath and shook his head. "I mighta saved your dad's life."

The reply shocked her. She stared at him, her voice cracking as she asked, "What do you mean?"

In typical Diaz fashion, he didn't give her an answer. He simply shook his head. As she formulated a further condemnation, she realized he was probably right. Her father could have become a murder victim like the other man. His arrest might have put her father out of harm's way for the night. Still, she couldn't hold back a sarcastic reply.

"He's doing fine, but just so you know, he's coming back to Rio Rojo with me and Patrick. You don't have to

149

worry about him taking up space in that damn empty shack anymore. He…" she stopped as she realized the opportunity he had given her by approaching her. Swallowing, she softened her voice as she continued, "But one thing…I know you don't like me or him…but, Mr. Diaz, I hate to ask you, but could you do something for me? Or maybe for my Aunt Lottie?"

Now she had his interest. He leaned toward her. "What?"

"Dad's things…"

Diaz started to shake his head, but she quickly pressed on. "I know you probably want to toss them or burn them, but please, don't."

"Why not?" he asked with a grunt. "He had no business squatting there with his crap."

His disdainful tone only strengthened her determination. "I know, but it's not all crap. He has a toolbox with his supplies to work."

He snorted at the word "work," but she rushed on. "We'll need to replace them if you throw them away." Freeda paused again, inhaling as she got to what she really wanted saved and returned. "And…and he has pictures on the wall…pictures of me."

Despite her best efforts, she couldn't stop the tears that formed in her eyes. "I bet you don't know what it's like to lose everything from your past…to lose every scrap of evidence of who you were…"

"I doubt your daddy cares about the past any more than I care about my own." His voice was surprisingly hard. His face showed no visible emotion.

Freeda didn't want to give in that easily, so taking a deep breath, she tried another tactic. "Maybe he's not always honest, but those photos mean something to him.

He's…he's kept them all these years, through all his traveling around. They're pictures of me when I was little…" she paused, choking back tears. "Pictures…of my mom. I can barely remember her before she went into the hospital. Please don't burn them or destroy them. It's all I have left of her."

His lips tightened and the dark glasses stayed pointed at her, but he stood so still, she knew she had to be reaching him. She rushed on, wishing her voice didn't sound so desperate, but she had to get past that hard shell of his somehow.

"Listen, Mr. Diaz, I'll pay to have the cabin cleaned up if that's what you want, even if I have to clean it up myself, but please…don't throw out his things. They're my things too."

He took a quick breath and turned away.

"The past, those pictures," she continued, her voice croaking. "You're right, I don't care about a lot of things…but I do care…about that." Tears spilled down her cheeks, and she lowered her head so he couldn't see them, but a clean blue handkerchief suddenly appeared in her line of vision. Freeda took it and wiped her eyes, chancing a glance up at him.

The very dark glasses remained fixed on her. "Yeah, okay," he said in his raspy voice that seemed even more gruff than usual. "I'll take care of it. I'll see to it that his personal crap is tossed in a couple of boxes and that it gets sent directly to *you*."

The emotion that flooded through her brought more tears, and Freeda used the handkerchief to wipe them away. She had not expected the brusque man to give in so quickly. It would have been an easy way to hold something over her head. She drew a huge sigh of relief as fresh tears edged into her eyes.

"Thank you," she said, reaching out for his hand, but he twisted it away. She realized she had reached for his gloved hand, the one he never used.

"But you keep him away from the ranch," he rasped. "He better not come back, or I'll see to it that he spends more than a night in jail next time."

Chapter Thirteen

After the tension and chaos of the previous day and night, the trip back to Rio Rojo was relatively quiet. Fergie napped in the backseat while Patrick found a radio station with soothing music to provide low background sound. Freeda and Patrick kept their voices low as they talked in the front seat.

"I like being on the move," she admitted. "What keeps you in New Mexico? I think you could probably get a great paying job anywhere in the country," she said.

Patrick glanced over at her and shook his head. "Those few years back east were enough to convince me I belong out here in the wide-open spaces. The pace is slower, less frenetic. There are years I don't like the winters, but the other seasons are beautiful," he said. "There's even a minor league baseball team that keeps me outside on warm summer nights. In the fall, the colors in the nearby mountains are beautiful, while the winters don't last so long they become tiresome. Many weekends I just take long walks or drive around the area. There's also plenty of history here. In many ways, it's as rewarding as what I learned back east."

She agreed with his assessment of the area. "I've had no trouble finding stories to write since I started to look for Dad." She cast a glance to the backseat where Fergie stretched out across the seat emitting a soft snore. "There's such rich history to this area, yet also so much that continues to change and point to the future. From prehistoric drawings to space labs, every time I come back I find something new to use in a story. I don't think I miss LA except for the ease of getting a tow truck."

"You simply write stories for different publications?" he asked. "You talked about that before, but exactly what do you do?"

"I write some stories, but not just for publications. I also shoot and produce video stories on a freelance basis. I have plenty of contacts back in Los Angeles who will give me assignments, but I also work on my own. I'll find a story and do it, and then offer it to them. Sometimes I send out queries to magazines. I've been able to develop plenty of contacts, so if anyone needs something, whether it's a story, a comment from someone or a picture, they call me to get a picture taken or send me wherever they might need me. It's less expensive than sending someone out from the west coast for one or two shots. They know I'm ready to go anywhere as long as they finance it and pay me when the story is done and runs in the magazine or airs on television."

His brow furrowed as he glanced over at her. "Do you make any money doing that?"

"I make more than enough to survive and I'm even able to set a little aside for the lean times. Mostly I like the freedom it gives me. I can't imagine staying in one place for too long."

"Freedom for Freeda," he teased.

"Hey, I like that. I could make that my motto," she agreed with a laugh. "Make up a t-shirt in one of the gift shops. I embrace every wonderful moment of that saying—Freedom for Freeda."

"Sounds too unsettled for me," he said, wrinkling his nose.

The morning had gone that way. With each passing moment she could see the differences between them. Now that the tension had lessened, and they were settled in achieving their temporary goals, she could see how different they were. She enjoyed his company, and in some ways Patrick even attracted her, but she could not ever see herself becoming involved with a man like him. Safe, predictable, certain of himself and everything around him. Boring.

The conversation slowed and eventually trickled away. Freeda took one final look at her father snoring in the back seat, leaned her head back on the front seat and fell asleep until the car slowed as they had entered Rio Rojo.

****

Patrick was drawn to Lottie Medina from the moment he met her. Freeda's aunt greeted him with a wide smile as though they were long time friends. Lottie was a willowy woman with bright blue eyes, a welcoming smile, and a disposition to match. Her long white hair still had blonde streaks of what was probably its original color and was tied behind her back.

"You must come to dinner tonight," she directed as he held out his hand. "I made a pot of beans yesterday, and I'm putting them into my famous chili recipe tonight. And don't you try to shake my hand, Patrick Sanchez. I've known your family for years and you deserve a big hug for taking care of my Freeda and bringing her home."

With surprisingly strong arms, Lottie pulled him to her and embraced him. She smelled of lilacs and flour, as though she had just been baking. She had not been at all bothered by the idea of having Fergie stay. The two of them greeted each other as old friends.

"Fergie, where the hell have you been, and why haven't you come by and stayed for a while?" she scolded him.

Fergie shrugged a thin shoulder and lowered his eyes. "Don't want to be a bother to you…" he said sheepishly.

"You're never a bother. I have plenty of room, and I'm always ready for company," she told him, waving at the two-story brick house. "This monstrosity has four bedrooms and what they used to call a parlor which I use as my sewing room. I don't know why you haven't come before, Fergie. Remember how we used to crash at our friends' houses in the old days when we were traveling? We'd just show up and sleep on the floor. Well, I have real beds available for all of you."

Fergie eagerly accepted her offer. "Thanks, Lottie, it'll be great not to have to search for the nearest outhouse," he replied with a laugh.

Despite her friendly manner, Patrick declined. He had no idea what his schedule would be for the next few days, and he wanted to be free to move about on his own. "I'm going to be busy at my grandfather's house so I may stay there."

"I don't think so," she replied, shaking her head. "Wait until you see the place. Anyway, you do what you think is best. I love guests, and the door is always open, but I'm not the type to force anyone to do something that is uncomfortable. I know how you bachelors prefer your privacy. Just understand that no matter where you decide to stay, my kitchen is always open. I'm up early in the morning and I make great omelets."

Her blue eyes sparkled as she spoke, and Patrick's opinion of her increased. If Diaz did have "a thing" for her as Freeda had suggested, Patrick could understand why. If he'd been any older, he might have given Diaz some competition.

From that point on, the day quickly turned into the disaster he'd feared. His first stop after leaving Lottie's house had been at the rental agency to get the keys to his grandfather's house.

"Don't think it's going to make much sense to keep the house standing." Fred Bennett said when they were introduced. The rotund lawyer appeared to be in his sixties. A half ring of graying hair wrapped around his shiny bald head. "The whole place has been pretty well ransacked and most of the inside of the house is gutted. Roof is about to fall in. The garage has never been much more than a pile of boards. Best idea is to dig it out and knock the whole thing down. Haven't had it rented in nearly a year."

"I understand," Patrick said. "I'll see what shape it's in before I make any decisions. What do you mean, about digging it out?"

"The place is right up against the hill behind it. Looks like old Naldo used that hill as a partial foundation for the back. Course you could do that in those days. Place was built before the turn of the last century. Today's building codes would never allow it. Whole mountain could slide down on the place, but hell, he also coulda dug into that hill even…who knows what's behind the place. I think that's why folks keep trying to get in there. People say the old man used to be a miner. He coulda dug a whole mine behind that house and nobody would know it. Hell, he used to come through town all the time with a tarp on his pick-up. He coulda been hauling out dirt."

Patrick drew a quick breath. He should have thought of that. One of his memories of his grandfather was an old mining helmet. The idea that perhaps his grandfather had tunneled into the hill behind the house and stashed something valuable there was probably what drove some of the treasure hunters.

"I'll take a look at the whole situation," he repeated. You're probably right. It might make the most sense to simply raze the house and sell the land."

The man agreed eagerly. "Sounds like a plan! Listen, we can probably find you some buyers for the property if you decide to go that route."

Patrick didn't reply, instead taking the keys from the man. "Thank you, I'll check over the property and get back to you."

The address was only a few blocks from the realty office. From the moment he turned onto the block, Patrick could see the house he remembered vaguely from his childhood. It was a small stucco structure in the middle of the block with a separate wooden garage that backed up to a hill. The appearance of the property itself appeared to be as problematic as he'd feared. While someone had cut the yellowing grass recently, nearly all the windows in the house and a small window in the garage were broken. Graffiti stained the light brick walls of both buildings. He pulled into the gravel driveway in front of the garage as a wave of sadness washed over him. He should have never let this happen. His grandfather had always kept the exterior of the house painted a light beige while the sills of the windows were usually painted a bright green with white shutters. The glass windowpanes had always been kept clear and clean, except at Christmas when the old man put lighted bulbs around the windows.

"I'm sorry, Gramps," Patrick whispered as a chill ran through him. He could remember coming to this house and always being excited to arrive. He had always been certain he'd get a shiny quarter from his grandfather. Later it had become a silver dollar, and once a gold piece. His grandfather had doted on him, taking him on long walks or telling him stories about "the old days."

Damn! He had to fix this. In that moment he doubted he could simply tear down the house. Whatever the repairs would cost, he wanted to rebuild. The stucco walls had been placed more than a hundred years ago, and the place...he stopped. No. He was reacting emotionally—like Freeda might.

Much as he hated the thought, the realtor had been right. It was probably best to raze the building and sell the lot. The stucco and adobe houses nearby were newer with neat green lawns and shady elm trees, unlike the patchy yellow grass and scrawny cedar bush on his grandfather's property.

With a heavy sigh, Patrick unlocked the door and walked inside. The interior was in even worse shape than the exterior. Many of the floorboards had been pulled up, and most of the fixtures in the bathroom were missing. The sink, toilet and tub were all shattered pieces of porcelain.

The place was a nightmare.

He drew up to his full height and blew out a quick breath. While he was disappointed by the mess, Patrick was also a little relieved. Fergie might be able to help clean out the house, but there was no way he would be able to live on the property. Freeda's father might have to remain with Lottie or Patrick might agree to get him a motel room for as long as he worked on the clean-up project.

His phone buzzed and Patrick glanced down at the the screen, not surprised by the number. He tapped his phone to answer, though he would have preferred his mother had given him a little more time to explore.

"Hello, Mom," he said, fighting to keep frustration out of his voice. "I'm here at the house, in case you're wondering."

"Hi, son, how does it look?"

"As bad as I thought. Uninhabitable. The guy at the rental place said the best idea is to knock it down, clear the property and sell it. I agree—"

"No!" she cried. "Not yet."

"What do you mean *not yet*? Mom, this place is a mess, and people are going to keep digging here. You should see the lawn and inside of the house. They trashed it, pulled up all the floorboards, tore out the walls. Looks like someone even camped out inside. They're lucky they didn't burn the place down, though I think there's not much wood left to burn."

"Maybe I should come see it," she offered.

He huffed, knowing that would only delay whatever they decided to do. "There's nothing you can do about it. Walk through it with me maybe…" he paused, hoping to come up with other excuses.

"But what about all his things: Pictures, belongings, things like that? I thought that you had his personal items cleared out years ago."

"Well, yes, I arranged that with the sheriff, but I haven't talked to him yet. I just got here."

"I hope he hasn't pulled a fast one. What about that other guy?"

"What other guy? You never told me about anyone besides the sheriff."

"Well, the other guy who volunteered to clear things out."

"Mom, this is the first time you've mentioned that. I've always talked to the sheriff who arranged to have his personal items put into storage."

"Well, okay, but what about the rancher who said he had known your grandfather for years? He agreed to go through the personal belongings with the sheriff and put everything in storage so I could get to it when I had time. I wonder if he could have found something or kept it…Damn! Maybe I shouldn't have trusted him."

Patrick sighed. He had never heard about any of this. He had always dealt with Sheriff Rafe Tafoya who had never said anyone else was helping. Why hadn't his mother told him earlier? It had been years since the estate was dealt with and settled. But maybe that was why she had been so adamant about his coming now. He wasn't about to conduct his own treasure hunt while they knocked down the walls of the sad old structure. He sighed. "Okay, that's it then."

"Well, check the safe-deposit box. We need to find out what happened to that bag of coins the old man had. Didn't he ever show them to you?"

Her certainty surprised him. Had she really thought he would simply walk into the house and find something valuable? If people had been searching for years and never found anything, what made her think he would discover something valuable the minute he walked in the door?

"Maybe I need to come up there," she added.

Patrick shook his head vehemently, even though she couldn't see him. "No, Mom, everything is fine. I'll take care of things. Besides, if there was anything valuable in the house, someone would have taken it by now."

"Maybe you should go back to the house…"

"Mom, I've told you. I'm here now. I've gone through it. It's a mess. Do you want me to text you some pictures? Unless I start digging out the walls that are still standing, I'm not going to find anything. Most of the interior is gutted."

She ignored his question about pictures. "Did you check the garage?"

"The garage? Do you think something might be in there?"

"The guy who helped me kept hanging out in the garage, like he was looking for something. I remember that specifically. Everyone else was obsessed with the house, but he appeared to be focused on the garage."

"Everyone seems to be obsessed with this place," he said with a sigh. "I met this woman yesterday who was from California, and even she knew about it. I stayed in Casitas last night and even people there had heard about him. As soon as anyone heard my name, they asked if I was related to Gramps."

"Woman?"

Damn, he shouldn't have mentioned Freeda. He could sense her immediate interest.

"What woman?"

"She needed a ride so I gave it to her. Her car had broken down along the highway. It's why I stayed over in Casitas last night and didn't get here until today. She needed some legal help." At least that was not totally a false statement, but he still felt guilty for the part that was untrue.

"Young?"

"Not teenage young. In her twenties. She was looking for her father, and we found him. He's going to help me clean out the house."

"Don't tell him about those crazy rumors, okay?"

"Sorry, Mom, like everyone else, he's already heard about them. But don't worry, he's harmless. Just a sad old guy in need of a job. I'm going to pay him to help me clean up."

"Well, don't tell him anything more than he already knows," she urged. "You'll only be asking for trouble."

"Like you did with the guy who volunteered to help?" he reminded her.

Her sigh was heavy and quick. "I know. I should have been more careful. He was spooky looking from the beginning. But kinda quiet, like he was just watching everyone. He spoke in a low, calming voice, though, like he was really sincere…"

"Sure, mom," he replied coolly. Then another thought rocked him. "Wait. What was his name? Did he tell you?"

"I don't remember. It was a years ago now. I don't think I ever knew his real name. He went by initials. I do remember that."

A chill ran through Patrick's body as his fear was confirmed. "D.V.?"

"That sounds right. D. D., I thought. I just remember everyone called him by initials. He had a black patch over one eye."

Patrick bit back the urge to correct her on the initials, but he knew now who the man was. Why had Diaz not revealed that to him when they met? A tightness grew in his throat. He couldn't talk any longer. He needed to think through this latest discovery. "Listen, Mom, I better go."

"Okay, I'll talk to you later."

He stared at the blank phone screen before looking up at the gutted walls of the living room. The phone call with his mother upset him more than he wanted to admit. So Diaz had offered years earlier to help his mother too? Why would he do that? According to Freeda, he had not been around for that long. Had he helped the sheriff with the clean up? Sheriff Tafoya had never mentioned who helped him clean out the house. He had only let Patrick know that everything had been handled. What might Diaz have found while carrying out his strange offer? What did the man *really* know about his grandfather? Could he be one of those treasure hunters as well? Had he found nothing years ago but now Patrick's presence offered another opportunity?

Perhaps he had been wrong about the man. He recalled how cold Diaz had been with Freeda and Fergie while being so friendly with him. Were there ulterior motives involved? Could Freeda have been right about him all along?

Patrick shook his head as though that would clear him of his thoughts. But in the end, he still had one more question—just what the hell was the story on Diego Diaz? Perhaps he needed to look into that strange coincidence.

Chapter Fourteen

Freeda smiled as she surveyed the table. A feeling of contentment settled her nerves. She couldn't recall the last time she had sat at a dinner table across from her father. Having her aunt present was a welcome addition. The other two men at the table, Patrick and her aunt's friend, Tony Gennaro, only added to the joyous feel of the gathering. After the past two hectic days, this evening was a welcome respite from her chaotic life.

She'd liked Tony from the moment they were introduced. She had seen him from a distance when she had been in Rio Rojo previously and had dined at the Italian restaurant he owned several times.

She had never talked to him then, but now it was clear that he and her aunt had become close since the last time Freeda visited. Tall, slim and with soft brown eyes, he had a sly wit that had her laughing almost from the moment he arrived. She enjoyed the easy way he teased her aunt, and the two appeared to enjoy each other's company. He had even welcomed her father, expressing interest in his travels, and Fergie visibly enjoyed the chance to talk about all the places he had visited. Her father kept them all entranced with stories of crossing the country many times

"A toast to Lottie's cooking," Fergie said as he held up a homemade tortilla and leaned over his bowl to inhale the spicy scent of chili. "If I remember correctly, we're in for a great meal. Raise your glasses to good company and fine dining. Finest cook in town, I'm certain."

Lottie laughed, lifting her wine glass. "Oh, now wait a minute. I know someone who would give me a run for that title. My chili may be good but wait until you get a taste of Tony's spaghetti. We'll have to visit his restaurant before you leave town, Patrick." She leaned to her side and touched Tony's arm. "It's still the best dish I know how to make."

"Here's to Lottie's cooking, and she's being modest," Tony added as they toasted the gathering. "I think she can give my cooks a run for their money, especially when she bakes bread."

"Maybe we need to do a taste-off," Fergie suggested.

"Yes, definitely." Tony agreed, smiling at Lottie. "You must all come to my place before you leave town. You'll be my guests."

"Now that sounds good to me," Fergie said. "I'm never going to turn down a free meal."

Freeda winked across the table at her father, pleased to see him engaging in the conversation. He had fluctuated between restless energy and exhaustion since their arrival at the house. After a quick shower, he had retreated to the bedroom where Lottie directed him and spent much of the morning and early afternoon sleeping. When he rose, he paced from one end of the house to the other, seldom engaging in conversation. He reminded her of a caged tiger longing for freedom. Could he be worried about Bob's murder? Had he witnessed something that night that might put him in danger? She wanted to ask him but feared his reaction.

When Freeda asked him to go with her to the nearest discount store to buy fresh clothes, he declined. After getting his sizes, she went alone and purchased several t-shirts, sweatshirts and three pairs of jeans. Luckily her grandmother had agreed to pay her credit card bill this month so she was free to fill the order without worrying her credit card might be over its limit.

The experience served as a wake-up call on her expenses, however. Now that she had found her father, she needed to make some decisions about her own future. Any time spent here in Rio Rojo meant another job she wasn't working in Los Angeles. Because she worked unpredictable freelance jobs, Freeda normally kept a close watch on her spending habits. If she stayed in New Mexico much longer she would need to find an income source, which meant producing a few stories in the area as she had done in the past. She had bragged to Patrick about her ability to find story sources and selling stories, but often finding opportunities could become a real issue.

But that was a problem for the future. Freeda forced her attention back to the table and away from her financial problems. Patrick was telling the others about the few times he visited his grandfather as a boy.

"I'm so sorry you barely knew your dad," Lottie said. "Berto could be a character at times, but I know how much he always wanted a son."

His gaze dropped as he shook his head. "I'm sorry too. He left when I was very young, a baby really. I have no memories of him, but I do have a few happy memories of visiting my grandfather. I recall that he liked to keep busy, and he loved to talk. He enjoyed teaching me things, like how to chop wood or how to fish, though I was too overactive to sit still with a pole. I preferred the business of video games." He paused, sighing sadly. "I regret that now."

Lottie reached over to pat his hand. "Well, while you're here, you should ask Rafe to tell you about your grandfather. He used to work with Rafe at times. I'll bet if you asked some of the others around town they'd be able to tell you more too. Some of the older generation may even remember back when he and his family ran the pawn shop."

"Yes, the pawn shop." Patrick sighed, looking toward the window. "I've heard a little about that. I understand he still had a lot of the old things that were pawned."

"Oh, yes. You'd think he would have sold them, but he kept things he really liked if they weren't reclaimed. He could have retired earlier if he had just sold everything and lived off the profits. And then, of course, there were all those old coin rumors."

"Coin rumors?" Fergie had been sitting quietly, almost dozing, but his head jerked up and his boredom disappeared.

Lottie laughed and slapped at his hand. "Oh, Fergie. That would be right up your alley. You're the one always searching for pots of gold. Surely, you've heard the rumors that old Naldo had a stash of gold coins buried in his back yard."

"That was *your* grandfather?" he asked, studying Patrick as though he hadn't seen him before that moment.

Patrick held up a hand in a stop gesture. "None of that is true."

"Maybe it's not true, but plenty of people think it

is," Lottie continued. "After he died, people kept looking for them. It used to drive Rafe crazy. He spent days and nights trying to keep people from digging around the yard or through the floors of the house."

"Old gold coins?" Fergie was fully alert, leaning toward Patrick. "In his yard? I thought they were buried out on the prairie."

Lottie laughed. "Oh, Fergie, don't you start too."

"I'm not startin' anything. But I hear other people talking...all the time."

Across the table, Tony shook his head and grumbled. "Lots of people have searched for those coins, and no one's ever found anything, or even proved that they exist."

"You don't believe in them?" Lottie asked, glancing back at him.

"No," Tony began, putting down his fork. "Old Naldo used to work for me at times. Cleaned up at night. Helped me re-paint the restaurant. Why would he do that if he had gold coins stashed in his back yard? But I don't try to talk anyone out of believing that. Those stories bring tourists to town in the summer and that means business for me." He winked at Lottie.

"As long as they don't rip up my grandpa's yard or break into the house, they're free to dig anywhere they want." Patrick's tone turned hard. "But those scavengers have made a mess of the house and the property."

"I feel bad every time I go by the house." Lottie heaved a heavy sigh. "I know it would have broken old Naldo's heart to see it like that. He was always such a tidy man. Cute curtains in the windows and if you went inside his house, his floors were always polished, everything dusted, the counters spotless. He kept a cleaner house than I ever could. If you need me to go over and help you, just let me know. I'll be glad to pack up some mops and buckets and help you to clean up."

"No need to clean," Patrick replied, shaking his head. "My mom and I are thinking of simply demolishing the house and selling the land once it's been cleared. I don't think it can be salvaged."

"Oh, Patrick, that's too bad. That house has been there as far back as I can remember," Lottie said. "When I was young, I'd walk by it whenever I needed to get away from town and go hike in the hills. I did that quite often in my teenage years. I knew I could park my bike in the yard or the porch, and no one would take it. Your grandfather knew it was mine, and he'd watch it for me if he was around. Naldo was a treasure himself. He kept that yard so beautiful—flowers every spring, the greenest, best cared for lawn in town my dad used to say. Sometimes he would pick a few flowers for me to take home to my mother. He said he liked driving by houses and seeing his flowers in the windows."

Though Patrick enjoyed her recollection of the grandfather he didn't really know, he doubted he would follow her desire to let the house remain standing. While stories about the past pleased him, they also reminded him of how little time he had spent getting to know the old man. He should have been the one leaving his bike at his grandfather's or going over to mow his lawn as the old man grew less able to do yardwork.

****

"Mark my words, that Patrick fella has a crush on you," Fergie said to Freeda. They sat outside on the swing in the backyard of Lottie's house enjoying the night air after the others had left.

Pleading fatigue, Lottie went to bed as soon as the dishes were done but Fergie appeared restless once the guests were gone. Fearing he might wander off and end up in another bar brawl, Freeda suggested they sit outside until they were ready for bed. They'd been sitting in silence, enjoying the evening until now. Patrick Sanchez was not a subject she cared to discuss with her father.

"No, Dad, he's a rich uptight attorney. Not my type.".

"Maybe not, but you know if you play your cards right, who knows what could happen…"

He left the rest unsaid, but Freeda only shook her head. She wanted to protest but she knew that would only lead to further teasing. Her father had always excelled at making remarks like that. It was one of the things she remembered from childhood that often irritated her. It wasn't simply the teasing, but the way he seemed to enjoy doing it as well.

"Yeah, right, Dad. He might have a *thing*," she said, "but he won't do anything about it. Mr. Patrick Sanchez is not the sort to want someone like me in his life for more than fun. When he decides to get serious, I can guarantee he's going to go after someone who will properly be submissive and drop dead gorgeous. Also, someone who is little Miss Debutante who will give tea parties for his partners' wives while he and the other guys in his law firm go out to play golf." She shook her head in distaste. "Not the sort of person I am ever going to be. Can you imagine me at some lousy tea party? Or giving one? He insisted on selecting just the right wine for us to drink tonight."

His laugh sounded hoarse, but his grin was honest. "You're quite a gal, Freeda. I may not see you much, but

I can see you have a lot of the Ferguson gumption in you. You're not afraid to step over the line when you need to or take a chance when everything is against you. That's a good way to be."

Freeda smiled at him and realized that this was the first time in years the two of them had simply sat around and just talked. Maybe it was the wine her aunt had served at dinner, or maybe it was the fact that tonight he knew where he would be staying, and the next day would not be fraught with anxiety of what problem the following day might hold. She was pleased at the thought that she might have helped to bring some serenity to him.

"Thanks, Dad. I like that idea," she said softly.

"But you're also resourceful and not the type to back down. I could see that yesterday. You're just like your mama. She wasn't the type to take any guff from any man. It's why we got along so well together..." Suddenly he snapped his fingers. "Damn!"

"What?"

"Your mama. I left my pictures of her at the cabin. Doggone it! They were the only pictures I have of her!" His voice sounded distressed, the most emotional she had heard him since their reunion the previous day. "Damn! We're going to need to go up there and get my things before Diaz tosses them all out. Maybe we can borrow Lottie's car tomorrow so you can take me back and get them and the rest of my stuff."

Freeda rubbed his arm, hoping to calm him. "Don't worry, Dad, I asked him not to throw them away."

His head snapped toward her. "When did you see him?"

"When I was waiting outside the courthouse this morning. He came by. I don't know why he was there, but I asked him not to destroy your things and to return them."

He blew out a harsh breath and shook his head. "He won't give them back. He's probably burning them right now and laughing as he does it. Damn, I shoulda thought of that before we came up here. Maybe we should go back there anyway. I know a way to sneak inside the fence, so they won't see me."

"Dad, are you serious? If Diaz catches you even close to the ranch, he'll have you arrested again. Don't worry. I'll have Aunt Lottie call him."

"Lottie?"

"She knows him quite well, I guess. Personally, I think he's got a thing for her."

"A thing?" His head jerked up in surprise. "Diaz and Lottie? Really?"

Freeda sensed his immediate interest. Perhaps she shouldn't have told him that, but as obnoxious as Diaz was to her, she owed no loyalty to the man. "He's always doing things for her, and whenever she's around, he's on his best behavior. You wouldn't recognize him. Maybe I should have warned Tony."

Fergie's eyes brightened as he lifted and lowered his eyebrows. "Well, well, what do you know about that? Never knew the patch man ever noticed any woman."

"Oh, he looks at her. So, how well do you know him?"

"Well enough to know he's a damn thief and liar. Man has more stories than I do. Only difference is his stories all come as a veiled warning. Hell, not even so veiled. He gets a kick out of taunting people."

"That's nice to know," she replied dryly. "I thought it was just me, and that he did it because he gets so angry at you."

"No. Or maybe it's just the two of us." Fergie said, laughing. "If the only good we ever do in this world is make that man crazy, I say we go for it."

Freeda giggled with him. She liked that idea too.

****

"What's on tap for today?" Fergie asked the next morning as Freeda and her Aunt Lottie seated themselves around the kitchen table. "Do you need anything done around here I can help with?" he asked, looking directly at the older woman. "I'm pretty handy with a hammer and saw. Also do yardwork if you need the lawn mowed or the trees trimmed."

Lottie shook her head. "You're a visitor, Fergie. You just need to sit outside on the hammock or relax in a lawn chair."

"Maybe I should go over and help Patrick," he offered before turning to Freeda. "What do you think of that? You want to go over there with me? See your boyfriend?"

Freeda jerked up in her chair. "He's not my boyfriend, Dad."

Lottie glanced up from the table where she had been scribbling in a notepad. "Well, if you're looking for work, Fergie, maybe you should come with me. I need to get groceries, and I have a few errands to run. What about you, Freeda? Anything on your agenda today?"

"I thought I might go over to the newspaper office and see Cere. I need to come up with some story ideas to pitch and she always has ideas."

"Are you going to take Patrick with you?" Fergie asked.

"Why would I take Patrick? He has plenty of work

he needs to do at his grandfather's place."

Fergie turned to Lottie. "You know, Lottie, she's right. He has a lot to do over there. He's been so good to me, maybe I should go help him."

Freeda rolled her eyes. "You just want to see that house and look for treasure."

"If I find anything he better be willing to share it with me and you," he replied with a wink. "Didn't you say you needed money?"

Freeda sighed. She should have known that treasure hunting was what would be on her father's mind. "I'm no treasure hunter, Dad. And no gold digger either," she added, twisting toward her aunt. "The two of you can stop trying to link me up with him. I just need to earn a living! I'll go see Cere."

"Speaking of linking up, what's the story with you, Lottie?"

The sudden shift in conversation surprised Freeda and her head jerked in his direction, concerned he meant to divulge what she had told him the previous night about Diaz' possible infatuation with her aunt.

"What do you mean?" Lottie asked, her gaze glued to her coffee cup, her face turning a light shade of pink.

Freeda spoke up in a teasing voice. "I think Tony really likes you."

Lottie waved a hand, though her flush grew darker. "We're simply two old classmates having a friendly relationship in their later years."

"Nothing wrong with romance at our age," Fergie added, lifting his cup toward her aunt. "But come on, Lottie, spill it. What's the deal with you two?"

"Tony and I have known each other forever. Believe me, it has always been friendship." She lowered her gaze.

Freeda watched her aunt carefully. Could she really not be aware of the interest men showed in her? "What about Diaz?" she teased.

"Diaz?" Her head jerked in Freeda's direction. "What do you mean?"

"Oh, Aunt Lottie, you can't be blind to the way he acts around you. He almost becomes a gentleman. Not at all like he normally is."

"Pfff…" Lottie rolled her eyes, her face turning a darker shade of pink. "We tease and joke a lot, but that cantankerous man would never be interested in an old lady like me. He'd pick someone young and lively if he was ever going to look at a woman."

"I don't think so," Freeda retorted. "He's always ready to help you. He won't go out of his way for anyone else, but for you, he practically takes off his cloak and says, please use this to walk across the mud puddle."

"Ooh, Lottie, sounds like you've made a conquest," Fergie added, shaking his finger at her. "Maybe you need to invite him to dinner some night."

Lottie's face grew pinker, but she shook her head. "Are you kidding? He'd complain about my cooking. The man is a whiz in the kitchen."

"Now how do you know that?" Freeda asked.

Lottie's face turned even pinker as her gaze shifted from one to the other before turning back to Freeda. "Several months ago, when he stayed in town—you know the ranch keeps a big house a few blocks over where he sometimes stays—well, he invited me over for breakfast." Her eyes grew large, and her smile widened. "He cooked steaks and eggs along with the most scrumptious green chili I've ever tasted. He still won't give me the recipe, but it reminded me of the way my dad made it back when I was a kid. Now if the guy did really like me, don't you think he would have given me that darn recipe by now?"

They all laughed, but Freeda still wasn't convinced that Diaz had no interest in her aunt. From the way Lottie blushed, she also wasn't certain her aunt was being totally honest about her feelings about him either.

Chapter Fifteen

Diaz was on Patrick's mind as he waited for Freeda to meet him the next morning. She'd called him to invite him to breakfast, but he was already at the Rio Rojo diner, so she gave him her own order and said she would be right over.

"Aunt Lottie and Dad are both early risers, and they've already gone on a drive around town," she told him. "I'm stuck here cooking for myself and I'll probably burn down the house if I even try to fry an egg."

"Aha! You were calling to invite me to *cook,* not to *eat* breakfast," Patrick replied with a laugh.

"Well, you are a bachelor, so I figured you'd know how to make eggs at least. I'm a horrible cook. I was raised by a grandmother who wouldn't let me come near *her* kitchen except to eat."

He chuckled. "Shows what you know about men. I usually have cereal when I'm on my own, though I've been known to whip up a mean omelet on weekends. See you in a few minutes. I'm at the counter, but I'll get us a table. And to really make your morning, your pal Diaz just walked in the door and picked up a newspaper. Should I—"

"Don't you dare to invite him to join us," she interrupted.

"Whatever milady wants. I'm at a place called *El Matador*. The woman at my hotel recommended it."

"I know just where it is. Didn't I mention it to you yesterday? Anyway, see you soon."

He clicked off the phone and waved at Diaz who had spotted him and approached the counter.

"Good morning, Patrick," Diaz said. "Where's you lady friend? Over at the jail bailing out Daddy again?"

After the discussion of Diaz the previous evening and Patrick's growing doubts about him, the comment provided another point of condemnation against the strange man. Diaz spoke with an edge to his raspy voice, making it easier to respond with a coolness of his own.

"I just spoke with Freeda, and she's on her way over to join me. I was about to get us a table." He got to his feet and Diaz placed the newspaper on the counter and took the seat Patrick vacated.

"What about her jailbird Daddy?" Diaz asked.

"He went driving with her aunt. But don't worry, I think he knows better than to go back to the ranch."

"Tell them both I sent my regards." Again, the tone was cool and filled with sarcasm.

"I don't think you need to worry about Fergie anymore," Patrick added. "He's going to stay over at Lottie's for a while."

The only reply from Diaz was a grunt as he opened the newspaper and shook it out on the counter in front of him.

"Look, Mr. Diaz, I know you think he's a lazy bum, but he is willing to work. He's volunteered to help me clean out my grandfather's house."

Diaz dropped the paper and whirled toward him. "You're kidding me."

"No. He doesn't even care if I pay him…"

His green eye widened, and he rasped out a chuckle

as he began to shake his head. "Damn, yeah, I'll bet he doesn't. But I wouldn't count on too much work out of the guy." His sarcasm grew more irritating by the moment.

"I know you don't like him, but he's not that bad a person. Just gone through some hard times in his life."

Diaz grunted. "Come see me again when he's done *helping you*," he replied shortly, lifting his good hand in a quote mark gesture.

Patrick had grown tired of the man's negative attitude. For the first time, he could see what frustrated others. "Fergie also offered to work for Tony Gennaro at his restaurant."

Again, the older man's head jerked up. "Gennaro? What does he have to do with anything?"

"He joined us at Lottie's for dinner last night, and Fergie offered to work at his restaurant either cooking or cleaning."

Diaz looked away, but Patrick could feel the agitation vibrating in the man. His jaw clenched as his hands curled into fists. but he didn't act on the anger. Instead, his eyes met Patrick's, while his lips curved into a cold, hard smile.

"Hell, I don't have time for this damn soap opera." He put down the paper and gestured toward the waitress with a lifted forefinger. "Hey, Jo, get me a thermos of coffee and a Special to go. I better get to work. I'll be back in a few minutes to pick it up."

With surprising speed, Diaz got to his feet and hobbled to the end of the counter without saying goodbye.

The waitress walked over to Patrick. "Wow, what the hell did you say to him? I've seen him get angry before, but I've never seen him so upset."

Patrick shrugged, still stunned by the man's reaction. "I have no idea."

****

The tense moments at the counter were still nagging at Patrick as Freeda slid into the chair across the table from him by the restaurant's front window.

"What is the deal with Diaz?" he asked as soon as she sat down. "He sat by me at the counter when I was on the phone with you, and at first he appeared friendly. Then as we were talking about yesterday and last night, it was like he switched personalities. Suddenly, he didn't have time to talk and had to be on his way. He ordered the waitress to change his breakfast to take-out and left."

Freeda chuckled as she waved a hand in the air. "Haven't I been telling you he's like a shape shifter? He can change his attitude from one moment to the next. One minute he's semi-pleasant, the next, he'll become a real jerk. Sometimes I think he does it on purpose, just to get a reaction. I think the man just likes attention—good or bad."

Patrick leaned toward her. "But why does he act that way?"

"Because he really *is* a jerk. He enjoys being obnoxious. He kept pulling that sort of thing on Cere and Rafe when they were trying to figure out that whole Marco Gonzales thing and who killed your grandfather."

"But he did know my father? I mean, my grandfather?"

"So he says. But who knows? We thought he killed your grandfather at first, but they could never prove it. And wouldn't you know it, when they finally got a confession from the real killer, Diaz was right there. Rafe has always said there's something hinky about his identity, but we never did figure it out."

"Hinky?" Patrick repeated with a laugh. "Hinky? Like what?"

She leaned forward across the table as though she didn't want anyone else to hear, although he doubted anyone could hear anything with the noise in the restaurant.

"Well, okay, Diaz once said he did time with your dad, but no one can find his fingerprints in the system. There's no record of any Diego Diaz in the prison records, according to Rafe."

A rush of coldness ran through Patrick. "I see. Do you think he switched identities?"

"I don't know. He does have a real driver's license and even a passport. Cere saw them, but she and I think they're false. However, Rafe says the man has a legal birth certificate. He's seen it, though I don't know why or how."

The waitress interrupted them as she delivered their breakfast orders. Once she refilled their coffee cups and departed, Freeda raised her hand to Patrick. "Enough of this negative chatter. Let's not bother with him and his moods. Let's talk about your grandfather."

"My grandfather?" The comment surprised Patrick. "Why would you want to know about him?"

"He's kind of famous, isn't he? At least around here? I told you I need to do a story I can sell."

The comment startled him, and Patrick immediately shook his head. "No, no. I am not going to let you exploit him that way."

"Exploit him? He was a legend! Let's tell his story. Don't you want people to know what a hero he was to everyone?"

"I don't think he was a hero. He was just an old man trying to make a living. Doing a story about him would only mean more people coming around and digging up the yard."

"But you're selling the place," she argued. "Heck, maybe a story could drive up the price."

Patrick sighed and shook his head again. *Damn, the woman was stubborn.* "No, Freeda, and I'm serious about this. I don't want to bring attention to his house or to him or to any damn legend. I am certain he would not have wanted that. He was an old man who lived a full life in a small town, just like so many others of his generation."

"Well, take me over there and show it to me anyway," she said with a shrug. "I want to see where that famous attorney Mr. Patrick Sanchez got his start."

Patrick chuckled at her comment, but he again shook his head. "Don't try to butter me up. I know you, Freeda Ferguson. You're up to no good."

"No harm in trying." She shrugged again and her gaze shifted toward the window. "Okay, no story. I would like to see the house, though, if you don't mind."

"I don't mind showing it to you, but no digging around, and no pictures. You leave your camera and your phone at home or in the car when we go."

Freeda grinned at him. "Yessir! Of course, sir! Freeda Ferguson at your service and on her best behavior, sir!" She attempted a mock salute, but at Patrick's stern stare, she turned away.

She was probably again thinking about what a sober jerk he could be, but Patrick wasn't going to change his attitude about his personal life or family story—not for any woman.

****

After two hours of difficult physical labor at the house, Freeda was ready for a break. "I was never cut out to be a cleaning lady," she complained to Cere on her phone as she shifted on an uncomfortable folding chair outside the house. "Are you certain you don't need any emergency help at the newspaper?"

"Maybe later in the week when we're getting ready to go to press."

"I'm willing to do re-writes or even wander around town taking pictures if you need anything. What about sleeping through a city council meeting? Or some city planning session? Even obits. I write a mean obituary. How about if I start a neighborhood feud? I'm good at that."

By now Cere was giggling full force. "Freeda sweetie, we haven't had one death in the last two weeks and every time someone gets into an argument or fight, the story gets around town in five different versions long before the paper is printed."

"Well, how about layout? Do you need someone to do that? Heck, I'll run the damn printing press."

"Things are done electronically now, my dear. You're way behind the times. Why don't you just tell Patrick that you're worn out?"

"Oh, hell no!" she cried. "He'd never let me get over that. He's a damn attorney who gets all his exercise in the gym, but now he suddenly thinks he's a muscle man, moving everything around. He's even showing up Diaz."

Cere's breath caught. "Diaz is there?"

"Can you believe it? He showed about an hour ago. You wouldn't believe how nice he is to Patrick. Hell, the guy came by to apologize to him for some reason, and then volunteered to help. Imagine that! *Apologized.* Who knew the man even knew the words 'I'm sorry,' or what they mean?"

Cere laughed with her. "This Patrick must be someone special. I need to meet him. Why don't you all come over to dinner tonight? That will give me an excuse to get off work early."

"Aunt Lottie and Dad were talking about going to *Gennaro's.*"

"Well, let them go. You can come over here and relax."

"Let me check with Patrick, but that sounds like a great idea to me. He might not feel like a formal type dinner so let's keep things simple."

"Are you kidding? Simple is what we do best here. Rafe will the love the idea of showing off his grilling abilities to a new guy."

"Well, warn him Patrick's not exactly the rough and tumble type. His shirts could stand up on their own coming out of the suitcase."

****

"Let's keep it to an early evening," Patrick said as they walked the three blocks to Cere and Sheriff Rafe Tafoya's house later that day. "It's been a long day for me."

"Aren't you happy Dad was there to help you?" she asked.

"Hmph! Like he helped. Mainly he wandered from room to room, looking under and around things. If I didn't know better, I would think he's just another damn treasure hunter."

"Patrick, he's trying to help, I'm certain of it. He

owes you that."

"Yeah, right. He keeps saying that, but then I find him lounging in the back yard or checking out the basement for the fifth time, banging on pipes and walls." He left the obvious conclusion unspoken.

"He's harmless," she insisted.

"Oh, that he is," Patrick agreed. "Just like he's helpless."

"He's my father," she reminded him in a hard voice.

He threw up his hands in a gesture of surrender. "I'm not going to argue. But you're not like him. I've never seen anyone as dedicated to trying to get work as you are, but I think Diaz is right about your father. He avoids work…" At her look of warning, he stopped what he was about to say.

She was happy to reach the front door and ring the bell. In another couple of minutes, she would have grabbed one of the little wooden deer statues beside the front door and clobbered him with it.

****

"How are you enjoying New Mexico?" Freeda asked Cere as they stood in the kitchen preparing a salad for dinner.

"I love living here," Cere said, looking toward the door to the dining room where they could hear her husband Rafe and Patrick arguing about great college football and baseball teams. "And Rafe is the ultimate good guy. I have no idea how I was so lucky to find him."

"The hand on the wall," Freeda reminded her. "Wasn't that it? The stain that brought you together?"

"And almost killed me," Cere said quietly, but she immediately perked up. "But in the end, it all turned out fine. I shudder to think what my life would have been like if I hadn't been so darn drawn to that old building in the hills."

"The Palladium."

"It's a pile of rubble now." Cere sighed and shook her head. "So sad. Sometimes Rafe and I go out there for a picnic, just to remember where we admitted how we felt about each other."

"Did they destroy the dance hall? Maybe I should drive out there and take some pictures before I leave."

Cere's eyes lit up. "Oh, yes, yes, you should. We could run the pictures in the paper. They didn't destroy the building. A few of the walls are still standing—well, leaning. It was originally built of adobe, so it didn't burn, just portions of the interior walls, plus the wooden floors and roof. But nature and people have knocked most of the rest of it down. Same thing with the old commune buildings just up the road from there."

"The commune? Where Mom and Dad met?" Freeda asked, her pulse rate growing quicker. "Is that still standing?"

Cere's shaking head immediately dampened her enthusiasm. "Unfortunately, no. Like the Palladium, only partial walls remain. Still, you should take Patrick up there before he goes back to Albuquerque. Wasn't that where his dad hid after he confronted Marco at the Palladium and then ran away?"

Freeda drew a quick breath. "That's right. Given the circumstances, I wonder if Patrick wants to see it, though. I mean, he's been in Albuquerque all these years and he has seldom come back here—even to see his grandfather. He doesn't know this town. But maybe old Naldo took him up there when Patrick was young, and he might want to see how it looks now."

Cere wrinkled her nose. "On second thought, maybe it's not a good idea to tell him."

"But he is curious about his father," Freeda said. "The man totally vanished after that night at the Palladium, and Patrick and his mom never heard from him again."

"Wow, think about it," Cere said suddenly, eyes widening. "Patrick's dad could have met your dad at the commune. Or even your mom."

Freeda had not considered that possibility. Both Rio Rojo and Casitas were small in population currently. How much smaller would they have been thirty-five years earlier? Both communities had been impacted by the commune. "Wow, wouldn't that be something?"

"Have you ever asked Fergie about his time at the commune?" Cere asked.

"Not really. Dad doesn't like to talk about the past as it relates to my mother. I think he still misses her too much."

"I thought they didn't meet there," Cere said.

"They didn't," Freeda said, shaking her head. "They met in California, but both had lived at the commune at different times. That was what drew them together, according to Dad's stories about the past. Both remembered what life had been like at the commune, and both wanted to come back."

"Wow, maybe that's why he keeps coming back here," Cere said. "Have you thought of that? That he wants to remember her. Isn't that romantic?"

Chapter Sixteen

The idea that memories of her mother was what drove Fergie to continually return to New Mexico intrigued and heartened Freeda. Being in Rio Rojo probably did remind him of his youth and his relationship with her. Knowing so little of her mother herself, Freeda liked the idea that Fergie might still want to remember those past days when the pair had fallen in love. She thought about the picture he had kept tacked to his wall. Hopefully Diaz would return it to him.

"We have to take your dad out to the old commune so he can see it again," Cere said, smiling at Freeda.

"Oh, yes! I think he'd like that," Freeda agreed. "I'll ask him."

Cere's eyes brightened as she gestured with a waving hand toward Freeda. "Hey, maybe I could do a story for the paper on his memories of the place. We can walk around the area and he can tell me what he remembers. Not many people still recall what it was like in those days. Most of the kids who lived there are long gone. People from town didn't go out there. If they wanted to get away, they wanted to be in another state, not our own mountains. What do you think? A retrospective from an old hippie."

"He might enjoy that. He mentioned something similar the other night. And his friends…" Freeda stopped. She'd been about to suggest also taking his friends from Casitas, but that probably wasn't a good idea—not after the barroom fight and the death of one of those men.

"Say, how about you take pictures for the story?" Cere added. "I'm certain I could even get you paid for them."

That suggestion made the idea even more appealing, and Freeda agreed enthusiastically. "Sounds good to me. I could use the money. I'll ask Dad about it tonight. I've been looking for an opportunity…say, maybe I could even sell pictures to one of the regional magazines. Would that be okay? Your paper would get them first."

"That's a great idea!" Cere agreed. "Some regional publications do features on 'old New Mexico.' I have a few contacts I could call and put you in touch with them."

Freeda's enthusiasm grew as she thought of the possibilities Cere was offering her. That could relieve some of her financial concerns about her extended time in New Mexico. "That would be great. In fact, the more I think about the idea, the better I like it—especially if there's a possible payday involved," Freeda said.

Cere laughed and tapped her arm. "I hear you, babe. We might need to borrow Rafe's pick up, though. I'm not certain how the roads are out there."

Another difficulty popped up in Freeda's mind. "Are you certain we can get even to the site? It's not on Tres Padres land, is it?"

"Oh, damn, I think it is…" Some of Cere's enthusiasm waned, but just as quickly she brightened. "Maybe I can have Mom ask D.V. He could take care of that, and he'll do anything for her."

"I get that impression," Freeda agreed. "You should

have seen how concerned he was about my driving her car. He was ready to call her just to make certain I hadn't stolen it. But when he heard it had broken down, he volunteered to take care of everything. And he did."

"Of course. He treats her like a queen." She touched Freeda's arm gently. "So don't worry, babe. If that's Tres Padres land, he pretty much controls who comes and goes in the back country, and I'm certain she will be able to talk him into it if I ask her."

Despite Cere's prediction, her words about D.V. controlling Tres Padres also presented Freeda with a new difficulty. "Well, now that may be another problem; Dad and Diaz don't get along. We might be better off just taking a chance and going…"

"Let Mom ask first," Cere said. "If he says no, then we take the chance and plead ignorance of the property boundaries if we get caught. That's how I get into places where I shouldn't be. If they throw us out, so be it. If they try to arrest us, well, I have an in with a very sexy sheriff." She punctuated her words with an exaggerated wink.

Freeda smiled in return. That sort of attitude was exactly what she loved about her cousin. As a news reporter, Cere had never been afraid of taking chances and accepting the consequences if she couldn't talk her way out of a situation.

"Tres Padres, here we come," she said. "Diaz be damned!"

****

"I'm sorry about your grandfather's house," Cere said to Patrick as they sat down to dinner. He had been telling them about the destruction he'd had to deal with since beginning to clean out his grandfather's house.

He winced as he replied in a dejected tone. "It's sad. I have only happy memories of visiting Gramps when I was young. I remember spending hours in the garage playing video games. But I also recall looking at all the articles in the newspapers that were pasted on the walls for wallpaper. I used to read them when I was a kid, and now, I wish I'd paid closer attention to them. Most of them are torn or faded."

Rafe laughed. "I know just what you mean. I used to like reading them too. I can't remember the prices on the ads, but they were crazy, like a dime for a soft drink or a quarter for a loaf of bread. They were as fascinating as the stories in the paper. Luckily, I can go through Dad's archives at the paper and find copies from the same dates. Most of them are preserved on microfilm or saved in a database."

"Technology rules," Patrick added.

The two men waved their utensils at each other, laughing, while Freeda and Cere exchanged smiles and shook their heads.

"The two of you are such *guys*," Cere said. "You remember the ads, but did you ever look at the articles around them?"

"The articles? There were articles?" Rafe asked, winking at Patrick. "I only noticed the ads."

Cere rolled her eyes and shook her head. "There were plenty of articles. Marco Gonzales put them up when he lived in the garage."

"The guy who made the bloody handprint on the wall?" Patrick asked, his face growing sober. "He lived there?"

"Yes," Cere said. "After he got out of prison, he had no place to go, so your grandfather took him in and let him stay in the garage. That's where he was living when he was killed."

"He probably took the money or coins everyone keeps trying to find," Patrick said.

Rafe tapped his forefinger on the table. "Exactly! Maybe that was what he planned to do all along. I mean, would you live in a garage in winter without a good reason? I've been thinking that for years, haven't I, Cere?"

"Yes," she agreed in a bored tone, rolling her eyes.

"Hell, he may have taken the money or coins when he ran off," Rafe added. "The question is, if he was leaving the night he was killed and he had taken the stash with him, where had he kept it until then? And what happened to it after he died?"

"He didn't have a stash, remember?" Cere reminded her husband in a bored tone as though the subject had been raised in the past. "Berto had been committing the robberies. *He* had the money, the st—" She stopped suddenly as though realizing what she was saying. Her smile lessened as she turned to Patrick and shrugged. "Sorry."

Freeda turned to Cere, speaking up to break the awkward silence that followed. "Have you done a story on the missing money?"

Cere blew out a quick breath. "We've done so many stories on the Palladium and that missing money I get bored reading them. It comes up every time someone gets lost or stuck out there. People still wonder what happened to the stolen money, but no one has found one lousy cent."

"It makes sense why no one has found the money if the old story is true. My dad took the coins and all the money and ran…and got away with it." Patrick's rasping voice was barely above a whisper, his eyes focused on the floor in front of him. He shivered and blinked before looking up at Cere. "Have you ever investigated that? Where my dad might have gone?"

Cere dropped her gaze before raising her eyes to her husband. "Sort of."

"We've never been able to establish where Berto went or what he did after he left the Palladium. I've never found any police or prison records for him anywhere in the state." Rafe waved his hand as though clearing the air. "And I'm not certain I want to look. He's been gone for years, and no matter what we come up with, if I bring it up again, that will only perpetuate more rumors and more theories. I've finally convinced Dad to stop doing stories on Marco Gonzales and that whole situation. That sad episode is all over. I say, let it stay buried with the damn coins or treasure everyone claims is out there. We need to focus on the present and the future, not on the past."

Freeda's gaze shifted from one man to the other. She could see their distaste for the subject. "I have one last subject that is out of the past, but it's more fun. I want to go up to the old commune. I remember people mentioning it when I was here the last time but seeing pictures of my dad and mom made me think about how they met because of it. I'd like to take some pictures of what it's like today."

"Don't tell your dad," Patrick added quickly. "You know what that will do to him."

"But he could tell me about life at the commune," she protested. "I'd love to see where he and Mom lived even if it is torn down. I could do a story on what life was like back then for people living in the commune."

Rafe was already shaking his head. "Won't do you any good. It's now private property," he reminded her.

"I told her that," Cere said. "She thinks she can convince Diaz to take her."

Patrick blew out a quick breath. "I doubt it." He turned to Freeda. "Are you serious about this?"

The doubtful looks should have dissuaded her, but their comments only made Freeda more determined.

"Yes, I am. How about this idea? I've decided to pitch it to him as a story that might bring more paying visitors to the ranch. And if he doesn't agree, I'll go over his head to the owners and convince them that a story with scenic pictures might bring them more visitors, good publicity." She turned to Rafe. "Now wouldn't you like that? Visitors who come to enjoy the country and spend money in town, rather than coming here for some old ghost or murder story?"

Beyond Rafe, Cere smiled and winked at her before turning to her husband and Patrick. "I'd give up arguing, if I were you, guys. My cousin has always been an ace at coming up with ideas and getting what she wants."

****

Patrick was not certain Freeda would be able to get what she wanted in the case of visiting Tres Padres, but he had no intention of trying to dissuade her. Let her face Diaz and try to get on the ranch property. He had his own problems to solve, but the time he had spent talking to Rafe had given him an opportunity to thank the sheriff for the help he had given years ago with Patrick's grandfather's house. The only jarring note was that Rafe confirmed that in the end, Diaz had finished the work.

"I like your cousin and her husband," he said,

hoping to clear his head of those troubling thoughts as he walked Freeda home later. "Rafe seems like a very down to earth guy."

"Oh, he is, and he'll make a great father. Cere told me they're thinking of having children soon."

"Makes sense."

She wrinkled her nose. "I don't know about that. To be honest, I can't see Cere as a mother. She's always been too much of a working woman, more comfortable pursuing a story, than chasing a couple of kids or changing a diaper. But who knows what love can do to a person?" She shivered as though the thought of children chilled her.

He chuckled. "You don't believe in love?"

"Of course I do, but not if it automatically means having kids. I doubt I'll ever be the motherly type. I'm like my father. I prefer to be on the go."

"You are not at all like your father," Patrick protested. "You take responsibility for what you do. I'd say you're probably more like your mother."

Freeda burst into laughter. "I doubt it but being here does make me want to know a little more about her. This area might not be where she grew up, but it is an area that she loved and longed to return to one day. Aunt Lottie says Mom always talked about how she wanted to live here when she decided to settle down. Dad once said she found her soul here, whatever that means. He always told me how much she loved the wide-open spaces. I didn't even know what wide open spaces were until I came to visit Cere years ago. What about you? Did you miss New Mexico when you were back East?"

"Totally. When I first got to Boston, I felt like I was closed in. Even driving outside the city felt boxed in.

There were too many huge trees so you couldn't see for miles like you can here. I felt like I couldn't find enough areas of open sky without going to the ocean. But being on the ocean felt too lonely. You had miles of big blue sea in front of you." He sighed heavily. "Don't get me wrong. I liked my time back east, but I was happy when I got off the plane in Albuquerque. I could see the outlines of the Sandia peaks in the distance, and I knew I'd come back to where I wanted to be. I could never live back east or even west for long."

"I understand that sentiment. I felt good when I first got here too. I liked the clean smell of the air, the grass, and the trees. You can smell nature here, not fumes." Freeda laughed as she recalled wishing she was back on the west coast just before meeting Patrick. How long ago that seemed! "At times in LA, I feel like the smog is thick enough to eat."

"I hear you. That's one place I doubt I'll ever visit for long."

"But if you come to LA, and we run out of gas on the freeway, at least there is cell coverage. You don't have to worry about when the next car might be coming by."

He leaned toward her and grinned. "But can you meet crazy, talkative ladies?"

"Or sexy lawyers?" she shot back, as they both burst into laughter.

"You want to see wide open, then look up," Patrick directed as his head tilted up toward the inky sky. "Have you ever seen a sky like that in Los Angeles? It's so clear, you can easily pick out the constellations. We get some amazing meteor showers, and it's easy to see them simply by driving to the edge of the city."

Freeda tilted back her head and studied the sky. She pointed to the one familiar feature she recalled from childhood visits to Rio Rojo. "Is that the Big Dipper?"

"Certainly is."

"It's such a nice night. We should go stargazing," she said, pausing on the sidewalk. "You can teach me the different constellations."

Patrick sighed sadly. He was tempted to take her up on the offer, but he had put in too many hours working at his grandfather's house. His aching shoulders reminded him he was no longer a teenager.

"Maybe another night. I had a hard day."

"I forgot." She punched his arm playfully. "Mr. Lawyer Man is used to spending his days cleaning up in the courtroom, not in a dirty house. That physical work must have worn you out."

Patrick chuckled, but his muscles protested that it was time to climb into either the hot tub at the hotel or into a comfortable bed. "I'd argue, but I'm even too tired for that."

Her fingers skimmed over his arm in a feathery touch. "I understand. Thanks for going with me to Cere's. Maybe we can go stargazing another time."

"Definitely. We'll go whenever you want. It's a date." He glanced down at her. Standing so close to her, he could smell the fresh scent of her lavender perfume. Her eyes shone in the dim light from the house windows. He put his hand on hers and lifted it to his lips. "You're quite a woman, Freeda Ferguson. Thanks for the fun evening."

Her impish smile was visible in the moonlight, making her lips too tempting to ignore. As she often did, Freeda took the moment out of his control.

"Then kiss me goodnight, Patrick Sanchez, before I go inside. Give me something fun to dream about tonight."

His heartrate increased but he hesitated instead of following her request. Leave it to Freeda to openly go after whatever she wanted. But then again, he had been wanting it too.

His body quivered with awareness of her closeness, the soft sound of her voice, the light scent of her perfume. He put his hand on her arm and gently pulled her toward him. She moved easily, putting her hand around his neck. The touch of her fingertips made him shiver with desire. Damn, he wanted her. He lowered his mouth to hers.

Her lips were soft beneath his as his heartbeat quickened and his senses came alive. The scent of her perfume overwhelmed him, along with the soft sensation of her moist mouth on his. He wrapped his arms around her, pulling her fully against him, as his body shuddered. She responded to his touch with a warm sigh, and she kissed him back, her lips parting as her tongue explored his mouth.

He longed to ask her to go with him back to his room, but the porch light suddenly went on, bathing the front porch in brightness. He released her with a soft sigh of regret, feeling like a teenager caught kissing on a first date.

"Damn."

He wasn't even certain who said it, but he let her pull slightly away.

"See you tomorrow," he said, sighing.

"I can ask Aunt Lottie to make pancakes." She tapped his chest lightly, making him shudder again. "Just don't bring your damn newspaper with you."

He groaned as he shook his head. "Much as I enjoy the idea, I better decline. I want to be at the house early. I'll call you when I get finished."

"Are you certain you don't want to take the day off and drive out to the commune?"

"Are you looking for a ride?" he teased her.

"Well, I hate taking Aunt Lottie's car out there. What if it breaks down in the middle of nowhere? I bet there aren't any nice lawyers driving around out there with spare water bottles."

Patrick shook his head and Freeda reached up and kissed him quickly on the lips before pulling back from him.

"Think about it," she said. "That house isn't going anywhere." Her eyes flashed in the darkness as she turned away and hurried up the sidewalk, her heels clicking on the cement.

Patrick stood on the sidewalk watching as she opened the door and stepped inside. She pushed back a lace curtain to blow him a kiss before turning and slowly walking away. Hell, he wanted to dance.

Still smiling, he climbed into his car. Every day with Freeda Ferguson held something new, and he was already looking forward to their next encounter. She was right—the house would still be there no matter what he did the next day.

"Damn you, Freeda Ferguson," he whispered to himself. "I'm going to play hooky tomorrow."

Chapter Seventeen

Freeda woke with a smile on her lips. She touched them lightly with her fingers thinking of Patrick's goodnight kiss for probably the hundredth time since it had happened. She had guessed the kiss might be coming as they walked, but still, she liked that he had seemed almost like an uncertain teenage boy trying to decide what he was going to do.

Just who was Patrick Sanchez? Confident man? Shy boy? He seemed to be parts of each, and she enjoyed that. Still, she had also seen the strong, determined side of him and she didn't for a minute think he'd be shy as a lover. That thought made her smile even wider.

She walked downstairs to find her Aunt Lottie and her dad in the kitchen, drinking coffee, with the remnants of their breakfast still on the table.

"Well, well, she's finally up," Lottie said with a laugh, getting to her feet. "I'll start your breakfast. What do you feel like?"

"Just toast and maybe a soft-boiled egg," Freeda replied. "Cere is still a great cook. I ate too much last night. If I stay around here for long, I'm going to gain a hundred pounds."

"Nah, I think you have your mama's genes," her father said, as she leaned over to give him a hug. "She could eat anything she wanted and never gain an ounce. Nervous energy, I used to say."

Her aunt laughed as she moved around the kitchen. "Like her brother, Del. No matter how much I fed that man, he never gained an ounce. Meanwhile I was constantly dieting. Still am at times."

"But you're looking good, Lottie," Fergie added. "Bet you're still fighting off the guys with a stick. Young and old."

A blush crossed her aunt's face, but Lottie laughed. "No sir. I've known most of the men around here who are my age since I was a kid. Jimmy Duran pegged me as a hard-headed girl in the sixth grade and I never lost that reputation. These guys know better than to mess with Logical Lottie."

"Including Diaz?" Freeda couldn't resist asking the question as she took the coffee cup her aunt handed her. "What was he like in high school? I bet he was a terror for the teachers."

"Diaz?" She pursed her lips as she shook her head. "I have no idea. D.V. has only been here a few years and has been a mystery since he showed up. He's one of those secretive types who refuses to say anything about his personal life or his past. Ask him a question and he won't give a straight answer, just a nasty retort."

"Even to you?" Freeda teased.

"Even me. Heck, especially me." She winked at Freeda. "It's why I like to give him a hard time back when I can. I dealt with recalcitrant teenage boys as a teacher. I keep telling him that's what he reminds me of, and it gets him every time."

That idea appealed to Freeda. Perhaps that's what she should try with him—treat him like a teenage boy. "Do you know how he met Patrick's father?"

Lottie stopped as she was about to pour fresh coffee

into her cup. "Who said that he knew Berto?"

"I think Cere told me once," she said, trying to remember how the subject had come up. "Maybe they met in jail or something?"

Lottie shook her head, still looking surprised. "He's never liked to say much about the past. I know he once said he was once put into a juvenile facility or youth home, but…well, I don't know. He changes the subject every time I try to bring up his younger years, and he's never mentioned anything to me about Berto. I've given up trying to get that man discuss anything when he doesn't feel like talking."

Fergie waved his hand in front of his face as though swatting away a pesky insect. "Enough about Diaz. He's not worth wasting our time. If you've got a lick of sense, Lottie, you'll tell that guy to hit the road. Your friend, Tony, is a much better prospect. At least with him you'll never go hungry."

Lottie's face turned a bright shade of pink. "Prospect? For what? I'm not eighteen anymore, Fergie, in case you haven't noticed. I don't need you to arrange my love life like you used to try to do in college."

"Don't be too sure," Fergie shot back. "Just remember, I set you up with Del."

"But I set you up with Helen first," she retorted, winking at Freeda. "We were all just casual friends, but your mom had a secret crush on Fergie. She was this shy little sweetie, always watching him but afraid to say anything to him. Fergie was everyone's friend, talking all the time, probably the most popular guy we knew. One day I grabbed Fergie by the hand and took him over to her in the cafeteria and properly introduced them, and the rest, as they say, is history."

"Yep," Fergie had watched her speak with a reddening face, but he sighed in agreement at her conclusion. "First, she starts off talking about the commune and when I took one look at those big bright black eyes, I jumped right in and never looked back." Grinning like a love-crazed teenager, he put his hand to his chest and shook his head.

"Like she would have let you look back," Lottie retorted. "Deciding to marry you was the only time she ever stood up to Nena, according to Del."

Freeda enjoyed their easy camaraderie and seeing her father so relaxed. "Now that's scary. Even my uncles don't have the nerve to stand up to her and they're in their sixties." Freeda winked at Lottie as they all burst into laughter.

"What are you going to do today, Dad?" Freeda asked as they finished breakfast. "Would you like to go for a drive? I'm going to look around for story ideas for the paper."

"I may have some business matters to conduct." Fergie turned his head away from her, looking out the window as he sipped his coffee.

Business? That surprised Freeda. What kind of business could he mean? He had no job. He'd been squatting on Tres Padres for a while. Could he finally have realized he needed to look for work?

"Wait, what do you mean by story ideas?" he asked, turning toward her suddenly. "Maybe I can help you."

That question surprised her even more. Normally he wasn't interested in what she was doing, though he often bragged about the result. "Well, I was thinking of searching for the old commune. I might do a story about it. Cere says there are people around who still remember it. She's going to get the paper to publish the story so I can get paid. Later I might offer a longer version of the story, or a photo spread to a national magazine. And, Dad, I could interview you for my story. You could tell me about what the commune was like when you lived there."

Fergie's head bobbed in approval as he stroked his chin. "Yeah, great ideas, but the commune was on what is now Tres Padres. I've tried to get up there several times. What makes you think you can go up there? You don't even know where it is."

"I was going to personally ask Diaz for her," Lottie said quietly.

His head jerked around to her aunt. "Damn, woman, you're brave. What makes you think he'll let her go near the ranch? He's so damn protective of that place, you'd think he owned it. He won't even let you enter unless you pay. He keeps saying *private property* like those mountains are his own damn land."

"It doesn't hurt to ask," Lottie replied with a shrug. "And you know D.V., he's like the weather in those mountains. You never know when it's going to change."

All three laughed, but Freeda hoped her aunt was right, and that Lottie could get the recalcitrant man to give his permission.

"Well, while you do that, I'll start the process by going over to the newspaper office," Freeda said. "At least I know Cere will be nice to me. I want to look over their files on the ranch's past and how it came into being as well as check on the origins of the commune."

"The Hollister family owned the property when I was growing up," Lottie offered. "When Mr. Hollister died, he left it to his sons, and they broke it up and sold it off in chunks until some eastern conglomerate tried to put it all back together, but then I think it got sold to someone else. I stopped following the business end years ago. Too confusing. You need to get that information directly from Diaz. Heck, you should interview him for your story. Let him explain it. If anyone knows about the ranch, he would."

Freeda wrinkled her nose. She didn't like the idea of having to be dependent on information from Diaz, much less interviewing him. Perhaps she could find out the information some other way.

"Damn good food, Lottie." Fergie spoke up suddenly, waving his fork. "Beats anything I've been getting lately."

"Those people at that Casitas diner are going to miss you." Freeda turned to her father and shook his arm playfully. "They were worried about why you didn't come in that morning I came looking for you and when they found out you were in jail."

"Yeah, well, they'll live without me. Besides, Lottie makes the best pancakes I've ever tasted."

Lottie refilled Fergie's coffee cup and ruffled his messy, thinning hair. "I also give decent haircuts, old man, and you could use one."

"Don't expect a tip," he retorted, "but you're free to cut my hair any time you want. What I really need is a fresh t-shirt. Mine are all ripped or turning gray." He pulled at his thin, dull blue t-shirt.

"How about if I take you shopping again?" Freeda offered. "I should have a paycheck deposited in my checking account for my last job today or tomorrow."

"I won't argue," he said, winking at her.

They both laughed, and again Freeda felt pleased

that her father seemed so carefree around her aunt. Their friendship had been forged as college students, and obviously both retained their mutual friendly affection. She enjoyed watching them interact. The easy interplay not only relaxed her after the concern of the previous days, but also allowed her to get a better understanding of her father. Fergie had been through hard times, but from what she had witnessed so far, much of it appeared to be of his own making. While he openly and easily expressed his feelings for her and her mother, when the chips were down, would he be there for her? Or would he expect her to take charge and protect him? She shivered slightly and reached for her coffee cup. Not knowing the answer disturbed her.

****

The sight of Diego Diaz surprised Patrick as he rolled another wheelbarrow of debris out to the back yard of his grandfather's house. As usual, the man wore his dark sunglasses even though the day was cloudy.

"Good morning. I saw your car parked out front and then saw you out here so I decided to stop by again to see if you needed anymore help." Diaz stepped around the debris in the back of the house. "How's it going?"

"Slow," Patrick admitted, pleased to be able to take a brief hiatus in the physical labor. "There's been so much damage to the house I've decided to demolish it and sell the property."

"Probably the best bet," Diaz agreed. "All this mess is so sad, though. That old man was a neat nut. He would have hated to see the mess it became."

"So I've been told by several people."

Diaz jerked his head toward the side of the house. "Have you seen the inside the garage?"

"I barely glanced in. It's worse than the house."

His deep sigh surprised Patrick. "Yeah, people did a real job on this place."

A sudden thought occurred to him. "My mom said you've helped to take care of the property and kept the damage from being worse. I appreciate everything you've been doing. Thank you."

"No problem," Diaz replied, waving a hand as though swatting away a fly. "The old man would have done the same for me. Hell, he did." He emitted an abrupt laugh.

"What about my dad?"

Diaz stiffened. "What about him?"

"How well did you know him?"

He shook his head as though not comprehending what Patrick was saying. "Who the hell told you that I knew your dad?"

Patrick drew a quick breath, stopping himself from admitting the information had come from Lottie. The man's sudden concern alerted him that he might be traversing in unknown, perhaps private territory. He turned away and shook his head. "I don't remember. Just someone I've met in the past couple of days."

"People in this damn town have always been big on spreading untrue gossip," he replied gruffly. "Talk too damn much sometimes."

"But *did* you know him?" Patrick pressed, studying Diaz to gauge the man's reaction.

He stared off into the distance and for a couple of silent moments Patrick didn't think Diaz was going to answer. Just when Patrick was ready to ask again, Diaz blew out a harsh breath.

"Yeah. It was a long time ago," he replied, pressing

his lips into a hard line. He paused, and Patrick didn't think he was going to say more, but with a sudden sigh, he continued. "We met in jail. It's not something I talk about much, so I'd appreciate it if you don't spread it around. Some people know I did time, but I was kid then. We were both there…kids serving time with hardened criminals. It's no wonder things turned out the way they did…"

"Do you know where he is now?"

The man stiffened again, his good eye blinking rapidly. The question appeared to startle him. His gaze bored into Patrick, his good eye blazing. "Now how the hell would I know that? Been a long time since I was a teenager, and once I got out, I wasn't anxious to ever see anyone I'd met there again."

Patrick could understand the man's rationale and decision. He had worked with enough people who were anxious to leave a troubled past behind once they escaped it. A slight twinge of guilt ran through him for bringing up what was probably a sore subject with a man who obviously worked to make that past go away. "I'm sorry. I'm being rude. It's simply…well…I've never met anyone who actually knew him…"

"Lots of people around here knew him," Diaz replied with a grunt. "You could probably ask just about anyone in town over the age of fifty. Not sure they'll talk about him, but you can ask if you're curious. He was quite the talker, always up to some new crazy idea in the time I knew him. Your dad was no dummy, but he was always looking for some new scheme that was going to make him a bundle of cash with minimal work."

Patrick sighed. Given his father's record, he doubted the ideas were on the legal side. How much did Patrick really want to know about the man? In the past, he had never tried to learn much once he discovered Berto had been in and out of trouble. What had caused Berto to choose the wrong side of the law? What had kept him hidden all these years? Could it be fear of facing or hurting people he might care about that had made him disappear? Or had he finally committed a crime that had locked him up forever? Would Patrick ever know? Did he really want to know?

"I guess now that I'm here, I have grown a little more curious," he admitted. "He seems to have simply disappeared. I know people probably didn't pay much attention to records in those days. I once did a check on him on the Social Security registry. I couldn't find anything except that he had a card many years ago. No work record after prison."

Diaz blew out a quick breath. "Makes sense. He probably changed his name. Some people don't want to remember their past mistakes. Want to leave them behind. Want to stay away from situations that got them into trouble. Lots of reasons people disappear. It's not hard to do if you know how, and that's one thing that's easy to learn in prison. Why did you want to know about him?"

Patrick sensed from the man's rapid response that he was growing more uneasy about the conversation. "I wasn't trying to pry. I was simply curious. Doesn't it make sense to want to know about one's father?"

Diaz studied Patrick with a watchful eye for several minutes before rasping out a reply. "You're a good kid, Patrick, and you've done a good job with your life so far. You have much more living ahead of you. Sometimes looking back can only cause problems and it's better to look forward. But, hell, you're a smart kid. You should be able to figure all that out for yourself."

Patrick wasn't certain what to say in response, but as usual, Diaz took the matter out of his hands. He suddenly reached into a shirt pocket and pulled out a folded piece of paper.

"I almost forgot the other reason I came over to see you. Do you mind giving this to your friend? It's a map of how to get to the commune. If you want, I can meet you out that way with a couple of ATVs to help you get to it."

Chapter Eighteen

"I'm feeling a little guilty," Freeda admitted as she and Patrick drove through the gate onto Tres Padres. "Dad may be upset when he finds out we came up here. He has wanted to re-visit the old commune himself, and now I'm going without him."

"We'll take plenty of pictures," Patrick replied, glancing at her. "And, besides, Diaz was pretty adamant about his not coming back onto the ranch. This trip is for you and your story, not a treasure hunt for him. If he's serious about wanting to see what the commune looks like now, the pictures should be enough to show him."

"I just hope we can find where the commune used to be without him." Freeda unfolded the map Diaz had given Patrick. She still couldn't believe he had actually provided it. "What if Dad refuses to talk about it because we didn't bring him?"

"He'll talk. Think about how many free breakfasts and dinners he'll get if his name is in the newspaper and he becomes a 'celebrity'," he replied with a quick laugh.

Freeda emitted a sad sigh. Patrick was probably right about that. The more time she spent with Fergie, the more disappointed she grew with him and his behavior. She had always considered him a wanderer who was pursuing a carefree life. Slowly she was beginning to realize his carefree behavior came at a price to others around him.

First, he had volunteered to mow the lawn for Lottie the previous day but broke the mower going over a rock on his way to the side of the house. This morning he had volunteered to cook breakfast and slept through his alarm so that when they awoke he was still fighting with the coffee pot. They ended up eating at the diner. That was followed by another trip to the discount store to exchange some of the clothes she had purchased for him because they didn't fit. The final result was that he maxed out one of her credit cards by getting more expensive items. Only her aunt's quick action, volunteering to help pay, had prevented an embarrassment.

Through it all, her father kept coming up with one excuse after another for why the bad things continued to happen to him. That was one area where she had to give him credit. Stories and creative excuses were where he excelled. Just when she felt she might grow weary of his antics, he charmed her with stories about her mother.

"Helen would have been so proud of you, baby girl," he had told her at lunch as they sat looking at pictures. "She was always so strong, so determined, so ready to make her mark in the world."

"And she would have made her mark," Aunt Lottie had agreed, pointing to a snapshot of Freeda's mother speaking at a peace rally. "You have her drive, and energy, plus you inherited her creative eye. I see that in everything you do, even arranging these flowers for the dining room table." She had flicked her finger toward a vase of flowers Freeda had picked and arranged from the garden.

Freeda's cheeks grew warm and she knew she had been blushing. She avoided looking in Patrick's direction, knowing his eyes were probably on her. She had lowered her head to look more closely at the picture of her mother. Why had she never seen these?

"Aunt Lottie, could we make copies of these?"

"Certainly, Sweetie. I still have the negatives somewhere. You choose what you want and I'll see that you get them."

"Was she ornery too?" Patrick had asked in a teasing tone, as though he wanted to lighten the atmosphere.

"Oh, yes." Lottie replied, laughing. "She kept us all on our toes, right Fergie?"

"Kept me going," Fergie had agreed. "Helen was the one who insisted we come back here and check out the commune that first summer. She was also the one who taught me how to hitch free rides so we could get here. Got us home too."

Freeda had felt pleased that they kept the atmosphere light. She glanced up at her aunt, smiling in appreciation. "Did you hitchhike too, Aunt Lottie?"

Her head jerked up from the album as she laughed. "Oh, no. My mom and dad were very strait-laced. They insisted I take the train. It took those two almost twice as long to get here." She had waved toward Fergie, laughing.

"But we arrived in one piece," Fergie added proudly. "And with plenty of stories to tell. Those were the days." He paused, sighing. "Not able to do that anymore. Hitching, riding the rails, now you're liable to end up with your throat slit…" His head had lowered, his eyes growing moist. "And for no good reason…"

Her father's lament touched Freeda. While he had perhaps been inconsiderate at times, he had also grown increasingly quiet the past couple of days, no longer as full of bluster as when they'd reunited. He was no longer as jocular and filled with bravado as when she'd first encountered him.

When Tony Gennaro had offered him part time work in his restaurant's kitchen, she was happy that he quickly agreed to consider it. Hopefully, he decided to accept. If Fergie could hold down a job nearby, he might stay around until she went back to California.

"Lockhart Lake, is that where we're headed?" Patrick asked suddenly, breaking into her thoughts. He pointed to an upcoming faded sign.

The sound of his voice jerked Freeda out of her reverie. She blinked, taking in their surroundings. They were in a small clearing, with a wide expanse of grass on either side. To the right, a less used dirt road branched off toward another stand of trees.

"No, that's where the Palladium used to be. I remember it from last time I was here. Have you ever been there?"

Patrick studied the sign, trying to remember it from the past, before finally shaking his head. "I don't know. Maybe when I was young. It doesn't ring a bell."

"It used to be a popular gathering place in the summer, but that was years ago. Families would come out and picnic in the daytime or camp out at night. There was an old dance hall that came alive on weekends. It also served as a community center. That's the building where Marco was killed."

"The hand on the wall," he noted in a soft voice. "No wonder that name sounded familiar. No, I've never been there."

"You didn't come out here as a little kid to see the bloody handprint when you visited your grandfather?"

"No. I heard about it, but I never thought about trying to see it. Sounded like it was a long way from town."

"Do you want to see the remains of the building? I don't know if the road is still drivable. It was in bad shape when I was out here with Cere a few years ago, and since it's all Tres Padres land now, I doubt the road has been kept up. Come to think of it, they probably demolished the building so people would stop coming out here to see it."

"Maybe another time," he said, his voice growing slightly hoarse. "Let's keep looking for the commune. It wasn't far from here, was it?"

"Five or six miles I think, and I'm not certain about the road or its condition either. Maybe we should have rented an all-wheel drive car."

"It'll be okay," he muttered, drawing a deep breath.

"What are you thinking, Mr. Sanchez?" she asked, leaning across the seat toward him. "You have been rather quiet this morning."

He had been quiet, but he also had a reason. Knowing she would ask again, he decided to be honest. "I've been thinking about my dad. About his choosing not to ever come back here." He gestured toward the blue line of mountain peaks in the distance. "He walked away from all this—from everything and everyone he knew. From the father who cared about him. I missed this whole state when I went back east, and I was only gone a few years. What did he find out there that has kept him…" He stopped and cleared his suddenly constricted throat.

He glanced over at her. She studied him, and he expected her to tease him. Patrick turned away quickly, fearing he might be on the edge of becoming emotional, but the moment quickly passed.

"I've been thinking about you and *your* dad…" he continued softly. "How he's so connected to this land, he keeps coming back here, even if it means getting into trouble. My dad was able to simply walk away and stay gone…"

Freeda was tempted to touch Patrick's arm in consolation, but she didn't want to break the spell of the moment. Instead, she stayed still and considered what he was saying—that his father had walked away and never returned, even to find out about what became of his son and wife. For an instant she felt sorry for this man who seemed to have so much materially, and yet so little emotionally. Perhaps her father might not be around all the time, but her grandmother had always made certain Freeda had a sense of a place where she belonged. Nena had always been around to guide Freeda and to show her someone cared about her.

"I understand," she finally said softly as the moments of silence stretched on. "I know Fergie keeps moving around and he's not the best father, but at least he turns up every so often. And I have my grandmother Nena who sometimes spoils me rotten." Tears clouded her eyes, and Freeda reached over to touch Patrick's bare arm gently. "I bet your father would be proud of you. Maybe he has thought of coming back. Maybe he's afraid because of the stories about him, or the stories Cere did on the Palladium. He could become a murder suspect. Have you thought of that? That could be one reason that has kept him away."

"Doesn't matter," he said, his lips pursing. "We can't change anyone else. We can't direct their lives. We need to focus on today and our own lives and keep moving forward."

"And you still have your mom," she added, hoping to make him feel better.

"Yes, that's true." He turned toward her, a grim look on his face. "Did I tell you she's talking about coming up here? Hell, for all I know we're going to get back to town and she'll be at the motel in the room next to mine."

The thought amused Freeda. "It sounds as though your mother is as flaky as my dad."

"In the opposite direction, maybe, but they're both the same in one way—unpredictable."

They burst into laughter, but Patrick suddenly slammed on the brakes, jerking the car to a jarring stop.

"What's wrong?" she asked, reaching out toward him.

He stared straight ahead. "It looks as if the road ends up there."

She leaned forward, studying the sudden rise in the terrain. "No, it doesn't. Can't you see where it goes?"

"There's nothing there. Look beyond the hill, toward those trees in the distance. Where is the road?"

Freeda scanned the grassy land in front of them. Beyond the next rise, she could see no sign of the dusty road. In fact, she couldn't see where it went past a dip up ahead.

He turned off the engine. "Let's check it out. I need to stretch anyway."

"Bathroom break!" she announced.

"I'll use the men's room on the other side of that stone," he offered, pointing at an outcropping of rocks to the left of the car. "You take this side and let me know when you're decent."

Freeda wrinkled her nose. She didn't like the idea of baring her lower body in the grass, but she had known the possibility existed when they decided to make the trip into the hills. Quickly she concluded what was necessary and afterwards wiped her hands with cleaning wipes she kept handy in her purse.

"I have extra wipes if you need them," she called around the boulder to Patrick.

There was no answer.

"Patrick?"

Still no answer.

Her pulse rate quickened, and she called out to him louder. She still heard nothing over the breeze rustling the grass and bushes.

"I'm coming to find you," she shouted. "I hope you're decent." She walked toward the rock, but Patrick emerged from the trees.

"I was right. The road ends just beyond the trees. That's where the Tres Padres fence begins," he said.

"But what about the commune?"

"It has to be on the other side of the rise. You can't see it from here. We may have to look into riding horses up there."

"Horses?" she asked uncertainly.

Patrick grinned. "Now, come on. Don't tell me you've never ridden a horse."

"Once. A long time ago when I was little. I'm no cowgirl," she admitted. "Don't tell me you can ride a horse, Mr. Educated in the East Lawyer Man?"

He shrugged and wrinkled his nose. "Well, it's been a while, but I've done some riding."

"When you were a kid with your grandfather?" she guessed as they climbed into the car.

"No. I dated a woman once whose family owned a ranch in the western part of the state. We used to spend weekends there, so I learned to ride. I can do it."

"Well, well, who knew? I guess I could try riding, if it's not for long," she said. "Maybe we should ask Diaz if he can set us up with a couple of horses. Though, knowing him, he'll demand to go with us."

"Perhaps I should go with him alone," he said.

"Oh, hell no! I want to go. I want to take pictures. I'll get through it somehow. Oh, hell, speak of the Devil…" She pointed out the window. "How the hell did he know we would be up here today?"

Diego Diaz rode out of the trees in front of them, sitting tall in the saddle. He could have been a cowboy from an earlier century, except for his very dark sunglasses

Patrick chuckled. "He reads your mind," he teased.

"I'm so glad we didn't bring Dad. He would have thrown a fit. Oh, damn, I wonder if he was watching me from behind the trees. I wouldn't put it past him."

"He's on the other side of the road. Maybe he was watching me," Patrick tossed back. He lifted a hand in greeting to Diaz as he rolled down the window. "We made it."

"So, you did," Diaz called back. "Road is going to change and get pretty bad past the next stand of trees. I brought up a couple of horses if you're ready to hit the saddle, though I also brought along a couple of cross-country ATVs if you prefer. You can leave them here when you're done."

"I vote for ATVs," Freeda chirped.

"Somehow I knew that would be your choice, so whatever the lady wants." Diaz winked at Patrick.

"Trailer is up ahead. You can leave the car here."

"Do you keep these for your ranch guests?" she asked as Diaz led her over to the trailer while Patrick found a place to park his car in the shade.

"We used to. Too many folks went crazy with them, and the liability was too high, so now we use them for work. Sometimes they're easier and faster to get around the ranch. We have a fleet of snowmobiles for the winter."

"So modern," she said and immediately regretted the sarcasm in her voice. Unlike his normal behavior he was being accommodating. "By the way, thanks for not pressing charges against Dad," she added. "Aunt Lottie told me this morning that you were dropping the trespassing charge."

"As long as he stays away," he replied curtly.

"Do you ever loosen up?" she asked.

"What?" The question appeared to catch Diaz off guard.

"I mean do you ever just talk with a person without a needing to make a nasty retort? Do you ever have just a normal person-to-person conversation?"

"Not many people worth having a normal conversation with," he quipped.

"See?"

A small hint of a smile lifted one side of his lips. "Someday I might have a normal conversation with you just to prove you wrong."

She laughed at the response. "What? You'd risk that just for me? Now, you're almost becoming normal."

"Only almost," he shot back. "Don't hold it against me."

Freeda turned away and smiled. Perhaps there were

good points to the man. Diaz had not only brought them the ATVs, but he had done it personally. Maybe he had come to make certain Fergie had not come with them, or perhaps he had done it for her aunt, but she had a feeling there was more to his appearance than simply being helpful. She didn't know his true motive and couldn't even guess it. That fact irritated Freeda as much as it intrigued her.

Chapter Nineteen

The commune site was little more than a series of log and adobe structures: some partially standing, some without roofs or lacking doors. None of the windows had glass, though a few had dusty shards that clung to frames. The remnants of a long wooden cabin stood at one end of the compound. Like many of the other buildings, the roof had fallen inside, and everything had the feel of a world long ago abandoned. Saplings had begun to grow inside some of the structures. The area had the feel of desertion. Even the old road was almost grown over with weeds. Only the ruts remained. Diaz had been right. They never would have made it in Patrick's car. She was pleased Diaz had left them on their own, instructing them where to leave the ATV's when they were finished.

"This could make a great story, but now I'm really feeling bad about not bringing Dad along. He's going to be unhappy we came out here without him," Freeda admitted again as she began snapping pictures of the forlorn structures of the old commune. "Heck, he might even be furious when he finds out we actually got to see the commune itself."

"He could have come up here already if he really wanted. He was living in that old cabin, and it's no more than a half a day's hike from here. He could have camped out or walked here anytime he chose."

Patrick was right, of course, but that didn't ease her

feelings of guilt. Diaz had given them directions that took them directly to the spot, and there was no way he would have done that for her father.

She studied the forlorn remains of a row of weathered wooden cabins, trying to visualize what the place might have been like in the past when the cabins were newly built and filled with boisterous young people—including her father, mother and their friends. The starkness of what would have been their living conditions surprised her. The cabins had rough wooden floors and she couldn't imagine how the group might have stayed warm in the winter. One large building had a broken earthen fireplace at one end. Water would have been pulled from a stream that ran nearly a mile from the compound. Toilet facilities were several squat outhouses located away from the main houses.

What had it been like to live there? The cabins were small and only meant for perhaps four to six people in one big room if they all slept in sleeping bags. She couldn't imagine room for more than three to four beds. In the middle of the structures, several logs were placed in a formation like a ring and what appeared to be an old fire pit was in the center. She could almost picture the group sitting on the logs on a summer evening, playing music on guitars or other instruments, and talking late into the night. What had drawn her mother and father? What might have made them choose to live in such primitive conditions? Would Fergie remember what drove them? Suddenly she wanted to talk to him, to hear what the area had been like in its heyday.

Carefully, Freeda photographed everything she could from different angles. To make the story really work, she would need to interview someone who had lived there. Hopefully her father would be willing to let her quote him on how the group had survived in the wilderness. The more she thought of that idea, the better she liked it. Fergie might enjoy a few moments of celebrity as the old hippie guy. It would also give him an idea of how she made her living.

"Got enough?" Patrick asked as she was about to make a second pass through the compound.

"For now," she replied, lowering her camera. "I would like to come back with Dad if I can convince Diaz. Dad can give me more of an idea of where everything was, and the daily life for folks who lived here. I'd love to get pictures of him walking around or pointing out things he remembers. That would give my story more oomph."

"*Oomph.* Now there's a journalistic term I don't recognize. I doubt I could use it in a trespassing case in court. 'Judge, she wanted to give her story more oomph. Please don't jail her or her father.' Anyway, I'm not certain that will ever happen," Patrick cautioned. "I know you want Fergie to see this, but I don't think Diaz is going to permit him to come back onto the property again. Your dad has worn out his welcome."

Patrick was probably right, but she would try anyway. She placed the camera into its case. "I have enough pictures. Let's go."

They again mounted the ATVs and made the short ride through the trees to where they had left his car. A small piece of paper was jammed against the front window.

"Great. He gave us a ticket for trespassing," Freeda said.

Patrick unfolded the paper and read it before holding

up and waving it. "Care to try the back way?" he asked after reading whatever was on it.

"The back way?" she questioned.

"Diaz left a map on another way to get back into town. We'll have to drive cross country for nearly a mile or so, but it looks as though it will take us less time. It's beyond that stand of trees." He pointed in the opposite direction of the way they had come.

"Perhaps he's hoping we'll get lost and drive off a cliff. I didn't see any other road listed on the map I had earlier."

"That map didn't show the road we came in on either," he reminded her. "This is all private property. Come on, let's try it. Don't you want to see how Tres Padres got its name?"

He handed the note to her. The first thing that shocked her was the writing. The script was neat and fluid, almost like it came out of a penmanship book. She studied the picture Diaz had drawn of a road that led south to the edge of the mesa and then directed them to turn west to a landmark of three cone shaped structures that appeared to be a rock formation.

Watch for the Tres Padres who protect the valley and the ranch, the note said.

"Is this serious?" she asked, holding up the note.

"Hell, I don't know," Patrick replied with a smile, "but it's easy enough to check out later. Anyway, they're a good landmark to guide us. Let's go."

She studied the ruts in the grass and shrugged. "It's your car," she said.

"It's leased," he quipped. "And I have good insurance. Come on, Diaz said there's a scenic view that will knock your socks off."

"Like he would know what kind of socks I wear," she shot back, rolling her eyes. "But sure. why not? I'd like to see what might knock off Mr. Negative's socks, not to mention seeing the Tres Padres. I had no idea why the ranch has that name."

The drive across the grass was as bumpy as the drive in had been, and as they reached solid rock, he stopped. The rocky ledge appeared to end only a few yards away.

"Are we about to drive off a cliff?" she asked, seeing the valley in the distance below them. "See? Diaz sent us this in direction as a way of getting rid of me once and for all."

"Maybe you, but I think he likes me," he teased, turning to wink at her. "Now where?"

She glanced at the note again. "It says to follow this ledge south until we come to the Tres Padres formation. It also says there's an awesome view of the valley from there. Wow, he actually wrote 'awesome?' Must really be something." She leaned forward to peer in front of them. The rocky area didn't simply stop, it appeared to drop off into nothingness.

"Are you certain he didn't instruct you to drop me off a ledge?"

"Don't worry. I won't do it." He grinned at her before guiding the car along the edge of the rock as the note instructed.

After crossing the next rise, the landmark formation came into view. Freeda gasped at the sight. The three cones of red sandstone rocks stood out in sharp contrast to the flat area at the top of the canyon. Perched on the edge of the hill, they rose proudly from the grassy plain as though they overlooked the land on all sides.

"Oh my gosh!" she exclaimed. "We have to stop

there. I want to take some pictures. Can you get me close to the base?"

"Your wish is my command, *milady*. Still wearing your socks?"

Freeda ignored his comment and was out of the car before it came to a complete stop. She began snapping pictures as soon as she had her settings ready and her best lens in place. Patrick followed her and they walked toward the edge of the hill.

The sight beyond the formation made Freeda gasp. If anything could be called breathtaking, this was it. The valley below them was green but dotted with trees, and in the distance she could make out the cluster of buildings that was Rio Rojo. To the west, the mountains rose like giant snow-covered bumps on the horizon. For a few seconds she felt dizzy, until she lowered her eyes. Perhaps Diaz had meant for her to become disoriented and walk off the rocks. She turned to Patrick, smiling.

"Diaz was right." Starting to walk toward him, her foot caught on an indentation in the rock and she stumbled, falling to one knee. She was about to comment that perhaps Diaz was watching her and making her fall when she caught sight of something that didn't belong on a rock in the middle of the wilderness—a round grayish-black object that was a little larger than a quarter. Her heart began to thump. That wasn't a quarter, but what would such a perfectly shaped object be doing in the middle of nowhere?

She reached down to pick it up. "Oh my gosh…"

"Found a coin?" Patrick teased as he stepped toward her to help her to her feet.

She held it out in the palm of her shaking hand. That was exactly what it appeared to be. Her breathing quickened as she studied it. The small, flat object was light and her heart thudded even harder as she scraped it with the fingernails of her other hand. "I…I think so."

He stared at it, taking it from her palm and holding it up. "What …the hell?"

Freeda scanned the ground nearby but saw nothing else. She glanced up at Patrick. "It's a coin, isn't it?"

He turned it over, also rubbing it between his forefinger and thumb. "Certainly appears to look like one." Taking a handkerchief from his pocket he wiped the object with it. "It is a coin, but not like anything I've ever seen."

She scanned the nearby rocky area. "Are there more? What would one coin be doing here in the middle of nowhere?"

"Beats me," he said, but he also began looking in cracks and in small indentures in the rocky ledge. For several minutes they searched, crossing the rocky plateau several times. They found nothing else.

Patrick studied the object again as Freeda made another pass along the rocks. His fingers shook slightly, but then he had felt shaky since she first handed it to him. The object reminded him of the old coins his grandfather had shown him years ago when he was a boy. Was this how his grandfather had come into possession of his coins? He recalled how the old man often had taken him out to the country on long walks. Being so young, Patrick had never paid attention to how they got to the locations or how they got back into town.

What he did recall was how his grandfather often walked with his head down whenever they stopped, studying the ground in front of him. As a child, Patrick thought he was watching for snakes, but the old man had found several artifacts that way—arrowheads and, yes, once he had found a coin. That was when he had recited the story of how the Spaniards had crossed this area on horseback, searching for cities of gold but left behind some of their own currency, which was useless. The native tribes preferred metal weapons or horses to little pieces of silver or gold.

Almost as though she could read his mind, Freeda's voice came to him.

"Is this how your grandfather found his coins?"

"I was just thinking about that," he admitted. "I'd be chasing bugs or butterflies, but he watched the ground. I always thought he did it to watch for snakes, but he once told me he did it to look for things from the past."

Patrick glanced around and another memory flashed from his past. He had once visited here—not on this ledge but in the valley below it, looking up at the rock formation. *Tres Padres.* The name had always seemed familiar to him, but when he was young and visiting his grandfather, he had thought it meant three Catholic priests might have discovered the valley, not the three rocks that overlooked the valley.

"My grandfather brought me here," he said. "Down below. He told me about the Spaniards and the gold coins they brought with them. Those coins were worthless to the indigenous natives, nothing but shiny trinkets. They wanted the horses so they could be more free to roam."

"I wish I could have met him. I wonder what he would think of this?" She held up the small round piece, giggling. "Now I have my own discovery."

He smiled at her. "You would have enjoyed Gramps—he was a real character." He paused, studying her before adding, "and I have a feeling he would have liked you too. He always said I was too serious, but he had a wicked sense of humor, and he loved to make things up, to tell stories. The two of you would have gotten along very well."

"Yes, I am certain I would have loved him," she replied loudly. Her voice echoed in the canyon, and she cupped her hands around her mouth and called out. "Hello? Hello, ghosts, are you out there?"

The sound echoed in the canyon, so she called out once more. "Echo, echo, echo!"

"Welcome to the canyons of New Mexico," he said with a laugh, enjoying her enthusiasm.

She called out again and then again, just as he had done as a child when he made the discovery. He watched her now for a couple of minutes and then turned away as a realization washed through him—one he wasn't certain he liked. Freeda Ferguson was getting under his skin. He'd been with her almost non-stop for only a few days, but suddenly the thought of life without having her constantly around was inconceivable.

****

"You can drop me off at the newspaper office," Freeda said as they passed the sign welcoming them back to Rio Rojo after their sojourn to the mountains. "I know you want to get back to working at your grandfather's place. I really appreciate your taking time off to take me out there this morning. That was just what I needed to get started on my stories."

"And just what are you going to write?"

She waved her hands in front of her. "I know. I know. No mention of our finding the coin to anyone. Do you think I want to start a stampede to Tres Padres? Earn that place more money than it is already raking in? I bet

Diaz would love that. He'd probably sit at the gate selling tickets and pocket all the money for himself."

"Actually, I'm certain he and the owners *wouldn't* love people going all over without regard for the cattle and digging up the property in their search for gold coins," he reminded her coolly. "From what I've seen of their guest operations, they regulate where people can go. There's a pamphlet at my motel that tells all about the place, and the emphasis is on *organized* trail rides, not unsupervised wandering."

Freeda sighed in sad resignation. They had been arguing about that prospect ever since leaving the hill where they had made their coin discovery. "Okay, okay, you're made your point twenty times already. Just drop me off."

He turned toward her, his face remaining grim. "Only if you promise…"

"I won't tell anyone about what we found," she replied, rolling her eyes and crossing her heart with her finger. "How many times do I have to promise you I won't say anything? You can trust me."

"It was on Tres Padres land. *Private land*," he reminded her for what was probably the tenth time. "We need to tell Diaz or arrange a…"

"Meeting with the owner of the ranch," she repeated in a childish voice. "I know, I know, *I know already.* But doesn't what we found show that Dad has been right all along? Can you now understand why he has been trying so hard to stay up there? And aren't you glad we didn't take the direction Diaz told us to take?"

"No, because the first map is what got us back into town," he replied in a matter-of-fact way. "Going the other way almost drove us off a cliff. If we hadn't stopped so you could take pictures, there's no telling where we might have ended up."

"Well, then I saved your life too. I hope that makes us even. And I hope you remember that it was Diaz who wanted us to see the Tres Padres. He probably was hoping we would end up seeing the holy maker."

To her surprise, Patrick burst into laughter. She had meant the comment as a mocking comeback, but he seemed to enjoy it rather than take it as a rebuff of his practical nature.

"*Touché*. I guess now we're *almost* even."

"What will make us even? Perhaps a night in bed?" she shot back.

The slight coloring of his face surprised her as he turned away. "That's not even funny," he replied, his lean face growing stiff. "I don't use women that way."

Yikes, he'd taken her teasing comment the wrong way. "Sorry," she said softly.

"Go take care of your pictures." His voice had become hard. "Work on your article for the newspaper or whatever it is you've been planning to do. Just don't mention finding that coin. I'll call you later. I want to get back to the motel and take a shower."

With his face so set and serious, Freeda couldn't resist a final dig. "Call if you need someone to wash your back."

His tan face darkened even further, making her pulse quicken.

"You're blushing, Mr. Lawyer man," she teased.

"Freeda!"

She clamped her mouth shut and climbed out of the car, closing the door with a little finger wave through the window. She smiled as he drove away. Had she finally spotted a weak link in Mr. Perfect, Mr. Serious Patrick Sanchez?

Chapter Twenty

Freeda's heart skipped as Patrick walked through the restaurant door and spotted their corner table. Tony Gennaro had seated her and the rest of the party a few minutes earlier. Patrick wore a beige blazer over a brown shirt. Damn, why did he always have to look so good? He caught sight of her and Lottie and waved.

"There's Patrick," her aunt said from across the table, waving toward him.

Beside her, Cere twisted around to look in the direction of the door, emitting a sigh. "I can't get over how you always seem to pick out the sexiest guys, Freeda. I meant to tell you that the other night. He is such a hunk," she said as Patrick walked toward them. "Who's the woman with him?"

Freeda's breath caught as he turned to a woman who was nearly as tall as he was. *Who the hell was that?* A bitter strand of jealousy ran through her until she noted the resemblance between them and realized the woman was probably twice his age. Her hair was black, like Patrick's; she was of medium height but that was helped by the black stiletto heels she wore. Her sleek blue pantsuit appeared to be made of silk as was the colorful scarf that streamed down the lapels of the jacket. Diamond earrings dangled from her ears.

"Maybe it's his mother?" Freeda speculated. "She does look a little like him."

Across the table, Aunt Lottie clapped her hands and beckoned toward the pair. "It *is* his mother. He told me she might be here this evening. I'm glad she was able to make it early. That's why I made certain we got the largest table."

"Any larger and we might as well seat the whole town," Fergie grumbled, breaking his second bread stick in half.

"I'm sorry Rafe couldn't come." Lottie turned to Cere, and her gaze went beyond her. "But I'm glad he sent his sister, Estella, in his place. The more the merrier I always say."

"I've become used to Rafe cancelling dinner plans at the last minute," Cere grumbled. "Life as a sheriff's wife." She squeezed the arm of the young woman seated beside her. "We've become frequent dinner companions. Of course, I stand him up just as frequently when we're on a deadline."

"We eat together then too," Estella lamented. "Only it's fast food or takeout."

Freeda had taken an immediate liking to Cere's sister-in-law from the moment they met at the newspaper office. Patrick had dropped her there after they returned from the trip to Tres Padres. Estella Tafoya had given Freeda the use of her desk and demonstrated how to use the computer to download the pictures she had taken at the ranch. Estella also arranged to have several printed for Freeda.

Pictures of the coin she and Patrick had found had not been among them. Freeda had uploaded photos she had taken of the coin onto a thumb drive and kept it in her camera case. She had not told anyone of their discovery. She hoped Patrick would keep it secret from his mother. Freeda sensed the woman's animosity from the moment they shook hands.

Geneva Sanchez studied her with very dark eyes ringed by thick mascara. The older woman's make up was perfect, giving her small light brown face a very sculptured, almost doll-like appearance. She was thin to the point of bony and wore black stiletto pumps. Unlike Lottie in her cotton slacks and blouse, Geneva wore a contoured silk suit that probably carried a designer label.

"Nice to meet you." Her voice was cool as her black eyes swept over Freeda, almost as though sizing up her worth. "You have kept my son very busy the last couple of days."

Freeda bit back a harsh reply. Somehow, she didn't think the woman would understand a dig at her son. "He's been very helpful. It's nice to meet you, too."

The older woman slid onto the seat directly beside Freeda, placing Patrick to her other side. Freeda doubted the maneuver was coincidental.

Dinner turned into a raucous affair with everyone sharing hilarious tales. Cere spoke of her life in the Los Angeles media compared to her current stint as a reporter-editor in Rio Rojo, while Fergie chimed in with stories about his cross-country trips. Tony Gennaro came over to join them for coffee and tiramisu as a small band began to play in background. Several couples got up to dance. To Freeda's surprise, Patrick suddenly appeared beside her.

"Care to dance?"

They had not spoken all evening, but her heart rate fluttered at the prospect of being close to him. "I guess I owe you one for being so kind to me," she teased with a smile.

"You owe me several," he teased back, winking. To her surprise, her breath caught in her chest at the shine in his dark eyes.

He took her hand and led her to the dance floor. Her face flushed as he put his arm around her and pulled her so close to him, she caught a whiff of his aftershave lotion.

"Your mom seems very nice," she said, trying to be polite, hoping he couldn't feel the rapid pounding of her heart. "Good taste in fashion."

"Only the best," he replied with a teasing grin as he leaned back to look down at her. "I've never seen her in cargo shorts or jeans."

"Did you tell her about…" She paused, unable to say the word "coin," but he was already shaking his head, his smile dissolving.

"I'm not going to either. I think the less people know about that, the better off we will be."

"I would like to go back there at some point," she began, but he was already shaking his head.

"Don't even think about it, Freeda. Not just yet."

He was right course. They finished the dance in silence. Unfortunately, when they returned to the table, the diners had turned their attention to where Patrick and Freeda had been that afternoon.

"I'm gonna get back out to that commune," Fergie said in a hard tone. "No way is Diaz going to be able to keep me out of there forever."

"Dad, don't bother. It's just a bunch of old destroyed buildings," Freeda protested, afraid to look over at Patrick. "I'll show you the pictures I took if you want to see what it looks like now."

"I know what it looks like. I've been out there

enough times. Where do you think I was camping before I moved into the cabin?"

"They're within their rights." Tony Gennaro's deep voice was surprisingly hard as he glared at Fergie. "We used to have one of those cabins out there in the summer, but the land was all leased from the ranch owners and those leases were cancelled years ago."

"They may have bought the property," Fergie argued. "But nature belongs to the people."

Freeda sensed a confrontation growing and took hold of her father's hand as the band struck up a new song. "Let's dance, Dad."

His lips drew into a thin straight line, but suddenly he shook his head. "You people will never understand. People may *buy land*, but they'll never truly own the earth." He stood and squeezed her hand as he led her out to the dance floor. To her surprise, he was agile and fluid as he guided her around the floor.

"Gennaro is as big a jerk today as he was thirty years ago," he said, looking back toward the table.

"You knew him then?" she asked in surprise. "The two of you didn't mention that the other night."

"I doubt he remembered me. I was just another one of the loser kids to him. But sure, he'd come out to the commune when I was there—hit on the women, drink with the guys. Like he said, his family owned one of the cabins over by the Palladium and Lockhart Lake. Just a few miles from there to the commune and he'd go out there like he was king of the damn world. Hit on all the girls and brag to them. Gonna be a big shot when he grew up, he used to brag. Well, now look at him. Where did he ever go? He's still stuck here, running a café just like his dad did. Hell, I coulda done that sort of thing if I'd wanted."

Freeda winced at her father's harsh assessment. Tony had been very nice to her aunt, and judging from all the customers, the restaurant appeared to be successful. "I can sort of understand his decision. He seems to be happy here," she said. "I guess you could say he is a big shot in Rio Rojo, and you said you might be willing to work for him."

He snorted. "Yeah, sure. His money will spend as well as any other employer. I just get upset that he loves to act like he's a bigshot. I've seen him a few times in Casitas. Heck, I saw him the other night when Bob got killed. He was having a cozy dinner with a very young woman. I almost asked him about her the other night at dinner, but I decided to keep my mouth shut because it's obvious Lottie likes him. But she's a big girl. She'll figure him out.'"

Freeda decided to change the subject. "Patrick and I drove by the old Palladium dance hall today, but we didn't stop to see it."

"Nothin' there but rubble now. I've slept inside the place a few times, but the ceiling's collapsed, gives little shelter from the cold."

"Dad, you need to stop that. Diaz will throw you in jail if he catches you on the ranch again. I swear he has eyes in the back of his head. He knew exactly where Patrick and I were going to be today. It was like he had been watching us."

"He probably was. He's a damn sneaky jerk, but I'm not afraid of him."

"I know, but—" she stopped and nearly choked. Across the floor, Patrick danced with Estella, holding the young woman in a very close posture. A surprising coldness ran through Freeda. Who had initiated the dance—him or her? Damn, it shouldn't bother her, should it? She had only known the man a couple of days, and she didn't know if he had a girlfriend back in Albuquerque. Besides, why would she be interested in him? He epitomized everything she disliked in a man. She couldn't imagine having to deal with someone who needed everything around him to be so damn perfect.

Fergie turned her away, and she felt his hand stiffen. He must have seen the other two dancers as she had. He glanced down at her, his brow furrowing into a look of worry. "You okay?"

"I'm fine," she lied.

"You're prettier than she is," he said, then suddenly grinned. "Want me to beat him up?"

Despite her unsteadiness, the comment drew a laugh from Freeda. She leaned back and smiled up at him. "Dad, he's thirty years younger than you, and I know he works out."

"Yeah, well, sometimes a man's just gotta do what a man's gotta do." His wink was as exaggerated as his grin, but it loosened the knot in her stomach.

Leave it to Fergie to make everything okay for Freeda in a very unlikely way. "Dad, I love you."

"Damn, didn't expect that," he replied winking at her. "But I love you too, Baby. You're getting more like your momma every day. You have her drive, her spunk, her smile. And you take good care of me."

His comments warmed her. Just as Fergie had noted about her, she had not expected his praise either. "We're all we have," she reminded him.

"Well, that will be enough for me, little gal, but you deserve a whole lot better. If I could find those damn coins, we could travel the world just like your momma and I used to dream about doing. You could take pictures…total freedom…she would have loved that idea."

Freeda drew a quick breath. Should she…she stopped herself from even taking the matter further in her thoughts. Telling her father about the discovery she and Patrick had made could only lead to disaster. Her dad would sneak back onto the ranch to check out the location, and Diaz would certainly put him in jail.

****

Patrick drew in the sweet floral scent of Estella Tafoya's perfume, but for some reason nothing about her enticed him. He'd agreed to dance with her only because he feared being rude if he turned her down when she had asked. Besides, a small part of him wanted Freeda to see him with someone else. Did his dancing with another woman matter to her? A part of him hoped it did, and yet another part of him feared hurting her. Damn, why was he suddenly so fixated on her thoughts and her wishes? It was as though she had slipped inside of him the minute she climbed into his car. Had it only been three days? Did love happen that fast? *Love?* Was he really thinking that?

"Freeda's a fun gal," Estella said. "I like listening to her talk. Cere says she's not afraid of anything. I wish I could be like that."

"I don't think it's a particularly good idea," Patrick said, smiling down at her. "She might be a daredevil, but I have a feeling there are times she gets in over her head."

"Don't men like women like that?" she asked with a teasing smile.

"Some men like women who know when to quit,"

he replied.

"Are you flirting with me, Patrick Sanchez?"

Normally he might make a suggestive remark back, but his eyes flickered across the floor to Freeda.

"Hello?" she said finally as he continued to look in the other direction.

"Sorry."

She burst into laughter. "No need to worry. I know a lost cause when I see one. I just hope she realizes what she wants before it's too late."

"What is that supposed to mean?" The comment surprised him. "Lost cause?"

"I'll let you figure it out," she announced, finishing with a giggle. "I like Freeda. I don't think she's as driven as her cousin, Cere, but they both know what they want, and they go after it."

"Now what the heck does that mean?" he asked, smiling down at her. He was beginning to enjoy chatting with the amiable woman. Her dark eyes danced with merriment. "You're a confusing woman."

"Not at all," Estella replied crisply. "Cere was so driven to find out about Marco Gonzales, she drove us all crazy. And now, here is her cousin, focusing on that area out near the old commune. What the hell are these people looking for anyway?"

"Who told you Freeda is looking for anything? She wants to find out about the old commune because her dad and mom stayed there at different times. It was what brought them together. That's what has her interested."

She seemed to consider the knowledge, looking toward the table. "That makes sense then. She pitched a story on the commune to my dad today." She paused before tilting her head back to look up at him, her eyes wide and sparkling. "And what about you, Mr. Sanchez? What are *you* interested in?"

Patrick grinned down at the young woman, wishing he could give her the answer she probably wanted, but his mind remained elsewhere. Her wide expressive eyes gazed up at him, and his gaze slid away. He couldn't afford to be distracted by another female.

"Just interested in cleaning out grandad's house right now," he replied, knowing he was probably disappointing her attempt at flirtation.

"My Aunt Rosalie lived out at the commune for a time, according to my mom," she added as though she hadn't noticed his lack of a flirtatious answer. "Then she took off, and never was seen again."

His head jerked back to her as another thought hit him. "I wonder if Fergie knew her. Do you know when she lived there?"

"No, I've never asked anyone about her. The gossip is that she was wild, dated bad guys, drifted off to the commune and never returned. Probably like a lot of the other kids who went there. They met other kids from other places and moved on hoping for a better life."

"Now it's a place of sadness," he admitted with a sigh. "All the buildings are torn down, but at least Freeda got the chance to see where her mom and dad once lived, even if they weren't there at the same time. Fergie keeps going back without asking permission, and the ranch boss keeps throwing him out."

Estella rolled her eyes. "Diego Diaz. Now there's an enigma for you. I've tried to do stories with him several times, and he keeps refusing. He won't even let me quote him. And pictures? He practically busted my camera once when I tried to take a picture of him. The next week he sends me a brand new, state of the art camera as a peace offering. When I tried to thank him, he acted like he didn't know anything about it. He's one crazy guy."

"I won't argue that," Patrick agreed. "He treats Freeda horribly, but he's been overly friendly to me. I'm not certain why."

She smiled up at him, her dark eyes sparkling with mischief. "Now can't you figure that out, Mr. Sanchez? I can. You're a very easy man to like."

He glanced down at Estella, wishing he could give her the flirtatious attention she seemed to want, but just as quickly, his gaze shot across the room where Freeda sat talking to Lottie, her hands gesturing wildly. He smiled at her animated posture, wondering what sort of story she was telling her aunt.

When they returned to the table, the subject had turned to the one thing he had hoped didn't come up— the visit to Tres Padres and the commune. Patrick was relieved when Estella again brought up her aunt, Rosalie, who had disappeared after living there for a time.

Lottie immediately continued the story. "She was my friend all through school. We started first grade together and graduated from high school side by side. Then she went out there and got involved with that group. I saw her a few times when she came into town, but suddenly she stopped coming around and then she just vanished." She turned to Patrick. "You know what, though, I think she might have originally gone out there with your father—" She stopped suddenly as though she realized what she was saying and turned to Patrick's mother. "That would probably have been long before he met you, Geneva. Did he ever talk about it?"

Geneva's lip twitched in irritation. "My husband

never mentioned he *ever* lived in a commune." Her voice was hard, her dark eyes focused on Fergie. "Maybe he visited once."

Fergie turned toward her. "That's kind of how it was back then. Kids from town might come out every so often for a day or two, or to go to a party, but they didn't stay long. Most of the kids who lived in the commune came from the east or the south, and some from around the world. Hell, different people from all over were coming and going all the time. That was a great way to live. We were on our own—doing what we chose. We took care of each other as long as we were together, but we also stayed out of each other's business when we wanted to move on."

****

"Hon, will you stop pacing? You're making me nervous."

Freeda jerked her head toward her aunt who sat nearby on a wooden rocking chair, Lottie's fingers busy on a needle point project. She had been working on it since they returned from the restaurant more than an hour earlier. The evening had been pleasant, but through it all Freeda had been aware of Patrick talking to Estella. The woman had been so nice to her at the newspaper office, but she turned cool once her attention zeroed in on Patrick at the restaurant. To make matters worse, Patrick responded eagerly to Estella's blatant flirting.

Damn him! Freeda squeezed her palms into hard fists, but just as quickly relaxed them.

Stop it! What hold did she have over Patrick? A couple of days of acquaintance? Several kisses? She was tempted to walk over to his hotel to see what he might be doing, but why? What excuse could she give him?

She thought of the coin they had discovered on their way back from the commune. Would he tell his mother about it? Could the woman be trusted with such a secret? Would he tell Estella about it?

Freeda turned to her aunt, looking for a way to distract herself from her concerns about the evening. "What did you think of Patrick's mother?" she asked.

Lottie's head jerked up from her needlepoint, and she laughed.

"What's so funny?" Freeda asked.

"She's frightened by you," Lottie replied with a wink.

"Me?" Freeda drew back in surprise. "Why would she worry about me?"

Lottie laughed again. "Come on, you don't know?"

"No."

"Oh, hon. Haven't you noticed the way Patrick looks at you? When you're around he never takes his eyes off you."

The thought landed in Freeda's brain like a quick slap across the face. "Really?" She had not noticed, but then again, she tried not to look at him too much. What her aunt was saying couldn't be true, could it? "Aunt Lottie, you're teasing me. I met him a couple of days ago. All we do is argue."

Lottie's face was filled with mirth, her eyes dancing mischievously. "Yes, hon, I am teasing, but I'm also serious. Some people don't take long to know what's right and who's right for them. I fell for my Del immediately. It was as though we had an instant connection. The moment I met him, all other boys grew pale in comparison and I think I told you, your mom fell for Fergie the first night they met. Some things are inevitable."

Freeda stared hard at her aunt, considering what Lottie was saying. Patrick and her? She shook her head. "I don't think we're inevitable. We make each other nuts."

"So? Del and I made each other nuts for years. We loved our disagreements..." she paused to give an exaggerated wink. "...almost as much as we loved making up."

"Was he the first boy you ever loved?"

Her aunt's smile vanished as she lowered her eyes. For a couple of minutes, she remained staring at the floor, her face set and pale, her lips pressed together in a firm line. She sat so still, her face and body so rigid, Freeda wondered if her aunt intended to answer. Suddenly her aunt's head lifted, and Freeda spotted moisture at the corner of her blue eyes. "No, Del wasn't my first love," she replied in a soft voice.

"Really? You had someone else?" Freeda asked in surprise. Cere had never told her this. Did her cousin even know about her mother's earlier love?

Again, Lottie's reaction was slow, her lowered eyes growing thoughtful as though remembering a vision from the past. "Del knew...I mean, he knew I'd had someone else in my past, but he didn't care. We loved each other and I've always known...he was the right man for me to marry..."

"But the other boy, do you ever wonder about him? Is he still around?"

Lottie drew a quick breath, as though exhaling the old memories. She lifted her hand, waving it. "He died years ago, and I don't think about it anymore. It was young love: quick, hot, exciting, thrilling." She shivered as she shook her head. "But a marriage wouldn't have worked for us. We were so different, so…I don't know. We didn't know ourselves, and we both knew that it would be a disaster…so it ended."

"Uncle Del was the love of your life?"

"One of them." She drew a deep breath and turned away quickly, as though she suddenly needed to be on the move. "I better get to bed. I think the wine has gone to my head. Good night, sweetie. You should call Patrick and wish him good night."

"Good night, Aunt Lottie. Maybe I will."

"And don't wait up for your dad. He's a big boy and he will be fine. I gave him a key."

Freeda grimaced. Giving her father a key probably was not a good idea. As much as she wanted to believe he was an honest man, she feared more that he might be irresponsible and lose it or lend it to the wrong person. Why had he insisted on going off on his own after they came home? Perhaps she should go looking for him. What if the person who had killed his friend came looking for him? Someone had already hit him over the head once. What if that person tried to attack him again?

Freeda sighed and shook her head sadly. No, as her aunt said, he would be all right on his own. He didn't know anyone in town, and Aunt Lottie had only given him twenty dollars. He couldn't get into much trouble with that amount of money. No one was going to rob him for it.

Still, Freeda felt uneasy. She waited until her aunt was upstairs and Lottie's heard the bedroom door close before pulling her cell phone out of her pocket. She tapped in Patrick's number, hoping he might agree to make a drive through town and check for Fergie.

After three rings it went to voice mail. Perhaps he was in the shower. She called the hotel and asked for his room, hoping he would hear the louder ring of a desk phone.

"Hello?"

Geneva's voice was a surprise, but Freeda summoned her most pleasant manner.

"Hi, Mrs. Sanchez. This is Freeda Ferguson. May I please speak to Patrick?"

"Hello, Freeda. And no, you many not. He's not here. He's staying somewhere else tonight."

A chill ran through her, but Freeda fought to keep her voice even. "I just wanted to thank him for taking me out to the commune today."

"I'll give him the message when I see him in the morning. Good night."

The phone clicked off.

Chapter Twenty-One

"Are you seeing Patrick today?" Lottie asked as she slid onto a chair across the kitchen table from Freeda the next morning. She gestured toward Freeda's nearly untouched plate. "Eat your eggs before they get cold, hon."

Freeda shook her head as she obediently lifted another fork of scrambled eggs. The bite would be as tasteless as the last, but her lack of appetite was not the fault of her aunt's cooking. She might not be seeing Patrick any time soon, but he had been on her mind all night. "He's been busy at the house and with his mother."

"That was a fun gathering last night," Lottie added. "I enjoy Tony when he's hosting a crowd. He seems to come into his own when he's able to entertain others. I think he gets bored when we're alone, though he's always been like that. Even in high school he preferred being around groups of people. I think that's why he has made such a success of the restaurant."

"Did you ever date him in high school?" Freeda asked.

Her aunt's cheeks turned pink, and Freeda laughed. "You did?"

"Oh, we went to a couple of dances together, but he was never interested in me. He dated my friend Rosalie for a while, but she was more interested in Marco Gonzales. Isn't that the way things go when you're young? The boys or girls you want always want someone else?"

"Marco? The hand on the wall guy?"

"Oh, yes, we all had crushes on Marco. Francis, me, and Rosalie. He had his choice of any girl in town, but that might also have been because every parent in town didn't want their daughters dating him. That's probably another constancy of growing up. You choose the partner certain to anger your parents."

"Did you go out with Marco?"

Her aunt's face turned a brighter shade of pink. "A few times…" She hesitated, sighing heavily. "But we never dated in public. I'd sneak out to meet him. He'd sing songs to me. I liked that, but my folks were like every other parent in town. To them, he was the town hoodlum. He wasn't the type to let anyone push him around, so he was always in trouble. To the girls, he was the guy we would all love to date, but we couldn't do it openly or we'd get grounded. He was witty, smart, charming and could sing like a lark. Like I said, he could make up his own songs. We all wanted to go out with him, so he was a magnet for the girls."

"Sounds like Patrick. Did you notice our waitress? Between her and Estella last night, they were climbing all over him."

"Can you blame them? Patrick seems like such a nice guy, both charming and witty, though I'm not certain I care for his mother. Perhaps I'm being tacky, but I kept feeling like she was looking at us like we were a bunch of back country hicks."

Freeda had noticed his mother's distraction. While Geneva Sanchez appeared to enjoy the conversation when it was pointed in her direction, the rest of the time she either wore a frown or her smiles were stiff. Throughout the evening, she had kept checking her phone or looking around the restaurant as though she could hardly wait to leave. The only times she had engaged with the group was when Freeda or Estella spoke to her son, and then it was usually to cut them off and get his attention back on her.

"Freeda?"

She jumped, realizing her aunt had asked her a question and she had not been paying attention. "Sorry, what did you say?"

"Thinking of Patrick?" Lottie teased, grinning at her. "I asked if you are going over to the newspaper office today. I'm certain Cere will enjoy spending time with you, just as I'm certain Estella is depending on you. I do like her, even though she kept flirting with Patrick last night. It was so obvious he wasn't interested."

Freeda's head jerked around toward her aunt. "What do you mean, he wasn't interested?"

Lottie laughed. "Now *that* woke you up. Did you think he was *interested*? He was watching you all through dinner. Estella is nothing but a flirt, always wants to be the belle of the ball. Been that way since she was a little girl, but I swear she's gotten even worse. I should have warned Patrick."

Freeda wasn't as certain about her aunt's observation regarding Patrick being disinterested in Estella. "He danced with her twice," she pointed out, unable to admit the woman might have taken him home and done more than dancing or flirting.

"Well, he danced with his mother twice, but he danced with you four times. The two of you appeared to be enjoying each other's company."

"He thinks I'm a crazy pest," Freeda replied glumly. "But it doesn't matter. I came here to see Dad, and I'm going to spend my time with him."

"Not today, I'm sorry to say. He left early this morning."

"Left?" Her head jerked up from her half-touched breakfast. "To go to breakfast?"

"It might be for longer. I made him a ham sandwich and he asked me to pack him food for later. He was wearing his backpack when he walked out the door. Didn't he tell you he might be leaving?"

A needle of fear poked at Freeda as she pushed away from the table. "He didn't say a word. How could he leave without saying goodbye to me? Where could he go? He doesn't have any place else to stay." Where would she find him if he left Rio Rojo? Diaz would never allow him to return to the ranch so he couldn't have gone there. Would he dare to return to Casitas after what happened to his friend, after he had been hit by someone? Fearfully she asked, "Did you give him any money?"

Her aunt grimaced, eyes lowering. "Not much. He didn't have any, and I didn't want to let him go anywhere without a few dollars." She reached out a hand toward Freeda but stopped as Freeda drew back. "I'm so sorry, sweetie, but it'll be okay. I also gave him my old cell phone and set it up so we can stay in touch with him. Do you want to call him?"

"But why would he leave?" Freeda asked, ignoring the question as her eyes grew moist. "Without even saying goodbye to me? No, he wouldn't just go. Not like this." She glanced around wildly, and then back at her aunt, unable to stop the tears from filling her eyes. Deep down she knew he would leave without saying goodbye.

He had done that to her in the past. "Why would he go?"

Lottie approached Freeda with tear-filled eyes of her own. "You might not want to hear this, baby, but yes, he would just go. And for no good reason other than he wants to move on. He's done it for as long as I've known him. Come on, call him if you want to talk to him and find out where he's headed. He'll probably tell you that so the two of you can keep in touch. At least you got to see him for a few days."

Freeda could no longer stop the tears from rolling down her cheeks, even though she knew her aunt was right. Her father had never been reliable, and he could change his mind from one minute to the next. She wiped her napkin across her face, drying her tears. "He seemed to have so much fun last night. We even danced together…"

"I know, but that may be enough for him, Baby."

Freeda shivered at that thought. Enough for him? A dance with his daughter and a couple of days? Perhaps she should have told him about finding the coin. That could have kept him around. He might have even asked her to drive him to Tres Padres to show him where she and Patrick found it. But why should something so worthless mean more to him than his own daughter?

"Maybe I should go too," she said in a strangled voice. "Get out of here and go back to California. It's stupid to think I can do anything to help him…what an idiot I am!"

Lottie patted her shoulder gently. "Now don't make any hasty decisions, honey. Didn't you promise Estella last night that you would be willing to help with editing at the paper today? Isn't she counting on you?"

Freeda's sudden epithet-filled reply made her aunt

pull back.

"Are you okay? What's wrong?" Lottie's placid blue eyes barely registered.

"Men suck!" Freeda cried. "They are all such a bunch of…" she stopped, fearing another tirade might alienate her aunt. To make matters worse, her phone began to chime on the table. She grabbed it, thinking it might be Fergie. However, when she glanced at the number she saw Patrick's name come up.

She pushed it across the table toward Lottie. "Can you please get that? If I answer, I might throw it against the wall."

Her aunt watched her closely as she lifted the phone and tapped the answer button. "Hello? Good morning, Patrick. It's Lottie. Freeda's away from her phone right now. Shall I call her?"

Freeda shook her head and waved her hands violently. "No!" she hissed.

"I could give her a message," she offered smoothly while watching Freeda. After a few seconds, she tapped off the phone and handed it to Freeda.

"He wants you to call him."

"He can go to hell!"

Lottie drew back in surprise, drawing a quick breath, her blue eyes widening. "What's wrong? Did he do something? The two of you seemed so happy together last night. And the way he watches you…" she waggled her eyebrows. "He doesn't take his eyes off you."

"I think you mean the way he ogled Estella," she retorted.

"Hmph, Estella," she snorted. "Like I said, she's the original flirt. Has half the guys in town thinking they're special. And, yes, I saw the way *she* stared at him. But I didn't see him looking back. And I bet when you go over to the newspaper office today, she will act like she barely noticed him. Her mind will be on this week's edition of the paper. That girl reminds me of Cere when she started out—driven by work but a big flirt when the men are around so she can get a jump on them."

"Well, yes, I remember Cere, but at least she settled down. Maybe that's what Estella is hoping for too—a nice guy, someone like Patrick."

"Maybe, but like I said, if Patrick was looking at anyone last night, it was you. Perhaps he was hoping to make you jealous?"

Freeda paused as she was about to let loose with another tirade. Could that have been the reason Patrick flirted with Estella? Could he be interested in *Freeda* but unwilling to show it? They seemed to have formed a connection even though they had only known each other a few days. She had already shared more personal information than she'd shared with other men she had known. She had even let her guard down around him several times emotionally. Much as he seemed to hate doing it, he had also shared his own sad, personal story with her.

Where had he been the previous night when she called his hotel room? His mother had sounded as though she doubted he would be back. Had he gone to see Estella? Freeda shook her head. It didn't matter. Despite all their personal interaction, Patrick had no commitment to her, but Freeda had made a promise to her cousin to help with editing at the newspaper today. Besides, she needed to earn money if she was ever going to leave Rio Rojo, and Cere had agreed to see she got paid.

"You're right," Freeda admitted with a heavy sigh.

"I better get over to the newspaper office before it gets any later." Reaching across the table, she gently stroked her aunt's arm. "Thanks for calming me down, Aunt Lottie. I need that every so often."

The older woman winked, grasping Freeda's hand and squeezing it gently. "Your mom would have done the same for me and Cere if the tables were turned."

"I'm sorry if I seem on edge," Freeda added. "I've been so worried about Dad, and now…he leaves…and he didn't even say where he was going?"

"Not a word, hon. Just took his knapsack and headed out, but I told him to keep the key I gave him yesterday in case he comes back while we're not around."

Freeda made a face. "I'm not certain that's a good idea…"

"I'm not worried. And don't you worry either. He'll turn up again. Probably when we least expect it."

Freeda gazed out the window sadly. Men! She didn't know if she was more agitated by her missing father or where Patrick had been the previous night.

****

Patrick glanced at his mother quickly as he directed the car toward the Matador restaurant for breakfast. "We should have called Freeda," he said.

"That girl is probably not even up yet. She looks like the type who normally sleeps in until noon."

Her negative comment didn't surprise him. Any time he exhibited more than a passing interest in a woman, she would find plenty of reasons he shouldn't be more than friends with her, much less develop any sort of relationship. He found himself smiling suddenly. If he and Freeda ever did become more than acquaintances, he had a feeling his mother would have her hands full trying to come between them. Freeda was every bit as determined as his mother.

"We should have picked up breakfast at a fast-food place and gone to your grandfather's," his mother said suddenly. "I want to see this place and get it all over with so I can go home."

He pointed across the street. "Not too late to do that. There's a coffee place on the next corner. Want to pick up some muffins and a container of coffee and head over?"

"Yes."

Patrick directed the car into a short line and ordered coffee and muffins. His mother was right. He needed to finalize the arrangements for his grandfather's house so they could leave Rio Rojo. The sooner he got away from Freeda Ferguson and the disturbing vibrations she set off in him, the better off he would be.

The more he thought about the situation between them, the more he became convinced she was not the woman for him. Much as he had enjoyed her company the past few days, she was too unpredictable and too unstructured in her life. He had been jolted to the core to realize how much he wanted her. But as much as he might desire her body or enjoy her company, he also knew she was never going to be the type of woman who would bring him a peaceful existence. In a different way, she was as headstrong and unpredictable as her father. He had been thinking of that ever since he'd realized how much he desired her during their trip to the mountains the previous day.

A life without her? It would certainly be much more calm than a life with her. Did he want to become involved with her? Even when he danced with her, he had held her like a fourteen-year-old might hold a girl at his first junior high dance.

He brushed aside thoughts of Freeda as he and his mother munched on their muffins and drank their coffee before getting fresh cups to drive over to the house.

"Oh my gosh, this is horrible," his mother cried the minute they turned onto the block and she caught sight of the forlorn house. "This will never sell."

"Exactly what I have been thinking," he agreed. "Even the property might be an issue. That hill is right up against the back of the house, and a brush fire could easily destroy it, or a bad rainstorm could bring a mudslide down onto the entire property. Who would want to buy it?"

"Well, the house has been here for nearly a hundred years," she noted, "And the hill hasn't come down yet, so that's not likely to happen. But it's so small, so…I don't know…I thought it was bigger."

"When was the last time you were here?" he asked.

"I don't know. Fifteen, twenty years ago, I guess."

A sudden thought hit him. "You didn't visit it when you came to the funeral for Gramps?"

Her gaze dropped, avoiding his eyes. "I never came to the funeral. I had to work. And since you weren't coming, well, I didn't think I would know anyone. Have you found anything of value inside?"

"No, Mom, and there are no secret hideaways in the walls. The place is made of adobe."

She waved a hand as though clearing away smoke from her face. "Demolish it. Bulldoze the whole damn thing. That garage is about to fall anyway. Get rid of it before it burns, and we get sued when it sets the whole block on fire."

"Adobe is not known for burning out of control," he remarked dryly. "Don't you want to go inside?"

Not surprisingly, she wrinkled her nose in a show of distaste. "Why bother?"

"To check for hidden walls or treasures?" He meant the comment as a joke, but she suddenly perked up, her dark eyes widening as she studied the house again.

"Do you think there are any?"

Patrick laughed harshly. "No, Mom. The walls were plastered over the adobe, and some are cracked. If he had anything hidden it would have been revealed by now."

"Well, this was a damn waste of my time," she replied shortly, waving her hand in a dismissal. "Drink your coffee and let's go see the realtor. Maybe I'll feel like going inside later. But don't count on it."

"Whatever you say." He preferred the idea that she might visit with the realtor and then choose to leave. He would accomplish more without her presence. "At least you got to meet Freeda," he said quietly.

She jerked up. "Freeda? That ditzy girl at the restaurant last night? The one with the crazy dad?" Her eyes widened as she stared at him. "Patrick, you can't be serious about that woman. You just met her a couple of days ago."

"Well, she is intriguing and fun…"

"Fun? She's a damn nut!" she interrupted. "So is her dad. Did you listen to him? Stories of buried treasure and hitchhiking across country? He might have seen it as freedom, riding the rails without a worry, but I saw it as a bum on the run."

Patrick hated to admit that he agreed with her summation, but at the same time, Freeda was not Fergie. She was struggling to work on her own and from what he had seen of her resourcefulness the past few days…he shook his head. No, her actions had not been resourceful. What would she have done if he hadn't happened to come along? Wave down the next car? Much as he had felt himself drawn to her physically or personally, the logical side of his brain knew they didn't have any future together.

His mother broke into his train of thought. "If you're looking for a nice lady, what about that pretty girl from the newspaper? She seemed bright and serious. Perhaps we should visit her to see if she can recommend a good realtor or a good junkman. She probably knows everyone in town."

Patrick agreed. Hadn't Freeda said something about working there with her cousin? Perhaps he would have an opportunity to see her. They drove the few blocks to the newspaper office in the center of town, but as Patrick maneuvered his car into a parking spot, his mother reached over to grab his arm.

"Wait, look there's a real estate office on the next block. Let's go there instead and see about starting the selling process."

"You don't want to go to the newspaper office and check on the various realtors in town?"

"Why waste time with one more step? Let's get this thing started."

Patrick guided the car back onto the street, driving by the newspaper office. Only as he passed did he see Freeda sitting at a desk near the window. Had his mother spotted her? Was that why she suddenly changed her mind about going there? His lips tightened as he turned away. He'd been criticizing Freeda for being so concerned about her father and his antics. He needed to take his own advice about clinging parents.

Chapter Twenty-Two

"Well, well. Miss Freedom."

Freeda jumped at the sound of the scratchy voice behind her. She jerked up her head to look into the shiny dark sunglasses of Diego Diaz.

"What are you doing here?" she asked in surprise.

"I came in to talk to Art Tafoya about brochures they're printing for the ranch. What are *you* doing here?"

She pointed her finger at the computer screen. "I'm helping Estella and Cere with writing and editing for the paper."

"That doesn't look like writing," he pointed out, flicking his finger at the computer monitor where one of the pictures she had taken at Tres Padres filled the screen.

Freeda sighed, but she couldn't help but laugh as well. "I should have known the minute I started goofing off you would show up with your master's whip. But I can do more than write. These are the pictures I took yesterday at the ranch."

His raspy chuckle surprised her and for a minute he smiled, not his normal cynical, sinister grin, but a genuine smile, showing very straight white teeth. He removed his sunglasses and leaned closer to the screen, his bright green eye examining the pictures as she cycled through them.

"Amazing. Where did you take those?" he asked.

"Near the old commune. I wanted to show the pictures to my dad. I'm going to make him copies so he'll know what it looks like now."

"As if he doesn't already know," he replied with a grunt, again pointing at the screen. "Where the hell do you think I keep finding him?"

A shiver ran through Freeda. She thought of the small wooden and adobe shacks. Why would he keep returning there? Was that where he had headed when he left Lottie's house that morning? It did offer limited shelter in the way of a roof over his head, but she couldn't imagine him trying to survive there in the winter. However, now as she thought back on the area as she studied the pictures, she realized one reason why he might keep returning.

"I can understand why he might keep going there…it's what brought him and my mom together," she said softly.

"Really?" He sounded surprised. "She lived out there with him?"

"No, they didn't live together at the commune. They were there at different times, but they had that experience in common when they met in California."

He leaned forward to study the pictures on the screen again. "Was she from around here?"

"No, she came from California to live at the commune."

"And that's why you were named Freedom," he said to her in surprise.

She gazed up at him, wishing she could understand what was behind that hard green gaze. Was he viewing her with skepticism or did the emotion of her admission even register?

"Got any more?" he asked, flicking a finger at the screen.

She tapped her keyboard to cycle through several more of the pictures, aware of his very still presence beside her. He studied each one but didn't comment on any of them.

"It was a beautiful setting in that valley," she said to break what was becoming an uncomfortable silence. "I can understand why someone might set up a camp there. I just don't understand how people could find it or come and go very easily. How did they get food or supplies up there in the winter? There's not even a nearby source of water."

"There was a stream that ran close to the place back then. A dam upstream closed it off. As for supplies, they followed an old trail down into the valley to a small general store. It closed not long after the commune was disbanded, and the trail has become overgrown. Now all that's left are the old buildings."

"How do you know all that?"

"Stories." His good eye closed in a wink. "I listen more than talk. Good way to learn."

She stifled the urge to roll her eyes. "What else do you know about that place?"

"They grew their own crops and kept sheep and chickens. They hunted deer. Not hard to live on your own if you know how to do it, and if you don't mind getting your hands dirty working or going hungry at times."

"I work," she protested, but he held up his good hand.

"I'm not belittling you," he replied coolly, eye still on the screen. "Like I said, those pictures are good. You have a good eye. Who knew you were such a smart, talented lady?"

He concluded with a wink, and Freeda stared at Diaz, so shocked she had no idea how to answer. After so many taunts, the man had actually complimented her?

In the awkward silence he dropped another bombshell. "You want to work for me?"

"Wha…work?" Her heart began to thud. "For *you*? Doing what?"

He pointed again at the screen. "I told you. The ranch is going to create brochures about the property and what it has to offer that we can send out or give away. I need pictures for advertising purposes."

A quick sensation of joy rushed through Freeda as she realized what he was offering. A paying job! "Are you serious?" she asked in a small, uncertain voice.

"You ever known me to joke?" he asked with a wry smile.

"Not in a good way," she retorted.

His sharp laugh surprised her as much as his offer had. "I'm not certain how long you intend to hang around, but if you're interested, give me a call." He pulled a card out of his pocket and put it on the desk. The card had a picture of the main ranch gate in the middle and his name and the ranch address and a phone number below it.

"You have your own cards?" she asked.

"Call anytime," he replied in his normal bantering tone. He suddenly reached into his pocket and pulled out an envelope.

Freeda's heart began to pound. She recognized the handwriting on the outside. She had seen that envelope on the desk in the cabin where her father was staying. Diaz dropped the envelope on the desk. "If I find anything else, I'll see that it gets it to you."

Her body went limp as her heart began to thump and tears edged into her eyes as she stammered. "D.V...I mean...Mr. know..."

Sudden movement across the room caught his attention, and he glanced up and gestured with his index finger. "Have to go meet Art. Think about whether you want to take the photos and let me know."

Freeda stared at his departing back as he limped across the room to where Art Tafoya stood at the door to his office.

She lifted the envelope and opened it, seeing several black and white photographs inside. The pictures of her mother and Fergie! Diaz had gathered them up and brought them to her, just as she had asked. Damn, who knew Diaz might be capable of being thoughtful?

"Are you okay? What did he say to you?"

Freeda jumped at the sound of Cere's sudden questions behind her. She whirled around to her cousin, waving the card Diaz had given her.

"You wouldn't believe it. He brought me my dad's pictures, and that guy just offered me a job."

"Really?" Cere's eyes grew large as they watched Diaz enter the editor's office. "Doing what?"

"As a photographer." Freeda waved at the still open computer screen. "He saw these shots I took yesterday at Tres Padres, and he wants to hire me to take publicity photos of the ranch. Isn't that crazy?"

"Not at all." Cere touched her shoulder gently and grinned at her. "You're probably the best photographer in town at the moment. Are you going to do it?"

"I don't know..." Freeda blinked, still trying to absorb what the offer meant. "I hadn't intended to stay much longer. Dad took off this morning, and I don't know if or when he's coming back. He could have gone out walking around town, or he may be halfway to Albuquerque by now. But I do need money and I don't have any jobs lined up."

"See? Is there any reason you need to get back to California right away? Didn't you say you were running low on money, and you might need your grandmother to send you some cash?"

The enormity of the job offer settled on Freeda like an exploding bomb. Her eyes met her cousin's.

"You're right. If I'm working for him, I can afford to stay for at least a few weeks, perhaps a month. I'll be able to see Dad, maybe even get Diaz to let him onto the ranch or to stay there if I use him as a helper…or at least think about it."

Cere laughed and winked again. "I was thinking maybe you could also work part time at your cousin's newspaper who could also use a good photographer."

"Yes! Give me an assignment. I'll start today!"

They both burst into laughter, but a sudden questioning voice stopped Freeda in mid laugh.

"Start what?"

She whirled toward the sound of Estella's voice. The woman watched them with cool, puzzled eyes, looking from one to the other, a smile on her face that didn't reach to her piercing dark eyes.

Freeda bit back a sardonic reply and swallowed hard as Cere informed her of what they had been discussing. To Freeda's surprise, Estella agreed eagerly.

"That is absolutely great news," she said. "An extra body around here means I can finally take time off. I'll be able to take that trip to Albuquerque for the balloon festival this year."

"Wait! That sounds like a perfect photo shoot for me," Freeda said, immediately wishing her voice didn't sound so brittle and challenging.

Estella surprised her yet again, grabbing her arm and squeezing it. "Oh, yes! We could both go. I can do interviews and write a story for the paper. You could take pictures. Dad would love it. I bet we can even get Eddie to take us up in a balloon. Maybe we could invite Patrick."

Freeda's fist curled involuntarily, but Cere took hold of her arm. Did she sense Freeda's anger?

"That would be perfect," Cere said. "Maybe I can convince Rafe to take some time off work and we could finally meet Eddie."

"Who is Eddie?" Freeda asked looking from one to the other.

"My boyfriend." Estella turned to Cere, her voice again growing excited. "Oh, did I tell you? Patrick knows him. They went to high school together. We may call just to tease him before Patrick goes home. That Patrick…what a sense of humor."

"Patrick?" The name came out as a croaking sound and Freeda cleared her throat as the rest of what Estella had just said registered. Estella had a boyfriend? Some of the tightness Freeda had felt since the previous evening disintegrated.

"Yes, Patrick had me laughing all night, though I don't think his mother likes any woman to be around her son." She leaned toward Cere and rolled her eyes. "Now there is one predatory female. I'm not surprised he's still single. I get the feeling she won't let any woman come within ten feet of her son before she gets out her claws."

She turned to Freeda, grabbing her arm playfully. "And I don't think she approves of her son's friendship with you at all…"

Cere turned to Freeda, smiling. "I got that impression too. Didn't you notice how every time Patrick tried to talk to you or said anything directed toward you, she interrupted or tapped his arm to pull his attention back to *her*?"

"She's scared of you, girl." Estella agreed, winking at Freeda. "Let me know if you need me and Cere to double team her so you can spend time with Patrick. I think she senses his feelings for you."

Feelings for her? Freeda's gaze slid from one to the other, uncertain of how to reply. Could they be right? Had the woman lied about Patrick not being able to take her call? Freeda *had* misjudged her father.

Could she be misjudging Patrick too?

****

"Are you certain you want to stay on?" Patrick asked his mother as they sat in her motel room after an early takeout dinner.

"No, I'm not." His mother yawned as she stretched out on the sofa in the suite he had taken for the two of them. "But then I should think you would be ready to go back too. Just demolish the damn house, get an appraisal on the property, and let that real estate guy and the bank handle the rest. We're not doing any good here, and the only good place to eat in town is probably that Italian place where we ate last night."

"You haven't dined at the Matador yet. We should have gone there for dinner or gotten something to go instead of fast food. If you want, tomorrow we could take time off and drive up to the mountains to the Tres Padres

Resort. Freeda and I drove up there, and the scenery is spectacular. Roads can be dicey, but heck, think of it as a vacation in the country. You might even enjoy the place."

"I doubt it. Bumpy roads make me car sick." She wrinkled her nose. "And we aren't here on vacation. We need to settle things as quickly as possible so we can go home. And speaking of Freeda, where was the dippy hippie today?" she asked in a derogatory tone. "After the way she was clinging to you last night I'd have thought she might show up at the house today to help us clean. I guess she isn't into hard work."

"She was not clinging, and I believe she *was* working today." He had not talked to Freeda since the previous evening, though he had called her several times and left messages each time.

"I thought she didn't have a job."

"Her cousin's family owns the local newspaper. She was going to do some editing for them."

"I didn't realize she knew anything about writing. I thought she was a photographer. Probably a bad one at that."

Patrick sighed. This was a side of his mother he had never liked. He had long ago stopped trying to please her. But he wasn't even dating Freeda. They had simply become friends. He drew a quick breath. No, friendship was not what had been on his mind for the past twenty-four hours. But he didn't want to hear about her faults either.

"She's a damn good photographer from what I've seen of her pictures. It's why she can work as a freelancer in Los Angeles. People hire her and pay her because they know they can depend on getting quality work." Perhaps he was overdoing the praise, but this was one time he didn't intend to back down on his mother's pettiness.

"Well, for as much as she was all over you last night, I'm surprised she hasn't bothered you today. Maybe she was afraid we would ask her to help us clean up the house."

"Like I said, she *was* working, and tonight she probably wanted to spend time with her dad."

"Oh, now there's another sweetheart. Damn, I can hardly wait to get back to Albuquerque."

He'd had enough of her negative attitude. "Then go ahead and go back home. I keep telling you that."

"You should invite that nice girl from last night to come visit us."

"Who? Estella? I barely know her. She was nice, but—"

"She liked you," she teased, squeezing his arm.

Patrick shook his head and turned away. He had enjoyed the other woman's company, but much as he liked talking to her, she had not appealed to him as more than a friend.

Appealed to him like whom? Freeda?

He shook off those crazy thoughts, just as he shook off his mother's idea.

"Please don't attempt to set me up with anyone here, Mom, like you do back home," he said. "I'm old enough to make my own choices. And I can handle things here on my own too. I hate to leave before the house is totally demolished and the property cleared, but you should go back tomorrow if you don't like it here."

Her head popped up as she shook her head slowly. "Do you think they'll find something when they tear it down?"

He fought to keep the exasperation at her reply out of his voice. "That isn't why I'm staying. I just want everything cleaned up. We also need to go through that safe deposit box."

"The lawyer told me he saw nothing in it but a bunch of old newspapers and a copy of the will that left you everything, which we had already seen years ago."

The will had had been written before his father disappeared but shortly after Patrick was born. Patrick had gone through it verbally with the attorney after his grandfather had been killed but he was looking forward to seeing the document now. Back then, seeing his grandfather's shaky signature and listening to the lawyer read the document had chilled Patrick. Why had there been no mention of his father or passing the property on to Patrick in case of his father's death? Had there been such virulent animosity between the two men that the old man had chosen not to provide anything to his own son? Had he totally broken his bond with Berto years ago? Why had Naldo left everything to Patrick and nothing to his son who might still be alive? Was that why Berto had never returned?

"This has been a total bust," Geneva grumbled, breaking Patrick's train of thought.

He glanced across the room at her. She lounged on the small sofa by the window staring outside. Patrick recognized that look. She was bored and anxious to be on the move.

"Whatever you decide to do tomorrow is fine with me. I think I'll take a walk."

"I'm going down to the hot tub," she said. "This has been a long day. I need to relax."

Patrick agreed with the idea of relaxing; he had been

feeling tense throughout the day. He had constantly checked his watch and his phone for messages—not that he expected to hear from Freeda. She had business to conduct with her cousin and probably her father, but still…he could hope to hear from her, couldn't he?

Walking away from the motel, he turned in the direction of Lottie Medina's house. Moments later, he turned onto her aunt's street as though that had been his destination all along. He debated what to say or what excuse to use as he turned up the walk and hopped up the steps.

Lottie Medina didn't appear surprised to see him when she opened the door, though her face was pale and worried. "Patrick, I'm so glad you're here. We can't find Fergie. He's disappeared."

Chapter Twenty-Three

"What do you mean, Fergie has disappeared?" Patrick's heart rate kicked up a notch at Lottie's words as he stepped inside the house. Freeda appeared from the living room, her face pale, her hands shaking. He reached out and caught a hand in his, squeezing it gently.

"Are you all right?" he asked.

She clutched his hand in return but did not answer his question verbally. Her eyes were red and watery. Normally the tough girl, Freeda appeared to be in pain.

"He left this morning," Lottie continued in a breathless voice. "I gave him my old phone and activated it for him. I even charged it so he could keep in touch. We both talked to him a couple of times, but now he's not answering, or replying to text messages. It has a tracker and when we checked, it looks like he wandered around for a while and then it stopped tracking."

"Maybe the battery ran out," he suggested.

Freeda shook her head violently, dropping his hand. "No, she had it fully charged for him."

Her concerned face confirmed what Patrick was already thinking, and as his gaze swung from Freeda to her aunt, he knew that both were probably having the same thoughts as his. Fergie had left town and returned to the one place he was forbidden to be—the *Tres Padres Ranch*—where cell service didn't work beyond the main area.

Lottie attempted a smile and waved at Patrick. "I'm sorry, I'm being rude. Let's not stand out here in the hall. Please, come into the living room and sit down. Have you eaten yet, Patrick? Where's your mother tonight?"

"Back at the hotel." He inhaled the warm scent of baking bread as he stepped into the living room. "We had an early dinner and she wanted to relax. She's probably in the hot tub by now."

"Then have dessert with us," Lottie said. "I've been baking all afternoon. I hope you like blueberry pie."

"Love it. With vanilla ice cream?"

"You know it!"

Patrick sat on the sofa, and Lottie held up a glass of white wine. "Can I tempt you with a drink?"

After the long day he'd been through with his mother and the house, he was ready to relax. "Yes, definitely. I'll have whatever you're drinking."

"A very nice and crisp Pinot Grigio." She filled a glass and handed it to him.

Freeda's face was pale and set as she sat back on an easy chair to his left. Patrick wanted to reach out to her and pull her across the small space to sit beside him. Instead, he held out his hand. Her face was pale, her dark eyes shiny, as though she had been crying.

"Are you all right?" he repeated.

She shook her head, but she took the proffered hand and moved to sit beside him. Her fingers were cold as she grasped his hand.

"I hate that dad is missing," she said glumly. "What if whoever hit him the other night comes after him again? What if he ends up like…"

She stopped before giving the name, but he knew the dead man, Bob, was on her mind.

He tightened his grip on her cold fingers. "You know he's not missing. We both can guess where he went. If you're so worried, next time you find him, turn on the tracking device he probably has on the phone so you can keep an eye on him."

She sighed heavily before replying. "We did that before he left. It stopped right at the edge of town like he knew we were checking on him."

Patrick stifled the urge to roll his eyes. While fearing her reaction, he couldn't hold back from expressing the truth they both knew. "That means Fergie turned it off. Cell service is iffy at the ranch, but it does exist. We saw that. Shutting down the phone is more likely, so no one knows he has gone back onto the ranch. But then again, cell service is hit or miss outside of town. Didn't we learn that ourselves the other day? It doesn't track very well at Tres Padres or on the road to Casitas."

Her hand jerked free from his, and she turned to face him fully. Tears shimmered in her eyes as they widened. "Why would he go back there, or to Casitas after what happened the other night?"

"Perhaps he feels he has unfinished business?" he questioned. "Or maybe he's trying to get back to the commune yet again. You didn't tell him about that coin, did you?"

"Of course not! I knew better than to mention the coin. I knew he would want me to take him to the spot where we found it."

"The coin? What coin are you talking about?" Lottie's gaze slid from one to the other, her eyes questioning.

Patrick grimaced as Freeda put her hand to her mouth. "Aunt Lottie, you can't tell anyone."

Lottie's eyes widened as she drew a quick breath. "You found a coin, or all of them?"

"All of them?" Freeda asked. "What do you mean?"

Her aunt shook her head and waved her hands. "I'm sorry, that's confusing. People find individual coins every so often, but I meant all the coins your grandfather was supposed to own. No one has even verified they exist."

"No, no, nothing like that," Patrick replied quickly. "We did find an old, worn coin when we were walking around in the hills on the edge of Tres Padres. That's all. I'm not certain it's even worth anything."

"Oh, no!" Freeda's head jerked up as her eyes widened. "Maybe Dad saw the pictures on my phone. I let him use it to make a call to someone last night. I didn't think of that, and he never mentioned it to me…but maybe…Oh, damn…"

"What?" Patrick asked.

"Diaz saw my pictures too. Now he may blame me if Dad goes back. He'll probably think I took him up there and dropped him off."

"When did you see D.V.?" Lottie asked, twisting toward her. "You never mentioned that."

"He came by the newspaper office when I was downloading my pictures of the old commune. He even complimented me on them and asked me to work for him. I was so excited about what I was doing at the newspaper I forgot to tell you that, Aunt Lottie."

"Work for Diaz?" A buzz of shock pierced Patrick—not only that Diaz might ask but that she had considered it.

"He wants me to take pictures of the ranch for a brochure."

"That's a great idea." Lottie smiled, clearly proud of her niece. "That's exciting, hon. What an opportunity for you. They send those brochures all over the country. I hope he's paying you well for them."

Freeda nodded, but her tears didn't stop. "That's not important if those pictures get Dad in trouble!"

"Now, don't worry. We'll find him," Lottie insisted. "Fergie's a big boy and he's gotten himself out of worse scraps than this thing with Tres Padres."

"He probably went back to the ranch." Patrick said. *Damn!* Why did Fergie have to be so stubborn? "I'll tell you what, if he doesn't show up tonight, I'll take you out to the ranch tomorrow."

"We could go—"

He held up his hand to stop what she was about to say. "It's a little late to go out there tonight, and I'll bet Diaz has put a double lock on that gate near where Fergie was living."

"Of course, let's not go tonight," she replied in a cool tone. "I wouldn't want to pull you away from any other social obligations."

Her cold attitude surprised him. "Is something else wrong?" he asked. "We pretty much wrapped up things at the house today."

Freeda simply stared down at the floor, ignoring his question.

Lottie reached over to squeeze her arm gently. "I think it's a good idea to wait until tomorrow, sweetie. You don't want to drive those roads after dark. I know we've been worried about him all day, but Fergie can take care of himself. He's been doing it a long time."

"Perhaps he went back to Casitas," Patrick added. "Do you know if any of those guys from the other day have contacted him or if he's contacted them?"

"How could they get in touch with him? He didn't have a cell phone. I don't know if he has their numbers and can call them now that he has a phone." She cast a glance at her aunt, whose face reddened.

"Maybe I made a mistake giving him a phone…" Lottie avoided her eyes, her face turning a shade of pink. "I just wanted him to be able to stay in touch with *us*."

Patrick shook his head, smiling ruefully at Lottie. "You had no way of knowing this could happen. Fergie is a grown up. He should know Freeda will be worried, and he should have used the phone to stay in touch with her."

"Don't you start on my dad," she warned, turning to her aunt. "May I borrow your car again?"

"It's still in the shop," Lottie reminded her.

"I know, but your…" she hesitated, and they all knew she meant Lottie's newer car.

Patrick put aside his drink and stood. "If he doesn't show up tonight, I'll drive you over there tomorrow. It's too late to search those back roads in the dark. I doubt you can find the right road anyway. If you want, we can drive around town and see if he's simply gone for a long walk. I just need to call my mom and let her know I'll be back late."

"By all means, get mommy's permission," Freeda retorted.

"Freeda!" Lottie turned to her niece with the look of a teacher about to correct a student. "Will you stop misbehaving? Patrick is being courteous. I'm certain Geneva appreciates having a thoughtful son."

Freeda bit her lip as she lowered her head. "I'm sorry. You're right. I'd appreciate a dad who thinks of others."

Patrick excused himself to go into the hallway to make his phone call. His mother answered immediately.

"Oh, Sonny, I was just going to call you. I'm heading out."

He glanced at his watch. "Heading out where, Mom? It'll be dark before you get to Albuquerque. I'd hate to think of you stranded on the road like Freeda was the other day."

"No, not Albuquerque," she replied with a laugh. "Did you know there's a casino just forty miles away? I met a nice woman in the hot tub, and she was going there tonight. She invited me to join her if I give her a ride over. I can go back to Albuquerque from there. It will be closer."

"You're going with a woman you met in the hot tub? Mom, you're sounding as bad as Fergie." He regretted the words as soon as they were out of his mouth, but she simply laughed.

"She's very nice, and probably ten years older than I am. I'll see you in a few days. Maybe I'll hit a jackpot or two and we won't need to worry about anything anymore. We'll give away that damn old house and let it be someone else's problem."

"Sure thing," he said, shaking his head as they said goodbye.

Fergie and his mother. What a combination of parents.

****

Freeda had moved into the dining room when he walked back from the hallway, and they took their places around the table. She gestured him to a seat across from her.

"How long has Fergie been gone?" he asked as he took his place at the table.

"He left this morning," Freeda answered. "Aunt Lottie said she fixed him breakfast and he told her he had a friend in town and he was going to meet him."

Patrick rolled his eyes. "This sounds like that last time up at the cabin when he was waiting for a friend."

"I know, but he hasn't called and he has been gone all day. We thought that maybe he was going to just see his friend and then he might come back, but…" Her eyes teared up again.

Without thinking, he reached across the table and caught Freeda's hand in his. He squeezed it gently.

"Why would he just take off for so long without saying a word or calling us to let us know where he is?" she continued. "He has to know we would be worried about him. Aunt Lottie said she was coming and going most of the day or working in her garden. She thought he had come back and was sleeping so she didn't check on him until almost four. Who knows how long he's actually been gone or where he went?"

"We know where he went," Patrick replied in a hard tone. "If he hasn't returned by tomorrow morning, we'll drive up to Tres Padres and look for him. And don't worry about me having other obligations."

She grimaced. "Unfortunately, *I* have other obligations. I promised Cere to work tomorrow. It's deadline day so I have to be at the newspaper office most of the day."

"Well, my mom and I finished most of our business dealings today. That's why she left tonight. I'll make a run up there and check, just in case."

Her head popped up, dark eyes growing wide as a

smile spread across her face. "Really? That would be great. I hate to keep borrowing Aunt Lottie's car—especially after what happened last time."

"I'll take care of it for you. Even if he doesn't want to come back with me, at least we'll know where he is."

Her smile widened, and for a second he was tempted to lean across the table, grab her, and kiss her, but he held back.

"You're a good man, Patrick Sanchez. If I'd washed my hair this morning, I'd kiss you."

"What?" The outright invitation took him by surprise, but he lowered his gaze to her lips. They were so damn tempting a shiver ran through him.

She seemed to notice his reaction and laughed. "That's some old saying, I think, but I probably have it all wrong. It goes something like I'd love to kiss you, but I just washed my hair, or I want to wash you out of my hair? I have no idea."

He drew a quick breath, hoping he wasn't making a mistake, stood, and walked around the table, stopping beside her. Taking her hand, he pulled her to her feet without any resistance. He watched the quick beat of her pulse at her neck as he leaned forward and caught her chin in his hand.

"Maybe you should kiss me anyway," he teased. He studied her lips for a couple of agonizing seconds before lowering his mouth to hers.

"Patrick…" His name came out as a breathless whisper as their lips met. Her lips were warm and full of promise as she pressed forward against him. He pulled away slightly and she laughed.

"Do you know how much I've been thinking about doing just that?" she asked.

"You have?"

"No." She laughed as he pulled back.

"You're a tease, Freeda Ferguson." His whole body tingled, and his lower regions were coming alive so he pulled back slightly so she couldn't feel the effect she was having on him. No need to rush things.

"I thought you didn't want someone easy," she retorted, but she stayed very still, almost tempting him to make the next move.

He leaned forward to touch her lips with his, teasing them with his tongue.

"Aunt Lottie is going to come in and catch us," she warned breathlessly.

"She likes me. I think she would approve."

"I doubt it. She's from the old school. Very proper."

"Well then, we better make this quick." He leaned forward and kissed her more deeply, tasting her as her lips opened under his, his hands moving over the tempting lines of her curvy body, that same body he had been studying and wanting for the past couple of days.

"Damn," she whispered, shuddering as he broke the kiss. "You're some good kisser, lawyer man."

"And that is just the beginning." He smiled down at her, his hand catching in her thick hair.

Unfortunately, across the room, the door to the kitchen opened. Lottie's eyes widened, and she put her fingers to her mouth, winked at him and backed out of the room.

Patrick took that as permission from her aunt and leaned forward to deepen the kiss, but Freeda suddenly pulled back.

"What?" he asked,

"I don't think this is a good idea." She put her hands

to his chest, holding him back as he attempted to pull her back toward him.

"Why not? Isn't this what we've both been wanting?" he asked, panting slightly. Was he the only one who had been seeing the growing attraction between them?

"I think…" she reached up and put her fingers to his lips. "I've been wanting you to kiss me, but I'm not as easy as your girlfriend from last night."

The comment caught him completely off guard. He blinked in surprise. What was she talking about? "Last night? What girl last night? I was with my mother."

Her lips pressed together firmly as she studied his face before answering. "Not according to her."

Patrick blinked and drew back from her, shaking his head in confusion. "What the hell are you talking about?"

Freeda's eyes remained huge and questioning. But was that hurt he also saw in their depths? "I called your room last night. Your mother answered…" she hesitated as though uncertain of what to say, but he suddenly knew what had happened.

"What did she tell you?" he asked through gritted teeth. "Did she say I was with someone?"

"Rafe's…"

He put his fingers to her lips to silence her and shook his head. "That's ridiculous! I went for a walk, and she damn well knew it! I'm sorry, hon."

She stared up at him, studying him, at first uncertainly, and then a slow smile spread across her lips, and she teased his lips with her fingers. "I'm not. That means she's worried about me. What have you been telling her?"

"More than I'm going to tell her from now on." He

could feel the tension lessen in her body, and he leaned down to kiss her again, enjoying the pleasure of her response, and the touch of her body against his.

"Mom's gone for the night," he whispered into her ear. "Maybe you might want to keep me company."

She jerked back and the stricken look on her face surprised him. "That won't work since Dad hasn't come back…I'd be too worried…I don't want to miss him when he returns."

Patrick didn't want to hear more. He knew what that meant. If Fergie didn't return soon, she would want to go looking for him. Patrick desired Freeda more than he'd wanted any woman in a long time, but he wasn't willing to play second string to a man who was totally unreliable and who kept hurting her. Round one had gone to his mother. Now it appeared round two would go to her father.

"Fine, we can have breakfast in the morning," he said, kissing her quickly before he changed his mind, but she shook her head as she pulled back again.

"Sorry, but I have to work tomorrow," she replied, grinning at him. "I'm employed these days, you know." Her face sobered, and she touched his chest lightly. "Besides, I'm not certain what will happen tomorrow. It all depends on Dad…"

Chapter Twenty-Four

Freeda's phone sang out its familiar ring tone, pulling her out of a restless night of sleep. She'd slept off and on, checking her father's room from time to time. He had not returned the last time she checked at four o'clock. The clock on the bedside table now read 7:05. She grabbed the phone from the table. Her cousin Cere's number flashed on the screen.

"Damn," she muttered. Cere should know better. Freeda had never been an early riser, but then another thought hit her. Cere was married to the sheriff. What if…

She tapped the phone screen to answer the call. "Cere?"

"Good morning, Freeda. I'm sorry to call so early, but I have bad news. Rafe just told me your father was picked up…"

Freeda shuddered at the news. Her dad was back in jail? Where would she get the money to bail him out this time? But then her cousin's other words filtered through her early morning foggy state.

"…badly injured. He's in the hospital in Casitas," Cere continued.

"The hospital…" Frustration morphed into a jagged blade of fear.

"Yes, apparently someone beat him up. Rafe says he was found by the side of the road just outside of town and taken to the emergency room there."

Her heart began to thud as fear swept through her. Freeda sagged into a chair. "Oh, no! How-how badly was-was he hurt?"

"Not necessarily life threatening, but he could have died if he hadn't been discovered and taken in to be treated. Rafe wanted me to call you and let you know."

"I'll get dressed and drive over as soon as possible."

What could have happened? Did the beating have anything to do with the murder of the other man, Bob? Or had Fergie stumbled into a new situation and angered the wrong person?

The questions buzzed in Freeda's brain as she pulled on her clothes, not bothering to shower. She rushed out of her room and down the stairs. The scent of frying bacon hit her as she hurried toward the kitchen. Her aunt stood at the stove, but Lottie's smile dissolved as soon as she saw Freeda's face.

"What's wrong, hon?"

"Dad is in the hospital in Casitas," Freeda blurted in a high, shaky voice. "Cere just called to tell me. I need to get over there. May I borrow your car?"

"Let me make this egg into a sandwich and I'll drive you," Lottie said calmly, touching her shoulder gently. "Did she say what happened?"

"It sounds like he was beaten up." Freeda shuddered just saying the words. "What if it was the same person who killed that man, Bob, the other night? What if the same person is after Dad now? He's been telling us someone knocked him down that night too."

"We'll let the authorities figure it out." Lottie turned off the stove, wrapped the sandwich in foil, and handed it to Freeda. "Let's go."

"You don't need to go, Aunt Lottie."

"Damn straight I do. Helen would never forgive me if anything happens to her child after I let her guy get beaten up. Besides, you're in no shape to drive. Look at how your hands are shaking. Hopefully you can at least get them steady enough to eat your breakfast on the way."

Freeda glanced down at her trembling fingers that could barely hold onto the sandwich and the bottle of apple juice her aunt had handed her. Aunt Lottie was right about her condition. She'd be lucky to get the food into her mouth, let alone make the drive to Casitas on her own.

Why had Fergie gone back to Casitas after what happened to his friend? For that matter, how had he managed to get there?

She was still pondering those questions as she munched on her sandwich, which had gone tasteless, as they began the half hour drive. "I should have been more careful," she said between bites. "Why did I let him go out alone? I knew I should have gone looking for him last night. But why would he go back to Casitas after what happened to his friend?"

"Stop blaming yourself, Freeda. He is not a child," Lottie replied shortly. "And you're not his mother. Fergie has always been the sort of person who gets into trouble easily. Sometimes he seeks it out himself, and you know that. He has always taken unnecessary chances."

Freeda could not argue with that assessment. How many times had she wired him money because he was "*in a jam*"?

"When we were in school," her aunt continued, "we

used to sneak out of the dorm, but he was always the one who got caught because he took unnecessary risks. I might speed all the time, but the first time he did it, he got pulled over for pushing his luck. Some people have bad luck because they don't know when to quit and go too far."

"My father is not a loser," Freeda argued.

Lottie glanced at her and reached out to rub her arm. "I'm sorry. No, Sweetie, he isn't. Your mother never saw him that way, and I'm glad you don't either. But you must admit he takes too many risks and bad luck just seems to follow him, or he keeps going until he finds it. Deep down, he's a sweet guy who would give you the shirt off his back or help anyone who might be in need. He doesn't deserve what's happening to him right now. You don't think it has anything to do with that man who was killed?"

Freeda shuddered. "I hope not, but that was the first thing that occurred to me and it's what frightens me the most. What if whoever killed that man also targeted Dad? They were all in that bar together, and the night ended in a fight. But why? If only Diaz would let him stay…" she stopped, shaking her head. She was stupid to expect the ranch to let him occupy its buildings for free. Besides, if someone was after her dad, what easier place to attack him and leave him for dead than an isolated location like that cabin?

"Diaz?" her aunt questioned suddenly. "What does D.V. have to do with anything?"

"He won't let Dad stay at the ranch or in one of the cabins."

"Of course not. They rent those cabins out for a pretty penny," Lottie reminded her, pursing her lips.

"They aren't going to let someone live rent free on the property simply to be kind. Maybe if Fergie worked there, he could stay in the worker cabins at the main compound."

"He would work if Diaz would give him a chance."

Lottie sighed as she shook her head. "Hon, I hate to be the one to tell you this, but our Fergie has already had that chance. Several times, in fact. He doesn't like to do the work. I haven't told you this before, but I've talked D.V. into hiring him three times—in the kitchen, cleaning up cabins, even as a night watchman. Fergie stole food, took supplies and sold them, and was found sleeping on the job several times." She shook her head sadly. "I had to give up trying to help him. I guess I should have told you that from the beginning, but you were so eager to spend time with him. I didn't want to hurt you."

Tears ran down Freeda's face, untouched. She didn't doubt her aunt's story. Sooner or later, she was going to have to recognize the bitter truth—her father had never been dependable or honest. He had always chosen the easy way out. Even the previous day he had simply left without telling her anything. Not even a goodbye.

"Hon, you have to stop living in a fantasy world," Lottie continued gently, reaching out a hand toward Freeda and rubbing the top of her hand.

"But he loves me…"

Lottie's eyes were warm and filled with concern. "Yes, he does. Never doubt that. You're the one dream he clings to, but I think it's also why he doesn't see you more often. He knows you're smart, enterprising, and successful, and he doesn't want to jinx you or hold you back."

"I could help him," she insisted.

"That's exactly the problem. It would break his heart. You are the one thing he cares about, just like he loved your mom. He would have done anything for Helen, but he couldn't. She took care of him until the end. Now he doesn't want to be a burden on you. You're all he has left of Helen."

Freeda brushed away the tears that kept coming. Her aunt handed her a tissue, and she wiped her face. "But I *want* to take care of him," she repeated.

"I'm sorry, hon, but that's the worst thing you could do. He hasn't forgotten that Helen had to take care of him even when she was dying. It would destroy him to think you might end up like her, looking out for him instead of yourself. You need to live your own life. That's the best thing you can do for him."

She smiled sadly at her aunt, but Freeda understood what she was saying. Fergie might want to take care of her, but he had never been able to do it. The only thing worse would be for him to think that *she* might be forced to look after him as her mother had done. Still, she could not desert him. He was in a bad situation at the moment, and she was determined to help him get through it.

"I'll live my life, but I'll also find out who hurt him and make certain that person goes to jail," she said. "I can do that for him."

"Be careful, sweetie. Don't put yourself in any needless danger," Lottie cautioned. "That would only make matters worse."

****

Patrick's call to Freeda to say good morning went directly to voice mail to his surprise. Had he been right not to press for more the previous night? Should he have pushed to take their relationship to the next level? He was ready—he had been thinking of her all night. He shouldn't be surprised she didn't answer. Freeda would make any decisions about their relationship on her own time.

At least he knew where she was if he wanted to see her. She would be working at the newspaper office. He would find an excuse to stop by after breakfast. Damn, he needed to stop thinking about her constantly. Turning his car in the direction of the Matador restaurant where he had eaten previously, he resolved to put her out of his mind. As usual, the gravel parking lot outside was nearly full. He pulled into a spot near the door, grabbed a newspaper from a rack, and walked inside. The warm scent of green chili and coffee wafted through the air and the small dining room hummed with activity. Most of the tables were filled so he turned to the counter, not surprised to see Diaz already occupying a stool. Patrick stopped at the vacant seat next to him.

"Good morning, is this taken?"

Diaz waved at it. "All yours, brother. Where's your ditzy companion this morning?"

Patrick's lips tightened in irritation. Why did the man have to continue to denigrate Freeda like that? "Probably working with her cousin again. I understand you don't consider her too ditzy to work for you."

Diaz winked at him with his good eye. "*Touché.* Yeah, I know she's not ditzy. Just like to keep her on her toes. Have you seen the pictures she takes? Pretty damn good."

"I saw what she did when we were out at the ranch the other day."

"She has talent. Like her mother."

"You knew her mother?" Patrick turned to Diaz in surprise. Freeda had never mentioned that. His understanding was that the woman had died years ago. Hadn't someone said Diaz came to Tres Padres only several years earlier?

The older man blinked rapidly as though he realized he'd made a mistake, and Patrick drew a quick breath. He'd watched enough witnesses on the stand who did the exact same thing when they realized they had said too much. Diaz was either lying or had divulged something he hadn't meant to say.

"May have," Diaz said in the enigmatic tone he normally used on Freeda.

Patrick nearly replied with a quick retort, but the waitress interrupted their conversation to take their orders. As soon as she moved away, Patrick turned back to Diaz, wanting answers.

"I've been thinking. According to Freeda's aunt, her mother lived at the old commune years ago. Was that where you met her mother?"

The older man's gaze swung down, focusing on his coffee cup of coffee as though he might be looking for an answer in the white porcelain surface. For a few minutes he remained silent, then he lifted his gaze to the wall behind the counter and shook his head.

"Never was into communes. Rich kids or dropouts who could take time off. As for hiring Freeda, like I said, I chose her because she has talent. I doubt she even realizes it."

His quick change of subject didn't go unnoticed, but Patrick didn't press him. Was there a reason Diaz didn't want to discuss the commune? It didn't matter. Patrick was more interested in what the man had finally noticed about Freeda. "Have you told her that you can see her talent?"

"I gave her a job," Diaz replied bluntly.

Not for the first time, Patrick could understand Freeda's frustration with the man. Diaz' flippancy was beginning to irritate him too. "What is it with you?"

Diaz' head jerked around to Patrick. "What do you mean?"

"Do you ever just answer a question without some sort of secondary meaning behind it?"

"Sometimes." Diaz' lips twisted into a wry smile. "If it's the right question."

The man was playing semantic games, but before Patrick could reply, Diaz asked for the sugar that was within Patrick's reach. He handed the glass dispenser to Diaz, trying to decide what might be the right question to ask. He watched Diaz as the man slowly stirred sugar into his coffee, tapping the spoon on the rim of the cup as though demanding attention.

"Not to change the subject, but how are things going at your grandfather's house?" Diaz asked.

"Very slow," Patrick admitted. "I haven't gone through the furniture that was put into storage yet. I'll do that today before I head home."

"Find any gold coins so far?" he asked, smirking.

Patrick flinched and turned away. "Don't start with the coins. Even the bankers asked about them yesterday when I went through his safe-deposit box."

Diaz laughed in his raspy way, but Patrick noted a sudden stillness in the man's demeanor. He had caught the older man by surprise.

"Naldo had a safe-deposit box?" Diaz asked, turning to him. "What the hell did he have to keep in it?"

"Not any coins, in case you're interested, and you have my permission to spread that around town. I'm tempted to take out an ad in the paper. Actually, all the box had inside it was some old newspapers."

"Newspapers?"

"From years ago." Patrick shrugged as he stirred sugar into his coffee, pretending disinterest, but the man's demeanor was one of growing tension. His foot had begun to tap on the footrest below the counter and his fingers had tightened their grip on his cup.

Why?

Patrick kept his voice steady as he replied. "They're meaningless as far as I can tell. I don't know why he would keep them, let alone have them in a safe-deposit box. I don't think he read them. They were so old he might have forgotten they were in there."

"Probably," Diaz said. "His memory had been slipping for years."

"He seemed to have a thing for old newspapers and magazines. He had plenty of them stacked in the garage."

"Makes sense. Insulation. Lot of old timers used newspapers and magazines to paper the walls or stack them as insulation. Speaking of the garage, have you dug around back there yet?"

"Should I?" He again watched Diaz out of the corner of his eye. The man had taken to tapping his good foot on the lower rung of the step below the counter. Was he nervous? For the first time since Patrick had met the enigmatic foreman, he could sense a strange vibration coming from him. Diaz normally seemed so calm, but now he appeared to be on edge. But even as Patrick inwardly debated the reason, the foreman flipped back to his normal mocking demeanor.

"Yep. Who knows what treasure could be hidden in the garage behind those papers on the wall?" he retorted. "Did you read any of those old crime stories? They can be pretty hilarious."

"Actually, there aren't many left on the wall in the garage. I think people tore most of them down to check what was behind them, which was nothing. It backs up directly against a hill. In fact, in places, he put adobe walls right up against the rocks of the hill behind it and then pasted on the newspapers."

"Sandstone rocks as foundation, newspapers as wallpaper," Diaz said coolly. "You gotta love that old man. He was definitely resourceful."

Their breakfast plates arrived, and as they dug into their eggs, Patrick again turned to Diaz. "You keep giving me advice about him, and I appreciate that. Everyone in town seemed to know my grandfather, but no one seemed to know him very well even though he lived here all his life. It strikes me as strange."

"Not really. Lots of folks in town saw him all the time, but he kept to himself."

Patrick studied Diaz for a moment as he recalled another fact he'd been told. "Someone said that you moved here not long before my grandfather was killed. How well did *you* know him?"

A slight tic in his lip alerted Patrick that he again had succeeded in making the man uneasy. Rather than confront Diaz, Patrick drew a quick breath and tried to make light of the situation. "Come on, what's your real story, Mr. Diego Diaz? What are you hiding?"

"Hiding?" The tic appeared again, and Diaz dropped his fork and drew up straight. He faced forward stiffly, contemplating the wall behind the counter for a couple of minutes before turning toward Patrick with a sly grin as he picked up his fork. "Now you sound just like your grandfather. Naldo always told me, 'Kid be honest, you can't hide from yourself.' Well that, plus other things. Why are *you* asking, Mr. Sanchez? Do you think I have something to hide?"

Patrick was beginning to understand why Diego Diaz could irritate Freeda. Just the intense scrutiny from his one dark green eye could be chilling, but Patrick wasn't going to back down. Refusing to fall victim to the strange man's quiet intimidation, Patrick kept his voice calm but challenging, staring back directly at Diaz. This was no time to be timid. "Don't we all have things we want to hide?"

Chapter Twenty-Five

To Patrick's delighted surprise, Diaz had no response to the blunt, direct question, simply staring back at Patrick with his hard watchful gaze, before suddenly chuckling. He broke off eye contact first, looking away, obviously not wanting to reply. Diaz took a bite of his eggs and chewed slowly, as though considering the question.

Finally, he turned back to Patrick. "Tell you what, Mr. Sanchez, if I ever decide to confess my deep, dark secrets, you'll be the second person I inform. Naldo would like that."

Patrick chose to ignore the reference to his grandfather. "Inform?" he repeated. On a hunch he leaned forward and asked the question he wanted answered. "Who will be the first?"

Diaz emitted a hoarse laugh and winked at him again with his good eye. "You are a sharp fella, Patrick Sanchez. Quick and smart. Your grandaddy would be very proud of you right now. I can almost feel him looking down on us and laughing at *me.*" He tapped his chest. "Are you certain you aren't actually that old *Viejo Reynaldo* reincarnated to force me to finally become an honest man?"

Become an honest man? Now what the hell did that mean?

They stared at each other for several seconds, like

two battling warriors, except their weapons were words. Patrick tried to decipher the meaning of what Diaz was saying, but in the end he decided there were more important issues to resolve at the moment other than figure out the enigma of Diego Diaz. Patrick waved his hand as though clearing away the subject.

"Enough of that. I do have one question about this whole situation with my grandfather, though I doubt you would be able to answer it."

Diaz grew still, his coffee mug halfway to his lips. "What?"

"Like I said, the safe-deposit box had no coins, just a bunch of newspaper clippings."

His head slowly swiveled back toward Patrick. "Yeah, so? Did you toss them?" he asked, lowering the mug to the counter.

"No. I asked the bank to give me an envelope so I could save them to read later. They appeared to be old crime stories from a newspaper or magazines. At first, I thought they might be about my dad, but they aren't. Because of that bunch of old crime magazines at the house, I figured perhaps he was into that sort of thing, like you said, or maybe enjoyed looking at the pictures. But that got me to thinking even more. My grandfather could barely read."

"Who told you that he didn't read?" Diaz asked, his brow furrowing.

"My mother told me years ago, and I'd forgotten it until Tony Gennaro mentioned it the other night at dinner. Why would he subscribe to all those magazines or save them if he couldn't read them?"

"Are you certain *he* subscribed to them?" Diaz asked. "Maybe he picked them up around town or someone gave them to him. He collected a lot of things that people threw out. In the old days he would sell them in the pawn shop."

"No, no, they went directly to him. I saw labels. They were addressed to him. He even still had the old subscription bills. He was a very neat, fastidious bookkeeper."

"You said he didn't read, but he kept financial records?"

"He couldn't read or write well, but he could add and subtract. He actually kept little notebooks detailing monthly records to pay his bills. Someone sent them to my mom when they cleared out his desk before it was sold. I'd forgotten about them until I recognized his handwriting on notes I found around the house. He was good at math and quite thorough. He couldn't spell very well, but he could add and subtract."

"Maybe he was better at reading than you realized," Diaz said. "There appears to be a lot you didn't know about your grandfather."

"And just how well did *you* know him?" Patrick shot back.

The harsh laugh that erupted from Diaz came as no surprise, but he evaded a direct reply. "Perhaps he liked to look at the pictures, or maybe there were naked ladies on the other side? Did you think of that? Maybe he didn't even intend to read them at all. He could have wanted to use them for wallpaper. Your grandfather saved a lot of things. You need to stop analyzing things so damn much. He was a simple old man."

Patrick turned away, considering what he was saying. His grandfather had papered the walls with old newspapers and magazines. But that brought up even more questions. How had Diaz come to know so much about him in the short time he had worked at Tres Padres? In some ways, his knowledge appeared more comprehensive than many of the others Patrick had met in town—people who had known him most of their lives. Could Diaz actually be a treasure hunter who cultivated his grandfather's favor while hiding his own selfish motives behind those damn dark glasses?

****

Diego Diaz was still on Patrick's mind when he slid into his car in the diner parking lot. Damn, that man was frustrating. But thinking of Diaz also reminded him of Freeda. Patrick checked his watch. Was it too early to call her? Would he be interrupting her work if he called? Perhaps she was available for lunch. Damn, he had to admit he suddenly wanted—no—*needed*, to hear her voice.

"You're getting too damn involved with that woman!" he said aloud, shaking his head. But was it such a bad thing? They enjoyed each other's company. Why not continue their flirtatious relationship? Why not share a few kisses or even a night or a few nights together? She didn't appear ready to settle down any more than he was.

Without further mental debate, he tapped in her number before starting his car. She sounded shaky as she answered, "Oh, Patrick, I am so glad you called. Dad was attacked in Casitas last night. He was beaten up. It sounds bad. He's in the hospital so Aunt Lottie and I are on the way to see him. We just pulled into the parking lot. I'll have to call you back later."

Freeda's voice sliced through Patrick like a long, sharp sword as her number disappeared from the phone screen. He sat for a few minutes considering what she had said.

Her father had been attacked in Casitas?

Damn! Patrick's chores in Rio Rojo suddenly no longer mattered. He needed to be in Casitas; he needed to get to Freeda. Patrick tapped in a message to her that he was on his way.

Backing out of the parking spot with his wheels spinning, he had to remind himself to calm down. The powerful car was ready to go as fast as he wanted, but he had no desire to end up in an accident that might hurt someone. Patrick forced himself to sit in the lot for a couple of minutes, thinking matters through before guiding the car onto the street and turning onto the highway that would take him out of town.

Why had Fergie gone back to Casitas after what had happened to him and his friend? How had he even gotten there? Had someone picked him up in Rio Rojo and taken him there only to beat him up later? But why would anyone attack him?

So many questions, and Patrick had no answers.

As he drove past the turnoff to Tres Padres, Patrick thought back on his breakfast conversation with Diaz. Had the strange man known about what had happened to Fergie as he sat answering Patrick with short, noninformative replies? He'd only asked about Freeda once, and he hadn't brought up her father at all. Was that because Diaz knew he didn't have to worry about Fergie trying to go back to the ranch?

Normally Diaz issued threats or made unpleasant remarks about Fergie. Why hadn't he given Patrick any warnings to pass on to Fergie? For some reason, Diaz had only been interested in what Patrick had been doing at the house and discussing his grandfather. Yet even those questions struck Patrick as unusual. Just how well had the man known his grandfather? Or had those questions been aimed at getting information about what Patrick had found at the house?

He forced himself to push aside his thoughts about Diaz as well as his concerns about Fergie, keeping the car at a steady pace as he drove. He wanted to call Freeda back and get the details on her father's attack, but it would be better to concentrate on his driving. Instead, he turned to a jazz station on the radio to calm his nerves.

But thoughts of Freeda and Fergie also brought him to memories of his visit with her to Tres Padres, and the discovery of the coin he and Freeda had found. Was that what had happened to his grandfather? Was that what the lonely man had been doing all those years when he walked the prairie—looking for coins? The old man claimed walking in the woods helped to clear his mind.

That was one lesson Patrick had always carried with him. Even now he would sometimes long to get away from the city and he would drive a few miles outside of Albuquerque simply to walk and think. He had not mentioned it to Freeda, but that was another thing he had missed those years when he had been back east—not simply the wide-open spaces—but the ability to get away from everything and everyone so easily. Sailing on the ocean could give him that sensation, but he'd never been able to endure the constant movement of the boat for long.

Thoughts of solitary walking also brought back thoughts again of his grandfather's eager face as he held up a coin for Patrick's inspection.

"The Spanish brought them."

The words reverberated in Patrick's head as they

had the day he'd made this drive previously. Now he knew the stories of finding coins in the prairie were true. How many others were still out there? Now he could understand why searching for them could become addictive to someone like Fergie who appeared to favor get rich quick solutions.

Had Fergie found any coins or treasures during his years of searching? Had he found anything recently? Could that be what had caused the attack? No, Patrick knew he and Freeda would have heard about it. Fergie was not the type to keep secrets. Even at the dinner at *Gennaro's*, Fergie had bragged about searching the prairies with his buddies. He had also listened eagerly to Tony talk about his searches around the area with a metal detector and his own lack of luck. To Patrick, the stories had sounded similar to those his grandfather had told him.

"Every so often you find something," Tony had told them, his voice quickening, eyes growing shiny, just as Patrick's grandfather's once had when he related his stories. "I remember the kids who lived in the commune used to brag about having a secret map that might lead to a cache of gold or Spanish coins. Crazy talk. I went with them a few times on searches, but it always ended with folks drunk or lost, and the next day we'd have to go out from town and find them before they died of exposure or dehydration."

"Didn't you ever look on your own?" Lottie asked him in a teasing voice.

"A couple of times," Tony had admitted, frowning. "It was a damn waste of energy, but back when I was young, it seemed like a great idea. Every time we went out searching, it was going to be the day we came home rich and moved to New York. All we ended up with was cactus needles in our socks."

"I remember Rosalie found some old coins once," Lottie said. "Just before she took off."

"Rosalie?" Fergie had swiveled to Lottie. "Who is she? Is she still around?"

"She was an old friend of ours from high school," Lottie had replied with a sigh. "She simply left town one day and never came back. I always hoped that meant those coins she found were valuable so she was able to use them to do whatever she wanted." Lottie continued in a suddenly sad tone. "We used to think perhaps she wasn't honest about how many coins she found. She was always talking about leaving and making it on her own. Remember, Tony? Didn't you used to date her?"

His angular face had grown stiff, his dark eyes thoughtful. "For a while, but she changed after that mess out at the Palladium…when that kid got killed. Someone said they saw her out at the commune. I never saw her after we graduated. Even her parents moved away."

"Kid?" Freeda questioned.

"She had a big crush on Marco Gonzales, the boy who died at the Palladium," Lottie explained, her facial muscles tightening, and her cheeks growing pale as her gaze lowered to the floor. "I also remember that."

"Yeah, but she was being stupid." Tony had blown out a harsh breath as he rolled his eyes. "Most of the girls in school had a crush on that young punk, and he treated them all like crap. But that's another dead subject."

The insensitive comment about the dead teen who might have committed suicide drew a silence from the others around the table, and Tony had appeared to realize his error in judgment. He had tapped both his hands on the table.

"Enough of this talk about the past. Let's talk about the future. I want to hear about Tres Padres and what they're doing out there these days. Freeda, Fergie, you have both been on the ranch lately. What's happening with the property? Sounds like they're turning it into an upscale tourist trap."

For the few seconds of silence after Tony's remark, Patrick had feared that Freeda might try to shift the conversation to the coin they had found, but instead she had turned everyone's attention to the pictures she had taken of the ranch.

"Mr. Diaz gave me permission to do a write up on it and he's going to pay me to take more pictures. He even said I can interview some of the guests if they're willing to talk to me."

"We're going to publish it as a feature," Cere had added from across the table. "Freeda writes wonderful personal stories. Tell them about that story you wrote on the artist colony near Abiquiu."

Patrick had expected Fergie to pay close attention to what Freeda said about her pictures and Cere's endorsement of how good her stories were, but instead her father appeared to grow bored quickly. The whole time she was speaking, he had sensed Fergie's restlessness.

Now the man had been injured, and she was off again to care for him. While Patrick admired Freeda's loyalty and concern, he also wondered if she could ever give that sort of devotion to any other man besides Fergie.

As though she knew Patrick was thinking of her, his phone buzzed and Freeda's phone number popped onto the screen. He tapped the phone to answer, and her shaky voice came on the line.

"How's Fergie?" he asked.

"On his way into surgery." She paused. "Oh, Patrick, you should see him. He was really beaten up. He seemed so small and helpless in that hospital gown. I just wanted to hug him."

"What the hell happened?"

"He doesn't really remember. I bet Diaz—"

Patrick cut her off. He knew what she was going to say. "Let's face it, there is no way Diaz could beat up Fergie on his best day. Fergie is taller and Diaz can barely use his bad hand."

"Well, all right, maybe not beat him up directly, but he could hire a couple of thugs to do it. You know he probably would do that without a blink of his good eye."

"There might have been more than one person?"

"Fergie thinks so, but he didn't see the attackers. He just knew the guys were big and they kept pounding him with a board."

Patrick shuddered at her words. "A board?"

"It was like they wanted to kill him, he says, and they might have succeeded if a car hadn't come around the corner and frightened them away. And to think we haven't really been believing him when he said someone hit him the night his friend was killed."

"He also admitted he was drunk that night and fell down."

"I bet Diaz is behind this," she said, ignoring Patrick's comment. "Even if he didn't do it himself. I just know it. No one will ever convince me differently."

He drew in a quick breath, hoping to calm her. "All right, I understand, and we'll talk about it when I get there. I'm only three miles away. I'll see you in a few minutes."

He tapped off the phone, her words echoing in his mind. Could Diaz have been behind the attack? Could the man have coolly ordered an attack on Fergie and then so easily talked with Patrick about Freeda that morning?

Patrick recalled what Diaz had said at their breakfast together about coming clean about his past and Patrick's grandfather's personal cautions to the mysterious man. Diaz had noted the old man's desire for Diaz to be honest. What had his grandfather known about Diaz? For that matter, why and how had they met in the past?

Who was Diaz exactly? He wasn't a native of Rio Rojo. Had the ranch done any sort of background check on him?

Perhaps the time had come for Patrick to make some inquiries about Diego Diaz himself.

Exactly who was the man?

Chapter Twenty-Six

A chill ran through Freeda's body as she entered the hospital room and glimpsed her father stretched out in the bed. His eyes were closed and while his breathing was steady, she knew the air came from the tubes that snaked into his nostrils. His body appeared so skinny and pale in the thin pale blue gown, his face gaunt, his hair a tumbled mess. Bluish bruises dotted his upper arms, while bandages crisscrossed both forearms and the side of his face.

Freeda grasped his limp hand, wishing she could hug him, but fearful she might dislodge the equipment that helped him breathe and monitored his heart. His thin hand was cold and lifeless.

"Dad, Dad, I'm here. Your little girl is here for you," she whispered, leaning close to him. With a sigh, she asked the question she had been asking herself repeatedly on the drive to Casitas, even though he could not answer. "Why do you have to be so stubborn? Why did you have to come back here when you knew it might be dangerous?" She felt as chilled as the cold hand she held.

Her aunt came up beside her and put her hand on Freeda's shoulder squeezing it gently. "He'll be okay, baby," she whispered, relinquishing her grip on Freeda to reach over to touch his bare bony arm.

"We're here, Fergie."

To Freeda she whispered. "We'll help him get well, hon. He'll be all right."

"I won't leave you, Dad," Freeda said in a loud voice, hoping that somewhere in his semi-conscious mind her father would hear her and recognize her presence. "We won't let whoever did this get away with it either."

The still figure gave no response, and after a few minutes the nurse came in to check on him. Freeda and her aunt sat in the room, silently watching and waiting. Lottie took out her phone and proceeded to play a game on it, but Freeda was too rattled to try even the most simple diversion. Only when she spied Patrick's car through the window turning into the parking lot did Freeda get to her feet.

"Patrick's here," she told her aunt. "I just saw his car enter the parking lot. I'll go meet him and be right back."

Rushing out the door, Freeda hurried to greet Patrick as he walked up the sidewalk toward the hospital. She wanted to throw herself against his lean, hard body and beg him to simply hold her, but she held back, fearing that might lead to a total emotional breakdown.

"What the hell happened?" he asked, his lean face troubled. He grasped her cold hands and squeezed them gently. Just that steady touch calmed her.

"He hasn't been coherent enough to say anything," Freeda said, her voice breaking. "He looks so little and bony in that bed, and he's all bandaged up."

"Well, maybe that will keep him out of trouble," he replied wryly.

After the emotion-filled time she had spent in the hospital room, a sharp sliver of anger sliced through her. Freeda jerked her hands from his, clenching them into fists.

"What they did to him was nothing to laugh about, Patrick Sanchez, and if you've come to lecture me or badmouth him, you can go right back to Rio Rojo or Albuquerque or go to hell, for that matter."

His face sobered, and he reached out a hand toward her again. "Freeda, I am sorry. That was in bad taste." He drew in a quick breath and when he spoke again, it was with a contrite tone. "How are you doing? Are you all right?"

"No," she admitted, and at that point, the dam holding back her emotions gave way. Tears came quickly, though when he reached out toward her, Freeda pulled back, still hurt by his initial attitude. She had been looking forward to his arrival and now, well, now she didn't know how to feel or how to react.

"It's that serious?" he asked.

She nodded, too choked up to reply.

"I'm sorry for being a jerk. I wasn't thinking…"

He reached out again, but this time he put his hand on her shoulder, squeezing it gently, and Freeda could not stop from responding. She craved the comfort of his touch, and she moved toward him, letting his arms wrap around her, holding her against his warm body.

"He looks so small," she moaned, her cheek against his shoulder. "He has scratches on his face and bruises on both arms…Who the hell would do something like that to a defenseless old man?" She collapsed against him, sobbing. He simply held her, rubbing her back gently, letting her sob, until she was spent and pulled away from him.

"I'm okay," she mumbled, but he took her hand and led her to a bench in the shade just outside the building.

"It will be fine," he said gently, keeping hold of her hand. "He will heal. I'm more worried about you." His dark eyes were warm as his other hand pushed back her hair from her wet face. "Are you holding up okay?"

"No, I'm a damn wreck," she admitted, attempting a weak smile, but it quickly dissolved into fresh tears. "More broken than Aunt Lottie's damn car."

He chuckled at her reference. "But you're still keeping that Freeda sense of humor. That's a point in your favor." He pulled out a handkerchief from his pocket and wiped her damp face before handing it to her. "You look fine...ready for action. Maybe not strong enough to battle Diaz, but ready for just about anything else..."

The name made her shiver, and she muttered, "Diaz! I know this is all his fault. Maybe he didn't personally hurt Dad, but he caused it."

"Did Fergie say that?" Patrick asked, his voice registering surprise. His face dipped into her line of vision. "He said that Diaz had someone attack him?"

"He's not able to say anything yet, but when I asked him if Diaz did it, he did sort of nod...like he heard me."

"Freeda..." he cautioned.

Freeda didn't want to argue, but she knew the man had caused her dad's predicament. "Well, even if Diaz didn't directly order it, you'll never convince me he had nothing to do with this. Why can't he let Dad stay in that cabin? I don't believe Dad would steal things or ignore work he was given."

"Who said that?"

"Aunt Lottie, but she's not a good judge of character herself. Look at how she's always talking to Diaz, practically flirting with him. She's getting all her information from that jerk, and he never has a good word to say about Dad." Her gaze swung toward the hospital, as her lips pressed into a straight line.

"Hon, I understand your loyalty to her father, but this whole situation may be more dangerous than we realized. First, your dad's friend is killed, and now this?"

"Tell me about it!" she cried. "You should see what they did to him…"

Patrick waved his hands to cut her off. "That's not exactly what I mean. Yes, he is in danger, but some of that he caused himself."

"What? How can you say that?"

"How can you not see that Fergie brings some of this drama on himself? He came back here after seeing what happened to his friend. Not only that, but he is willing to use people around him, even you. He obviously has done it with Lottie if she's becoming fed up with him."

"No! She's fed up because she's been listening to Diaz, and believing his complaints against Dad," she argued. "She said Diaz told her Dad wouldn't work, and that he had been stealing things from the ranch. She's getting her information from the wrong man."

Patrick's face turned grim. "Freeda, she's right. We saw it that day at the cabin. He's living in their housing for free, burning the wood stacked up outside, and I'll bet using the supplies that were put there for the workers. He didn't seem concerned about leaving anything behind, so you know all the furnishings didn't belong to him…" Patrick stopped as fresh tears edged out of her eyes.

She wanted to reach up and cover his mouth to stop his words, to silence his accusations against Fergie. But deep down she knew Patrick was right—her aunt too.

Freeda buried her face against his shoulder as he wrapped his arms around her and held her close to him. She didn't like showing Patrick her weakness, but the feelings that had been bottled up inside her demanded an exit, and currently, he provided the closest solution. Leaning into his arms, she let her emotions burst to the surface.

****

"How did your mom and dad meet?" Freeda asked hours later as she and Patrick sat at a table in the hospital lunchroom sipping coffee and eating tasteless sandwiches—not that anything might taste good at the moment. Her aunt had remained in the room with Fergie.

The emotional turmoil of the situation had gripped Patrick almost as much as it had appeared to grip Freeda. He could see the pain that enveloped her, and the breakdown outside the hospital earlier had cut him deeply. While he feared for Fergie, his main concern was what the situation was doing to Freeda. She had demonstrated how strong she could be, and she had to have been bothered to give in so completely to emotion as they sat outside the hospital. He had held her until she regained her composure. Only then did she pull away from him.

Taking few deep breaths, she became as cool as usual. After taking him inside, they had stayed with Fergie until Lottie ordered them to take a break.

. Now, even with emotional turmoil swirling around them, he was surprised by her sudden personal question about his parents.

"What?" he asked. "That's what's on your mind right now?" He lowered his cardboard coffee cup and glanced across the table at her. As usual, Freeda was totally unpredictable. With so much chaos swirling around them, how his parents met was what she had on her mind?

"I'm curious," she said softly, hazel eyes imploring, not backing away from the question.

"What does that have to do with what's happening right now?" he asked and immediately regretted the abrupt reply given the sudden tightening of her lips and the immediate pallor that crossed her face.

"I really appreciate what you're doing for me, Patrick. You know my dad's a flake, and I'll be even more in debt to you when this is all over, but after meeting your mother, I'm curious about *your* parents." She paused, studying him. "You're not at all like your mother so you must be like your father. I've been thinking about it ever since I met Geneva. She seems so steady, I don't know, so together. And you talked about how hard she worked. It sounds like she really has her life together."

Patrick turned slightly, avoiding her eyes. He was beginning to think she knew exactly how to needle him. Since her earlier outburst in the parking lot, she had been on edge, acting as though her emotional breakdown had not occurred. But it had, and he could not forget the pain that had surged through his own body and psyche as he held her close to him, letting her sob until she was spent. That had been several hours ago, and she had been fighting back against her show of weakness ever since.

Now, he couldn't keep the hard tone out of his voice as he replied to her blunt personal question. "Do I need to remind you that my father was a petty thief who spent a good portion of his adult life in jail?"

"I guess I hadn't thought about it that much.

Everyone talks about how kind your grandfather was, what a good man he was." She studied him for several silent minutes until Patrick began to feel uncomfortable.

"Something wrong?" he finally asked, fighting to keep the irritation out of his voice.

"No, just thinking about how crazy this world is. You're not at all like your dad, Patrick, just like I'm not like Fergie," she noted softly. "Well, maybe a little. Dad and I always seem to get caught up in these crazy predicaments."

"Fergie causes his own trouble," he replied in a cold, blunt tone. He regretted his harsh reply immediately, but as usual, Freeda surprised him.

"That's what I'm learning the more I'm around him." She sighed softly as she shook her head, and her body shuddered. "I always thought his life on the road must be carefree, fun, and filled with adventures. Who wouldn't want to escape societal necessities whenever one wants? But now, what I also realize is that while I might be a little like him in getting into strange, unusual predicaments, deep down, I don't want to need or to rely on the kindness of others. I don't like needing someone else to get me out of tricky situations. Aunt Lottie has been letting me use her car. You've been driving me around. My grandmother helps finance me when I hit low spots. That's not right..." she paused, sighing. "I need to say *enough is enough* and stand on my own, or I'm going to end up like Fergie, always depending on someone else for handouts. I can't live like that anymore. Except I don't know..." she stopped, sighing heavily.

The raw pain in her voice sliced through him. Patrick wanted to reach across the table and take her hand and squeeze it, to show her that he understood her turmoil. He knew what it was like to have to live down a father's reputation and then to fight to succeed on his own. His father had been missing Patrick's entire life and had been known as a petty thief who had done time in jail; hell, perhaps he had even killed someone. Fortunately, the people he worked around every day did not know that. But *he* did. And that knowledge always seemed to rear its ugly head at the most inopportune moments. On the other hand, the people in Rio Rojo knew about his father, but those Patrick had met appeared to equate him more with his grandfather—the kindly man who was there for everyone.

"You're not like Fergie, Freeda, just like I'm not like my father or mother. I could see the difference in you the other day when you were taking pictures. Fergie doesn't like to work, and he uses the people around him. You are talented and devoted to what you want to do. You took time to set up your shots the carefully and now you keep volunteering to help Lottie. Heck, you're ready to work hard on your own to see that you get what you want. Your biggest problem is that you don't know when to quit. That's why you sometimes end up out on a limb. Even Diaz sees your drive and ability."

"Diaz?" She wrinkled her nose and shook her head. "He'll never give me credit for anything."

Patrick smiled at her warmly. "You're wrong about that. He gave you credit for your talent when we talked this morning. Plus, he gave you a job. Diaz strikes me as the sort of man who does not do favors or gamble on people. Why would he take a chance on you if he didn't think you could do the work?"

"Oh, all right," she replied, rolling her eyes. "That much is true. When did you see Diaz this morning? Did you go out to the ranch?"

"We ran into each other at breakfast, but I'm beginning to understand why you find him so damn frustrating. He's curious about what I'm doing at my grandfather's place—more than he lets on. It wouldn't surprise me if he was one of those people digging around the house."

"Really?" Her eyes widened. "What makes you think that?"

"Well, he knew all about the old newspapers Gramps used as wallpaper in the garage. He even knew what was behind the wall. Supposedly he helped clean out the place originally, but to know what's behind a wall?"

"What is behind it?"

"A thin layer of adobe followed by solid rock. Tell that to your father. Anyway, it didn't hit me until this morning, but I realized that no one in town appears to be friends with him. Why was my grandfather the only person he got to know very well? Or did Gramps even know him? One minute Diaz talks about him like they might even be friends, but he also keeps asking questions about what *I* know about Gramps. This morning he even asked what was in the old man's safe-deposit box. Now why would that be any of his damn business?"

"Treasure hunter alert!" she announced, waving a finger and smiling for the first time since he had arrived. "I've been warning you not to trust him."

"I know. I know," he admitted with a sad sigh, shaking his head. "It looks as though you might have been right all along. How did he know about my grandfather having my picture on the mantle and who I was? I didn't think about it when he told me the other day. I thought they must be friends, but when I talked to Mom yesterday, she never heard of him until he volunteered to help clean out the house. Most everyone else I've talked to since I arrived has told me he came to town a couple of years ago, and the two never had much contact before my grandfather was killed. How could he have known Gramps so well if he came to town just before Gramps was killed? The old man didn't travel."

"That's all very weird, but not surprising. That whole town is strange, and everyone seems interconnected. You remember Estella? Well, of course you do." She batted her eyes playfully at him. "Her mother spent time at the commune just like my mom and dad."

"I think a lot of people did. I think even my dad went out there."

"Not many natives did, according to Estella. She said her mother was ostracized after she went. And it was even worse because she got pregnant, so she had to come back home. Or maybe she got pregnant, so she went out there. I forget."

"Sounds like you made a friend," he teased.

"Nope." Freeda shook her head vigorously. "I don't think so. Yesterday she liked most of my pictures, and the job I was doing, but she threw a fit this morning when I said I had to come to Casitas today because my dad was in the hospital. And it was worse when I told her that you were coming over too. Of course, that reaction might not be work related, *Patrick.*" She spoke his name breathlessly. "That's how she always says you name. *Paaatrick?*" Freeda burst into a fit of giggles.

He was in no mood for teasing, his jaw tightening. "Let it go."

"Of course." She spoke again in her playfully breathless tone before turning serious. "Say, when the two of you were flirting…oops, I mean talking the other night, did she tell you her mom might have helped your dad when he left town?"

His head jerked to her. "What? No, she never said anything about that."

"I meant to tell you last night, but we got sidetracked…" She shivered, her eyes avoiding his, before turning back to him. "When she told me about her mother going out to live at the commune for a while, she also mentioned that her mother took your dad and one of her friends out there. Apparently, her mother and your dad were *very* good friends back then. If you really think things through, she could even be your sister."

A jolt ran through him, but Patrick shook his head. "Now you're being silly. My mother has never mentioned anything about Dad living in a commune. He moved around all the time, but a commune? That doesn't sound right, even when he was young."

"Maybe she doesn't even know. But go through the steps logically, Mr. Realist. These local families have all lived around here forever. They grew up together. They slept together. They married each other."

"What does that have to do with her mother?"

"Well, that was the only thing that changed for a while. It brought in all these young people from around the country. You said your dad liked to travel. Wouldn't it make sense he would fall in with these kids from around the country, or go off with some of them and never come back? My mom came out here from California. Fergie came from the East. When they met in school in California, the commune in New Mexico was what they had in common."

He considered what she was saying, but he still didn't believe the commune had anything to do with his family. "Perhaps it affected your parents, but Gramps lived here all his life. My dad was raised here, though I can understand his being interested in kids from other parts of the country."

"See? I've heard that same thing from lots of people. Everyone knows someone who knew someone who stayed at the commune for a while, or folks who live around here now because they came to the commune and stayed in Rio Rojo or Casitas to make a new life. You lawyers all love to talk, but you don't listen to people unless it's for a damn case. Me, I love to converse, but as a journalist, I also recognize the importance of listening. I've learned that often one learns more by listening."

He waved his hand at her to stop. "Enough with the lectures. Now *you're* talking too much but not saying anything. What does any of this have to do with my father?"

"See? You're still not listening. Perhaps he was like Estella's mother and wanted to get away from town. After his best friend, Marco, dies, what if he wanted more than anything to get away? Remember, they didn't know if Marco shot himself or if someone killed him. Your father could even have been a suspect if he was killed. There were rumors about Berto being hired to kill Marco. Maybe he needed to hide after Marco's death because he was afraid he might be blamed, and so he went to the commune. When he left there, he went off to a whole new life and married your mother. Then he moved on again. No one from town knew what happened to Berto after he left town except your grandfather. Have you found anything in your grandfather's papers that might indicate where your father went? No letters?"

Patrick shivered, thinking of the boxes that were stacked in his grandfather's garage. Upon opening them, he had found a variety of junk—everything from old buttons to used up tubes of ointment, along with old newspaper clippings and old letters. From whom? He hadn't bothered to look through them at the time. Could he find answers there to what happened to his father?

As for why the old man kept them, that was easily answered by the fact that his grandfather obviously loathed tossing out anything personal. But then again, the old man couldn't read well. Why might he keep something he needed someone else to read to him?

"There were some old letters," he admitted in a low voice. "I probably need to check through them."

She perked up, watching him with wide hazel eyes. "Do you want me to help you?"

Her offer surprised him. "Why would you want to do that?"

"Why not?" she asked, her smile widening. "You've been helping me so much. You're doing it right now. Let's just say I owe you one. Heck, I owe you several!"

"Are you certain you're not simply another treasure hunter?" He meant the comment in a teasing way but regretted the words as soon as they were out of his mouth.

Freeda's face froze, her chin quivering, as her eyes grew troubled. She stared at him for several minutes before twisting away to look out the window, as though the empty street outside was the most interesting sight in the world.

Patrick grimaced and pounded his fist against his leg. Damn, that had been a stupid thing to say, even if he was teasing. "I'm sorry," he said softly.

"You may not believe it, but I do eventually pay back people who help me, Mr. Patrick Sanchez," she replied in a soft voice.

"I know. I believe you."

"I want to help you because it's not simply paying you back," she added. "It's because of you and your own father."

"What?" Now he was confused, but her earnest face kept him from protesting further.

"I've spent so much time trying to find out where my father is, but you don't appear at all curious about your own dad. Don't you ever wonder where he might be? What he's doing? The answer could be in those letters. Why wouldn't you want to read them? Heck, I'll do it for you, if you'd prefer to simply let them sit there untouched."

Despite the tension in the air, Patrick reached out his hand toward her. She hesitated for a minute or two, studying it as though it might be something foreign. Slowly she reached out and took his hand and squeezed it. Once again Freeda had touched a part of him he didn't know existed. Why was she the only person who had ever seemed capable of doing that?

"Thank you for offering," he said gently, squeezing her hand back. He held it for a minute and then stood and pulled her toward him. Her scent was so familiar, so overpowering at the same time her touch seemed so right. This could get to be a habit.

Chapter Twenty-Seven

Freeda's heart began to thump as Patrick held her close. Why did this feel so good when she was going to have to let him go again so quickly? She leaned against him, her arms around his neck, wishing she could cling to his hard, muscular body, but that had never been her nature, and she didn't think he would want it either. She was surprised the normally reserved man had been so openly affectionate in public. Slowly she released her hold on him, and he did the same.

"Thank you," she whispered, keeping her head lowered as she pulled back. "Sometimes a good hug is the solution to any question."

Tender long fingers brushed away the tears that had spilled over.

"I'm here and available. Patrick Sanchez is at your service, milady, and I'll be here as long as you need me," he said in a voice barely louder than a whisper.

Another quick rush of emotion ran through her, and Freeda smiled impishly up at him, ready to break the poignant moment. "Unless a certain newspaper reporter gets there first."

He studied her face for a moment and then laughed, leaning back to gaze down at her. "Now, what is that all about? I like her, yes, but I am not interested in her. She has a boyfriend in Albuquerque. I know him."

"Ah, yes, *Eddie*." Freeda emphasized the name in a

playful voice. "I've decided I like him already." She grinned up at Patrick, not wanting to mention she, Cere, and Estella had talked about inviting Patrick to join them for a possible weekend in Albuquerque. What if he decided he didn't want to see her once he returned home? Was there someone else back in Albuquerque that he was dating? How long did she intend to stay in New Mexico anyway? True, she wanted to be there for her father, but sooner or later she would need to get a job that paid more than the small amount she was earning at the Rio Rojo newspaper office working part time.

Besides, with her father's life in danger she had no time to obsess over sexy lawyer, Mr. Patrick Sanchez. Unfortunately, for the past couple of days, even as she tried to establish a relationship with her father, the handsome lawyer had also been on her mind—his touch, his scent, the sound of his voice, his smile. She shivered as she gazed up into his dark eyes. He also studied her.

Suddenly he reached out and touched her face gently with his long fingers. "Seriously, though, how are you doing, Freeda? I've been concerned about you." Again, he turned a teasing conversation serious. "How are you holding up? You look fine, you always seem fine, but I worry about you…just remember I'm here for you."

Her heart rate fluttered at his words, and she fumbled for the right answer. "Thank you for coming." Her voice came out as a breathless whisper, but she was lucky to get that out. Emotion choked her, and she was relieved at his comment that he would stay with her.

At the same time, a part of her was questioning whether she should continue to be so dependent on him. She had never allowed herself to be dependent on any man, and she wasn't certain she ever would. She had gone through her haphazard life on her own. The days may have been hectic and unpredictable, but she enjoyed the sense of freedom that allowed her.

Could the two of them ever become more than the casual friends they'd been for the past few days? She tried to shake off thoughts of a future with him. She couldn't afford to get sidetracked. Right now, the only future that mattered involved her father's life. While they stayed out here joking playfully, he was fighting for his life a hundred yards away.

"I should go back up to check on Dad," she said.

"Good idea." His fingers lingered on hers as they walked up the steps into the lobby of the Intensive Care Unit where her father still lay in a hospital bed, his thin body looking shrunken to nearly a skeleton.

Lottie stood as they entered his room.

"No change," she said, "I'll grab a bite and be right back."

"Take your time," Freeda said.

Her aunt seemed tired, her face pale and stiff. For once, the lines stood out on her face, and her eyes appeared sunken with dark circles below them.

Freeda squeezed her arm. "You should get some rest too."

Her aunt smiled and nodded. "I'll be back but call me immediately if anything changes."

Freeda sank onto the chair beside the bed while Patrick took the other chair in the room. The only sound came from the hissing machine that pumped air into her father's body. A screen flashed out his vital signs every minute. He still appeared as pale as the sheets. His face was drawn, his eyes closed. Small dark blue bruises had become more visible on his face and on the skinny arms that protruded from the sheets.

His arm twitched suddenly, and she gasped and took hold of his hand. "Dad? Dad, are you awake?"

His hazel eyes fluttered and slowly blinked open, though they didn't seem able to focus. A slight smile came to his thin, chapped lips. He licked them before speaking in a raspy, nearly unrecognizable voice.

"Freeda...baby...you...didn't have...to come."

Tears filled her eyes. He recognized her! "Of course, I had to come! How are you feeling?"

His eyes slid beyond her to Patrick, and he lifted the hand and gave him a weak wave. "Paaatttrick..."

"We're here for you," Patrick said, stepping toward the bed.

"How are you feeling, Dad?"

He puffed out a quick breath. "Tired..."

"Do you know what happened, Dad?" she blurted.

He closed his eyes, and she feared he was going to fall asleep again, but slowly he again licked his lips and choked out a few words. "Got jumped...got... attacked...hit...beat up...someone...grabbed me...from behind..." he paused, running his tongue over his lips again. "Didn't see him...Probably...Diaz..."

"I doubt it," Patrick replied, from beside her, his voice cool, his face hardening.

She jerked her gaze to him, willing him to be silent with a hard stare. "It would be just like him."

"Did you hit him back, Fergie?" Patrick asked.

Fergie attempted a half-hearted smile. "Coupla good blows. Across the face. He'll be sorry." He again tried to smile, but his lips went stiff, as though he might be in pain. He gestured toward the tray beside the bed. "Water?"

She picked up a plastic pitcher and poured water into a plastic cup on a tray beside the bed. She put on a plastic cover and held the cup to him, helping him get the straw into his mouth while she held onto the cup.

"Okay, you don't need to talk, Dad. Just rest. You'll be okay. We can talk about what happened later when you're feeling better."

Her eyes met Patrick's. "Diaz!" she muttered, but he only shook his head. A rush of anger ran through Freeda, but she wasn't going to argue with him here, not in front of her father. She slid onto the chair beside the bed and took his hand again. "I'm going to stay here, Dad."

"Could it have been the same men who might have killed your friend or the person you said attacked you the other night?" Patrick asked behind her.

Fergie's eyes widened, but he shook his head.

"Diazzzz," he insisted, waving away the cup. She quickly took it from his shaking fingers and put it on the tray as a nurse came into the room, her plump pink face frowning.

"Now, now, don't disturb him. He needs rest."

"But he woke up," she said.

"He has gone in and out of consciousness several times for a few minutes. But he needs to rest," the woman insisted.

"May I stay here?" Freeda pleaded. "I don't want to leave him. He needs help drinking."

"We have a constant watch on him, but he needs to sleep more than anything. He has to get his strength back. It won't do him any good to make him talk or upset him," she said, moving to the bed.

"Let's step outside," Patrick suggested.

Freeda gave her father's limp hand one final

squeeze. "Just know we're here, Dad, and we're not going anywhere. No one is going to hurt you again. We'll be right outside, and I'll be back in a little while."

They stepped into the corridor, and Freeda couldn't contain her tears any longer. They rolled down her cheeks unchecked until Patrick stepped forward and handed her a handkerchief. She took it gratefully to wipe her eyes, still crying, and he wrapped his arms around her and held her close to him.

"Don't worry, hon," he said, gently caressing her back. "The important thing is that he's waking up, and he's going to be all right. Like the nurse said, he needs to get his strength back."

"Diaz did this," she said as a shiver ran through her. "I knew it. He won't get away with it. I'll see to that."

"Freeda." His voice was cool, and its timbre echoed with doubt.

She pulled back from Patrick. He was wrong and she was not having any part of his denial.

"You heard Dad!" she replied coldly, shaking with frustration and anger. "I believe him! It was Diaz!" She spoke through gritted teeth, her voice determined. "He might even have killed that guy the other night too. Oh, I know he probably didn't do it himself, but he has money and power. He runs Tres Padres and probably gets free use of that truck he drives. He could afford to personally hire someone to do the job."

Patrick watched her, his lean face set, his full lips pressed together in a firm line. She could read the skepticism in his solemn eyes.

But his disapproval didn't matter. Patrick would never convince her otherwise.

****

Diaz.

The name reverberated in Freeda's brain long after she left her father's hospital room. He had not said much beyond their initial conversation when she and Patrick were allowed back into the room. She and Patrick didn't talk either, as Lottie joined them. The three of them sat silently with magazines. Her father's status did not change, and he did not reawaken.

Finally, after several hours of sitting silently by his bedside, Patrick convinced Freeda to take a break. He agreed to sit in the room and promised to call her if her father awakened again. For Freeda, the next hour dragged by as she roamed the hospital grounds.

"Diaz," her father had said. The condemnation kept coming back to her. Could the man who had been so gentle with her aunt be so brutal that he would leave her dad bruised and battered by the side of the road? Could he have been so cunning that he had arranged for someone to come after her father? Why would he do that, simply because of Fergie's persistence in staying at the ranch? Those questions haunted her thoughts now as she walked around the outside of the hospital.

Could Diaz be so treacherous as to offer her a job, flirt with her aunt, and then viciously beat her father within an inch of his life? She didn't doubt that he could lie. Diaz seemed to delight in making veiled threats or hinting at events and then questioning them later. She had witnessed his devious nature first-hand. He even did it with Lottie, though her aunt seemed to laugh off his antics as meaningless.

"It's just the way he is," Aunt Lottie had said.

Freeda was tempted to tell Lottie about her father's claim, but in the end decided to hold back. She still wasn't wholly certain if he meant to blame Diaz. He had simply said the name, but it could also have meant he was to blame for throwing Fergie off the ranch and putting him in harm's way.

Another, personal reason held her back from making the charge. If Diaz was to blame or hated her father, why had the man tried to help her? Why offer her work at the ranch? He had to know her father would use her presence as an excuse to get back onto the property.

Like Patrick, Freeda also questioned the reality of the smaller, physically challenged man attacking her taller father or Bob. How had that been possible? Her recollection of Bob was that he stood over six feet tall and appeared tough and fit when he threatened her father. Diaz stood closer to five feet eight or nine. She could see Diaz attacking Fergie if her dad had been drinking, but Bob? Perhaps the man had been too drunk to defend himself. Could that have allowed Diaz to overtake him by surprise? Had the same thing happened with her father?

"Are you okay?"

She jerked up as Patrick fell into step beside her. "I'm fine, but you didn't leave Dad alone, did you?"

"Your aunt told me to come out and keep you company. I think she's worried about you, and so am I. You barely ate any lunch. I know hospital food is not exactly tasty, but you need to keep up your strength."

"Don't play parent…" she began, but he cut her off.

"Someone needs to." He rubbed her arm gently. "You should have someone in your life to treat you special."

Freeda turned to him as tears came to her eyes, but she didn't care what he might think. She was an emotional wreck at the moment. "Are you volunteering?"

Patrick stared down at her and she could see a sudden shift in his dark eyes as he studied her.

What was he thinking? She immediately regretted putting him on the spot and cut him off as he opened his mouth to speak. "I'm sorry, that was unfair. Besides, I can take care of myself, and my aunt and my cousin both treat me very special."

"All right, maybe you deserve extra special treatment." His smile was warm, and the twitch at the corners of his full lips increased her pulse rate.

Touching his arm gently, Freeda grinned back at Patrick. "You've become a very kind friend in the past few days, Mr. Sanchez."

He put his other hand on hers, squeezing her fingers in return. She was afraid to look into his eyes to see if she could decipher what he might be thinking. Yes, he was a friend. She had known him for only a short time, but she had become closer to him than most men she'd dated for longer periods. Freeda focused her gaze on the distant hills, avoiding direct eye contact.

"You really do deserve someone to treat you well, Freeda," he said gently. "You may not realize it, but I think you are a very special lady. I've only known you a couple of days, but I've learned that."

An impish smile came to her lips, and she tilted her head up at him. "Have you ever considered vying for the position?"

His body jerked, and Patrick stopped walking. She turned to tease him and was surprised at the intense look in his dark eyes as he studied her. For an instant their gazes met and held.

A rush of awareness ran through her, and she wanted nothing more than to reach out and take his hand, to touch him, to wrap her arms around. To let him be the one who cared about her; the person who treated her special. Damn, she wanted him to reach out to her too, to grab her, hold her and never let go. Instead, after a couple of awkward moments, he turned away.

"The man who gets you is going to be lucky," he said in a hoarse, choked voice.

A small stab of disappointment dug into her, but she refused to show it. Freeda turned to her normal weapon against pain—sarcasm. "Really? Lucky to get a loudmouth who loses things and is never certain of what she's going to do next? Not to mention not knowing what she might say. Whose father is…" She stopped as emotion overwhelmed her. What a time for her normal shield of sarcasm to stop working!

He turned back to her and lifted his hand to brush her cheek gently. Freeda hated that he was feeling the tears that spilled from her eyes, rolling unchecked down her cheeks. Surprising her, he reached out and pulled her against him, holding her tightly, one hand rubbing her back gently.

"I'm sorry for crying," she said, turning her head down, "But, but…I'm so worried about my dad…" At least it sounded good. It even sounded like an honest way to explain her sudden emotional behavior.

"He'll be okay," he said gently.

"Someone is after him. I just know it." she whispered against his shoulder.

"I know it too. I've been thinking that I should call the sheriff and see that he has a guard. Hell, if he won't do it, I'll pay for one myself."

She almost choked at his comment and pulled away to look up at him in surprise. "You would do that for Dad?"

His dark eyes were warm as he brushed his fingers across her wet face. "Wouldn't you do the same for me?"

She agreed, ready to move away from their tense, emotional moments. "If I could afford to drive a fancy car, I would."

He tapped the tip of her nose. "See?"

"You're a good man, Patrick Sanchez," she said gently.

He leaned down and dropped a quick kiss on her lips before tapping her nose again. "Don't you forget it."

"Never," she replied, suddenly shivering. No matter how many men might come into her life, she doubted she would ever forget this particular one. Was there anything she could do to extend her time with him?

****

The afternoon passed slowly, with Freeda, Patrick, and her aunt trading time sitting in the hospital room beside Fergie so that he would never be alone. They picked up books to read from the hospital gift shop and waited. For Freeda the hours were agonizing, but as she sat thinking about the past few days, she became more convinced that her father's presence in that hospital bed was due to Diaz. The name muttered by Fergie grew larger the longer she waited.

"That doesn't make any sense," Patrick said, shaking his head the next time she posed the possibility. "Why would Diaz risk his job or his freedom like that?"

They sat at a table in an Italian restaurant in Casitas, the warm scent of tomato sauce and garlic filling the air. The chatter of other diners accompanied with the muted strains of a mandolin provided a backdrop of friendly conversation. Freeda had barely touched her lasagna, but Patrick had finished off his steak and ordered dessert. She had been enjoying the evening with Patrick but when she brought up the comment that had come from her father, his smile dissipated.

"I don't know, but it *does* make sense!" she argued, her fingers playing with the stem of her empty wine glass. "Think about how much he hates Dad. Why? Because he keeps slipping onto the ranch? That's a stupid reason to hate anyone, but Diaz does. And what about that other killing? Dad's acquaintance from the other night? Maybe Dad saw something…Maybe he learned something, and now someone wants to keep him quiet. Can't you see that? Someone is out to hurt my father, maybe even kill him!"

Chapter Twenty-Eight

Freeda's comment didn't really surprise Patrick. Her anger and concern had seemed to grow with every hour they spent at the hospital. At times she paced in an agitated manner, at other times she had attempted to read, but she kept looking away, staring out the window instead. Until now she had kept her thoughts to herself.

"Are you trying to blame that murder a few days ago on Diaz too?" he asked. Patrick knew he was probably making a mistake in prolonging the discussion, but he wanted her to see reason.

Freeda's face hardened, her lips pressing together in a tight line as she thought things through before finally speaking. "Could be. He's a much more likely suspect than Dad should be. He told me he hadn't seen that Bob guy in years."

"But they argued," he reminded her. "We *saw* it. Did Diaz even know the man? Why would he have any reason to hurt him? And how would he do it? That guy was twice the size of Diaz. If he was going to kill him, he would have shot him, not beaten him to death. How the hell could he beat up Fergie either? Fergie is much bigger too."

Her eyes went down to the table as she folded and refolded her napkin carefully, avoiding his eyes. Finally, she lifted her face to confront him, her voice hard. "If Dad was drunk, if that man was drunk, it would be possible. I've been thinking about this all day, Patrick, and it's the only thing that makes sense."

Patrick shook his head, looking away as he blew out a quick breath. He shouldn't have continued on the subject. Freeda had seemed so vulnerable for most of the day, and he had found himself growing more worried about her and fearing the growing sensations that she engendered in him.

But this?

Claiming that perhaps Diaz might have attacked her father or killed someone? He had no desire to defend the man, but her idea was crazy. As the manager of Tres Padres, Diaz wielded a good amount of power. Why would he put his job in jeopardy over a couple of men who could easily be dismissed or who might simply be passing through?

In frustration Patrick posed that question to Freeda before adding what he felt should be the final argument. "He's in charge of everything at Tres Padres, so why would he risk his life and future to cause problems for a couple of men drifting through the area? All he would have to do if he wanted to kill them was to take them onto the ranch they keep trying to access, kill them there and bury them in the hills. No one would ever find them, at least not for a few years. They're drifters. No one would miss them."

Her answer was a blank stare at first but then she shook her head. "On the contrary, it makes perfect sense."

"Why?" he asked.

"Because of *who* they are—two drifters travelling through. No one is looking for them or worried about them."

"But why kill them for something that could be so easily accomplished by simply calling the sheriff and having them arrested for trespassing?" He leaned toward her, again shaking his head. "Makes no sense. They have no money, so theft is not a motive. I don't think he would kill someone simply because they're camping on the ranch."

"Maybe they knew something about his deep, dark past. Maybe they recognized him from a wanted poster or something. Dad doesn't trust him. He thinks Diaz has been in jail...I think Cere said something like that too. Oh, damn! I'd forgotten that. I need to ask her about it."

Patrick started to protest again, but then he paused. Was what she was saying possible? Exactly what did *he* know about Diaz? Given his dislike of Fergie, Patrick could understand why her father might make that accusation. Thinking back on the breakfast conversation, Patrick realized that he had begun to have questions of his own. How had Diaz received the injuries that hurt the left side of his body and damaged his eye?

"Do you trust him?" she continued.

Patrick dropped his gaze from her earnest face. He couldn't give her a direct answer. "You don't trust him so you're making up things about his past," he replied softly though he could feel more shadows of doubt forming in his mind.

Her breath quickened, as Freeda shook her head. "No, no, think about it. He's in charge of so much. What if he's embezzling or something? What if Dad found out?"

"I'm certain they have bookkeepers or auditors watching the money," he replied calmly. "I don't think he would be able to steal from the owners without their knowledge. He takes care of the property, not the financial records. You've been reading too many mystery books or watching too many crime dramas. How would Fergie or that guy Bob compile any financial information they could use to hurt Diaz?"

"Maybe he's keeping a secret stash somewhere on the ranch, or he's doing something illegal—like growing or making dope, and they found it when they snuck onto the property."

"Whatever might be going on at the ranch is not our concern. Let the authorities handle it," he repeated, shaking his head.

"Authorities…I wonder if Rafe or Cere know anything about him," she continued. "When we first came here, Cere didn't trust him, but now she seems to be fine with his friendship with her mother. Maybe Aunt Lottie knows something. He flirts with her all the time, but I wonder if he's said anything about his past. Personally, I think he has more in mind with her than just a mild middle-age flirtation."

"What, like her money? Hon, like I keep saying, he's in charge of a multi-million-dollar property. I bet he's making more money than she did teaching school for two or three years."

Freeda waved her hands as though she might be clearing away smoke. "Okay, okay, maybe he's not after *her* money, but you're right. Those people at Tres Padres have basically put him in charge of a huge operation. Shouldn't *they* be told about him?"

"Be told about what? Freeda, you're thinking too hard. I'm certain they would have run a background check on him when they hired him for the job. Besides, what does any of this have to do with your father?"

"Diaz hates Dad. Maybe Dad knows something about his past. We should ask him."

Patrick sighed and shook his head. "Believe me, if your father knew some damaging secret about Diaz, he would have used the threat long ago in order to be allowed to stay at the ranch. I know you love and believe your father, but I don't think he is above blackmail to get what he wants. Think about that."

Freeda lowered her head as though she was considering that possibility. After a few silent minutes, she jerked up again. "Well, maybe he *just* found out something—maybe that guy Bob told him something before he was killed, and Dad checked it out, and that's why he is in that hospital bed fighting for his life."

Patrick didn't have an answer. She could be right about that. Before he could frame a reply, Lottie and Tony Gennaro appeared at the door. With a sigh of relief at changing the conversation topic, he waved them over.

"Well, well, gone over to the opposition," Tony said with a smile as he approached the table. "This restaurant is my main competition."

Freeda ignored his jibe. She was surprised to see her aunt outside the hospital, and her heart began to thump faster. "Aunt Lottie, who's with Dad?"

Her aunt's face lowered and turned a light shade of pink as Tony stepped forward. "He's sound asleep, so I convinced Lottie she needed to take a dinner break." He pulled out chair for her aunt. "Mind if we join you?"

"Not at all," Patrick said, standing also.

Freeda glanced from one to the other as she pushed away from the table. They were treating this as just another social outing, but Lottie's presence meant no one remained at her father's bedside. "I should get back to the hospital…"

Lottie put out her hand to stop her as Tony tapped the back of her chair and slid into the chair next to Freeda. "Now you sit back down, hon. He'll be fine. He's asleep and the nurses come in every few minutes. Finish your dinner."

"But Dad's alone," she protested. "What if he wakes up?"

"He won't wake again for hours. Besides, he needs his rest," Lottie said calmly. "And I'm going back right after dinner."

Freeda's gaze shifted from one to the other. Patrick gestured with his hand, indicating she should sit again. How could they all be so calm?

"What if whoever attacked him…" she began, but her aunt again waved her hand, cutting her off.

"Please stop worrying about him being in danger. D.V. has hired a guard to stay outside the door. No one enters but the names on the list we left him."

A shiver ran through her, but she sank back onto the chair. "Diaz hired a guard? That could be even worse."

"Not at all," Lottie replied calmly. "The guard is very dedicated. Big as a horse, and he takes the job seriously. He almost didn't let Tony into the room."

"She had to come out and rescue me." Tony grinned and winked at Lottie. "That's why I convinced her to come out to dinner. Those hospital meals are nasty."

Freeda still wasn't convinced. "But what if Diaz—"

Tony again waved off her protest. "Stop worrying. Diaz has more trouble on his hands right now than worrying about a sick man trying to trespass on Tres Padres. Word is they found a skeleton up in the hills near the old commune. A woman's body."

"What?" Freeda jumped as Patrick also jerked up in his chair. "A body?" she asked, barely breathing.

"They're thinking it might be the remains of someone who once lived at the commune," Lottie said, taking her napkin off the table and carefully arranging it on her lap. "That happens every so often. I've heard that if someone got sick or died up there, they simply buried them in their favorite spot. People are always finding bones."

"Much more common than finding coins," Tony agreed with a smirk.

Freeda shuddered at the thought of a body simply buried in the woods. "Where did they find it? I wonder if it's close to where we were, Patrick."

"Could be," Lottie said. "It's a good thing you went out there a couple of days ago, Freeda. I think they're going to close off that area completely for a while. You'd never get up there now to take pictures."

"Won't be good publicity for Tres Padres either," Tony added in a cool tone. "Maybe it will keep Diaz busy, and he can focus on ranching instead of bringing in gullible tourists."

"Now that wouldn't be good for *you*, Tony." Lottie said, tapping his hand playfully. "Don't you count on those *tourists* to visit your restaurant?"

"I suppose." He agreed grudgingly. "But I'm not going to worry about this place as an alternative." He held up a long card printed with the restaurant's wine list. "My wine offerings are much more preferable than theirs."

"The service is superior too," Lottie said, smiling at him before her face turned serious again. "It is sad, though, about finding that body. Practically a skeleton, I guess. I wonder how they will ever identify the person."

"DNA perhaps?" Patrick offered. "Not certain how they would find a match even if they can do that."

"I hope it wasn't someone from town," Lottie continued, her face turning sad. "So many of the kids we knew who went up there never came back to town again. They'd go with kids they met, just take off with them to different parts of the country. Do you remember, Gary and Bill, Tony? They left and never came back."

"Rosalie, hell, even Berto, your dad, went out there for a while," Tony added, glancing across at Patrick.

"But my dad didn't disappear after his days at the commune," Patrick said glumly, his face tight. "He went to Albuquerque where he met my mom, but I suppose that's what happened with most of those kids. They went off to new lives, like Fergie." He turned to smile at Freeda.

"Certainly, and it was memories of the commune that brought Fergie and Helen together later," Lottie pointed out. "Actually, Patrick, your dad did come back for a while after being at the commune. Do you remember, Tony?" She turned to him, but he shook his head.

"I don't remember him being around at all after high school."

"I think you were probably away at college then. It was the summer Marco was killed. Some people said they thought he took off because he might end up the same way."

Tony's lips pursed. "The summer the town went to hell," he said glumly.

Without thinking, Freeda reached out and grabbed Patrick's hand. He smiled across at her and squeezed her hand in return. She knew that was a tough memory for him.

"That commune wasn't a good thing." Tony continued. "Brought in too many drifters, strangers." The edge to his voice brought Freeda back to the present.

"Stop it, Tony," Lottie said suddenly, her face growing hard. "Those were mainly good kids who just wanted to find themselves. Kids went out there looking for a way of life that wasn't nearly as easy as it was for those of us living in town. They had to grow their own food, cook over open fires, find ways to keep warm in winter. They made their own clothes. We had it easy until we went out on our own."

Tony shook his head dismissively. "Maybe, but earning a living is not easy either. Sometimes freeloading can be a whole lot easier."

Freeda kept her gaze pointed at the table as she slipped her hand from Patrick's. She wasn't certain if Tony meant her father or perhaps, her. Was that how Patrick viewed her too? That she was a freeloader? She couldn't look up at him to see what might be in his eyes.

Dinner was strained, Freeda picking at her cold lasagna as her aunt and Tony ate their meals, but Freeda made it through the evening. Her mind remained on what might be happening at the hospital. Had her father regained consciousness? As they finished dessert, Freeda announced her wish to go back to her father's bedside, but Lottie immediately shook her head.

"You need to go over to the hotel and get some rest. I'll go back and sit by Fergie's bed. Why don't you come relieve me around midnight? I know I'll never make it through an overnight shift."

****

Freeda felt anxious the minute she and Patrick reached her room at the hotel. She texted her aunt for an update on Fergie's condition, and Lottie called her.

"He's sleeping comfortably," she said, "So you get some sleep. They have brought in a very comfortable chair for me, so if you want to come later to relieve me, that's fine."

"I'll be there at midnight," Freeda announced. "I can also sleep there, and you need your rest too." She punched off her phone and slid it into her pocket as Patrick turned on the television set with the remote.

"I enjoyed the evening. Your aunt is a very entertaining lady. If only she was a few years younger…" He winked at her, but she was in no mood for teasing.

"I feel bad that we left Dad alone for so long."

"Well, now your Aunt is there. He'll be fine. What he needs more than anything is to rest."

"I should have gone instead," she lamented.

"You've been there all day, Freeda. He's getting the care he needs. I hate to say it, but aside from your aunt's house, it's probably the first night in a long time he hasn't had to wrangle a place to sleep."

His joking tone irritated her. "That's cruel, Patrick. Now you sound like Tony."

He blew out a quick breath. "All right. I know. Bad joke. But Fergie will be all right, Freeda. He's getting the best care possible."

"But who did it? And why? That's what frightens me. What if they try to hurt him again? The police don't even seem to be concerned. They barely asked me any questions this afternoon. I want to know who Dad was with yesterday, who might have wanted to hurt him.

Why didn't they even ask about that?"

"They asked about friends and acquaintances."

"They need to question Diaz," she said coldly. "When I suggested that, they stared at me like I was crazy. But you heard Tony. Even he agreed with that. No matter what his position is, Diaz should have been first on the list of people to be questioned."

"But as Tony also told us, Diaz wouldn't do the job himself if he wanted someone taken out. He would have paid someone to do it." Patrick walked over to her and put his hand on her cheek. "You need to let that theory about Diaz go, hon, or we might never find out who really attacked your dad."

Her gaze shifted up to Patrick, and as their eyes met, she felt some of her tension slip away. She leaned into his hand, and he took her hand and pulled her to her feet. He wrapped his arms around her, pulling her close. For a few minutes she leaned against his chest, listening to the rapid thumping of his heartbeat under her cheek, enjoying the touch of his hands in her hair and caressing her back.

Damn, simply being close to him wasn't enough— she wanted more. Taking a deep breath, Freeda lifted her head and put her hand around his neck, pulling his lips down to meet hers. The kiss was soft at first, but he quickly deepened it, probing her mouth with his tongue. She pushed herself to him as his hands ran over her body, moving up to caress her breasts, making her shiver.

He pulled back quickly at her reaction, and she moaned as his hands fell away from her.

"This…isn't right," he said hoarsely, gazing down at her with bright troubled eyes. "I don't want to take advantage of your vulnerability."

Freeda stared up into Patrick's troubled eyes, her body quivering with a desire and longing she had not felt in a long time. "Stop talking like a damn lawyer," she replied breathlessly. "I want you. I need you right now, and it has nothing to do with vulnerability. It has to do with you being a sexy man and me being a woman."

"Hon, I don't want to use you…"

"But maybe I *need* to *use* you," she protested, pushing her hand down along the front of his pants, feeling his hardness through the thick cloth. She caressed him with her fingers. "Patrick, right now, I need to know there are still good things in the world, things that make me happy…people who can make me feel alive…oh, so damn alive!" She emphasized her words with a squeeze, and he shivered too.

Chapter Twenty-Nine

"Damn you, Freeda," Patrick said hoarsely. He dropped his lips to hers again, then deepening the kiss. He opened his mouth to thrust his tongue into hers. His hand slid along her breasts.

Yes, the time for talking was over. It was time to let their bodies do the communicating. She needed him, and she wanted him right now more than she had ever desired any man. She pulled at the buttons of his silk shirt as his hands slid under her blouse and into her bra, touching her nipples with his fingertips, turning them into hard pebbles.

"Damn you," he said again. "I do want you so much...I-I need...you..."

They collapsed onto the bed together, pulling off each other's clothes, running their hands along bare stretches of skin, until their bodies fully joined.

For Freeda the sensations were something she had always guessed were possible with him. In her mind, she had been desiring him almost from that first day, she realized. She had wanted to be with him, to feel his long fingers caressing her, his pouty lips bringing her pleasure, and now it was happening. And it had not been because of his car or how he dressed or even the way he walked and talked. She had felt a strange, instant connection to him, something she had never felt before with any man.

"Patrick, did you ever think…" she started, but his lips claimed hers.

"Yes, damn, I've been wanting you," he said gently. "Almost from the first moment I saw you jumping up and down by the side of the road."

"Because my boobs were bouncing," she teased, tapping his cheek with a playful slap. "That's what you saw. Admit it, big boy."

"I plead the Fifth."

"Figures, Mr. Lawyer."

Laughing, he kissed her again, deepening the kiss until they were both gasping for air. Moments later, they moved together, enjoying the pleasure of their bodies. When they both sank back onto the bed in satisfaction, Freeda couldn't help teasing him. "Don't think this changes anything, Mr. Lawyer Man. I still owe you for that ride."

He leaned down to kiss her lips quickly, playfully. "Does that mean I get to keep trying to collect?"

"Anytime, big boy," she whispered. "Anytime."

****

Freeda's footsteps echoed on the deserted sidewalk as she walked toward the hospital. She clutched Patrick's blazer tightly around herself, pleased he had argued with her to take it. The summer evenings were growing colder. Soon fall would be making its cold presence known, even on the plains of New Mexico. Mostly, though, she liked carrying the scent of Patrick next to her.

He had been as much of a vibrant and satisfying lover as she had thought he would be. The moments they had spent together still made her body shudder. They had showered together, but even that had led to another bout of lovemaking. How the hell would she ever say goodbye to him in a few days? Should she try to stay in New Mexico for a little longer? She had nothing waiting for her back in California, except work.

"And rent," she added out loud. Freeda sighed heavily. She was being totally stupid. A few kisses from Patrick, and she was suddenly feeling like her whole life was on edge. She could arrange a way to stay in New Mexico living with her aunt, working for Cere. Freeda would be here for a while anyway if she committed to complete work on the photography assignment Diaz had given her.

But would that still happen now that those bones had been found at Tres Padres? She shivered, thinking about what they meant. Human bones, according to what Tony had said. She nearly tripped as she stepped off a curb.

"Get your head back into the game," she muttered. "Your dad needs you. You can't afford to get sidetracked by the first sexy guy who comes along with his fancy clothes and fancy car. You don't need that."

But not thinking about Patrick brought her back to an unnerving present.

The night was dark, no moon in the inky black sky. She felt alone on the deserted street, lit only by a dim streetlight on one corner. Didn't anyone go anywhere after dark in this little town? Of course, it was almost midnight. A few houses in the distance still had lights on, but the whole town appeared to be asleep. A car engine roared to life in the distance, but she saw no sign of anyone nearby. The downtown area was silent, the streets empty. Most of the businesses had turned off their neon signs hours ago. Even the windows of the café where she and Patrick had frequented was dark. Only the dim glow of indoor nightlights came from the large windows that opened to the street. This town definitely rolled up the sidewalks at night.

Damn, perhaps she should have wakened Patrick to come with her or give her a ride. No! Freeda shook her head to shake off thoughts of him and their moments of passion, but she couldn't stop the silly smile that seemed plastered to her face.

Patrick Sanchez! Who could have guessed? She had enjoyed him, enjoyed his touch, his body. But if she wanted a relationship with him, she needed to show him that she could function on her own—that she was more than that ditzy woman who lost things and always seemed to be in need of help or crying.

The sound of the car engine drew closer, erasing thoughts of Patrick, bringing her back to her current predicament. Who knew a small town could suddenly appear so menacing? Dark windows could mean someone hiding inside watching her. The dim shadows from the buildings could hold someone waiting to pounce.

"Stop it!" Freeda muttered. She was going to spook herself. After all, hadn't she walked through dark, quiet streets in cities before? Heck, she'd even walked alone on the beach at midnight. Walking a few blocks to the hospital should be no problem.

Besides, Patrick had been on the go so much lately because of her. He needed to rest. Fergie was her problem. She felt bad enough about her aunt volunteering to spend the evening with him at the hospital, even though Tony had offered to drive Lottie back to Rio Rojo. No, her aunt needed relief, and Freeda had promised to be at the hospital to relieve her. Freeda was determined to come through for once.

The sound of a car approaching provided an almost welcome distraction. At least someone was still out and about in this sleepy town. Lights flashed behind her, and Freeda instinctively moved closer to the building. She waited for it to pass but realized the driver was slowing as the vehicle grew closer.

She started to turn toward it, thinking perhaps Patrick had decided to pick her up. The lights hit her full force, nearly blinding her as she glanced back. At the same time, the car engine revved, its wheels spinning on the pavement.

That wasn't Patrick's sleek car. It appeared to be a larger SUV. Freeda whirled away, spotting the entrance to an alley. As the car sped toward her, she dodged behind a lamp post and then behind the edge of the building at the beginning of the alley.

The vehicle's brakes screeched and then roared past. *What the hell?*

Everything happened so quickly she didn't see the car clearly. Freeda barely had time to grasp the meaning of it coming toward her. Had it meant to hit her? But even as Freeda absorbed what had just happened, the car slowed, and its brakes squealed as though it was coming to a stop. But it didn't stop. Tires screeched and headlights appeared on a building on the opposite side of the street.

The damn thing was doing a U-turn, intending to come back!

With her heart thumping wildly, Freeda twisted her head from side to side, looking for a place to hide. Quickly, she ran further into the alley as the headlights of the car flashed across the street and then whirled in her direction.

She ducked behind a garbage can, hoping it hid her as the bright headlights shone across the wall behind her.

Who was doing this? Could it be Diaz? Was he coming directly after her as he had her father and Bob, the man who had been killed? But she wasn't drunk, well, perhaps a little high, but she had her faculties about her. Freeda remained still, making her body as compact as possible as headlights played across the area beside her. Could the person see any part of her? For long moments it stayed there, its lights illuminating the area. After a few minutes, it backed up and drove slowly away.

Freeda waited, her breath still coming quickly, now more from fear than from running. She inwardly debated whether she should come out of her hiding place and was about to take the chance when headlights suddenly flashed again across the wall. At this rate she would be there all night, hiding, hoping the person didn't finally get out of the car and come looking for her.

Her phone buzzed in her pocket. Oh, no! She wanted to get it out, but to do that might alert the person driving the car. He or she would see her movement or the light of the phone. The car waited. It appeared to be a hulking monster at the end of the alley.

Maybe she could make out a license plate. She squinted into the headlights but the plate on the front had no light over it. She only saw that the vehicle was big, and not a compact car. Did she know anyone with a car that big?

Patrick…

No!

That wasn't his car, and there would be no reason

for him to chase after her or want to hurt her. They had been alone so much in the past few days. Stood on that ledge overlooking the valley together. He had made love to her. Touched her so gently, kissed her and caressed her in ways no man ever had. He had been so kind to her for the past week and so loving in the past couple of hours.

But still she shivered. Had she been hoodwinked by his physical interest? Could there have been secrets about his grandfather or father that he feared she might discover and expose? Her cousin, Cere, had been attacked when she tried to do a story on the old dance hall because of a long-kept secret.

But what secrets could Freeda possibly know?

Could there have been some hidden message or clue in her pictures that she wasn't seeing? Or was it because someone had learned of the coin she and Patrick had found and was going after her for it? Who might have seen it besides Patrick? Had they already come after him too?

Or had Patrick discovered the coin's true value and decided he wanted it for himself?

No!

This was undoubtedly someone hired by Diaz or even Diaz himself behind the wheel. He had tried to attack her father and now he was coming after her. Why? Hadn't he asked her to work for him? Or was that offer simply a way to make her less wary of him?

For long agonizing moments she waited, hidden in the shadows, trying to think of who might want to hurt her. She went over scenarios, thinking about the people she had met recently and who might want to see her, and her father gone.

The street beyond the alley stayed silent. Finally, she took a cautious step out from her hiding place. The night remained quiet. No sound of any kind came to her except the soft whisper of the rubber soles of her shoes on the pavement. She walked slowly to the end of the alley, not wanting to venture back onto the main street. Poking her head around the corner of the building at the end, she held her breath.

The street was relatively dark: silent and empty. Muted lights came from the windows of nearby buildings, and the streetlights lit up every corner. She stepped onto the sidewalk, listening for any sound, but all she heard was the hushed whisper of her running shoes on the cement. She remained in the shadows, running from one protected spot to another, ready to drop behind the nearest garbage can if any headlights shone nearby. Finally, after an agonizingly slow journey, she had to step out into the light to walk across the parking lot of the hospital.

"Freeda?"

She jumped and cried out as a soft, rasping voice came from behind her. Whirling around, tears came into her eyes. *Of course.*

Here he was—the man she should have known was involved.

Diaz!

Chapter Thirty

Freeda held her purse in front of her, wishing she had another weapon to use for protection. Even a vial of perfume would work to squirt in his face, but she had emptied her purse of everything except her wallet and phone. She didn't even have a lipstick tube.

"Stay...stay away from me." Her voice came out in a shaky, breathy whisper.

"What the hell? Are you all right?" he asked, reaching out with his good hand.

"Don't you touch me," she cried, finding her voice. "I'll scream. Scream to bloody hell. I'll wake the damn dead."

He held up his hand in a stop gesture. "Hey, I'm not going to hurt you. Lottie wanted me to look for you. She's been calling your phone, and Patrick said you left the hotel twenty minutes ago. Where the hell have you been?"

Shivers ran through her. She lifted her purse again, crying out in a voice so shaky she barely recognized it as her own. "Don't you come near me!"

"Hey, no problem." Again, he held up his hand. "But what is wrong?"

"What the hell are you doing here?" she asked shakily. "Shouldn't you be-be out chasing dead bodies? You-you didn't do anything to my dad, did you?"

"Your dad is doing fine. No change, but he's coming

along, according to the doctor. They say he's going to be okay."

"What do you care?" she cried.

His raspy chuckle surprised her. "Good. Good, now that's the feisty Freeda I know."

Freeda ignored his attempt at humor. "I'm going into that hospital," she announced, wishing her voice didn't sound so shaky, "and you won't touch me or come near me or I'm going to start screaming bloody murder."

He remained very still; his palm raised. "I know, I know. I get it. Go right ahead. I'll watch until you get inside…"

Her heart pounding harder than a bass drum in a parade, Freeda ran beyond him, knowing he couldn't get to her with his bad leg. All the same, she kept glancing back over her shoulder to make certain he didn't come toward her. He watched her with a furrowed brow, and a fierce frown, but he let her get inside the lighted hallway of the hospital before he even moved.

Only when she burst through the door of the hospital did Freeda feel safe. She let out a heavy sigh of relief as she glanced down at her shaking hands. She fumbled for her phone, but suddenly her aunt appeared at the end of the corridor and came down the hall, her face slipping from smiling to concerned as she grew closer.

"Freeda, what's wrong? You look like hell. I'm so glad you're finally here. I've been worried. Hon, are you all right?"

Freeda shook her head and collapsed into a chair as her aunt sat beside her.

"My god, your hands are shaking." Lottie said, grasping her fingers and squeezing them tightly. "What the hell happened? I talked to Patrick a few minutes ago and he told me you should have been here already. I sent D.V. to find you. Where have you been?"

"Diaz…"

She shook her head, not comprehending. "What about him? Did he find you?"

Freeda shivered, not certain how to say what she thought or even if her aunt would believe her. "I think…think…he came after me…tried to run me down."

Lottie's face went pale, shaking her head in disbelief. "Hon, I don't think so."

"He did," Freeda insisted. "I know…it was him."

"What happened?" Lottie squeezed her hand, running her hands over Freeda's, trying to calm her.

"A car…tried to run over me…"

Lottie began shaking her head as soon as the words were out of Freeda's mouth. "Sweetie, it couldn't have been D.V. He's been sitting beside me in your dad's hospital room since I came back from dinner. He left the room a couple of minutes before you came into the hospital. Didn't you see him in the parking lot as you walked in?"

Freeda stared at her aunt in shock, shaking her head. She began to shiver. "No! He couldn't have…" she stopped. Her aunt had to be right. Diaz had been coming from the hospital when she saw him, not from the parking lot. He wouldn't have been able to get to the hospital and come back out in the short amount of time it had taken her to walk there.

If Diaz hadn't done it, then who had tried to attack her?

Freeda shivered at the thought that someone might have wanted to hurt her. Or perhaps simply scare her?

Why? She had no idea, except that whoever had done it had an evil intent in mind. Of that, she had no doubt.

****

"Freeda…Freeda…"

She woke with a start, jerking straight up in the hard chair, blinking at the sunlight that filtered in through a window. Morning had come. How long had she been asleep?

"Freeda…" The voice was harsh, raspy, and for an instant she feared Diaz had come into her father's hospital room.

Had she dozed off and allowed him to come in and hurt her father? Her head swung toward the sound of the disturbing voice.

No, Fergie still lay in the hospital bed. Tubes emerged from his nostrils, while a machine beside the bed flashed his vital signs. His eyes fluttered, but they appeared to rest on her when they opened. He reached out a scrawny, shaking hand.

"Freeda…baby…"

She hopped up from the hard chair where she had spent most of the night as suddenly relief swept through her. Hurrying to the bed, she stretched out a shaking hand to her father. Soft rays of sun filtered through the window blinds. Morning had come, and he was awake again.

"Dad? How are you feeling?"

"Like…hell," he said in the raspy voice she barely recognized.

Freeda grasped his rough hand in hers. "I'm so glad to see you more alert!"

His smile was sad, and his fingers trembled. He

licked dry, chapped lips and motioned toward a stainless-steel pitcher and cup on the rolling cart beside the bed.

"Wa...wa...water."

Freeda poured a small amount of water into a paper cup and held the straw out to him. He took a couple of sips, licking his chapped lips before finally waving it away. She put the cup on the rolling cart and pulled it closer to the bed so he could reach out for it whenever he needed to take a drink.

"I'm...glad...you're here..." he said in his raspy voice. "You look just...you reminded me of Helen..."

Tears filled her eyes at his comparison of her to the mother she only knew through photographs. Brushing her hand across his bony, stubbly cheek, she replied softly. "You loved her."

"Yes, yes...I did. I still miss her...every day."

"I bet, but you got to spend time with her. I miss her all the time too." Tears ran down Freeda's cheeks, but she ignored them, preferring to keep one hand on his cheek and holding his hand with the other.

"She had your laugh...your sweet smile...and she...always ...helped me..." Tears formed in his unfocused eyes. "I dream her...all the time. I loved her..."

"I know. I love you, Dad."

"I know...our Freedom...our baby..." He attempted a smile as he weakly squeezed her hand. "But...sweetie..." he took a quick breath. "You...have to let go...live your life...while you're young."

"No, Dad, I won't leave you."

"No, never. You won't ...leave me..." A shaky hand touched his heart. "I have you...here...always."

She feared bursting into tears that might not stop so

she turned the subject away from their emotional conversation. "Who did this to you, Dad? Was it Diaz?"

His eyelids fluttered and to her surprise, he shook his head.

"Who?"

His reply was to hold out his hand and gesture to the tray again. "Water…"

She picked up the water cup and again held it out for him, giving him the straw while she held the cup. He took another couple of sips, before waving it away.

"You're going to be okay, Dad," she said. "And I won't leave you, I promise. We'll get you better and you can go home…" she stopped. Where did he live exactly? "Maybe you can come back to California with me…" Again, she paused. Could such an arrangement work? She was constantly on the move for her job and never home for very long. Freeda shook her head—she would figure it out. Somehow they would fit into her two-bedroom townhouse. She could convert her office space into a bedroom and he could stay there. Nena might grumble at first, but Freeda would see to it that he never went hungry, and at least he would have a roof over his head and not have to worry about being attacked again.

His lips turned up in a smile and he waved a hand in the air. "Don't know if I want to leave here," he said in a voice almost as raspy as that of Diaz. "Meals provided…clean bathroom…" His hand pushed down on the sheet under him. "Clean, comfy bed."

"Dad…"

He chuckled and coughed before waving for another sip of water. "I know…"

"First, we need to find out who did this to you," she said. "Was it Diaz?"

He shook his head, closing his eyes. "Nah, guy had two good arms."

The response surprised Freeda. "How can you be certain? Do you know who it was?"

His eyes grew clouded, as his brow furrowed. "Not sure, but it doesn't make any sense."

"Who else, then?"

He shook his head and waved a shaking hand. "Don't…don't worry…about it."

"Dad, we can't let the person get away with it, not even Diaz. Did you see the man?"

Again, he didn't reply beyond assuring her of one fact. "Not…not Diaz…" he insisted.

"But how do you know he wasn't behind it?" she asked, surprised at his adamant denial.

"He…found me…got me here…got help."

Her aunt had said the same thing, but she still had trouble accepting that possibility. It remained the last scenario she could imagine. Why would Diaz get help for the man he appeared to despise so much? That didn't make sense.

"Damn…jerk coulda left me there…" her father continued. "I coulda died like…Bob…but he saved me…dammit…"

"He certainly did." A small, dark man in a white coat stood at the open door. He entered, carrying a clipboard. "If we hadn't gotten Mr. Ferguson here when we did, he wouldn't be talking to you now. How are you doing, Fergie? I'm Doctor Tony Fernandez. I met you last night, but I bet you don't remember."

He touched Fergie's arm and checked the readings on the monitors over the bed before donning his stethoscope and listening to Fergie's heart.

"Not...feelin' so good," Fergie replied in his hoarse voice. "Doc, this is my daughter Freeda."

"Is he going to be all right, doctor?" she asked.

The man nodded as he began to write on a clipboard he had taken from the wall behind the bed. He checked Fergie's arms and the bruises on his body before turning to Freeda. "He'll be fine, but he wouldn't have been if he had stayed out there much longer." He pulled away the blanket and peeled down her father's gown, revealing a mass of bandages. "He was bleeding heavily," he continued.

Freeda gasped at the bandages that crisscrossed his chest. She had not seen them before when she had been in the room.

"His stab wounds were pretty deep. Yep, sliced up pretty badly. Had to be a big guy. From what the police say, he was dragged from the street behind a building, then left there. Your dad was lucky someone spotted him before he lost more blood. His wounds could have been fatal."

A shiver ran through Freeda as the horror of her father's attack totally revealed itself to her. How close had her father come to death? Why had he stubbornly insisted on returning to Casitas? The doctor completed his check of her father's injuries and stood back, nodding.

"You stay still, Mr. Ferguson, and let us take care of you. We'll have you on your feet and out of here in no time."

Fergie attempted to smile, his thin lips curving up. "Not going anywhere, Doc. It's good to know where I'm going to be sleeping tonight and having some cute young lady bring me my meals instead of digging through trash cans."

The doctor patted his shoulder. "Just rest," he replied, winking at Fergie. "And don't chase the nurses. They can run a lot faster than you can right now." He turned and left the room.

"I'll be right back," Freeda said, hopping to her feet.

"Take your time, hon," Fergie said hoarsely. "I'm not goin' anywhere."

Freeda followed the doctor into the hall and caught up with him. "Doctor, I know you told him he'll be okay, but will he? How long will he have to stay in the hospital?"

"At least a few days. No injuries to vital organs, but they did cut him up. A couple of deep wounds. We need to give them proper time to heal."

"Doctor, I hate to ask this, and I know this probably isn't your area, but someone…attacked him. What if…the person who…" Freeda paused. She didn't know how to ask the rest of her question, but he finished it for her.

"Tres Padres has a guard stationed at the end of the hall. No one gets into your father's room without permission."

"*Tres Padres*…Mr. Diaz arranged that too? I know he had hired someone for last night…but?"

He shook his head. "Not just last night. He has arranged a guard to remain in the hospital until your father is released." The doctor touched her arm gently. "You don't have to worry about his safety, Miss Ferguson. Your father will be very safe here, and our staff will get him back on his feet."

Freeda turned and walked back into the room. Her father had not moved, but he still appeared to be so helpless and vulnerable that she wanted to cry. How long would it take him to be all right? Would he ever be his old vibrant self again, able to walk wherever he wanted and be free to come and go as he pleased? She knew his freedom to travel or move around had always meant more to him than anything else, including his own daughter.

But she would not deny him that opportunity to remain free and be on his own. Now more than ever she needed to stay near her father until he was able to function independently again and be that free man she loved. She would help him get his life back and find out who had tried to hurt him.

Everyone could say whatever they wanted, but she was convinced the manager at Tres Padres was to blame for her father's condition. Diaz might not have the strength to have done it himself, but he had the means and probably the will to hire someone to do the job. And now he was taking charge of the people who would watch over her father. She had to be more on her guard than ever. She was not going to give Diaz another opportunity to hurt her father.

Chapter Thirty-One

Patrick touched the side of the bed as he woke, groggily hoping to feel Freeda's soft body next to him. He came fully awake, remembering that she had left to relieve her aunt at the hospital. She'd sounded rushed when she called to tell him she had reached the hospital and he'd immediately fallen asleep, still smelling the scent of her perfume on the pillowcase.

Damn! He had wanted to wake with her beside him, wanted to hold her for a few minutes at least, to be warmed by her body. He shivered at the thought of their lovemaking before he'd fallen asleep the previous night.

Now the bed felt cold and empty, though he could still smell her perfume on the sheets. Hell, he felt empty inside. He'd hoped to wake finding her back next to him, perhaps even waking him to another bout of lovemaking. He shivered at the thought of their bodies joined together, the touch of her soft hands, the feel of her smooth skin underneath his hands. Damn, he wanted her.

For the first time he could remember, he had not wanted to wake alone. He wanted to see her smile the minute he opened his eyes.

Damn! Who knew he could become so dependent on a woman—not in the material sense, but her physical presence—in such a short time? He had known Freeda for almost a week and now he was having trouble thinking about how his life would continue once she was gone. He longed to hear her voice, her laugh, smell her perfume, feel her body against his skin. He picked up his phone and punched in her number. She answered in a cheerful voice.

"Patrick? Good morning. Dad woke up a few minutes ago! He went back to sleep, but I think he's going to be okay."

"How about you? How are you doing?" he asked, softening his voice. "I've missed you."

"I…I missed you too…" she replied, though she sounded less enthusiastic than he felt.

Several times in the night he had wakened, reaching for her before remembering she wasn't there, but wishing she could be next to him. Right now, he wanted to see her face, hear her laugh when she teased him.

"Are you up for breakfast?" he asked. "I'm buying."

Her heavy sigh provided a quick reply. "I don't want to leave Dad alone while he's asleep. Aunt Lottie should be coming over in a little bit. She called me a few minutes ago."

A wave of disappointment hit him harder than expected. "Okay. I've been neglecting my running, so I'm going to take my morning jog, then head over to that cafe where we had breakfast the other day."

"You don't want breakfast in the cafeteria here?"

Her request disappointed him. Why did everything have to be about her father? For once he felt stubborn— and perhaps a little jealous? "Not really. I'll check in with you before I head over in case you want me to pick you up."

"Fine, but please don't wait for me. I don't want to leave him alone."

"Do you want me to bring you something?"

"I'll be fine Patrick. I can get something from the cafeteria when I get hungry. I don't want to leave his room," she insisted.

Patrick hung up, shaking his head. Why did Freeda have to be so damn tied to Fergie? The man would probably take off the minute he got out of the hospital.

****

Muted music met Patrick as he opened the door of the café where he and Freeda had eaten only a few days ago. The small room was as crowded as it had been the last time he and Freeda visited for breakfast. Chattering diners filled the room with the constant buzz of voices, while the clatter of plates came from the kitchen. The warm scent of coffee and the tangy aroma of chili wafted from the window behind the counter. Patrick took a spot at the counter next to another open stool. Hopefully, Freeda might change her mind and come over. He was studying the menu when someone slid onto the vacant seat beside him.

"Well, well, this is getting to be a regular breakfast habit. Good morning, Patrick."

He turned as Diaz placed a newspaper on the counter and picked up a menu from the nearby dispenser. To Patrick's surprise, he was not wearing his normal dark glasses, but the black eye patch and his watchful green eye gave Diaz a more sinister appearance than he normally had. He flipped over a coffee cup and gestured toward the waitress. Patrick wanted to point out that the seat beyond Diaz was open and to take it in case Freeda came over, but why bother? Diaz would make a snide remark and remain in his place. Patrick didn't feel like tension or drama this early in the day. Actually, he wasn't certain he wanted the company of this particular man either, but to suddenly leave would only make matters worse next time they encountered each other.

"Good morning," he said, attempting a smile as he stirred sugar into his coffee.

"How's Fergie?" Diaz asked as the waitress filled his cup.

The question was simple, but given his normal attitude toward Fergie, the man's sudden show of concern rankled him. Did he really care?

"He made it through the night and has regained consciousness," Patrick replied curtly, not certain how much to tell him. "He can't identify the person who beat him up, but the doctor says that memory may come back to him. Freeda said you helped get him to the hospital."

Diaz shrugged as he put down the menu. "Man was hurting. Needed help." He shrugged again as though it might be the most natural thing in the world to help a man he didn't like.

"I also hear this wasn't the first time you've helped him out."

"Really?" His good eye blinked and an eyebrow rose. "Where the hell did you hear that?"

Patrick smiled grimly. He felt like he had the upper hand. "Just something I heard." Two could play at the lack of information game, but he didn't want to talk about Fergie with Diaz. Luckily the waitress interrupted them to take their orders. Both opted for the daily breakfast special and as soon as she was gone, Patrick turned to Diaz, ready to change the subject from Freeda and her father's condition.

"I heard they found some human bones on the ranch yesterday. Anything new on that? Have they identified the body?"

Diaz wrinkled his nose and shook his head. "Some commune kid, I think. That happens every so often."

"Kind of an inconvenience, though, isn't it?" Patrick replied, thinking of what Tony Gennaro had said the previous night at dinner. "That won't be a good sales pitch for bringing tourists to the ranch, I would think. I mean, who wants to stay at a resort where bodies start turning up? And how will you ever find out who it is, or does that matter?"

Diaz grimaced, but he took another sip of coffee before answering. "It matters, and DNA can work wonders these days."

"You need to know where to start, though."

Diaz turned toward him and fixed him with his good eye, a hard look that was so piercing it chilled Patrick to his bones. "Maybe with you?"

"Me?" He shuddered. What the hell was the guy up to now? "Why me?"

"Rosalie? Your dad's sister?"

"My dad...had a sister?" Patrick started to ask if he was joking, but the older man's face remained rock hard, his jaw set. "No one has ever told me he had a sister." And Rosalie? He had heard that name. But where? Damn, he hated the way this man played games with personal knowledge. He used it as a weapon and right now Diaz was wielding it against him. Diaz leaned back to look at him. Could he be pulling one of his teasing games?

"You didn't know that? Your mom never told you?" Diaz asked.

Patrick inhaled sharply, shaking his head. "Never...does she even know?"

"No, now that you mention it, probably not," Diaz

said, suddenly sighing. "Naldo never claimed her. But just how well did your mother know Naldo? Or your dad, for that matter?"

Once again, Diaz had managed to turn a situation in another direction, and it was one he didn't like. Patrick's irritation increased. "Exactly what are you implying?"

"Nothing. Just asking."

Patrick wanted to reach over and knock the smug man off the stool as his cold hands began to shake slightly. Exactly what secrets did this man know? As usual, Diaz did the unexpected.

He held up a hand in a stop gesture. "Sorry, didn't mean to rock the boat…I'm just being an ass," he said, his raspy voice going suddenly soft and hoarse. "Forget I said anything."

Patrick turned to study him, but as though he knew what he had in mind, Diaz twisted in his stool away from him, staring down at the counter as though the flecks in the dull green Formica might be the most fascinating things in the world.

"What did you mean about my dad having a sister?" Patrick asked again.

Still Diaz said nothing, his head remaining lowered, his lips pressed together.

"Diaz?" he said in a hard tone. "Maybe I haven't been around here much, but don't I deserve to know the truth about my family? I'm a big boy, I can handle it."

The older man stayed still for several more minutes before finally turning to face Patrick with a grim smile. "The truth is, sometimes I say too damn much. That's exactly what your grandfather loved to tell me…'Boy, sometimes you don't know when to keep your damn mouth shut.' And, as usual *Viejo* Naldo was right. You should have had time to get to know him better. He would have loved to talk to you. And you would have loved to talk to him. He knew ethics much better than any damn law book. Knew history better than any encyclopedia. Old man always had sage advice."

Patrick inhaled sharply, feeling defensive, knowing Diaz was right. He should have visited more, but this man had no idea about his relationship with his grandfather. While Patrick would always carry that guilt with him, he wasn't going to let Diaz mar the happy moments he had been able to spend with Gramps. Besides, why had Diaz changed his mind about Patrick? When they met several days ago, he had been friendly and spoken differently. Was it because of his growing friendship with Freeda and her father?

"I *did* talk to him," Patrick said defensively. "Even when I was back east, I'd call him from time to time. And when I was young, he walked me all over the hills around here. Told me stories about the past. He loved to talk about history. That is one thing I'll never forget about him. I remember that I was never bored talking to him. He always had stories to tell, and when you're a kid, you want to hear them."

Some of the tension left the man's body as he smiled grimly. "Did he tell you about the explorers and their golden coins?" Diaz turned to him with a sudden grin, not his normal sinister look, but an actual friendly smile.

Despite the sudden attempt to turn the conversation around, a sudden chill ran through Patrick. "How did you guess that?"

Diaz fixed him with his shiny, mysterious stare. "No guess. He told them to me too. Old man loved to talk about the past. Not recent past—historical times. He checked books out of the library—"

"I didn't think he could read," Patrick interrupted.

"Not much. But he could read better than you realize. Just didn't like people to know it. Worried people might take advantage of him so he kept that to himself. People thought he only looked at the pictures, but the damn old man knew more than any of those damn books."

Patrick felt as though he had been punched in the stomach. Of all the things Diaz had said so far about his grandfather, including the mysterious claim about his father having a sister, this was the most unique.

"Exactly how well did you know my grandfather? I heard you arrived just before he died?"

Diaz avoided his gaze, grimacing. He drew a quick breath as he lowered his coffee cup, blinking rapidly, and his breathing rate increased. His head dropped down and his gaze focused on the cup in front of him. The silence between them grew as Patrick waited for the answer. After a couple of tense moments, he turned back to Patrick, his green eye soft, almost liquid. "I knew him…but not as much as I would have liked…"

Patrick sat in stunned silence, uncertain what to say as Diaz lowered his head again, blinking. Now what the hell did *that* mean? *Not as much as he would have liked?* Diaz took a couple of quick breaths and sipped his coffee, his lean body tense.

"What the hell does that mean?" Patrick asked.

Diaz smiled sadly and shook his head. "Get me drunk some night. Maybe I'll tell you."

For a change, the rigid man didn't seem as tough and hardened as he normally appeared. He stayed rigid until the waitress provided a distraction as she approached with their orders. She placed them on the counter, but Patrick was not ready to let go of the conversation. As soon as she stepped away, and Diaz lifted his first forkful of eggs, Patrick again turned to Diaz, ready to resume their conversation.

"I think it's time you stopped playing games with me and gave me some straight answers. You owe me that much. Maybe I didn't know my grandfather very well, but if you knew him at all, I think he'd tell you that too."

To Patrick's surprise, the stiffness left Diaz, and he chuckled, nodding his head as he took a bite of bacon. He seemed to consider Patrick's remark as he chewed before finally turning to him, still grinning.

"Yep. He sure as hell would. As for how well I knew him, well, I'd have to say we went back years. From the time I was a little kid, I'd see him every so often."

"But you didn't live here…"

"Nope. But it's a big valley. Old Naldo didn't simply run a pawn shop in Rio Rojo. He traveled around this whole area, looking for bargains, making deals. That old man got around."

"But you also knew my dad. Freeda said you…were in prison with him?"

His face darkened and Diaz considered the question as he chewed. "It was a long time ago."

"But you got out and got work…"

Diaz grimaced, keeping his gaze focused straight ahead, avoiding his eyes. "So, they tell me. Got away from the bad life at least."

"And *my* dad?"

He sighed and gave a small shake of his head, as he turned toward Patrick. "Have you ever looked for him?"

Patrick turned away, wishing he didn't have to make

the admission. "No."

For a couple of minutes, both remained silent, focusing on their food until Diaz finally put down his fork.

"Doesn't surprise me at all you became a lawyer. Your dad was smart. Good head on his shoulders. Just kept falling in with the wrong people and chose to use his intelligence in the wrong way."

Wasn't that what his mother kept telling him? She felt that Berto could have made something of himself— if he hadn't gotten in with the "wrong crowd." If he hadn't chosen to disappear from his wife and son. "Do you think so?"

"I *know so*, not that I'm much of a judge."

"I've often thought of looking up his record. Trying to see where he is now."

Diaz shook his head, lowering his fork that was halfway to his lips. "Don't bother. It wouldn't do you any good."

"Why not?"

Diaz dropped the fork with a clatter and turned to him. "You won't find him that way. Like I said, Berto was smart. He wanted out of this valley. He kept talking of going to Vegas, of making a killing."

"And he had all that money he made from killing a man," Patrick said, wishing it didn't sound so derisive.

"Hate to be the one to have to tell you this, son, but if Berto had known about you, he wouldn't have chosen the money. Man might have been many things, but he was never the type who was going to desert his own son."

377

Chapter Thirty-Two

Damn! *Who was this man?* Patrick had never heard that before. "Why would you say that?"

"Because it was all he wanted," Diaz replied bluntly, his gaze steady on Patrick. "Said it all the time—all he wanted was to find the right woman and settle down. Have a bunch of kids."

"But he left my mother…"

Diaz turned to him with a cold, unsettling look. "Are you certain?"

The accusation sat between them like an unexploded bomb.

"What are you saying?" Patrick asked, his heart racing, voice breaking as he lowered his fork. "That my mother didn't tell him about me? That was why he left us? Why he never came back?"

Diaz studied Patrick with his hard green eye for long seconds, but suddenly dropped his gaze and shook his head. "Hell, I don't know. It's none of my damn business anyway. Maybe you should ask her."

A hot rush of anger ran through Patrick. The man was playing one of his head games, and this time Patrick was the victim. "How the hell would you even know about any of this?" he asked coldly. "That was all in the long ago past."

Diaz laughed, a soft hoarse sound, dropping his fork on his plate with a clatter that barely made a distinctive sound in the noisy café. "No, I guess I wasn't around here. All I know is what I see now. And right now, I can hear your grandfather telling me to shut up."

"If you do know anything about my father, I would like to hear that," Patrick insisted. "He was in prison. What happened when he got out? He married my mother, but then what? Why did he take off like he did? I can understand his disappearing if he killed a man, but from what I've heard, everyone thought Marco Gonzales' death was by suicide. So why did he run away? Where did he go? The truth about the burglaries he supposedly committed didn't come out until a few years ago. Do you know about any of that?"

Diaz shook his head, his face down. "Not really, but it doesn't surprise me that he was able to disappear so easily and stay hidden. New identities were much easier to come by back in those days. You could have two or three identifies if you wanted. All you needed was to know someone with a good enough printer."

"Like you?" Patrick challenged, knowing he was being unfair, but wanting to do something to break the man's equanimity while discussing his own father's checkered past.

Diaz's harsh laugh was a surprise. So was the sudden wink of his good eye as he glanced over at Patrick. "Money and power. That's all it takes to hide things and to find out things. How do you think I know so much?"

"You…were in prison?" Patrick studied Diaz, trying to read what was in that good eye, but the hard look on the man's face made him feel cold inside.

Their eyes remained locked for a few seconds, but then a sudden bark of a laugh rang out as Diaz turned away. "You think I'd admit anything illegal to anyone? Especially a sworn ward of the court who would probably turn me in if I admitted any illegal thing?" He licked his lips and shook his head. "Nope. I plead the fifth Amendment."

Patrick pressed on, knowing he would probably never get an opportunity to question the man this directly. "Freeda claims the sheriff has never found your fingerprints on file. If you did time with my dad, why is that?"

"Simple enough," he replied with a shrug. "I was a kid when I knew your dad. My record was expunged. They did things like that back in those days. If you didn't kill someone or stayed clean for several years, and knew the right people, you got a break. I did my time, got out and I've been clean ever since. No need for my fingerprints to be on a record or file anywhere. I cleaned up my act, as they say."

"You think that could have happened to my dad?"

He shook his head and his mocking smile dissipated. "Unfortunately, he was not in juvie when he did his last stint. He was older. Not much, but a couple of years. Sometimes they put those younger guys in with us, rather than with the hard-core bunch. Strange times back then."

Patrick was tired of the man. He wasn't going to play mind games with him any longer. He took a final bite of his eggs and put down his napkin.

"This has been interesting, but I need to get going. Freeda will be wondering where I've been for so long."

Patrick reached for his check, but Diaz was much quicker to move and snatched it off the counter. "Go check on Freeda. This is on me."

He almost refused, but instead his gaze zeroed in on

the man's good eye. "I appreciate all you keep doing for me. But I'm not like Freeda's father. I pay back the people I owe."

Diaz smiled at him, but it was a hard grin, as cold as the look in his green eye. "You owe me nothing. Anything I might do for you I consider repayment for what your grandfather did for me."

****

"Freeeeda?"

Her father's voice croaked as he held out a hand in her direction. Freeda hopped up from the chair where she'd been for the past eight hours and rushed to the bed.

"Dad! You're awake…"

He licked his lips. She held the drink to his mouth and he sipped at the straw weakly, alternating with short, harsh bouts of panting, but then waved it away, falling back on the bed.

"How are you feeling?" she asked.

He winced and attempted a smile. "Won't…won't be dancin' anytime soon."

His lean face still had a grayish tinge and his eyes looked unfocused, but at least they were open, and he knew she was there for him.

"We'll do that later," she promised, smiling as she squeezed his hand, careful not to disturb the tubes that were connected to it. "I'm so glad you're awake. We've been so worried about you."

He attempted a smile, but it didn't reach his hard eyes.

"Do you need anything? Should I call the nurse or the doctor?"

He shook his head slightly as his fingers gripped her hand.

"Dad, I don't want to pressure you, but do you know who did this?"

Again, he shook his head, his eyes appearing to grow unfocused before he closed them.

Damn, he probably didn't want to think about those moments. Or maybe he didn't even remember. She sighed and rubbed his limp hand before grasping it. "Well, you just rest. We're going to be right here with you, so don't you worry."

"I…I…love you, baby," he said, as a tear rolled out of his eye. "I…want you to know…"

"I do know. I've always known that. And I love you too, Dad. We'll get through this, and I'm not going to leave you. I won't let anything bad happen to you again, I promise. Patrick and I will make certain of that…we'll take care of you…"

He attempted a smile, but it froze on his chapped, bluish lips. "I…I know…my…little girl…"

"And your little girl will always be here for you, okay?"

His eyes fluttered, and he squeezed her hand.

"Are you all right? Is something wrong?"

He licked his dry lips, and his hazel eyes focused on her. "You need…need…to do something…for me…"

"What, Dad? I'll do anything you want."

"Find…get the money…get it before he does…get the map…"

Freeda gasped at the hoarse words. "Money? What money? What map?"

"Money isss real…" he gasped. "He doesn't know where it is…Bob…moved it…"

She squeezed his hand. "What are you talking about? What did you find? What money? What happened to you?"

"Isss by the curve…Bob…ssaid he ffffound it… reburied it…drew a map…" He twisted suddenly, his eyes wide and wild as he looked around. "My clothes…pants…where…are…my pants? The map…"

"Dad, I have no idea where your pants are. What are you talking about? You need to calm down…"

"No…" He shuddered as he tried to turn again and rise, but he didn't have the strength. "My…. pants…"

"Why do you need your pants?"

"Map in…back pocket."

The door jerked open suddenly, and a tall, thin, gray-haired nurse swept into the room.

"Well, our patient is awake," she said, crossing quickly to the bed as Fergie fell back, breathing heavily. She waved Freeda away from the bed. "Please, let me check on him. He shouldn't be moving around. Did he just wake up?"

"Yes."

Fergie's breathing was labored, the reading on the screen showing a wild up and down pattern on his heart.

"You need to calm down," the woman said, stepping between them, forcing Freeda to release his hand. "Can you step outside, please? You're upsetting him."

"Ffff…find it…" Fergie insisted behind the woman.

The nurse waved again at Freeda, her eyes fierce. "You're upsetting him," she repeated. "Please go before he has another episode."

Freeda didn't want to leave her father, but she didn't want her actions to hurt him worse. Someone had put him in that bed, and she needed to find out who had done it, but first she needed to let him know she would follow his instructions.

"You'll be okay, Dad, and I'll take care of things. I won't let anyone hurt you again."

He smiled weakly from the bed; his energy spent. As Freeda leaned around the nurse to gesture to him with a small wave, her phone suddenly buzzed in her pocket. Glancing down, she saw Patrick's name flash across the screen.

She stepped into the corridor and punched the button to answer the call, but it had already gone to voice mail. She immediately called Patrick back.

"Patrick, Dad's awake," she announced, giggling, unable to curb her excitement. "He's even able to talk a little…I think he's going to be okay. I just left his room so he could rest."

"That is amazing news. I'm on my way over to the hospital right now. I'm sorry I didn't get there earlier."

"That's fine. I'm just glad I didn't leave. I would have missed Dad waking up. Now he just needs to rest. How was your breakfast?"

His deep sigh of exasperation said it all. "Disastrous. I spent half an hour sparring with your pal Diaz."

"Oh, yuck," she replied, unable to suppress a chuckle. "That couldn't have been a fun experience. Sounds like he was as pleasant as usual."

"And then some! Hon, I owe you a huge apology. I've seen recalcitrant or lying witnesses, some downright strange people in court over the years, but I never witnessed anything like what I just went through with him. That man is hiding something. I will no longer hold you back from arguing with him or complain when you feel frustrated by him. He knows more than what he has been saying. The problem is, I have no idea what the hell he's even lying about or why."

She shivered as she clutched the phone tighter. "Do you think he might be lying about Dad? About the attack on him?"

"Who knows? I can simply guarantee he is lying about numerous things."

"Well, you can tell me all about it as we drive out to our assignment."

"Assignment?"

"Yes. We need to go back out to where we were the other day, to the old commune. Dad says he had a map that he left in his pants. I just need to find them, but they're probably around here somewhere. Once he goes back to sleep, the nurse should let me back in, and I'll check the closet in his room."

"Why? Do we even know what we're looking for?"

"No, but Dad says this whole thing with him and that guy Bob who was killed involves some map that leads to something valuable that is hidden out there near the commune. We need to find it before whoever hurt him goes after him again or hurts someone else."

"Freeda, this sounds crazy. You need to tell the sheriff. Let them figure it out."

"Don't start lecturing me. You and I found that coin. We know there could be something out there, and I'm going with or without you. I'll borrow Aunt Lottie's car and go on my own if I have to."

Patrick's sigh came across the phone. "I'll be there in a few minutes."

****

"Do you know how crazy this is?" Patrick asked as he guided the car over the same gravel road they had travelled a few days earlier. He didn't want to make the trip, but he had let her talk him into going immediately so that she could report back to her father. He might make this trip once to appease her, but he didn't intend to keep doing it. She had been waving a rumpled piece of paper when she climbed into the car, claiming it was a map. Since then, she had been studying it intently, not saying a word.

"I'm not going to make this habit," he added, trying to capture her attention.

Her sudden lighthearted giggle as she reached over to rub his arm lessened his irritation. He enjoyed seeing her upbeat attitude after the few days of pain and uncertainty she had endured. This was the giddy, chatty woman he had first gotten to know, and he enjoyed her even more, knowing they now shared a special connection. Part of him wanted to stop the car and reach for her, to simply hold her against him for a few minutes.

"It's the last time," she replied, tapping the paper. "We shouldn't have to come out here again after today, but I want to get this done so we can tell Diaz and whoever is after Dad that there is no reason to beat him up again."

"You don't know that's the reason he was beaten. What is that map supposed to lead to anyway?"

"The gold coins everyone is supposedly looking for, I suppose. What else could it be? And don't tell me again that Diaz has nothing to do with any of this or with my dad being in that hospital bed."

Patrick was not going to argue. "That man has more secrets than anyone I've ever met."

"Oh, you finally figured that out?" she retorted in an "I told you so" tone. "What changed your mind?"

As they drove, he told her about the strange breakfast he had shared with Diaz, and the man's unusual comments about the past and about the father Patrick had never known, but whom Diaz appeared to know so well.

"There are so many hidden layers to that guy." He shuddered as he recalled their conversation. "I don't even want to consider what they mean."

"Just how I've always felt…" She sat up straighter and waved at the window. "There's the turn we made when we were out here last time. Don't miss it!"

"Are you certain we shouldn't keep going straight? That leads to the old commune, remember?"

"You're right. Keep going then. If we don't find another turn, we can come back."

"What are we looking for anyway? Did he give you any idea?"

"Not really, but he said it was just beyond the turn."

"But which turn? Going where?"

"By the commune," she insisted.

"But that was the turn to the commune. How will we know when we've found it if we don't know what the hell we are looking for?"

Patrick waited patiently as Freeda studied the lines of the crudely drawn map before shaking her head.

"This is confusing. The only landmark I know is the main ranch house and the road to the commune we followed when we visited the other day. I guess I wasn't listening as closely as I should have been." She held up the map that had been drawn in pencil. It was smudged in places so he couldn't see how they would ever be able to make sense of it.

"See, here's the main road we're on." She pointed to a dark line on the map. "Here's where we went toward the old commune the other day. See those little squares. Those would be the buildings. And then I think this little line is where we went toward that ledge overlooking the valley, above the view of the town of Rio Rojo. Those drawings look like those Tres Padres formations. But see this mark a little bit over toward the other side of that ridge? I think that's where we're supposed to go." She held up the map to indicate a tiny, smudged penciled-in X on the drawing.

"Something is buried there?" he asked, his frustration growing.

"That's what he seemed to indicate." She flung up her hands in frustration "I don't even know. He just said to look there. At least I think that's what he said."

The whole expedition was beginning to appear to be a losing effort to Patrick. He sighed in exasperation. "Freeda, this sounds like a wild goose chase. We *were* by the commune. We didn't see anything. We *were* by the ledge…" he stopped but she filled in the rest.

"Where we found that coin. This X isn't far from there." She pointed toward another mark on the map. "That's where those rocks are that overlook the valley where we ended up stopping."

Patrick turned to her, smiling, as his heart rate increased. He glanced at the map again, anticipation running through him. "Yes," he agreed. "And if we don't find anything we'll go back over to that ledge where we were the other day."

Her eyes widened and then settled on his lips as a shiver ran through him. "Yes," she said in a hoarse whisper. "Maybe…maybe…well…you know, right there at the top."

Patrick laughed as he reached over to touch her soft, pink cheek.

"No maybe," he said. "That's where I realized I was

falling in love with you."

Her eyes widened. "You…" Tears glistened in her hazel eyes. "Patrick…I don't think I knew it until last night how much I loved you…but then I've always been one step behind you."

He winked at her. "As long as you realized it. That's what is important."

"Yes!"

How fitting would it be to return and make love near the spot where he had first realized his growing feelings for her. Afterward, they could sit atop the rocks and just talk, looking down on the valley below—maybe discuss their future and what they might be able to work out to stay together.

"Later," he said. "That's a promise."

Patrick turned off onto another road, trying to recall the exact route they had taken that led them to the rocks. Was this where they had turned the last time? To make matters worse, another car suddenly came up behind them. How long had it been back there? Had he been so obsessed with Freeda that he hadn't noticed it approaching?

"Damn," he muttered. Did the driver think they were heading to the main ranch house? Where was it going?

"What's wrong?" Freeda asked.

"Someone is coming up behind us. Hopefully they turn off soon."

"I don't think there's much out here, or maybe they think this is the way to where those bones were found the other day. Turn off up there and let the car go by."

"Good idea." Patrick guided his car to the edge of the road to give the other driver room to come around, but instead, the car pulled up behind them.

"Damn, it's Tony," Freeda said in a voice filled with frustration as she looked through the back window. She hopped out of the car and waved at him. "Hi, Mr. Gennaro, I think you're on the wrong road."

Patrick watched in the mirror as her smile suddenly slid from her face and her eyes widened. His mind filling with apprehension, he opened the door and hopped from his seat. The sight of the gun in Gennaro's hand turned Patrick cold.

"What the…"

"Get back in the car," Tony said, pointing the gun at her as he opened the back door. "You too," he directed Patrick. "You drive."

"Where…" Patrick began.

"We're going back to where you went the other day, the edge of the canyon. You know how to drive there, right?"

Patrick shivered, recalling the sharp drop of the canyon wall. "Why?"

"Why do you think?" Tony asked sarcastically, his lip curling up in a snarl.

"You followed us," Freeda said as she slid into the car and Gennaro climbed into the seat directly behind her. "Why?"

"What did your damn dad tell you?"

She blinked in surprise, shaking her head. "My dad? Told me about what?"

"Bob told him where the money was buried, didn't he?" Tony said, his face hard as stone, his gruff voice nearly unrecognizable. "Fergie wouldn't tell me where it is, but he found it, didn't he?"

Patrick was as shocked by the harsh tone as the solution to the mystery of the past few days fell into place, except for one detail. "What money? What the hell are you talking about?"

"The money Berto stole. Isn't that why Fergie linked up with you?" Tony asked in his strange unfamiliar voice. "To get the money and coins Berto and Rosalie were using to run away? Those were her bones they just found. They'll figure that out soon enough. And you may own the old coins, but the money they stole came from all of us in town. I figure the old man's damn coins should be enough to pay that back with interest. That is all *my* money now."

A cold ribbon of fear weaved its way through Patrick's body. Damn, why hadn't he seen that? He recalled their dinner conversations where Tony had more than once asked about his father and grandfather and where they liked to walk when they went out to the hills. Tony had also mentioned the ledge overlooking the valley one night. Why hadn't Patrick remembered that?

Patrick looked down at Freeda, seeing the fear growing in her eyes, but also he saw determination. She was not going to let this man get the better of her without a battle.

And neither was he. As they arrived at the ledge and climbed from the car, Patrick reached down and took hold of her cold hand and squeezed it.

"You won't get away with this, Tony," Patrick said, his eyes remaining on Freeda's taut face.

"My dad will get out of that hospital and pound you to a pulp," Freeda shouted in a hoarse voice.

Tony laughed sharply and gestured them forward. "Go ahead and make all the damn noise you want. No one out here is going to hear you. But don't wear out your energy. You're going to need it to dig your graves."

"Is that what *you* did to Rosalie?" Patrick asked as pieces of another mystery began to fall into place. Hadn't Diaz said she had been killed and buried somewhere?

That appeared to confuse Tony. "Who told you that?"

Patrick wasn't going to reveal his source, but the man's voice told him that was exactly what had happened. "You brought her out here…"

Tony shook his head, his white hair flying around his reddening face. "She came out here to help Marco," he growled, his voice growing hoarse. "And ended up helping Berto escape instead. Damn fools! Those bastards kept *my* money! And then she refused to tell me where they hid it!"

"But what does my dad have to do with any of this?" Freeda asked, her voice cracking. "Or that man, Bob?"

"Bob! That damn fool recognized me the other night. He knew I used to come out here with Rosalie years ago, probably even knew what I did to her. But they're gone now, both of them, so it doesn't matter. Your dad remembers me too. And sooner or later he was gonna put me together with Rosalie. As for the two of you…once you dig up that money, you're going to get lost and drive off the ledge where you were making out the other day. And then it will all be over."

"You won't get away with this," Freeda cried. "Dad woke up today and he'll tell them."

"Damn old fool. You think anyone will believe him? They didn't believe his claims of being attacked the other night either."

Freeda shivered. Her father had been telling the truth all along. He *had* been attacked and she regretted doubting his story.

"He's nothing but a worthless drifter. I'm president of the town council. Respected businessman. You think they'll believe a babbling hippie who barely has two nickels to rub together most of the time? He won't even make it out of the hospital. I'll see to that."

"Aunt Lottie…" Freeda began, but he cut her off.

"She won't figure it out. Lottie's a softie. She'll be too hurt, probably even blame herself. I'll make certain she gets through the pain." His lips curled in a sinister grin, his eyes growing hard as granite.

"You're forgetting Diaz," Patrick said in a flat voice, and Tony's smile disappeared as his head jerked around toward him.

"What about Diaz?" he demanded.

"He knows, or he'll figure it out." Patrick's voice was flat, accusing.

"Damn Diaz is too besotted with Lottie to see anything else. Just like his old friend, Marco, was. But I'll take him down. He won't…"

A rifle shot reverberated from behind them. Tony stumbled backward, a surprised look on his face as another shot sent his body jerking backward until it toppled over the edge of the rocky ledge.

Freeda's heart thudded as she whirled in the direction of the sound where the shots had originated. She was not surprised when the man they had just been discussing stepped out from behind a nearby tree, but her heart rate only increased.

Were they his next victims? Her breath was coming fast, but he lowered his gun as he came toward them.

"Diaz…" she said shakily, realizing she had nothing to fear from him as he smiled at her grimly. She had never been so happy to see the disagreeable man as she was at this moment.

"What are you doing here?" Patrick asked.

"Patrolling the ranch," Diaz replied without missing a beat. "That's my job."

****

"How did you know about Tony?" Freeda asked Diaz after he had called for the sheriff and an ambulance. "He's always been such a nice man. Or did you know?"

"I've suspected him for a while. He comes up to the ranch quite a bit. Has…uh, had…dinner in the main dining room with various female guests. Even came for tea sometimes. I haven't told your aunt, but he loves to make friends with the older women."

"My dad said that to me too…" Freeda admitted.

Patrick was shaking his head as he walked to look over the cliff. "I think he's dead…he's not moving. I'll go down and check." His face was pale as he turned to Freeda. "I'm with you. I never suspected him." Patrick hopped onto the flat rocky ledge and disappeared over the edge.

"I should have figured this out sooner," Diaz said softly. "I saw him at the ranch the day that first guy was killed,"

"But you never told anyone." She immediately regretted the accusing tone of her voice, but it was short-lived as he reverted to his normal tone.

"Your dad was in town too," he added.

"Don't start with that…My dad is fighting for his life."

"Gennaro was also in town the night your dad was attacked. And he normally didn't come to Casitas at night because he worked the restaurant. Very coincidental that he might be around both nights people got attacked, huh?"

Freeda had no answer. What would her aunt say? "I feel bad for Aunt Lottie…"

"I know…"

"Be kind to her, Mr. Diaz. She likes you."

His only reply was a forced smile and then he turned and walked toward the edge of the hill where Patrick had gone. She sank onto a rock, her hands still shaking, knowing she needed to call her aunt and let her know what had happened. She doubted she would forget this day for some time to come.

****

"Your dad has a job if he wants one," Diaz said as he slid into the empty seat beside Freeda at the diner counter in Casitas. "I'm looking for a storyteller, someone who spins tall yarns about life in the old days or life at the commune. I've never known anyone better at making things up. The job comes with a salary, free meals, and a cabin near the main house where there is shuttle service to and from Casitas and Rio Rojo. You have one too, if you want it."

Three days had passed since her narrow escape with Patrick at the ledge on the Tres Padres anch. She turned to smile at the man who had been her nemesis for so long, but whom she knew she could never repay now. He had saved her life—along with the life of the man she loved.

A warm river of contentment rushed through her, as she recalled Patrick's admission that he cared about her. Cared, hell, he said he loved her! Would she ever get over that? No, and she would never risk changing that fact. She loved Patrick, and she would do anything to keep him in her life. She tilted her head to lean on his shoulder as she replied.

395

"I'll think about it," she told Diaz. "But I have no idea what I'm going to do now. I know Dad would love the job."

Patrick squeezed her knee as he leaned around her. "Sorry Diaz, but I have other plans for this special lady."

Diaz glanced at Freeda and smiled. It was more of a crooked grin, but for once his green eye was twinkling at her instead of appearing be accusatory or harsh or disapproving. "Well, well, I think old Naldo would like that." He winked at Freeda. "You take good care of my favorite lawyer, or I'll turn up on your doorstep. And you know you don't want that."

Freeda grinned as she shook her head. "Don't worry, Mr. Diaz. My traveling days are almost over. Patrick and I are going to California to get my belongings, and then I'm coming back to Albuquerque. Mr. Tafoya has promised to put me in touch with several media outlets so I can get back to work, and Patrick has made me the ultimate offer."

"So, you're staying in New Mexico? For how long?" Diaz asked.

Patrick reached over and took Freeda's hand, squeezing it gently. "For as long as she wants," he said, kissing her hand. Had it only been a few days since this unpredictable, boisterous miracle of a woman had wandered into his life? So much had changed, but he wasn't sorry. He had known he wanted her, and now she had agreed. He wasn't going to let this man ruin things. "You can visit us in Albuquerque any time."

Diaz looked from one to the other, but in the end, he shook his head. "Don't get into the city much. Never did like being in too large a crowd. If I leave here, I'm liable to shrivel up and melt into a puddle like a wicked witch or a ghost." His quick wink didn't bother Patrick for a change.

He leaned forward toward Diaz and said in a low voice. "We're not finished. I do want to talk to you… in…uh…private…again someday and learn more about my grandfather…and…his life…and…what might have happened to my dad…"

The older man drew a deep breath, nodding, but then he stepped back and eyed Patrick critically. "I understand your curiosity, son, but if you don't mind a word of advice, stick to the present. That past is dead and better forgotten. Let it go. That's what your grandfather would have told you if he was here." A slight, crooked smile crossed his face. "Believe me, I know. That past is as dead as the ghost of Marco Gonzales. Live for the present and build for the future."

Patrick almost protested, but instead he twisted his head to look down at Freeda as she grabbed his hand and squeezed it. His heart swelled as she smiled up at him, her eyes dancing with delight.

Diaz was right. A few days and nights had changed his entire life. He didn't know what was ahead, but that didn't matter. For the first time in years, he was not concerned with what might go wrong. He could handle whatever came along to challenge him. He had found the right woman to share those possibly chaotic days and nights. He was ready to move forward. Lifting Freeda's hand, he kissed it. Live for the present and build for the future, Diaz had just said.

Patrick's smile grew wider. "I intend to do just that."

Epilogue

Diaz watched Patrick and Freeda walk out of the diner together, holding hands like two teenagers. With a final wave toward him, they climbed into Patrick's car just as they had done the first day he helped Freeda and met Patrick. Far from being the strangers they were that morning, today they drove happily toward their future.

As the vehicle became smaller, Diaz turned away, rubbing his chin in thought. The voice of Patrick's grandfather, old Naldo, suddenly reverberated in his head, words the old man had told him years ago. *"The past is dead. son. The time has come for you to live for the future."*

Diaz glanced solemnly toward the surrounding hills that had become so familiar to him. Perhaps he should follow the advice he had just given Patrick. Maybe the time *had come* to stop living in the past and start living for his own present, his own future…

No, his future was not nearly as rosy as theirs could be.

But again, the old man's voice seemed to come to him. *"The past is dead. Stop waiting to live."*

Yes, the past was dead. The time had come to unearth the final truth that had remained buried for so long with a dead man's secrets.

A word about the author...

Rebecca Grace is an award-winning former broadcast journalist who worked in television newsrooms from Denver to San Diego, Seattle, Las Vegas and Los Angeles. Currently she writes mystery and romantic suspense fiction often based in the world of broadcasting. Her first book in this series was DEAD MAN'S RULES, and she is presently writing the next installment, DEAD MAN'S SECRETS. Her novella, SHADOWS FROM THE PAST, was turned into an audio book. www.rebeccagrace.com